Perfect Mess

M.J. FOX

Published by FoxJam Books

FoxJam Books

www.foxjambooks.com

ISBN: 979-8-9924014-0-0 (paperback)

ISBN: 979-8-9924014-1-7 (ebook)

Cover Design by Gowtham Thangaraj

Edited by Breana Bowles

This book is a work of fiction. Names, characters, places, and incidents are the product of the author's imagination or are used fictitiously. Any resemblance to actual events, locales, or persons, living or dead, is coincidental.

To Janis

Thank you for making my mess perfect.

The best laid plans of mice and men often go awry.

— ROBERT BURNS

And sometimes they careen off a steep cliff and explode in a cataclysmic inferno.

— MARY BURNS

Prologue

It was Janet's idea to go. We wore fancy dresses, got our makeup and hair done. Ralph even bought corsages. Janet said, if we didn't do it right, we'd regret it. Janet said we'd remember that night for the rest of our lives.

She wasn't wrong.

I was only seventeen. Algebra was brain torture invented by evil scientists. Every night before bed, I played whack-a-mole with a tube of Clearasil. Dad called me beautiful, but none of the boys agreed.

It was the end of the night. Colored lights danced across the ceiling. The DJ brought things down a notch, a slow song, one everyone knew. Couples drifted to the dance floor. I didn't want to dance, I was fine just standing there alone.

Jack moved like a shark in dark waters. I didn't see him until it was too late. I wondered why he looked at me. Jack Thompson was a god. I was less than nothing.

His wavy blonde mane held his crown. When I met his eyes, they were full of secrets. "I brought you something." He pulled another crown from behind his back. "For the queen." Jack offered his hand like a prince at the royal ball. "Will you dance with me?"

Logic and reason deserted me. *So young. So stupid.* That was the last time I let my heart rule my head.

We danced, and the world stopped. Time was unfathomable and intangible. Like algebra. At some point, Jack pulled me closer, his hands pressed against my back.

When the music stopped, I realized a crowd had gathered. They were cheering, cheering for me! I swam in a sea of adulation, a rock star everyone adored.

"Come on, Mary," Janet came out of nowhere, snatched my hand.

"Janet?" I didn't understand.

"We have to go." Her eyes blazed but her voice trembled.

A voice cried out, "Long live the queen!"

"Now!" Janet yanked me through the mob as Ralph cleared the way.

More voices joined the first one, "Long live the queen! Long live the queen!"

Janet dragged me after her. Where? Why? I didn't know.

"Everything's going to be okay," she said. *What are you talking about?*

The chant spread through the room like a virus, "Long live the queen! Long live the queen!" Giddy gawkers pressed in from all sides.

"Where are you taking me?" I snatched my hand back.

Janet's eyes begged me. "Anywhere but here." *But I like it here!*

As Janet pulled me after her, the faces took shape. Like looking through a camera lens twisted into focus. The people surrounding me weren't cheering, they were laughing. Those weren't smiles, those were sneers.

Janet grabbed my hand back, and this time, I let her whisk me away.

Ralph ushered us into the bathroom. We stopped in front of the mirror, where Janet ripped the crown off my head. Ralph tore away something taped to my back.

"Ralph? Janet?" Nothing made any sense.

Ralph held up a paper sign, the thing taped behind me.

Queen of the Geeks

"I saw Ashley give it to him," said Ralph.

"Jack put it on you." Janet spewed impossibilities.

"He wouldn't have." I tried to replay it back, but everything was a blur. "He couldn't have."

"He did!" As Janet cradled me in her arms, I realized I was crying.

"Stay here." Ralph yanked on the bathroom door handle, but it wouldn't budge. "It's locked."

Laughter came from behind the closed door. A voice, "See you later, geeks!"

We stayed there all night. Eventually, the school janitor came along, everyone else long gone.

I'd like to say what happened that night didn't change me.

I'd like to tell you I forgot all about Jack Thompson and I simply moved on.

That's what I'd like to tell you.

But then you'd miss all the good stuff.

Chapter One

T he ass stood in the middle of the road, munching on a tuft of grass poking out of the dirt. It lifted its head and stared at us, but never stopped chewing.

Ralph held up his hands in a gesture of peace. "It looks wild."

"It's not wild," I hissed. "Probably." Janet and I had already stopped. That was on purpose. If the creature charged, it would get Ralph first. I wondered if farm animals could get rabies.

"What do we do?" Ralph averted his gaze, as if making eye contact would set the beast off.

"Turn around and go home." Janet had been mopey since we left.

"We're not going home." I pointed past the ass, where a big red barn loomed on the horizon. "We're almost there."

It was the site of our twentieth high school reunion, a ranch in Chuluota, land of cow gates, pickup trucks, and banjo players. Possibly albino ones. There was definitely going to be a lot of bullshit. And not just the kind that comes out of the animals' butts.

"I don't even want to go to this stupid thing." Janet was growing more irritated by the second. Whenever Janet got annoyed, her left eye would twitch, then wink involuntarily. It was kind of hilarious in the right situation. Sometimes I liked to provoke her just so I could watch. But this was not the right situation. I needed Janet to be in a receptive mood for my plan to work.

"One of us should shoo it," Ralph offered.

"Shoo it?"

"You know, shoo." Ralph made a shooing motion with his hand to illustrate the technique.

"It's too hot for this." Janet winked.

She was right. The temperature was ninety degrees and rising. The humidity made the air feel like a sauna in hell. My freshly waxed armpits dripped sweat like a faucet.

You're probably wondering about that plan I mentioned. The plan, simply, was to hook Janet up. I'll leave the specifics of the hooking and the upping to your imagination.

"We'll just go around it," I said. I refused to be deterred.

To our left was a ditch filled with stale, murky water. Likely chock full of snakes and alligators. It's a well-known fact that any standing water in the state of Florida contains at least one creature or thing you don't want biting you, slithering on you, or swimming up your nose.

On the right, barbed wire lined an overgrown pasture. Cows were grazing. And mooing. Possibly laughing. The smell of fresh manure wafted in on the breeze. A hand painted sign warned, "Trespassers Will Be Shot!"

Getting shot seemed like it would be less painful than getting eaten by an alligator, so we crept along the fence to the right, giving the ass a wide berth. It still hadn't moved, other than the chewing, and some occasional pooping.

"Is that foam on its mouth?" Ralph pointed at the ass.

"That's not foam, it's drool." Truthfully, from a distance, I couldn't tell.

Now, some might say hooking up at a high school reunion is a bad idea. In fact, Ralph said that exactly. So did my hairdresser and the cashier at Publix. I, however, thought it was a good idea. A great idea. So that's what we were there to do.

"Mary, you don't have to do this." Janet planted her cowgirl boots firmly in the road, arms crossed, eye winking.

"Oh, but I do." You see, I knew Janet better than she knew herself. We had been best friends since the first grade. Sleepovers. Summer camps. Girl scouts. We'd had each other's backs through thick and thin. But being friends with Janet was like riding a roller coaster with backward flips and loop-d-loops. It was exhausting.

"You need a distraction," I said. "Don't you want to see all our friends?"

"I didn't have many friends," Janet replied. She looked like a toddler who dropped her ice cream cone.

"I didn't have *any* friends," said Ralph.

You see, if you stop and think about it, high school reunions are the perfect place for a hookup. With divorce rates what they are, statistically speaking, at least half the people there would be single, damaged, and emotionally vulnerable. The ones who were still married, with kids and jobs and real responsibilities and stuff, were too busy or too tired to show up. It really narrowed the field.

The ass looked back up and we all froze, backs pressed against the barbed wire. It stared at us, still chewing and drooling. Possibly foaming. Definitely pooping some more.

"How is it even scientifically possible to produce that much crap?" Ralph whispered.

"I don't know," I said. "Ask Justin Bieber."

"Hey, I like Justin Bieber." Janet winked again.

"Exactly."

I should also explain why Janet needed a hook-up. There were many reasons. But the latest one happened the week before, when she caught her boyfriend Stan cheating on her with some girl from work. I never liked Stan. If Janet would have listened to me, she never would've started dating him. But Janet didn't listen to me. With men, she never does.

So of course "Stanet" had ended in a train wreck. Just like I knew it would. And not just a little train wreck. A big train wreck. Like one of those trains carrying barrels of toxic waste flew off the tracks, flipped over a bunch of times, and then exploded in a mushroom cloud. And then the people in the little town down the river glowed neon green for the next hundred years.

The past few weeks had been especially brutal. Every time Janet got her heart broken, it was the same thing. Binge watching Bachelor show reruns. Random teary outbursts. Tubs of rum raisin ice cream, spiked with real rum. She wouldn't snap out of it until she met someone new. Hence Operation Hook-Up-Janet.

"Hurry, it's distracted." The ass bent down for another bite and we scurried past it.

With the ass behind us, we continued down the road. We didn't make it far before Janet pointed at the thunderclouds forming in the distance. "I should go back and move my car before it rains."

Parking for the reunion was in a muddy field a few hundred yards from the ranch gates. That's why we had to trudge down the dirt road, in the heat, across ass infested territory. And Janet drove a Toyota Prius, which I was pretty sure didn't come standard with four-wheel drive for off roading.

I looked at the gathering storm clouds and then at my watch. It was getting late. All the best hook-up candidates were going to be taken if we didn't hurry. "Your car's going to be fine," I said. Worst case, Ralph and I would get an Uber.

By that point, we had reached the big iron gates to the ranch. A sign read, Circle H. "What do you think the H stands for?" I used my cheery voice to stoke some enthusiasm.

"Hell," Janet and Ralph said together.

This close to the festivities, we could hear music and laughter rolling down from the barn. A rabidly enthusiastic "Yeeeeeee Haaaaaa!" rang out from somewhere inside. "Come on you guys, this is going to be fun." I did my best to sound optimistic.

Little did I know how wrong I was.

"OH! MY! GOD! IS THAT MARY? MARY BURNS?" A rhinestone encrusted woman charged.

Before I could run, she scooped me up in a rib cracking hug. "It is you!" I felt my feet lift off the ground as the air squeezed out of my lungs. "My word, you haven't aged a bit!" The woman held on to me like I was her personal flotation device in the middle of a stormy sea. Who she was, I had no clue.

When the woman finally released me, she snatched a polaroid camera and blinded me. FLASH! When my eyesight returned, my shell-shocked expression of terror materialized on film.

"For our Now and Then wall." Behind the mystery woman, photos of other surprised reunion guests were pinned on a board next to their corresponding yearbook photos from high school. It looked like a post office wall full of mug shots, except instead of taking the pictures back at the police station, the police had jumped out from behind a wall and yelled "Surprise!" right in the middle of the crime scene.

When I pulled my eyes away from the wall of photographs, I saw the rhinestoned woman looking at me and smiling. "You remember me, don't you?"

I had to wait for the yellow and white rings to fade. She wore more eye shadow than the lead singer of Twisted Sister.

"It's Cristy."

Blink.

"Cristy Carson."

Blink.

"We sat next to each other in Culinary."

Blink.

I still had no clue who Cristy Carson was. But I didn't want to disappoint her, so I pretended to play along. "Oh, right, Cristy? Cristy Carson." I even raised my voice a couple of octaves to make it sound more authentic.

This kind of thing actually happened quite a bit. Even though I did everything in my power to brainwash high school from my memory, most of the people in town looked back on those days with fond remembrance. And since 99.9% of our small town senior class still lived in the area, it wasn't uncommon to run into each other now and then.

"Oh, and there's Janet! I should have guessed you two were still inseparable. Two peas in a pod, you two." Janet and Cristy got their hug on, then Cristy added Janet's pictures to the wall right beside mine. At least Janet had time to shield her eyes.

"What about me?" Ralph asked, striking a pose.

Cristy frowned. "I'm sorry. Who are you again?"

"Ralph," he answered.

Blink.

"Ralph Stein."

Blink.

"The Jewish goth kid everyone pelted with dodge balls."

"Oh yes! Ralph Stein! You look less ..." Cristy searched for the right word. "Pale. And sickly." Cristy pretended to smile, but not very well. Then she snapped his picture. "Now don't forget your hats." Cristy passed out large styrofoam cowboy hats from a nearby table.

"We get hats?" Janet's mood seemed to brighten.

"Yee ha!" Ralph slipped his hat on right away.

"Oh, no." I waved Cristy off. "I'm not wearing that."

"Oh yes, you are." Janet stuffed the hat on my head. Not gently. "This was all your idea. If I have to be here, you're wearing the hat."

"I look ridiculous." I yanked the hat off, my head already itching.

Cristy butted in. "Don't worry about how you look, Mary, live a little. Who knows, you might have some fun." My memory of Cristy returned. She had been on the Activities Committee, the student club that organized all the pep rallies. Cristy was one of those people who was always smiling and happy and trying to force other people to have fun. *So annoying.*

"Put the fucking hat on, Mary." Janet smiled. But it was a scary smile, so I did.

Cristy resumed hugging and blinding other guests, while we took a moment to gawk at our old yearbook pictures.

I'll be honest with you. The first thing I did was look for a picture of Jack. As my eyes scanned over the pictures, I allowed my brain a moment to process a thought. Was I scared his picture would be up there on that wall? Was I scared that it wouldn't? After so many years, I think a part of me wanted to see Jack again just to prove to myself and everyone else that I wasn't the same person I was before. *So young. So stupid.* The kind of person people like Jack played for a fool. But then, if I'm still being honest, I think another part of me was petrified. What if he did show up and did something to prove that nothing had really changed at all?

"Hard to believe that was twenty years ago." Ralph's voice yanked me back to reality.

Janet said, "It seems like just yesterday, but a lifetime ago, too."

She was right. So much had changed. With Janet and Ralph, for sure. Back in high school, Janet was a late bloomer. The shy girl. Thick glasses. A face full of freckles. Now, she had a kick ass figure and her dream job working with books all day.

Ralph was a real turnaround story, too. After an ill timed booger picking incident in the sixth grade, Ralph was now a big time divorce lawyer and went to the gym five days a week. Whenever we would go to the beach, he got more head turns than Janet and I combined. Like an ugly caterpillar with an inhaler, Ralph emerged from the cocoon as an Armani suit-wearing butterfly.

"So Janet, see anything you like?" I swept my hand toward the photographs like a game show hostess revealing fabulous gifts and prizes.

"Seriously, Mary, I already told you. I'm never dating again. I mean it. This time for good."

She didn't mean it. "What about that one?" I pointed to a classmate's surprised face on the board. Based on his "now" picture, he still had all his teeth. Mostly.

"Ned Bailey?" Ralph looked unsure.

"What's wrong with Ned?"

"He was that kid who ran the Spirit Committee," Ralph answered.

"So?"

"He was very ... spirited."

"I'd say Janet could use a little extra spirit right now." The look Janet gave me confirmed it.

"I don't think Janet wants the spirit Ned offers, or to put it another way, Janet isn't the type of person Ned would prefer to give his spirit to." Ralph pointed across the barn where Ned was happily sharing his "spirit" with a few of our male classmates. Only male classmates.

"Fine. What about that one?" I pointed to another set of photographs that looked like the before and after pictures used on a hair loss treatment commercial. Except in reverse.

"Harold Demings?" Once again, Ralph had a tone.

"What's wrong with Harold Demings?"

"He was that crypto investor," said Janet.

"Fantastic. Not only is he not too horrible looking, he's probably rich too."

"He scammed old ladies out of their retirement funds." I could tell by her face it was going to be a deal breaker. I spotted Harold on the other side of the barn, ladling a fresh cup of punch. If you looked closely, you could see the tracking monitor poking out under his pant leg.

"Look," I said. "This is our twenty-year reunion. Every guy here is staring down the barrel of forty years old." Ralph and Janet did the math in their heads, nodding.

"At our age, any man who's single is divorced, because he was never marriage material to begin with, or he didn't get married because no sane woman would go anywhere near him with a twenty-foot pole." Ralph looked offended, but I plowed onward. "We're dealing with a low bar here. Very low. Like down here." I bent down and made an imaginary line in the air at my ankles.

"You're going to have to adjust your expectations." It wasn't the most motivating thing to say, judging by the scowl on Janet's face, but it was the truth. I mean, that's why I didn't waste my time with relationships at that point. Single men my age were a lost cause.

As we made our way past the registration tables, it was clear the reunion committee went all out. A Garth Brooks cover band, Rolling Thunder, played from a portable stage. Garth's doppelgänger was singing about Friends in Low Places, flush with whiskey and beer, where everyone was going to be okay.

"You smell that?" The scent of charred meats drifted over from the buffet tables. I heard a rumbling. It was Ralph's stomach, or a squadron of B52's taking off outside.

"Is that foam or drool?" I teased.

"Quite the turnout." Janet gazed in wonder, her mood thawing.

"Probably the free beer," I explained.

"Free beer?" Ralph's neck moved so fast the foam hat boomeranged on his head.

———

WE FOUND THE BAR OUT BACK ALONG A PATH OF mondo grasses and flagstone. Whiskey barrels served as tables. Glowing lights swooped down from the trees.

"Wow." Janet's eyes sparkled with wonder. Flannel clad bartenders dispersed a steady stream of red solo cups. There were lots of smiles. Lots of laughs. The mood was good and getting better by the second.

"They even have a chocolate fountain." Janet pointed at the dessert table, smothered with treats.

"And pony rides." Ralph was warming up, too.

It was true. There were pony rides. With actual ponies being ridden. A weathered, leathered ranch hand helped riders climb into their saddles. It was hard to determine which group was more terrified, the humans or the ponies.

Once Janet saw the chocolate fountain and the ponies, her mood completely flipped. She was no longer winking, she was smiling.

"See, this isn't so bad." I pointed at a pony for visual reference. "When you fall off the horse, you just have to climb back up and ride again."

Jason Rosenbocker, former captain of the lacrosse team, whose once infamous six pack had since grown into a full sized keg, hoisted up into a saddle, then tumbled over the other side. We heard the thud all the way across the yard.

"Sometimes it's better to just stay down," said Ralph.

"What about you, Mary?" Janet aimed a sharp glare in my direction. "You never get on the horse at all."

"That's because she's waiting for Mr. Right." Ralph made a little quote-thing gesture with his fingers.

"No," I corrected. "I'm waiting for Mr. Perfect." Which was true. I was waiting for Mr. Perfect, who didn't exist. Accepting that all relationships were doomed to failure made things much easier because you didn't have to get your hopes up.

Janet wagged her finger at me. "You can't pick love, Mary. Love picks you."

"If love worked, I'd be out of business." As a divorce attorney, Ralph was always a pessimist with matters of the heart, one of the many reasons he never settled down.

"I thought we came out here to get drinks." I had to get our mission back on track.

"Yes," Ralph and Janet answered, once again in unison.

I figured the sooner I got Janet hammered, the sooner she would stop being so picky, and we could begin with the hooking and the upping. And then, with the night's mission complete, I could go home and change into pajamas and binge watch Alaska survival shows while consuming my body weight in ice cream.

When we got to the bar, Janet ordered a cider. Ralph picked a pilsner, and I opted for the blood orange sour. I was a sucker for a pucker.

"Oh my God, oh my God, oh my god!" Janet squealed like a twelve-year-old girl at a Jonas Brothers concert having a seizure. "Look at the baby cows!" I swiveled my head to where Janet was pointing. There was a whole pen of cows just past the pony rides.

"Oh, my goodness, they are so freaking cute!"

They looked like cows to me. Only smaller. Though even from thirty yards away, I could tell that they emitted the same amount of stink as the ones that were fully grown.

"Look, you can feed them a carrot." There were tin pails hung along the fence. People were pulling carrots from the pails to feed the not fully grown but fully odored cows, a practice I found both stupid and disgusting.

Janet, however, was all-in. "You want to feed them a carrot? Let's go feed them a carrot. I'm going to go feed them a carrot."

Drinks in hand, Ralph and I moseyed our way over to the cow pen, where Janet had already grabbed a fistful of carrots. "Here, try one." Janet tried to hand me a carrot.

"No. Thank you. I'm good." A sign on the gate read, Warning! Do Not Lean on Fence! I took a few steps backward to ensure a safe distance.

"Look how cute they are." Janet patted one of the miniature cows on its head.

I wrinkled my nose after getting a strong whiff of hay. "You have a thing against cows?" Ralph asked.

"No. I don't have a thing against cows. Specifically. I just don't like animals."

"What animals?" Having already distributed her first round of carrots, Janet stuck her hand in a pail and removed another fistful.

"All of them."

"What about panda bears?" Ralph was holding his carrot by the very tip, a wise precaution to avoid being bit. "Everyone likes panda bears."

"I'm allergic to bamboo."

Janet finished feeding a cow her carrot and stepped back from the fence. It was apparently still hungry because it tried to squeeze its head through the gate to come after her. "No, no Simon. You'll spoil your dinner."

"Who's Simon?" Ralph looked as confused as I did.

Janet pointed to the cow. "He is."

"How do you know his name is Simon?" Ralph made the mistake of asking.

"Because that's what I named him."

"You can't name a cow," said Ralph. As a divorce lawyer, arguing with everyone about everything was ingrained in Ralph's DNA.

"I just did."

"He's not your cow."

"He's not yours either."

I said to Janet, "You know Simon is going to be somebody's hamburger someday, right?" In hindsight, it probably wasn't the best thing to say. You know that scene in The Exorcist where the little girl spins her head around and spews green vomit? That's how Janet looked.

Then she burst into tears.

Ralph and I exchanged a look. He made a "what the hell was that" gesture. I shook my head and shrugged.

I had to do something. People were staring. "Janet?" Gingerly, carefully, I executed a conciliatory pat on the back. "I'm sorry I said that thing about the cow. I mean ... Simon."

"I love him," Janet wailed, the tears rolling down her cheeks.

"You love Simon?"

"No Mary, I love Stan. I don't give a shit about the stupid fucking cow. I love Stan. He was my one true love."

It was the same thing every time. Janet always fell head over heels for the wrong guy. "Stan was a jerk," I countered.

There was a faraway look in Janet's eyes. "He was great in bed."

"Yes," I agreed. "With other people."

The tears started back again. "Now I'm going to be miserable and alone forever."

"You won't be miserable and alone forever. Miserable maybe. But you won't be alone. You'll never be alone." I put an arm around Janet's shoulders, pulling her close. "Because you've got me."

"Best friends forever?"

"Forever," I agreed. Eventually, the faucet of tears slowed to a trickle.

While Janet and I held each other in a warm embrace, and by warm, I mean hot and stifling, I took a moment to consider my options. Maybe I was pushing her too hard. Maybe my hook-up plan was wrong and insensitive. Maybe I should just give her time to heal at her own pace.

"I'm sorry about all this, Janet. I just wanted to help." All Janet's crying had made the top of my shirt damp. And I was pretty sure she got snot on my sleeve. "Tell you what," I said. "Let's all go back to my place. I'll make a whole sheet pan of nachos. With jalapeños. And extra sour cream."

"Sour cream gives me gas," Ralph interrupted.

"Nachos with jalapeños, and absolutely no trace of sour cream."

"Maybe watch a romantic comedy?" Janet said, releasing me from her hug.

I flinched. Romantic comedy movies. Ugh. "Sure. Anything for my best friend."

"Thank you, Mary. Thank you, Ralph." Janet paused a moment. Then she said, "But I don't want to go home. Not yet." She looked at her watch. "We came all this way, and it's still early." She knocked back the rest of her cider. "If a single man with no criminal convictions walks by, no matter who it is, I'll at least give him a chance."

"You will?"

She took the red solo cup out of Ralph's hand. "Maybe you're right, Mary. Maybe with the right distraction, I'll forget all about Stan. And how he cheated on me, maxed out my credit card, and never filled my car up with gas. And ruined my favorite white blouse when he threw it in the washer with his stupid, ugly red Manchester United socks."

She threw back the rest of Ralph's drink, then drank mine. "Who knows? Maybe I'll get lucky this time. I'll just put my fate in the hands of the universe. Let the universe decide."

And that was it. The point when everything everywhere went horribly, horribly wrong all at once. In hindsight, it was my plan's fatal flaw. The Achilles heel. Putting things into the hands of the Universe. Because the Universe is a bitch. And she didn't just have Janet's fate clenched in her iron grip. She also had mine.

Janet handed me back my empty cup. "Of course I have one small condition." Janet drummed her fingers together, like an evil supervillain planning world annihilation.

In the distance, I could hear the Universe laughing.

Chapter Two

Before I could bend over and let the universe have its way with me, I had to fulfill my end of Janet's deal. I didn't know it at the time, but it was a deal with the devil.

"Go on," Janet urged. "He won't hurt you." Janet was forever the optimist. She was delusional, but optimistically so. Ralph had his phone out so he could record.

I held the carrot out in front of me as far as I could reach. Simon pushed the entirety of his baby cow weight against the gate, trying to get to the carrot. The gate bulged outward. A few more pounds of pressure and I think it would have burst.

"Now you're just teasing him," Janet scolded. Simon's long pink tongue flicked through the bars.

I inched closer. "I'm not teasing him. I'm just trying to avoid getting my hand mauled."

"He won't bite you." Janet stepped on the bottom rail of the gate for added height and leaned over the fence. She patted Simon on top of his head. "See? He's friendly." The baby cow mooed appreciatively, tilting its head and leaning into Janet's patting.

I eyed Simon, looking for any sign of aggression. He licked his lips. Whether he was eyeing the carrot, or my fingers, I couldn't be sure. In the distance, thunderclouds rumbled, which in hindsight was a clear portent of doom.

I took a deep breath.

I made my peace with God.

I leaned in toward Simon and I …

"Hey, is that Jack Thompson over there?" Ralph pointed across the yard.

My head whipsawed like I'd been smacked hard across the face, following Ralph's line of sight. My eyes locked on him instantly. Like a submarine captain staring down a torpedo.

It took me a moment to realize my mouth was hanging open. The entire time I had been staring at Jack Thompson, Ralph and Janet had been staring at me. They looked at me the same way they had looked at the ass on the road. *Was she just going to just stand there drooling? Or was she going to charge?*

"You okay?" Janet looked at me as if I was about to jump from a tall building.

"Of course I'm okay. Why wouldn't I be okay?" The ninety-two degree air felt like it was ninety two hundred. Straightening the foam hat on my head, I said, "I'm not a teenager anymore Ralph, I'm a fully grown adult woman. I'm the number two agent in the number three real estate firm in all of Central Florida. I have my own Netflix account. I even have a 401k with company matching. I don't even know what that means, but I have one and my company matches it."

"You don't seem okay," Ralph said.

"Yeah. Like the opposite of okay," said Janet.

Somehow, I pulled my eyes away from Jack. "Actually, you know what? I'm better than okay. I'm great. I can still do downward dog in yoga class without rupturing my spinal cord. I have all my original teeth. Plus, guess what? I still fit in size six jeans." I lifted my shirt to show them.

"Your button is loose," said Janet.

I yanked down my shirt. "I'm still wearing them, aren't I?"

"Do you want us to call 9-1-1?" Ralph asked. "Your face is the color of an infected pimple."

"Look, Mary, nobody would blame you if you were still upset after what he did to you." Janet's eyes narrowed as she watched Jack get some sort of blue colored drink from the bar. "I know I would be."

"That was twenty years ago," I said. "Ancient history. I'm not the type to hold a grudge."

Ralph rolled his eyes. "You're exactly the type to hold a grudge. Grudge-holding is your secret superpower."

"Not sure that's a secret," said Janet.

"Well, I hope you really are over him, Mary," said Ralph. "Because he's looking this way."

I froze. Maybe if I held perfectly still and didn't breathe, Jack wouldn't see me. Like a chameleon that blends into its surroundings. A chameleon wearing a neon orange foam hat.

Then Janet did the unthinkable. She waved.

"What are you doing?" I gasped.

"Waving."

"Now he's walking over here," Ralph warned.

It felt like my eyeballs were sweating. I snatched Ralph's sunglasses out of his front shirt pocket and tipped the foam hat down to cover more of my face. "How do I look?" The stains under my armpits were now the size of apocalyptic black holes.

"Like Robert Duvall in *Apocalypse Now*," said Ralph, humming Ride of the Valkyries. "I love the smell of panic in the morning."

"That's not panic." Janet wrinkled her nose. "I think one of the cows got into the baked beans."

While Ralph and Janet continued to debate the root cause of the toxic cloud of farm odors, I turned around, scanning the barn yard for a means of escape. The ponies were twenty, maybe thirty yards away. If I was quick about it, perhaps I could ride off into the sunset.

"Mary?" The voice came from behind me. "Mary Burns? Is that you?" A man's voice. "Wow, after all these years."

I turned back to confront the voice, a voice that belonged to Jack Thompson.

He looked like he just stepped out of a cigarette ad in an old Playboy magazine. Was he always that tall? A red checkered shirt clung to his deltoids. His denim wrapped butt was the shape of a ripe peach. Ready to be plucked. Then plucked again in the shower. And plucked a third time after breakfast in bed. With waffles. And pancakes. *So that's what twenty years of high octane testosterone does to the human body.* He wore a hat. A real cowboy hat. Black, of course. Not the neon orange foam the rest of us fools were wearing.

I glanced back at the ponies, but my window of escape was now closed. Nailed shut and mined with heavy explosives.

"It's me, Jack." He held up his hands like he just reappeared after a magic trick.

I knew I was staring, but my eyes told my brain to mind its own business. His jaw was a cement block. His forearms jackhammers. He wore a big silver buckle on his waist, just below a washboard of chiseled abdominal muscles. Just above his bulging ...

"Ouch!" Janet elbowed me in the ribs.

Jack must have mistaken my mental paralysis for a lack of recognition. "You remember me, right?" Of course I remembered Jack Thompson. Jack Thompson still haunted my nightmares.

I scrunched my face and played dumb, which really wasn't hard for me in that moment.. "Hmmm. Jack? Um, yeah, sure, I think so. Jack Thompson, right?"

Ralph rolled his eyes.

Jack looked older, of course. Well aged like a fine wine. In high school, his body perfectly combined an all-state quarterback and a Greek god. Twenty years later, Jack had the body of ... well, an all-pro quarterback and a Greek god. Clearly, he owned a gym membership. And a team of full time personal trainers. And a testosterone injection machine.

"Janet, good to see you again." Jack flashed his million-dollar smile, the one that made girls' panties melt. "Been a long time."

Janet's eyes answered, "not long enough."

"And you're Ralph, right?" Jack extended his hand. "Didn't we play dodge ball together?"

Ralph's hand disappeared into Jack's giant maw. "I'm not sure play is the right word."

"Good times. Good times."

"The best," Ralph's mouth agreed. His eyes expressed a sentiment similar to Janet's.

When Jack turned back, I felt his eyes sweep over me. "Mary Burns. Wow." A muscle in his jaw twitched. "You look great." His cheeks flushed. "Amazing." *Was that the tip of his tongue on his lip?* Apparently, the Universe had her hand on the temperature dial and cranked things up another notch. I began sweating in places I hadn't sweated in for years.

"Are you going to stab me with that?" Jack pointed to my carrot, the one I was supposed to feed Simon.

I realized I was holding it aloft, like Norman Bates standing outside a motel shower. "No, of course not." I yanked the carrot behind my back. Maybe if Jack Thompson hadn't been so distracting, I would have heard the hungry moo behind me.

"I guess I couldn't blame you if you did. After what I did to you. That's why I was hoping you would be here today," said Jack. "I was hoping we could talk."

"You want to talk?" In the distance, another rumble of thunder rolled in with the setting sun. A storm was coming. "You want to talk to me?"

"So I could apologize," Jack explained. He smelled like raw hide and sawdust and the pheromones of uncircumcised bulls. "Maybe make it up to you somehow. If you'd let me."

My pitiful brain scrambled to keep up. Did Jack Thompson just ask me out? My Hook Up Janet plan took a steep dive off a high cliff, crashed, and burned. Nothing left but the ashes. It was time for a new plan. And in this new plan, Janet wasn't the one hooking up. I looked around for a fire extinguisher I could use to douse my crotch.

Perhaps it was the hand of God reaching down from the heavens. To give me the finger. Perhaps it was karma, and I was Genghis Khan in a former life. Or maybe the Universe had a grand master plan and my role in that plan was to endure eternal suffering.

Everything that happened next happened in slow motion.

I heard a *MOO.*

I heard a *SCREAM.*

I heard a *CRASH.*

I turned just in time to see Simon head butt the gate, the same gate Janet leaned against when she was patting Simon's head. The same gate with the sign that explicitly said-

Warning, Do Not Lean On Gate!

Fed up and disgusted by my carrot taunting, Simon took matters into his own hands. Or hooves, I suppose, in his case.

It would have been nice if this was the part of the story where Jack Thompson swooped in, scooped me up in his big, brawny arms, and dashed me off to safety. And then I, ever-so- grateful, leaned in close and we shared this amazing fairy tale kiss. But that's not what happened.

What really happened was the herd of cows, led by Simon, broke loose from their pen.

They started coming.

I started running away.

I should have dropped the carrot.

I didn't drop the carrot.

I kept running.

They kept chasing.

I turned back, only for a second, to see how close the cows were.

I didn't see the dessert table.

Until it was too late.

When I opened my eyes, a flock of canaries orbited my cranium. It was hard to tell what part of the mess was the remains of the chocolate fountain, and what part of the mess resulted from the cows eating the chocolate fountain.

Ralph said, "Holy cow."

Janet said, "I'll go find a doctor."

Jack said, "You found one. Right here."

And that's when the hero really did swoop in to save the day.

"You're a doctor?" After hitting my head, I wasn't sure I heard him right.

Jack swept aside the mangled chocolate wreckage and dropped to one knee, boot planted in a smashed apple pie, jeans smeared with brownies. Possibly cow poop.

He leaned in close, almost on top of me. Face to face. "How many fingers am I holding up?"

I glimpsed a fancy watch under Jack's checkered cuff. Rolex?

"Mary?" Jack had manicured fingernails. Cuticles oiled. Nail plates buffed. "Can you hear me?" His moisturizer must have been made of cashmere and baby duck fluff. "Are you okay?"

Hold on. I stared at Jack's fingers. Long fingers. Slender fingers. Bare fingers. Jack Thompson wasn't wearing a ring.

Jack leaned in closer, giving me a closeup view of his flawless face. The dimples on his cheeks were as big as moon craters. "How many fingers?" He smelled like cake. I really, really, really wanted to lick him.

I counted Jack's ringless, manicured fingers. "Three."

It must have been the right answer, because he smiled. I'm not sure how it got there, but one of those super soft hands took my hand, pulling me upright. It was even softer than I could have imagined. So many baby ducks must have given their lives. Every spot where our fingers touched sent a surge of energy through my entire body. Like a bolt of lighting that set my vagina on fire and fried every nerve ending in my brain.

Not young. Still stupid.

"I'm just going to take your pulse." His fingers traced up to my wrist. "Your heart rate is elevated." *No shit.* "Is it okay if I examine you?" *Absolutely.* "I want to make sure nothing's broken." *Break me Jack, please!*

Jack probed me for injuries. "Does this hurt?" *Not physically.* "How about this?" Soft fingers tested my ankle, then worked their way up my leg. "Or this?" Jack wrapped his hands around my kneecap, his thumbs sinking into the muscles and tendons on all sides. The pressure sent tiny earthquakes up into my hips, the aftershocks rippling across my pelvis. Jack gently pressed against my ribs. "You could have broken a rib."

It wasn't my ribs that were broken; it was my libido. Pushed over the limit after years of neglect. Logic and reason abandoned me. Replaced by horniness and lust. If Jack had asked me in that moment to follow him behind the barn, strip naked, and bend over a hay bale, I would have done it for sure.

"I think I'm okay." I was about two seconds away from having an orgasm.

Jack helped me to my feet, then gave me another good looking-over from head to toe. "Nothing broken, so that's good." His eyes seemed to linger again, his teeth sinking into his lip. Probably because I was smeared in strawberry frosting and speckled with sprinkles. "But there's a chance you might have a mild concussion. We should get you to the hospital just to be sure."

Again, thunder rattled the darkening sky. A growing breeze twisted the leaves in the trees.

"I called an ambulance." Janet plucked a rice crispy treat out of my hair.

"You want me to ride with you?" Jack held on to my arm again, keeping me steady on my feet.

"I got her from here," said Ralph, swooping in for support.

Jack handed me his business card, *Dr. Jack Thompson.* "Just in case."

Ralph rode with me in the ambulance while Janet fetched her car. The plan was for her to meet us at the hospital. I felt fine, physically, really, only my pride was bruised. But Jack insisted I get checked.

At the hospital, Ralph waited with me as I filled out the insurance papers. He waited with me for an exam room to come free. He waited with me until the doctor came.

I ended up being fine, of course. All good. Just like I said. When the nurse finished stapling all the paperwork, Ralph helped the wheel chair guy push me down to the curb.

As we waited for Janet, Ralph sat down beside me. "You smell like cow." Despite smelling like a farm, Ralph let me lay my head on his shoulder. When he saw the tear on my cheek, he rubbed my back.

"I can't believe Jack Thompson is a doctor," I said.

Ralph shook his head. "I thought he'd be running a puppy mill or something."

"Seal clubber." I wiped the snot dripping from my nose with the back of my hand.

"Seal clubber?"

"Someone who clubs baby seals for their fur."

I pulled Jack's card out of my pocket, turning it over in my hand. *Dr. Jack Thompson.* I still couldn't believe what happened. Part of me hoped it was all a bad dream, but Jack's business card was proof it was real. I sat there on the curb staring at his phone number like it was some kind of algebra equation. Or a winning lottery ticket. Maybe the combination to a treasure filled vault. "He wasn't wearing a ring, you know."

Ralph gave me a funny look. "You had time to notice that, did you? In between getting trampled and running for your life?"

"His hands were literally on my body. Next to my boobs. Beside my crotch. Hard not to notice his fingers when they were actively probing me."

"At least he didn't give you mouth to mouth."

Janet never showed.

Chapter Three

As soon as my alarm went off the next morning, I snatched my alarm clock off the bedside table and hurled it across the room. I was supposed to get up early to meet the new painter at Aunt Catherine's house, but my head felt like a herd of cattle stomped all over it, so I decided to sleep in.

Eventually, I had to get out of bed to pee. While I was sitting there, I checked my phone to see if Janet had called. She hadn't. *Weird.* I thought best friends were supposed to check in on you after a near death experience.

I saw a text from the new painter, though. He was waiting for me. Judging by the number of texts, he had been waiting a long time. And not patiently.

I texted him the door code and told him to get started. All the paint and supplies were already there, left behind by the last painter, painter #4, the one who quit when I asked him to touch up the hallway again because he still hadn't painted over the paw prints.

For some reason, I couldn't seem to find a competent painter who could get the job done, with each excuse or mishap even crazier than the last. Some people accuse me of being a perfectionist. Okay, many people. What can I say? I have high standards.

I texted the new painter I would get to Aunt Catherine's house as soon as I could. Technically, it wasn't Aunt Catherine's house anymore, it was mine.

Aunt Catherine was my father's mother's sister. She never got married. *Smart woman.* Never had kids. *Really smart.* My father was her only nephew. When she wrote out her will, he was her only next of kin. But since he wasn't around when she died, everything she owned went to my father's only next of kin. Me.

Still sitting in the bathroom, I considered the possibility that getting screwed over by cosmic forces was hereditary. You see, my great Aunt Catherine got thrown under the bus. Literally. She was ninety-nine years old. Smoked like a chimney, drank like a sailor, ate like a diabetic pig. And despite it all, she was in perfect health. Except her eyesight.

One rainy Tuesday, on her way to bingo, she stepped off a sidewalk in front of a bus full of schoolchildren. Wham! What a way to go. You make it ninety-nine years in this life and then you get plowed down a week before you turn one hundred. That's the Universe for you.

My phoned binged. The painter replied with a thumb's up emoji in response to my last text telling him I would get there as soon as I could.

Still sitting in the bathroom, I took an exploratory sniff of my armpit. Notes of hay. Barn. Cow fart. The scent of the previous day's disaster stuck to my body like cow flavored super glue.

I stripped out of my pajamas and jumped into the shower. I squeezed half a bottle of cucumber melon body wash into a luffa and scrubbed my skin raw. If I still smelled like cow farts after all this, at least the farts were from a cow that ate a lot of cucumbers and melons.

After showering, I got dressed and made myself a banana kale protein shake for breakfast. It was disgusting. So I dumped that and toasted two frozen waffles instead. I drowned them in maple syrup and covered them in whipped cream. Then I added half a bag of chocolate chips and rainbow colored sprinkles.

There were enough calories on my plate to feed a third world country.

———

I GOT TO AUNT CATHERINE'S HOUSE A LITTLE AFTER noon. Aunt Catherine had spent most of her life working in a factory embroidering souvenir T-shirts for tourists. The hours were long; the paychecks were small, and the vacation time was non-existent. It was like the Florida version of a sweatshop in China. Though she told me once they had a nice dental plan.

After saving every penny she could, Aunt Catherine bought her first and only house on an oak lined street in downtown Sanford. The house had a wrap around front porch and a big backyard with a pool.

I'm sure it was lovely when it was brand new. I bet when she first bought it, it was a dream come true. But after almost fifty years, without a single upgrade or refresh, it was now on the nomination ballot to be officially added as the tenth circle of hell. The foundation was crumbling, the trim was rotting, and between the overgrown weed garden, cobweb crusted windows, and creepy looking rusted fencing, it looked like the set of a horror movie.

As I pulled into the driveway, I saw a white van parked on the street in front of the mailbox. Except it wasn't just on the street. Two of the tires had gone up over the curb and were now sitting on the front lawn. My landscape guy, Leo, had put in new sod just last week. New sod which was now being mushed by van tires. Worse, there was a trail of stomped grass clearly visible between the van and the front door. As if someone, a painter perhaps, had marched back and forth across the front lawn multiple times carrying a ladder and heavy cans of paint. The green grass was already turning yellow. I had to remind myself to breathe.

I snarled as I put Charlotte into park and turned off her ignition. Charlotte, by the way, was my car. A red-head. That is an

Imola Red BMW. Premium package. Comfort package. Technology package. Top of the line all the way. Could I afford her? No. But in real estate, it's not just the house that has to keep up appearances. Success breeds success. Or more specifically, the appearance of success makes potential clients think you know what you're doing.

Charlotte was like the car version of a trophy wife. A lot of upkeep, secretly hated me, and as a short-term lease, would only stick around until the money ran out. If I didn't flip Aunt Catherine's house quickly, Charlotte would be shacking up with another owner soon.

With the economy and the housing market the way they were, costs were up, materials were scarce, and good help, painters especially, were in short supply. My renovation was well over budget and let's just say my bank account didn't have a lot of wiggle room for cost overruns and schedule delays.

I left Charlotte in the driveway and marched down the sidewalk toward the van, taking care not to step on the newly installed, newly trampled sod. As I got closer, I could feel my temperature rising. And not just from the sweltering heat.

I know what you're thinking. It's just a little grass, right? Wrong. You see, everyone knows the number one rule in real estate is location, location, location. But what is less known, though almost as important, is the number two rule of real estate. Curb appeal, curb appeal, curb appeal.

Not once in all my years selling houses did a prospective buyer gush about the steel reinforced concrete foundation. In the history of real estate, not one time did a buyer offer above asking price for the type K copper plumbing. People didn't care about what's on the inside. It's the outside that counts. Looks aren't everything, they're the only thing. What seals the deal are high end fixtures. Feng Shui furnishing. A gourmet kitchen.

Speaking of curb appeal, once I got a better look at it, the new painter's van definitely did not have curb appeal, or any type of appeal at all. It was a hunk of junk. Dents and rust covered the back bumper. Scratches streaked the door like it had sideswiped a telephone pole. One of the side windows was cracked. *Was this thing even road legal?* Stenciled lettering on the side of the van read Wright Touch. Right touch? Looked like the wrong touch to me. I hoped the new guy could paint better than he could drive.

I turned back toward the house, fully intending to give the new painter a piece of my mind. That's when I noticed the front door standing wide open. My mouth dropped. I could hear the the air compressor on the side of the house spinning faster than the engine on a turbo charged jet. Dollar bills with little wings on them were billowing out the front door.

I BURST THROUGH THE DOORWAY AND SCREECHED TO A halt.

What. The. Hell.

The inside of Aunt Catherine's house looked like a murder room. Tarps on the floors. Duct tape piled on a table. Plastic sheets covered the windows so nobody could see inside.

"Hello." The voice came from behind me. I spun around, almost face planting into a wall of flesh. Pectoral flesh. Shoulder flesh. Jaw flesh.

I looked up. A pair of eyes looked back down at me. Steel-grey eyes ringed in sea-foam green. Like tiny whirlpools in the middle of the ocean, sucking wayward ships into the depths of oblivion.

"Sorry, I didn't mean to scare you." His eyes locked onto me. Sharp eyes. The kind of eyes perfect for stalking prey. And those shoulders, big enough to heave heavy sacks. He was tall, too. Enough vertical length to peer over fences. Arms etched in muscle. Arms that could shovel for days.

As soon as my life finished flashing before my eyes, my next thought was, he's kind of cute for a serial killer. I held my breath as the serial killer's eyes floated over me. His jaw ticked when they brushed over my chest. Like he was wondering how I would taste with a side of fava beans.

"Mary Burns?" His smile made a dimple pop in his stubbled cheek. "You don't remember me, do you?"

Mister, if I ever met you before, I sure as hell wouldn't forget. I stood there gaping long enough to make it awkward. He knew my name, but there was no way we ever met. I wouldn't have forgotten a face like his. A body like his, either.

"It's Gary."

Blink

"Gary Wright."

Blink

"From high school."

It took a couple of seconds to piece it together. But when I did, my mind was officially blown. I had to grab on to the doorframe to steady myself. *The man standing in front of me was Gary Wright?*

"We had a biology class together, remember?"

Of course I remembered Gary Wright. How could I forget Gary Wright? The memory of Gary Wright was like a toe fungus that wouldn't go away. But not just because Gary Wright and I were in the same biology class. And not even because he squirted formaldehyde from a dead frog all over my favorite Red Hot Chili Peppers shirt when he sliced open its stomach.

I remembered Gary because of Janet. Janet talked about Gary Wright ... every ... single ... day. Every day I had to hear about what kind of t-shirt Gary was wearing. Usually something involving Star Trek or hobbits. Every day I had to suffer through a play-by-play of conversations they had in the hallway. Janet was obsessed with Gary Wright almost as badly as I was obsessed with Jack Thompson.

"I know I look a little different," said the imposter, pretending to be Gary.

A little different? How about a lot different. How about there was no way that the man standing in front of me was the same kid

Janet was in love with back in high school. If Jack Thompson was the official high school alpha male stud, Gary was his polar opposite. A geek among geeks. Dweeb among dweebs. A loser with a capital "L."

"You're Gary Wright?" I continued to stare at him in disbelief.

Gary shrugged. "I guess puberty was kind." *No, puberty deserved a standing fucking ovation.*

That's when I noticed all the red. Splattered on Gary's overalls. Dripping from ... Oh. My. God ... dripping from Gary's knife.

"Um ... is that blood or paint?" I calculated the distance to the still open doorway, ready to bolt, depending on how he answered.

Gary looked down at the smear of red across his chest, then grunted in amusement. "Probably both. My hand slipped when I was trying to pry open the paint." Gary plucked a rag from his tool belt and wiped the red from his blade.

I heard a tiny knocking sound in the back of my mind. Like my subconscious knocking on the door so my regular conscious would let it inside.

Red blood.

Red paint.

Why was he opening a can of red paint?????

"So what do you think?" Gary pointed to the wall behind me.

I took a moment to gather myself before turning, drawing a slow breath through my teeth. It was one of those times when you know it's going to be bad, but you're not sure how bad. Like when you get pulled over for speeding in a school zone. Or right before you put your W2 numbers into TurboTax.

Next to the front door, on the wall, was a large splotch of red paint. Not the entire wall, thankfully, just enough to provide a sample of the horrors that a full painting would unleash. The paint was the color one might paint a barn filled with pigs. Or a baboon's butt. Or a prostitute's lipstick.

When I hired Wright Touch Painting to complete the painting work in Aunt Catherine's house, I left a very detailed, very specific voicemail with the details of the job. I also sent a two-page email. And several clarifying texts.

After the incidents with my first two painters, not to mention the beige not greige incident with Painter #3, I even ordered and paid for all the painting supplies myself.

"Well?" Gary smiled ear to ear, like a proud toddler who brought home an ugly finger painting from daycare.

"Greige." My voice squeaked out as a whisper.

"Excuse me?" Gary looked confused.

"Greige," I said again. "Everything greige."

"Greige?"

"You were supposed to paint everything greige."

"Everything?"

It took effort to unclench my fists as I forced a smile through clenched teeth. "Greige is crisp. Greige is clean. Greige goes with anything and everything goes with greige. Greige."

Blink

Gary looked at me like I was speaking Swahili.

I glanced again at the swath of ugly red paint. When I first walked into Aunt Catherine's house, I thought I had accidentally walked into a serial killer's murder room. If only that had been the case. At least then someone else would have gouged my eyes out. Now, I was going to have to do it myself.

"I figured this room could use a pop of color," said Gary.

Slowly, I turned, taking my time to let my brain fully process the words that had just come out of Gary's mouth. "A pop of what?"

"Color." The smile dropped off his face when he saw my face. "You know, spice things up a bit?"

"I didn't realize that when I hired a painter, I was hiring a decorator too." I could feel the migraine forming. Like a serial killer stabbing me in the hypothalamus with a paint scalpel. "I was very specific when I hired you," I said. "Greige. Everything greige. Greige in the hallways. Greige in the bedrooms. Greige in the kitchen." I pointed to the stack of paint cans stacked against the wall. Every single can was greige. "Where did you even get red paint?"

"I had it in the van. Leftovers from another job. I figured I would put a little on the wall so you could see how it looks. I don't know, I think it compliments your grayish-beige color nicely."

It may have been the paint fumes, or the lingering effects of a cow hoof to my head, but at that point, I very much needed to get a breath of fresh air before my head exploded, which would have been terrible because then the rest of the wall would be colored red too. From brain matter.

I turned back around and began moving toward the door.

I never saw the ladder.

Nor did I see the can of red paint perched on the top step of the ladder.

The can of paint that was still open.

The can of paint that was not closed. You know the movie Carrie?

Yeah.

That.

TURNS OUT, PAINT IS EVEN HARDER TO GET OUT OF your hair than cow manure. While I rinsed off in Aunt Catherine's shower, Gary fetched spare clothes from his van, which comprised an extra set of the burlap textured painting overalls and a vintage concert T-shirt. Normally, I never would have entertained putting either piece of clothing on my body, but I had nothing else to wear and I wasn't about to get wet paint all over Charlotte.

"You like Justin Bieber?" Gary called through the locked bathroom door.

"No," I yelled back. When I looked at myself in the mirror, my braless nipples jut out of Justin Bieber's forehead like a set of erect devil horns, and the coarse material of the overalls chafed my cheeks. Not the cheeks on my face.

When I opened the door, Gary was waiting for me. To his credit, he tried not to laugh. To his detriment, he failed.

"Is there a specific reason you keep an old Justin Bieber T-shirt in your van?" I asked.

"Long story," he replied.

If the overalls were baggy on Gary, they were ten times baggier on me. Luckily, Gary had duct tape. Lots of duct tape. He even let me pick my color, silver, black, or red. Gary suggested red. I told him where he could stick his red duct tape. So he handed me the black. Did you know you can use duct tape to make a belt? Suspenders too.

Gary followed me back down to the foyer, where he had already cleaned up and painted over the red with a coat of primer. "Better?"

I glared at him. By that point, my emotional stability sagged even lower than the duct tape strapped overalls. In my mind, I waved a white flag. "I'm going to call it a day," I told Gary. "Go home and change. Into another person entirely, if possible. One who has better karma." I pointed to the wall where the red paint was now covered over with white primer. "Greige please. Just greige."

As I headed down the driveway, still wearing the borrowed overalls and T-shirt, Gary called after me. "Say hi to Janet for me."

Chapter Four

The pickleball crowd was out in full force that night. By the time I got there, the courts were already overflowing with players. In the summer heat, you had to go really early or really late in the day to avoid the peak potency of the sun.

Luckily, Janet got there early and put her paddle in the queue, saving our place in line. I found her sitting on a bench, then plopped down beside her. "You abandoned me."

"Technically, you abandoned me," Janet pointed out. "You and Ralph left me there by myself."

"They took me away in an ambulance," I said. It was a good excuse.

"Paddles up!" Mabel, one of the regulars, waved us over. Each game was played to eleven, two against two. The winning pair stayed on the court to play the next challenger, while the losers were banished back to the benches.

Janet and I lined up on one side. Mabel and her partner, Dick, on the other. "You need a warm-up first?" Mabel called over the net.

"Sure," I said. "Just a couple of swings to get loose." I was probably going to need more swings than a couple. After going home and changing, I had tried taking a nap. But between the nightmares about cattle stampedes and drowning in a red sea of paint, it was hard to get any rest.

Turning to Janet, I said, "You were supposed to meet us at the hospital."

Janet leaned over in a ready position, twirling her paddle in her hand. "I would have met you at the hospital if my car hadn't gotten stuck in the mud."

Mabel swatted the ball over the net toward me, and I swatted it back.

"Your car got stuck?" Dick volleyed the ball toward Janet.

"Yes." Janet tapped it back. "Which is exactly what I told you would happen, but you wouldn't let me move my car, so everything is your fault."

I scrambled to my left to slice a backhand toward Mabel. "You could have called at least. Checked in on me."

Janet had to retreat to chase down a lob. "I did call." The ball rolled out of bounds, breaking the flow of play.

I had checked my phone at least a dozen times. Janet's number never showed. I was sure of it.

"You two ready to get your butts whipped?" Mabel tossed the perforated pickleball from one hand to the other, a wicked grin on her face. Mabel was well known throughout Central Florida pickleball circles as a notorious trash talker, despite her advanced age of seventy-two. "I hope you two put your big girl panties on today because Dick and I aren't messing around."

"Well, technically, we are messing around," said Dick. "But you know what she means." He playfully swatted Mabel's butt with his paddle. Ironically, I was the one who first introduced Dick and Mabel during a lesson over at the Senior Center. They hit it off right away and had been together ever since.

"You serve first." Mabel threw the ball over the net to Janet.

Janet got into position. "In fact, I called you about ten times."

I lined up behind the baseline beside her. "The only calls I had last night were from "Unknown Number." About ten of them.

Janet bounced the ball on the ground to serve. "That's because I had to use another phone."

WHACK.

The ball sailed over the net, and Dick smacked it back at me. Besides the trash talking, Dick and Mabel were also renown for their lethal strokes. Dick was a "banger", shooting balls hard and fast. Mabel was more of a "dinker", playing low and slow. Together, they made a formidable opponent.

"Whose phone did you use?" The ball landed right in front of me and I started the forward motion of my swing.

"Jack's."

THWACK!

My shot sailed over the net, over Mabel, over the fence, and into the retention pond next to the parking lot. "You used Jack's phone?"

"He let me borrow it. Since mine was stuck in the mud."

"How did you get both your car and your phone stuck in the mud?"

"How Mary? Well, let's see. Maybe because my best friend insisted I go to some stupid high school reunion in the middle of nowhere with insufficient parking. So I had to park my car in the middle of a cow field which turned into mud as soon as it rained. And then when I called a tow truck I slipped and my phone went flying. But it was dark so I couldn't see anything and now my phone's gone."

"You two okay?" Mabel looked over in concern.

"We're fine. Your serve." I tossed Mabel a new ball and settled into position.

As Mabel served the ball toward me, Janet said, "I'm just glad Jack was there to rescue me."

The ball bounced, and I swung hard, completely missing.

"One nil!" Mabel called. In pickleball, you only get points when you serve.

"So Jack helped you get your car out of the mud?" I asked.

"Not exactly." Janet said. "It was stuck pretty good. We called a tow truck on the ride home."

"Ride home?"

"Yeah, Jack drove me home. Thank goodness he was there."

I couldn't believe what I was hearing, Jack Thompson drove Janet home? I didn't know what to think. Surely, he was just being nice, except Jack Thompson wasn't nice, Jack Thomson was evil incarnate. *Wasn't he?*

We continued playing, blocking and parrying, dinking and banging. During an intense rally, I had to duck to avoid Dick's forehand giving me a lobotomy. We exchanged another round of serves and another round of points. Mabel smashed a line drive forehand, and I completely whiffed. I was off my game, distracted by what Janet told me about Jack. Turns out, she was just warming up.

"Did you know he never got married?" asked Janet.

I picked myself up off the pavement after tripping over my paddle. "I saw he wasn't wearing a ring when he was checking me for damages. How do you know he's never been married?"

"He told me when we stopped for coffee."

"You stopped for coffee?"

"I bought him a coffee for helping me out."

Janet lobbed the ball over Mabel's head. "Although drinking caffeine that late probably wasn't a good idea because then we were up for hours."

Mabel chased down Janet's ball and hit it back. I watched helplessly as the ball bounced right between my legs for another point. "Hours?"

Janet shrugged. "Just a few. Then he drove me home." Janet returned the next serve, clearly oblivious to my inner torment. *Surely she didn't spend all that extra time with Jack on purpose?*

The ball landed deep on my side and bounced high. I smashed it back at Mabel as hard as I could. Somehow, Mabel got to the ball in time and sent a blistering shot back. I barely got my paddle positioned in time to protect my crotch.

"You okay over there?" asked Janet. "You seem a little off."

She was right. Not only was I was off my game, I was out of my mind. After what happened at the reunion the previous night, and then what happened with Gary Wright earlier that day, my mental health was on life support. Janet telling me about spending time with Jack Thompson wasn't helping.

Not that I was jealous. Of course I wasn't jealous. There was no way Jack would be interested in someone like Janet, so there was nothing to be jealous about. Janet was too innocent and nice for someone like Jack. It would be like a shark dating one of those cute little Dorie fish from *Finding Nemo*.

After the next point, we switched sides, and I switched the subject. "Guess who I saw today?" I asked Janet.

Janet dinked to Mabel. "Who?"

"Gary."

"Gary who?"

Mabel dinked it back.

"Gary Wright."

The ball deflected off Janet's paddle higher than she expected and Mabel pounced, blasting it back at her feet. The ball went straight through Janet's legs for another point."

"I hired him to paint Aunt Catherine's house. He told me to tell you hi." It occurred to me in that moment that we never found a hooking up prospect for Janet during the reunion. *Perhaps ...*

"Well tell him I said hi too."

"I'll do that." Maybe after I figured out what I wanted to do about Jack, I could revisit my original plan to hook up Janet. And this time I had a potential target.

With the two of us distracted, Dick and Mabel were true to their word. They whipped our butts. Nothing like getting your ass kicked by senior citizens to finish your day.

Touché Universe. Touché.

A<small>FTER PICKLEBALL</small>, J<small>ANET AND</small> I <small>SAID OUR GOODBYES</small> and then I went home and showered. After changing into my pajamas, the pair with the grumpy cat on the front, sticking the middle finger of its paw up, I realized I was hungry, so I called Ralph.

"Hello?" Ralph sounded tired.

"Hey it's me."

"Me who?" *Irritated too.* Ralph was in one of his moods.

I said, "I thought you were going to stop by and check in on me? Make sure I wasn't still suffering from cow trauma."

"Are you still suffering? From cow trauma?"

"A little." I rearranged the pillow that was jabbing me in the back. "On your way over, can you stop by the Thai place?"

"I never said I was coming over. And if I was, that's out of the way. Plus, I don't like Thai food."

"Make sure you get extra pineapple in the pineapple fried rice. Love you!"

While I was waiting for Ralph to deliver dinner, I dug out my old yearbook from the closet, flipping through the senior class pictures. I found the "T's". Specifically, "Thompson". More specifically, "Thompson, Jack".

His perfect smile, perfect skin, perfect face stared up at me from the page. Every high school has one. Captain of the football team. Prom king. Voted best looking, most athletic, and most likely to succeed. All the girls want him. All the guys want to *be* him. That guy at our school was Jack.

So ... I have a confession to make. Back in high school, I was kind of a stalker. Truth be told, I was obsessed. My teenage hormones worked overtime 24 hours a day, 7 days a week. I did everything I could to get close to him. Was he out of my league? Of course he was. Did it matter? No. I even tried out for cheerleading. Can you imagine? Me being cheerful? I only did it to get close to Jack.

As I flipped through the yearbook, a picture of prom caught my eye. There was Jack. With Ashley Griffin. The crowned king standing arm in arm with his witch, I mean, queen. Every high school has one of her too. Captain of the cheerleading squad. Boobs like a swimsuit model. The girl voted most likely to marry some rich, wrinkled old guy and then smother him in his sleep.

Ashley must have known what I was up to back then. As squad leader, she put me on top of the cheer pyramid during practice. And then her cronies, Heather and Britney, "accidentally" dropped me. I was on crutches for the rest of the season.

My brain held hostage by bygone memories, I never heard Ralph come in to my apartment. He saw the yearbook open in my lap. "That can't be good. Please tell me you're not still obsessing about Jack."

"Me? Obsessing? Don't be ridiculous." I needed an alibi fast. On the yearbook page opposite the prom pictures, there was a group photo of the chess club after they won some sort of prize. Gary Wright was in the picture, so I said, "I was looking up Gary Wright."

Ralph cocked an eyebrow. "The dungeon master?"

"Dungeon master?" Now my eyebrow raised. After twenty years, thankfully, most of high school, other than Jack Thompson, was a blur. I had almost forgotten that Janet had made us join the Dungeons and Dragons club senior year.

I slid over on the couch and Ralph settled in beside me. We flipped through the pages until we found a group photo under the heading, "Dungeons and Dragons Club." There I was, in some sort of green tunic and aluminum foil armor, holding a wooden axe in one hand and my crutches in the other. I also had a horned helmet on my head like an acne-faced viking.

"Remember?" Ralph pointed at the picture. "Janet was Periwinkle Bumblefoot, the kindhearted halfling. I was Gwain Goodfellow, the lovable bard. And you were ..." Ralph rubbed his chin and looked sideways contemplatively. "Who were you again?"

For the record, Ralph was being an asshole. He knew exactly who I was. He just wanted to hear me say it.

"Gronk," I mumbled.

"I'm sorry, what was that?"

"Gronk," I said again. "A half-orc barbarian."

"Oh, yes." Ralph's glee turned to euphoria. "With the pink magic shield."

"It wasn't pink, it was purple," I growled.

Ralph continued thumbing through the yearbook. "Hard to believe Gary's a painter now. I always figured he'd end up a rocket scientist or a brain surgeon or something."

"Yeah, well, he may have been one of the smart kids back in high school, but he's a real screwup now. The next time I see him, I'm going to fire him." If anyone deserved to be fired, it was Gary Wright. Dumping paint all over me. Trampling my sod. Running up my electric bill. Not to mention, painting my greige wall red! I had already been through five painters. What was one more?

I closed the yearbook and buried it in the back of my closet. The past was the past, and that's the way I intended to keep it. No more thinking about Jack. And certainly no more thinking about Gary.

For the rest of the night, Ralph and I ate pineapple fried rice and watched scary movies. After Ralph went home, I admit I pulled out my yearbook again. I flipped to the back, where friends and acquaintances scrawled farewell messages. I found Jack's message. On the very last day of school, he had come over to me and asked if he could sign it. For some reason, I said yes. I stared at it for what seemed like hours. Despite all my best efforts, Jack Thompson still haunted my head.

I'm sorry
Jack

Chapter Five

The next morning, I got up early so I could get over to Aunt Catherine's house before Gary could do any more damage. As soon as I verified that he finished doing what I had paid him to do, my plan was to fire him on the spot.

Since it was on the way, I swung by the real estate office to grab some paperwork. My inbox was swamped with invoices, and my voicemail was packed with messages. One of my clients wanted to lower her asking price, so I had to go in and edit the listing. One of my mortgage brokers had a question about an application, so I had to track down a tax form. The next thing I knew, it was time to order lunch. Someone suggested tacos so, well, obviously I had to stick around for that.

While I was scraping up the last bit of the guacamole with a tortilla chip, Bonnie, one of my coworkers, told me about her trip to Oahu and how she hiked up the side of a volcano. Not to be outdone, Joyce told us about her cruise to Iceland and how she hiked across a glacier. I explained I didn't have any vacation plans because I spent all my time renovating my dead Aunt Catherine's house. I left out the part about being broke and alone, although I'm sure they filled in the blanks.

When I finally made it over to the house and pulled in the

driveway, I saw Gary's van parked on the street. I noted his tires weren't crushing the grass. *Good.* What I was not pleased to see was the torrent of water gushing down the driveway.

I threw Charlotte into park and immediately saw the source of the flash flooding. It was a hose, spewing water down my driveway, into the gutter, and then parts unknown down the street. There was so much water the neighbor across the street started building an ark. Or he was just fixing a panel on his fence. One of the two.

I jumped out of Charlotte to investigate. There was a bucket beside the running hose filled with brushes and rags. Things a painter might use. I briefly considered dousing myself so I wouldn't explode. Following the hose, I found Gary hunched over in the backyard, uncoiling it from the reel.

I froze as soon as I saw him, unable to move, unable to think, unable to breathe. It was like a supervillain zapped me with a freeze ray.

Gary. Wasn't. Wearing. A. Shirt.

His overalls were dripping from a clothesline behind him. His boots were propped on the grass. The only thing on his body were paint stained cargo shorts and flip-flops. And the cargo shorts were barely on him. They sagged in the front, revealing the elastic band of his underwear. *Fruit of the Loom.* Above that, lines of hard muscles climbed up his body to his ribs.

While the outside of my body froze, the inside of my body was very much on fire. My lungs shifted into high gear to take in the sudden gulp of oxygen. My veins had to quadruple their capacity to accommodate all the rushing blood. I don't know how long I was standing there before he noticed me gawking.

"Mary? You okay?"

My brain was still frozen because instead of confronting him about my escalating water bill, what came out of my mouth was, "I forgot your Justin Bieber T-shirt." Apparently, missing shirts were top of mind.

Gary stood up from where he was bent over the hose, hair

dripping, rivulets of water cascading down the hard lines of his chest. "No problem." He shrugged his broad shoulders. "Just bring it next time."

There was no way the man standing in front of me was the same dungeon mastering, chess playing geek from high school. Unless lugging cans of paint and hoisting ladders was the optimal exercise for the pectoral muscles. And the glutes. I had seen Gary's arms and shoulders packed into the overalls already, but now set free with no encumbrance, they looked sculpted out of marble.

Gary bent over to pick up a dark blue T-shirt draped over one of Aunt Catherine's pool chairs. His butt was so tight I could have bounced a quarter off it. Which I really, really wanted to do. When he looked back over at me, his jaw twitched. "You want me to bring you a chair so you can sit down or something?"

As much as I could have spent the rest of the day, the rest of my life really, watching Gary carry heavy things, I said, "No, I'm fine, really. I just came over to check on the paint." Somehow, I kept from slobbering.

Gary smiled, showing off his perfectly white, perfectly straight teeth. Nestled between his perfectly pink, perfectly shaped lips. "Okay then. Follow me."

As I followed him to the back door, Gary slipped his T-shirt over his head and smoothed it down his muscle lined stomach. It read Yale across the front, right where his nipples would be. I assumed he had found it at a thrift store.

"I just finished so your timing is perfect."

That's not all that's perfect.

Once inside, Gary swept his hand from wall to wall like he was doing a reveal in one of those home improvement shows. "See? Greige. All greige." I made my way through the house, critically inspecting. True to his word, the entire house was now a blank, greige slate. Not a trace of red, or any other color. It was like we were in an old black and white movie before they invented color film. It was glorious.

"You know, I almost bought a house in this area," Gary said as

I ran my finger along a wall, feeling for any imperfections in the texture.

"You did?" *Yeah, sure,* I thought. Aunt Catherine's house was in the good part of town. Within walking distance of the revitalized downtown, where every weekend there was a new wine festival, street fair, or art show. Over the decades, the oak trees had grown as big as buildings, shading the brick lined roads. It was the part of the town where doctors and lawyers lived. Not painters.

"I heard the schools are some of the best in the area. Who knows, maybe someday I'll be your neighbor."

"Sure," I said. *When hell freezes over.*

Gary waited for me to finish my inspection of the wall paint. "So you really like it?"

Begrudgingly, I nodded. "It's not horrible." Despite Gary's earlier missteps, I had to admit that the walls looked pretty good. Granted, it wasn't rocket science, but Gary obviously knew how to use a paintbrush. Perhaps I had been wrong about Gary. Maybe hiring him wasn't such a bad idea after all.

"Shall we take a look at the kitchen now?" I asked. Once I verified Gary had completed his work in the kitchen, we would be able to shake hands, complete our transaction, and then go our separate ways for good.

"So about the kitchen …" Gary started.

Alarm bells began blaring. My dad, like Gary, had been a big Star Trek fan, the original show, with Captain Kirk. We used to watch the reruns together all the time. It was like when the Klingons showed up and the guys in the red shirts started running around, the screech of the red alert echoing throughout the starship.

"What about the kitchen?" My eyes turned the same color red as the wall used to be. And the shirts of the Star Trek guys.

"I was thinking …"

I didn't let him finish his thought. Nor did I complete any thinking of my own. Instead, my legs started moving toward the kitchen. Naturally, I assumed the worst. He had painted the walls eggplant purple. Or the ceiling was now stenciled with rainbows. Perhaps he painted a mural of unicorns frolicking in a gumdrop forest.

I burst through the kitchen door. To my horror I discovered the kitchen was ... still exactly the same as Aunt Catherine left it. Pink cabinets. Formica countertops. Avocado green linoleum. But as bad as each of those things were, the worst of the worst was the wallpaper. Pink rose blossoms and scrolling green vines. It gave off a serious grandma vibe. A grandma's grandma even. My kitchen guy, Gus, was scheduled to rip the cabinets out with a sledge-hammer and a crowbar. But getting rid of the wallpaper was the job of the painter. Gary's job. A job he had clearly failed to do.

Behind me, I heard Gary say, "I think we should keep the wallpaper."

"We?" An image of Gary as a hockey player formed in my imagination, weaving and spinning as he skated down the ice in the middle of a frozen pond. After a heat wave in July. With sharks swimming underneath. The ice Gary was skating on wasn't just wafer thin, it was translucent.

I pointed an accusing finger at Gary's muscled chest, trying not to look at his muscle-y-ness. Muscle-y-ness that was still very evident beneath his thrifted Yale T-shirt. "Do you always have this many personal opinions about the jobs you're hired to do?"

"Let me explain."

"There's nothing to explain," I fired back. "Gus is installing brand new slate grey cabinets at the end of the week. You know what goes great with slate grey?"

"Greige?"

"Greige."

"You know what does NOT go great with slate grey cabinets?"

Gary bit his lip. "Pink and green flower wallpaper?"

I cocked my finger at his face. "Bingo." You might say I was about to lose my patience at that point, but that would imply I had any patience to begin with. I took a deep breath. Janet always said that taking a deep breath was calming. It gave you time to think before you said something you'd regret later. As I was breathing deeply, I thought of several things I wanted to say to Gary and I knew I wouldn't have regretted saying any of them.

"Just hear me out." Gary pointed to the back wall of the kitchen, a wall covered in pink roses and green vines. "You see that wall over there?"

I decided I needed a few more deep breaths. "Let me guess. It needs a pop of color?"

"Actually no. More of a color ... blend."

"Color blend?"

"Color blend," Gary confirmed. "A merging of palettes. Sometimes, two colors that don't seem like they would go together end up complimenting each other nicely."

I took more breaths. Many more. "Right." I nodded. It was to acknowledge that I had heard Gary's words, not to signal agreement.

Gary placed a hand on the wall like he was touching a sacred relic. "It's just so ..."

"Hideous?" I asked.

"Original," he said.

"Deplorable."

"Genuine."

"Gruesome."

"Unique."

"Repulsive."

"They don't make it like this anymore."

"Thank God."

I'm not sure what Gary thought he saw on my face that made him keep talking, but he kept talking. "I found a few colors we could merge. Tie in the pinks and greens from the wallpaper with the slate cabinets and the greige."

Now I've made many bad choices in my life, and there have been many hard lessons that I've learned over the years. In the fourth grade, I didn't fully apply myself in Mrs. Fitzgerald's

English class, which she thoroughly documented in my permanent school record. As a teenager, I snuck out of church in the middle of Pastor Hanson's sermon to make out with Billy Hanson in the confession booth. In college, Janet and I accidentally joined a cult because the guy handing out the pamphlets was super cute, and there was a promise of donuts. But in hindsight, those were nothing. Hiring Gary Wright was the biggest bad choice of them all.

I took another breath. Not because I was trying to control my emotions. I just had nothing left. I said the only thing left to say at that point. "Gary."

"Yes?"

"You're fired."

Gary tilted his head sideways. For a moment I thought he hadn't heard me, because his face scrunched up like he was trying to listen to something faint and distant. Finally he said, "What was that?"

"I said you're fired."

"No."

"No?"

"No, I mean, what's that noise?"

"It's the noise of you getting fired."

"No, the other thing."

"What other thing?"

"Listen."

At first I heard nothing. Then I did hear it. But I had to hear it a second time before I could wrap my head around what I heard.

Meow

My ceiling was meowing. The sound was faint, but unmistakable. Then I heard more sounds. Scurrying footsteps. Random thumps. The gnawing of tooth and claw on exposed wood.

Meow

A creature had infiltrated Aunt Catherine's home. Gary

returned from his van with a ladder, two flashlights, and a thick pair of gloves.

I had been hoping for a bazooka and a flamethrower. Vagrant vermin haunting the attic were even worse for resale value than ugly kitchen wallpaper and red walls. The beast had to go.

"Where's the attic?" Gary asked.

I pointed up.

Gary rolled his eyes. "I mean the access door to the attic."

After a quick search, we found the access door in the hallway ceiling. And by "we", I mean Gary. He set his ladder underneath.

"Can you hold this for me?" I held on to the ladder with both hands. When he climbed to the top, I got a good view of his butt. I pretended to read one of the warning labels on the ladder step when he looked down at me. "You better take a look." *I have been.*

The inside of the attic was dark, hot, and smelled like buffalo. We scanned the darkened corners with our flashlights. The space was tight, so Gary had to get down on all fours to venture deeper. I looked at his butt again.

"A lot of old boxes up here." Gary's flashlight illuminated a wall of boxes stacked floor to ceiling. "Was your aunt ever featured on one of those hoarder shows?"

"No," I said. "But she was a guest one time on a public access show about knitting."

I hadn't even known the boxes were there. After the house cleared probate, I did a massive purge, packing anything sentimental into storage, to be given away or thrown away later. I hired an estate company to sell off the rest. The only piece of furniture left was Aunt Catherine's bed, because apparently no one wanted a dead woman's old mattress. It was still sitting in the bedroom.

I took a step toward the boxes, planning to investigate.

Creak

"Careful," Gary warned. "These old houses can be tricky. Make sure you step on the crossbeams so you don't fall through."

Sticking to the narrow lengths of wood was easier said than

done. You'd have to be an Olympic gymnast and a contortionist to navigate all the rafters and ceiling joists.

"There! I think I saw something!" Gary pointed with his flashlight. I swept my flashlight over, but the only thing I saw were shadows. Whatever critter was lurking here, it must have had extensive ninja training.

I put my hand on a support beam to steady myself and came away with a fistful of spider webs. The place gave me the creeps. I just wanted to find the invader, extract it, then get the heck out.

Meow

The sound was louder now. Like it was close. Like it was watching us. And waiting for the chance to leap out of the darkness and devour us whole. "Sounds like a cat," Gary said.

"What kind of cat though? Bobcat? Wild cat? Panther?"

We both turned when the sound of scurrying came from the far corner. "Sounds like it's coming from over there." Gary aimed his light toward the farthest corner of the attic. The darkness swallowed it whole. "One of us should check it out." I looked at Gary and he looked at me. Neither one of us moved. Gary sighed. "Fine."

The roof slanted sharply the deeper we went. Gary had to get down on all fours and belly crawl to get underneath the angled timbers. While Gary played Twister with the support beams, I decided that the best thing for me to do was keep looking at his butt.

Eventually, Gary got tangled up in a crisscross of two by fours. "I can't get all the way over there," he said. "I'm too big." He looked back at me expectantly. As in, expecting me to crawl over and join him.

"Oh no. I don't like small spaces. Or dark spaces. Or spaces with cats."

Meow

"We can't just leave it there," said Gary. "What if it gets trapped and then starves to death? That would be horrible."

"Good point," I admitted. "Dead cat smell is a real turnoff for potential buyers."

"I meant horrible for the cat." Clearly Gary had never smelled dead cat before. I hadn't either, but I caught a whiff of wet cat once and I could only imagine that dead cat was even worse.

"I'll watch your back," Gary said. "Promise." He flashed a smile that was supposed to be reassuring, but instead of being reassuring, I found it disappointing.

I much preferred the idea of watching Gary's back instead of him watching mine. "Fine."

We switched positions, playing limbo with a beam. As Gary slid past me, we found ourselves pressed against each other, face to face. With no air circulation up there, his Yale T-shirt was damp with sweat. *Maybe he should take that shirt off again.*

I was so distracted by the thought of Gary taking his shirt off, I almost missed the flash of fur streaking through the darkness.

Meow

"Grab it!" Gary pointed.

I spun on my heels to snatch it.

Whack

My forehead smashed into a two by four. The world spun. Off balance and dazed, I reeled backward, falling between two of the ceiling joists.

Crunch

When I looked down, I saw my butt had punched through the attic floor, and what I would later learn was Aunt Catherine's bedroom ceiling. My knees were tucked under my chin in the same position one might end up in after falling through a toilet seat.

"Don't move." Gary held up his hands like he was casting a spell of paralysis. I couldn't have moved if I wanted to. My butt was wedged in tight.

Creak

"Here," Gary leaned forward, keeping his feet perched on the crossbeams. "I'll pull you up." I grabbed onto his outstretched hands. "There. I've got you."

As a real estate agent, I've had my fair share of handshakes with brawny, able-bodied, man's men. Carpenters, plumbers, landscapers, electricians. Alpha males who work all day with their hands. Hands that felt like you were shaking a strip of sun baked rawhide coated with sandpaper. Gary's skin was as soft as a baby butt lathered in lotion. *What kind of painter hands were those?*

"Okay now." Gary braced his feet. "I'm going to pull you up." We locked our hands. "On the count of three, okay?" Gary squatted over me, every hard line from his hamstrings and quadriceps standing at attention. I had to close my eyes to avoid looking at his crotch.

Creak

"One. Two. Three!" Gary yanked me up by both arms, forearms rippling from the effort. My butt popped out of the ceiling hole like the cork from a wine bottle.

As I rose from the floor, Gary backpedaled, nimble feet tiptoeing along the beam. I fell into his arms. And for one moment, time stopped. Our eyes met. We both stopped breathing. Our quivering lips poised less than an inch apart.

"I've got you." His voice was breathless.

"I know." So was mine. He held me like he would never release me. And in that frozen moment, that was perfectly fine with me.

That's when the frozen moment thawed. And once time started moving again, it moved at the speed of light. With the momentum of my body crashing into his, Gary took one last step back. One irrevocable step in reverse.

Creak ... Crack ... Crunch

Eyes wide with horror, Gary tipped backward. I tipped with him. I went from horizontal to vertical to horizontal again. All I could do was grab onto Gary's shoulders and ride him like a toboggan down an ice slicked slope.

Our tangled bodies crashed through the ceiling in Aunt

Catherine's bedroom and landed right in the middle of the king sized bed.

I was still holding onto him as the last remnants of plaster dust drifted down from the ceiling. The room looked like a blizzard had blown through.

"You okay?" Gary's face was caked with white powder.

I could feel his heart beating in his chest as I laid on top of him. Mine was beating just as hard. "Physically, I think so. Mentally, I'm not so sure." For a few moments, I didn't move. I wasn't injured. I just didn't want to get off of him. "You?"

Gently, Gary rolled me onto the bed. He winced as he sat upright. "My spine is broken in at least six places."

I propped myself up on my elbows. "I think I saw an old bandaid in the bathroom."

Gary plucked a piece of insulation from my hair.

"Is that asbestos?"

"I think so."

Meow

Chapter Six

While I scoured my contact list to find someone available for emergency ceiling repairs, Gary resumed the search for the felonious feline. He found it outside on the roof, near one of the open air vents leading into the attic. We watched from the backyard as the cat licked itself for a good ten minutes. At one point, it lifted a paw and seemed to give us the finger.

After pleasuring itself, the cat sauntered over to a nearby oak tree and effortlessly leaped onto one of the outstretched branches. It climbed down to the ground, then strut across the yard toward the neighbor's house. It turned back to look at us one final time, a smirk on its whiskered face.

"That cat is an asshole," I said.

Gary shrugged. But he didn't disagree with me.

In the neighbor's yard, the cat went to the back door where there was a bowl of food and water waiting. It nibbled and sipped a bit, then flipped its tail our way. After that, it resumed pleasuring itself out in the open, where everyone could see. ASS-HOLE.

That's when the back door opened, and a woman stepped out on the porch to refill the cat's food and water. I decided I was going to put an end to the cat trespassing once and for all. I marched over, Gary at my heels. "Is that your cat?" I called, ready to give this woman a piece of my mind.

"No, it's not," the woman said. It wasn't the answer I was expecting.

"Then whose is it?" I countered.

"You the new owner?" The woman jabbed a finger at Aunt Catherine's place.

"Technically."

"Then, technically, it's yours." The woman scooped the cat up, noogied its head, then stuffed it into my arms. The cat didn't look any happier with the situation than I did.

"I've just been feedin' it time to time," said the woman. "Ever since Cathy passed. She's a real bitch, that one."

Gary and I exchanged a look. I can't say I knew my great aunt well, but it seemed harsh to call her a bitch, considering she was dead.

"Not Cathy," said the woman. "I mean the cat." The neighbor woman thought about it for another minute. "Well, actually, Cathy too."

The cat started squirming to wiggle out of my arms. So I squeezed it tighter. Which only pissed it off more.

"Its name is Purrfect, 'cept with a PU instead of a PE. Purrrrr-fect." The neighbor woman purred the name as she said it, then pointed at the collar. "See?"

I pushed aside a clump of fur so I could read the tag. Purrfect must have thought I was going to strangle her, because she sank her claws and teeth into my flesh. The tag on the collar did indeed read Purrfect, and listed the address of Aunt Catherine's house, which, technically, was now mine.

"Cathy loved that flea bag more than anything."

Gary looked at me like my doctor had just given me a cancer diagnosis, and was trying to assess which of the five stages I was in.

For the record, it was denial. "It's fine," I said. "I'll just drop it off at the shelter on my way home."

Gary, the neighbor woman, and Purrfect all looked at me like I had suggested we steal the donation box for the special needs children from the orphanage and use it to tip strippers.

"Ha ha. Just kidding," I said. None of them looked like they believed me, especially Purrfect. Which was smart of her, because I wasn't kidding. I wasn't kidding at all.

"I'm sure you and your husband will give her a lovely home," said the neighbor woman, as she headed back toward her own yard.

"Oh. No. He's not my husband," I said.

"Well, that was emphatic," Gary mumbled, just loud enough for me to hear.

The neighbor woman didn't seem to believe that either. She had a twinkle in her eye and a knowing smile on her face. Even though she didn't actually know anything.

"We're not married," I said again.

"What you kids do with your relationships these days is your own business," said the neighbor woman, as she turned and walked away.

"There is no relationship," I called after her. "There is no business!"

Purrfect thrashed in my arms as the neighbor woman disappeared into her house. In case her feelings about me holding her were not already clear, she let out a long, woeful moan.

"Perfect," I said.

"No, purrrr-fect," Gary purred.

"Cute." Purrfect twisted in my arms and I had to use both hands to keep her from escaping. I knew that if I put her down, she would make her way back into the attic, where enough damage had been done already.

"I better take her home." I had yet to find a ceiling repair specialist, but it was difficult to make calls when you were trying to wrangle a squirming cat. "You know anything about fixing large holes in flimsy ceilings?"

"No. I'm actually not very handy." *No kidding.* "Besides, I think you fired me, remember?"

Actually, I didn't remember. I had forgotten about firing Gary with all the bedlam and chaos. "Oh yeah. Right." I felt bad about firing him, but then I remembered his aversion to greige and his wallpaper fetish. Not to mention dumping paint all over me and throwing me through a ceiling. I was well within my rights to fire him. He was lucky I was too lazy to leave a Yelp review.

Purrfect made a sound like an ambulance siren that was running low on batteries. I had to get her back to my apartment before she clawed open my jugular.

"Thanks for ..." I racked my brain for something I could say to finish the sentence, but my mind was all blank. I went with "... guilting me into taking in a sociopathic cat."

"You're welcome?"

We stood there looking at each other as the silence went from uncomfortable to awkward to weird.

Gary looked like he had something else to say. Whatever it was, I had no interest in hearing it.

I turned and walked away

"Maybe I'll see you around," Gary called after me.

"Maybe," I called back. *Not in a million years.*

I made my way back to Charlotte and tossed Purrfect in the back seat, eager to put my brief relationship with Gary Wright far behind me and head for home. You know how you hear people say that cats always land on their feet? It isn't true. When I tossed Purrfect into the back of my BMW, she bounced off the back seat cushion, then landed on her head on the floor.

"Sorry." She made another moaning sound, then hissed. That one, I suppose, I deserved.

As we pulled out of the driveway, I activated the child safety locks. I figured they would work on cats, too. I didn't think Purrfect could open the car doors, but I wasn't taking any chances. Before shifting into drive, I tilted the rearview mirror to look

Purrfect in the eyes. "You be good back there, okay? For example, don't pee on anything." In hindsight, I should have been more comprehensive in my instructions.

When I first got Charlotte at the dealership, I had splurged. All the options. Upgrades for days. I wanted Charlotte dressed to impress. One of the more expensive options I splurged for was the luxury seating package, which added the multi-contour Napa leather seats.

Named after the company that developed the unique tanning process, a company located in Napa Valley California, I imagined it must somehow involve the cattle ranchers hand feeding the cows wine grapes as the cows reclined on a red cushioned sofa, with a bowl of fresh fruits beside them, so their hides got extra soft and squishy. Napa leather was the seating option of choice for discriminating luxury car buyers.

Turns out, it was also the leather of choice for disgruntled cats. Not to sit upon, but to eat. When I got home and opened the back door, my upgraded seats looked like they had been slathered in honey and then fed to a den of grizzly bears.

"Bad kitty! Bad!" Purrfect looked up at me with her big blue eyes, batting her eyelashes.

Meow

Which in cat language, roughly translates to "fuck you".

INSIDE MY APARTMENT, I GAVE PURRFECT THE GRAND tour. "There's the kitchen. That room back there is the bedroom. This is the couch." It was a small apartment.

Despite being a real estate agent, I didn't own a house of my own. You see, home ownership is a lot like having a relationship. There's a lot of upkeep involved. A lot of maintenance. Things break. It's better to keep it temporary. That way, when things inevitably go sideways, you simply move on to the next project.

Once Purrfect made herself at home, curling up on my bed

and getting cat hair everywhere, I opened up my laptop and ordered a cat carrier from Amazon. One with a lock. My plan was to put a "Free Cat" post out on social media, and if there weren't any takers, I would drive her down to the shelter. Somehow, Purrfect must have known what I was up to because she hissed at me from under the kitchen table.

I was about to close my laptop when Amazon generously suggested that I should also buy a scratching post. I didn't want scratch marks all over my furniture, so I clicked "yes". Then Amazon suggested a litter box. Absolutely. Cat food. I suppose. Cat treats. Just this once. While we're at it, how about a catnip stuffed, mouse shaped chew toy? You only live once. Unless you're a cat. Then you live nine times. After spending three hundred and seventy-two dollars, I had officially spoiled Purrfect. Rags to riches in a day.

"Happy?" I called into the bedroom

Meow

"Right back at you."

That night, I woke up sometime after midnight with the weird feeling that I was being watched. Because I was. Purrfect sat on the nightstand, staring at me in the dark. Probably trying to figure out how to smother me in my sleep.

I pulled the pillow over my head, but I could still feel her eyes on me. "What do you want?"

Meow

I threw the pillow, but she ducked, and I knocked over a lamp instead.

Meow

"Are you hungry?" She just sat there. "Thirsty?" Still, she sat.

I held up my hands, palms open, so she could see that I was unarmed. Slowly, gently, I extended an open hand. Purrfect braced herself, but held her ground.

I brushed her cheek with my fingertips. Miraculously, she didn't flinch. I placed my hand on her head. Not only did she not recoil, she seemed to lean into it.

Emboldened, I went all-in. My fingers caressed her ears. They were as soft as velvet. No, softer than velvet. Napa leather soft.

I let my hand sink into the fur behind her neck. She arched her back as I stroked her from head to tail. She didn't groan. Didn't hiss. I tried another long stroke, then another again.

As soon as I removed my hand, she stepped toward me. Her head nudged under my chin. She cuddled up against me. And then fell asleep. I don't know how long I just laid there, listening to her purr. How nice it must be, I thought. One moment you're holed up in some dark attic, all alone, just fighting to survive. The next moment, someone swoops in to take care of you. Spoil you. Give you their love. Even if maybe you didn't exactly deserve it.

Like me.

Chapter Seven

T he next morning, when the alarm went off, I was already up scouring the Internet for clues. The plan had come to me in the middle of the night, in between the tossing and the turning, a vision forming as I stared at the ceiling above.

Ever since the reunion, memories and thoughts about Jack Thompson had wormed their way into my brain. I had spent the past twenty years trying to forget him and what he had done to me, but one chance encounter now had me spinning, his words bouncing around in my head.

I was hoping we could talk.

So I could apologize.

Make it up to you somehow.

If you'd let me.

The smart thing for me to do would have been to rip up Jack's business card, have a hypnotist erase all my memories, and then join a convent in Tibet.

Then it occurred to me. That's what the old Mary would have done. Run away and hide. Curl up on the bathroom floor in the fetal position and let life kick her around. But I wasn't the old Mary, I was the new Mary. And the new Mary didn't back down from a ... *fight? Challenge? Super hot, once unattainable guy who, for some strange reason, showed a hint of interest?*

The truth was, I had no idea what was going on or why it was happening. Was I still physically attracted to Jack Thompson? Of course. *Who wouldn't be?* Was I intrigued by the potential possibilities? *Guilty as charged.* Did I want to prove to myself that after twenty years I was no longer the Queen of the Geeks? *Bingo.*

It wasn't that hard to find him, although the list of people with the name Jack Thompson was surprisingly long. After adding a filter for the keyword "Winter Park", the town listed on Jack's business card, I found a reference to a Dr. Jack Thompson in the blog archives of Modern Podiatry.

Now I know what you're thinking. Because I thought the same thing. A podiatrist? What kind of man enjoys spending all day looking at feet? Feet are all wrinkly. They can be hairy. A lot of times they smell. But then I realized something. A man who knows his way around a foot is bound to give one hell of a foot massage.

After closing my laptop, I glanced over at the bed where Purrfect was curled up against the pillow. She glared at me as if I was to blame for interrupting her beauty sleep.

I hopped in the shower, shaved everything that needed shaving, then shotgunned an entire banana kale smoothie.

After applying my best make-up, I doused myself in perfume, then wiggled my way into the sexy red dress I saved for special occasions. The one that showed off my calves and made my ass look like I did squats every day.

"I'll be back in a couple hours," I told Purrfect.

A whisker twitched.

"I filled up your dish with cat treats." My strategy was to bribe her with food to mitigate the inevitable cat-tastrophe the inside of my apartment would endure. Like a cat-nado. Or a purr-icane.

"Just try not to destroy anything. Please." She didn't make me any promises.

TRAFFIC WAS LIGHT THAT EARLY IN THE MORNING, SO it was easy to get across town. I had an appointment at the nail salon, the first appointment of the day. I ordered something off the VIP Deluxe menu called the Velvet Cucumber, which, coincidentally, was also the stage name of someone Janet and I met on a road trip to Fort Lauderdale back in college.

"Mimosa Mrs. Mary?" The receptionist presented a tall glass of fizzy refreshment on a silver tray.

"It's Miss. And yes. Thank you."

Sinking deeper into the massage chair, Vivian, the nail technician, buffed my cuticles, wedged cucumber slices between my toes, then propped my feet up on a soft velvet pillow. The candy red polish was a perfect match for my dress. A slathering of cucumber lotion made my feet smell like spring.

"Another mimosa, Miss Mary?" Vivian dug her thumbs into the back of my calf muscles, firm hands kneading away like she was making a loaf of sourdough.

I checked my watch. I still had plenty of time before my big date. "Why yes, thank you, don't mind if I do." Sixty minutes of VIP Deluxe pampering does wonders for one's mental state. By the time the vibrations from the massage chair subsided, the emotional traumas of my recent ordeals had all washed away on a velvet pillow boat in a river of cucumbers.

After tipping generously, I left the salon and scoped out the tall glass building across the street. I couldn't help but smile at my own clever brilliance. Strategically, I had booked my pedicure appointment at that salon because of the proximity to that building. A five-minute walk later and I was there.

As I walked through the parking lot, another red BMW caught my eye, almost the same color and model as mine. The personalized plate read, DRMEOW. *A fellow cat lover? Hmmm.*

As I got closer to the building, I saw a directory listing the business occupants. My heart skipped a beat. There it was, on the right-hand side, in gold lettering near the bottom of the marble slab.

Suite 250. Jack Thompson, M.D.

Like I said, C-L-E-V-E-R B-R-I-L-L-I-A-N-C-E.

I took several deep breaths, then made my way to the front desk of Suite 250. I scribbled my signature on the sign-in sheet. My hand shook so badly from nerves it was even less legible than usual.

The receptionist looked up at me from behind the desk. Her name tag read, "Susan". I tried to smile but when I glimpsed myself in the plexiglass, my face looked like I was about to barf.

"Do you have an appointment?" asked Susan.

"Yes," I replied. *Why was my voice two octaves higher?*

"And your name?"

"Mary. Burns. Mary Burns. With a B. And an M."

Susan frowned as she reviewed the schedule. "Your appointment is at three thirty."

I smiled and nodded.

Susan looked down at her watch, then back up at me. "It's only ten thirty."

"I like to be prompt."

Susan handed me a clipboard stacked with paperwork. "Have a seat and fill out these forms. You'll hand them to Dr. Thompson once he comes in. We'll call you in a few ..." Susan looked down at her watch again. "... hours."

While I was filling out the paperwork, I took peeks at the other patients when they weren't looking. There was a young couple holding hands, the anxiety clear on their faces. Like they were waiting for some critical life alternating diagnosis. Was it a hangnail or a bunion?

There was a pregnant woman who looked like she was about to explode. Her feet were so swollen she wasn't wearing shoes, only socks. Maybe a severe case of athlete's foot.

I don't know if it was Purrfect waking me up in the middle of the night, the relaxing chair massage, or the three consecutive mimosas, but it wasn't long before I found myself unable to stifle the yawns. I decided it wouldn't hurt to rest my eyes. Just a little bit. Just a momentary respite.

I MUST HAVE FALLEN ASLEEP, BECAUSE WHEN I OPENED my eyes again, the waiting room was empty and I was alone. Except for Jack.

I saw him standing by the door that led back to the exam rooms. A crisp white doctor's jacket hung on his shoulders, like a superhero's cape. A stethoscope hung around his tautly muscled neck. There was a twinkle in his eyes. He looked at me like he had x-ray vision.

"Hello Mary." I didn't just hear his voice, I felt it in my bones. "Are you ready to come?" Jack held the door open wide.

Following him on wobbly legs, Jack led me back to an exam room. All the nurses must have already gone home.

Jack motioned to the exam table. "Sit," he commanded.

I obeyed.

Jack walked over to stand in front of me, looking me over from head to toe. He smiled again, then dropped to his knees, sending my pulse into heart attack territory. "Give me your foot."

I did.

"I'm going to remove your shoes," he said. "Then I'm going to need you to spread your legs."

My head was nodding up and down before I even realized it was moving.

"Is it okay if I touch you now?"

I wanted to tell Jack he could do anything and everything to me, but my voice no longer worked.

Jack gently grasped my ankles, fingers like feathers on my skin. He removed my shoes, prodding muscles and bones and tendons. I closed my eyes as a gasp slipped out of my throat. I could feel his touch working up the inside of my calfs, underneath my dress. My muscles melted in his palms.

Our eyes locked. He flashed that smile again, sending my heartbeat racing. Boiling blood rushed through my body in a torrent.

Jack's hands smoothed past my calves and then up over my knees, kneading into my quadriceps, cupping the back of my hamstrings. He played the nerves on my thighs like a master violinist performing a symphony.

He moved closer. His body now pressing against mine. I could feel his breath on my inner thigh. See his lips quivering, a hair's breadth from my skin. Hear the rasp in his throat as he tugged my dress up to my hips.

Just when I felt like I was going to erupt like a Yellowstone geyser dormant for a thousand years, his fingers moved even higher. Teasing. Probing. I felt a finger slip under the edge of my panties, now moist from the inferno which was raging between my legs. His other hand came in behind me, squeezing the flesh of my bottom and pulling me closer to his mouth.

"I want you Mary. I need you. I need you now." Every muscle pressed against me was hard and pulsing, like a tightly coiled steel spring. "Do you want me Mary?"

"Yes," I moaned. "Yes Jack, take me. Take me now, please!"

"Mrs. Burns?" A voice echoed from the darkness. "Mrs. Burns? Are you awake?" I opened my eyes to find a nurse standing over me. She was young, blonde, and pretty. Her name tag said "Kelsey."

I needed a moment to regain my bearings. When I looked around the crowded waiting room, all the other patients were staring at me.

Every. Single. One.

"Was I snoring?" Instinctively, I wiped the drool from my chin.

The pregnant woman across from me slowly shook her head, then said, "It wasn't snoring ... exactly."

"It was more of a moaning," said the mom sitting with her teen daughter, who still hadn't blinked.

"Do you need anything Mrs. Burns?" Kelsey's face looked like she was trying not to smell a fart.

"It's Miss," I said. "I'm not married." The pregnant woman, the mom, and the teen daughter all nodded as if that fact was already well understood.

I followed Kelsey out of the waiting room and into the hallway. She pointed to a scale. "If you could just step there."

"You're weighing me?"

"For our records, yes."

"Does the doctor see this?"

She made the fart face again. "Is there a problem?"

"No problem." I handed Kelsey my car keys, then I took off my shoes and handed her my phone. I considered stripping naked to shed a few extra pounds, but assumed that would be frowned upon.

Once I stepped on the scale, Kelsey meticulously documented my measurements while I cursed the bowl of ice cream and nachos I had the prior night. To be clear, the nachos weren't on top of the ice cream, although they were in the same bowl.

"Right this way." Kelsey started down the hall, her tight ass swaying back and forth. "So what brings you to see Dr. Thompson today, your annual checkup?"

"You're supposed to get checked annually?" I looked down at my freshly painted feet, confused. I had never heard of annual foot exams at the podiatrist office. *Maybe, because they DON'T ACTUALLY EXIST!* That should have been my first clue that something was amiss. But in my blind rush to see Jack, I missed one tiny little detail in my scheming.

Kelsey wore her fart look again. "You don't get regular checkups?"

"No, this is my first time. I thought people only went to this type of doctor when they had a problem."

"Problem?" Kelsey's fart look kept getting worse.

"Yes, you know, like a fungal infection or funny smells."

Kelsey stopped. "You have a … fungal infection? Or funny … smells?"

I laughed her off. "Me? Oh, no. No fungus here. And the last time I sniffed down there everything smelled normal. I mean, you know, as far as I can tell." The expression on Kelsey's face should have been my second clue that something was off. It was a mixture of terror and, well, more terror. But I was too busy looking at my perfectly pedicured foot to notice so I blindly barreled ahead. "Mine is just a little sore. I've been taking on so many new clients lately. Maybe I just wore it out. You know how it is, right?"

Kelsey looked like she had no idea "how it is," at all.

"It's always in and out, this way and that way, back and forth. And of course they want me to do EVERYTHING. I'm always bending over backwards for everyone."

Kelsey opened her mouth as if she was going to say something, but then she just made the fart face instead.

"You'd be surprised what some clients demand these days. I mean, sure, the money's good, but it would be nice every once in a while to prop up my feet and relax. Let them do some of the work for a change."

Kelsey pointed to the open door of an exam room. "You're in here."

"Are you married?" I asked.

Kelsey hesitated for a beat before answering. "Single."

"If you're ever in the market, I help a lot of single women," I explained. "I know some like to try the self service route, but you'll get better results with a professional."

Kelsey took a long step back to let me pass by, careful not to make skin to skin contact.

As I stepped into the exam room, I noticed the inclined chair with the paper cover and the stirrups sticking out. My initial thought was that it was strange that a podiatrist would use the same chair to examine feet that a gynecologist used to examine vaginas.

But I didn't really get it until Nurse Kelsey pointed to the paper gown folded on the chair. "Everything comes off. Well, except for your shoes. It's not like he's going to be looking at your feet."

I realized the magnitude of my miscalculation when I saw the framed medical license on the wall. "Jack Thompson, M.D. Certification in Obstetrics & Gynecology". I realized the enormity of my error when I saw the life-sized plastic vulva on the desk, right beside the box of rubber gloves and commercial grade tube of lubrication.

Nurse Kelsey pointed again at the paper robe. "Doctor Thompson will be right in." If she had been wearing a silver crucifix, I think she would have been holding it up at that point and dousing me with holy water. But since she apparently didn't have her exorcism kit handy, she just shut the exam room door and fled.

Once again, somewhere out there in the cosmos, I heard the Universe laughing.

In hindsight, I should have done a little more research. In my rush to find Jack, I had missed a few key details. If I would have searched a little longer, perhaps a little more thoroughly, I would have discovered that Dr. Jack Thompson, Podiatrist, practiced medicine in Winter Park, *Colorado*, most likely specializing in ski accidents and snow shoe injuries, not Winter Park, *Florida*.

And perhaps, if I had been a wee bit more thorough in my investigative efforts, I wouldn't have paid two hundred dollars for a VIP Deluxe Velvet Cucumber just to have the man who had been tormenting my dreams for over two decades get up close and personal with my unwaxed hoo-haw in a desperate plot to talk to him again.

Obviously, I couldn't let Jack see me like that. I had to escape.

As I was sneaking past the front desk, I overheard Susan, the receptionist, talking with Nurse Kelsey. "That's the last of the appointments for today," said Susan. "Jack took the rest of the afternoon off."

"Must be nice to make your own rules," Kelsey said. "What's he up to this time?"

I had to get down on all fours when she glanced back toward the hallway.

"Oh, you know, the usual." They both giggled like it was an inside joke. *Where was he going? Or who was he going to see?*

My original plan was to escape Jack's office, sneak down to my car, and then keep driving until I hit Canada. But after eavesdropping, I decided on a new plan. A plan that involved me finding out what Jack Thompson was up to. A plan where, perhaps, my $200 Velvet Cucumber wouldn't go to waste after all.

Chapter Eight

T he Winter Park Golf and Racquet Club was a three hundred and fifty acre private property, nestled amongst the alligator filled lakes, snake filled palmettos, and mosquito filled bogs of Central Florida. With a PGA Tour caliber golf course, a resort style pool, and a half dozen bars and restaurants, all stocked with cold beer and at least seven flavors of chicken wings, it was the local playground of Central Florida's middle-class elite; the car crash lawyers, Botox surgeons, and time-share executives who called the greater Orlando area home.

I followed Jack to the guardhouse, which sat just outside the front gate. Sitting a few cars back in line, I watched Jack flash his membership card, and the guard waved him through. When I got to the gate, I flashed my best smile. The security guard seemed unimpressed.

"I suppose you need to see my membership card?"

The guard's face was a blank slate. His name badge said "Leonard."

I dug through my purse. "Let's see here. Costco membership. Punch card for Starbucks. Voter identification card. Let me guess, Republican?"

Leonard's face still didn't move.

"Hmm," I stalled, still playing the part of looking through my purse. "Here's a coupon for a free chicken sandwich. It's all yours if you let me through." I flashed another smile. Leonard did not look sympathetic. "I must have left my membership card in my other purse."

Leonard growled. "You got a driver's license?"

I handed it over.

Leonard glared at it. "Mrs. Mary Burns."

"It's just Miss, actually."

Leonard studied my driver's license like he was looking at one of those mugshots of America's Most Wanted they put up in the post office. He looked for me on his computer, and, as expected, didn't find me because I wasn't actually a member.

"Look," I said. "I'm just going to be honest with you here. You know that guy in the red BMW a couple cars ahead of me?"

"You mean Doctor Jack?"

"Yeah. Doctor Jack. I'm here to see him."

Leonard huffed. "You some kind of stalker?" His glare got glare-ier.

"Stalker? Me? No." I waved my hand in dismissal. "Of course not. I was just ... following him. He was supposed to get me in."

"He didn't say nothing." Leonard raised an eyebrow.

"That's because he doesn't know that I'm here."

Leonard rubbed his chin. "So let me make sure I understand. You're following him. But he doesn't know it."

"That's right."

"That's the literal definition of stalking." Leonard gave me a good, hard look. "What do you want with him anyway?"

It was a good question, a question I wasn't sure I could even answer myself. Demand he apologize for humiliating me in high school? Ask him if he was sorry for scarring me for life? Rip off all my clothes and use his hard body to relieve decades of sexual frustration?

With my brain momentarily paralyzed, my mouth went rogue. "I want to show him my feet."

As a security guard at a fancy-schmancy country club, Leonard had likely heard all kinds of excuses from people who wanted to sneak in. But, judging by the look on his face, that was the first time he had heard that particular excuse. "You want to show him your feet?"

"I spent almost two hundred dollars on this stupid pedicure to impress him, and now I just want him to see my feet."

Leonard nodded, as if what I was saying made any kind of sense. "What exactly does a two hundred dollar foot look like?"

I slipped off my heel and stuck my foot out the window. "Velvet Cucumber."

"Looks velvety. I can smell the cucumber from here. Nice."

"Thanks."

"What kind of chicken sandwich coupon?"

"Chicken King." I dug it back out of my purse. "Good for one Crispy Original or Spicy Deluxe. I see you as a Crispy Original."

Leonard held out his hand. I gave him the coupon. He gave me back my license. "Actually, I'm a Spicy Deluxe man. Can't judge a book by its cover, Ms. Mary. Never assume."

Once the gate opened, I saluted Leonard and drove through.

AFTER SEARCHING THE CLUBHOUSE, THE WELLNESS center, and messing up some guy's birdie putt on the sixteenth green, I spotted Jack's car parked near the driving range. Jack himself was blasting balls into the stratosphere from a driving bay.

After a quick stop at the pro shop, I reserved the Pro Package in the bay next to Jack's, which included a bucket of drinks, a basket of balls, some rental clubs, and a nice pillowed bench for relaxing.

Before taking my position, I watched Jack for a bit from afar. His stroke was incredible. Smooth. Elegant. Firm stance. Firm ... everything.

I took careful note of how Jack's hips thrust forward and the muscles in his arms rippled every time his club arced downward and impacted the ball, sending it high to the sky in a long, lazy loop. Watching Jack was like watching a gazelle. If gazelles wore tight checkered pants that enhanced their crotch bulge.

I adjusted my new golf skirt so it would show off my legs and tipped my new golf visor to shield my eyes from the sun. I had stopped by the pro shop for a quick costume change. Satisfied I looked the part, I took my place on the mat.

My bay was to Jack's left, which meant that I was behind him when he tee'd off. I watched him hit another ball, this time up close. Those checkered pants were really tight. When he turned to reach for another ball, I pretended I had yet to notice him, busying myself with selecting a club.

"Mary?" His voice angled toward me. "Is that you?"

I looked up, face full of surprise. "Jack?" The pitch of my voice was as high as my arced eyebrows. "What a coincidence!" *Hee-hee, coincidence, my ass.*

Jack strolled over to my bay, smile widening with every step. "How are you doing?" He looked me over from head to toe. Checking for damages I assumed.

"Me? I'm great. Never better."

I filled him in on all the details of my ambulance ride, my hospital visit, and most importantly, that I tested negative for rabies.

"So you play golf?" asked Jack.

I splayed my hands, highlighting the new golf outfit I bought from the pro shop. "Of course I play golf. I love golf. I play golf all the time."

Jack was clearly impressed. "Let's see what you got, then."

"Huh?"

Jack pointed to the rubber tee at my feet. "Show me your swing."

It was at that moment that I realized the flaw in my strategy. You see, my relationship with the game of golf could best be described as love-hate, with a current emphasis on the hate. The problem was, golf is a game you play outside, in nature, with the heat and the humidity and mosquitoes the size of woodpeckers.

I was more of an inside hobby person. Inside hobbies, like watching television. And snacking. And fish simulator games on my phone.

It wasn't always like that, though. I used to love golf. I started playing when I was only six. My dad taught me all the important stuff, how to putt, how to drive. How to pop the top off a Budweiser on the side of a golf cart. Playing golf was kind of our thing. One year, we even came in third place at the Daddy Daughter Tournament, down at the public course. But then, after he was gone, well, I hadn't picked up a club since.

Jack stood there waiting and smiling and showing off his perfect white teeth.

"You want to see my swing?" I poked the artificial turf with my six iron. Jack nodded. "Okay. Sure. Why not?" There are certain life skills that, once you master them, they remain in your repertoire of life skills for the rest of time. Polka dancing, for example. Whistling. Riding a bike. Golf is not one of those skills.

With Jack watching my every move, I placed a ball on the tee. My heart was pounding, my head was racing, and my palms were so sweaty I could barely hold on to my club. The way Jack scrutinized everything I did, you would think I was about to tee off at the Masters.

I took a deep breath. *I can do this.*

I laser eyed the ball, replaying all the lessons my dad gave me when I was a kid. *I can do this.*

I blocked out the distraction of Jack's golf pants. *I can do this.*

One more deep breath. *I can do this.*

I started the swing of my club. Glancing over out of the corner of my eye, I saw Jack smiling as the head of my six iron raced down to meet the ball.

The smile seemed to falter a bit as the head of the six iron breezed right over the ball, failing to connect.

The smile turned to concern as the six iron rocketed away from my sweat slicked grip and sailed high into the air.

The smile turned to a frown as the six iron splashed down into the pond on the near side of the closest green. A flock of ducks took flight.

When I looked back over at him, Jack was staring. "I always hated six irons." Avoiding eye contact, I selected a five iron and got back into position, as if I had meant to do that all along. Wiping my sweaty hands on my new skirt, I readjusted my grip. I set my feet and squared my hips. I prepared to try again.

"Wait." I felt a hand on my shoulder. The touch of breath on my neck. Jack stood next to me. "You're too rigid," he said. "Here, let me help."

Jack stepped around behind me. His hand tracing down from my shoulder to the middle of my back. "Bend forward a little." Gently, he tilted me forward. At the points where his fingers pressed against my body, it was like lightning bolts, tingling up and down my spine.

"You also need to loosen your hips." His hands moved down my body, cupping me around the waist. Long-lost sensations bubbled up like a hot spring.

Jack planted his foot between my legs. "Move your feet out a bit." I could smell his cologne. Oak barrels. Vanilla beans. Earthy musk. "Spread your legs a little wider. Stick out your butt."

It wasn't just my palms that were now slick with moisture.

"You're still too tense. Here." Jack's firm hands found my shoulders. He squeezed, and he rubbed, fingers probing my flesh. Every muscle melted. Nerves exploded like fireworks.

My throat made a noise that made the guy in the bay beside us blush. "Oh my God," I said. "Where did you learn how to do that?"

"I spent a summer in Bangladesh studying massage," Jack explained. "Among other things." *Of course you did.*

Summers in Florida felt like the inside of a pizza oven, wrapped in a hobo's blanket, stuck in the middle of a python infested, hurricane flooded swamp. I didn't think my body temperature could get any hotter, but with Jack that close to me, I was worried I would ignite him.

"Other things ... meaning ... golf?"

"No, that was Paris. I gave lessons to housewives to put myself through culinary school. I tried the chef thing before I went into medicine."

My brain tried to calculate the probability of my mouth putting together a coherent sentence. It came back under two percent. My mouth went for it, anyway. "You were a chef?"

"I still am, technically. Soufflé is my specialty. Chocolate, of course."

"Of course." My knees were now jelly. All my girl parts too.

"Now try again." Jack put a fresh ball on the tee and stepped out of the way.

"You're sure?"

"I believe in you."

Just because people believed in things didn't mean they were true. I used to believe in a lot of things. Decency. Fairness. Love. And look at where that got me. If Jack wanted to believe in something, he would have had better luck with Bigfoot. Or U.F.O.'S. Or Justin Bieber releasing a new single that didn't make you want to poke out your eardrums with a Q-tip.

"Sometimes you just have to go for it."

Nervous, well, more like petrified, I wiggled back into position, taking another deep breath before positioning my hips over the ball. Focused and vigilant, I set my stance. I made sure my grip was firm but relaxed. I leaned my chest forward, and, as Jack had commanded, stuck out my butt.

Jack gave me a thumbs up.

One more deep breath, then I swung my club.

This time, with the help of Jack's up close and personal instruction, my club contacted the ball. I should clarify the word "contact," because my version of contact in relation to, say, Tiger Woods, were two very different experiences.

At the front of the driving range bay, there was a small border along the lip leading out into the open air where golf balls soared out to the greens. I must have grazed the top of the golf ball with my club because instead of traveling up and out toward the target flags, my ball shot straight ahead.

The ball beamed the bay border.

Blasted back toward the bench.

Banging the beverage bucket.

Then bee-lined into the basket, bouncing balls all over the bay.

My original ball, the one that had started on the tee, rolled to a stop at my feet.

I heard slow clapping behind me. When I turned, I saw Jack smiling. "That was either the best shot, or the worst shot, I've ever seen."

Chapter Nine

Mercifully, Jack suggested we put away the golf clubs and grab a coffee in the clubhouse. "Before anyone gets hurt," he said.

Returning from the counter, he set my pistachio latte down on the table in front of me then sat down. "Look, Mary." Jack cleared his throat. "Back in high school ..."

"No," I held up my hand. I didn't want to hear it. Things were going relatively well at the moment and I didn't want any talk about the past to ruin it.

"I need to say this." Jack leaned forward. "I'm really sorry for what I did that night at prom. It was stupid. It was mean. My girlfriend ..."

"Ashley Griffin." Her name lingered in my mouth like cyanide.

"Yeah. Ashley. She was jealous."

I thought he was joking. "Ashley Griffin? Jealous?" Ashley Griffin had everything. Looks. Friends. A pearl colored Nissan Maxima for her seventeenth birthday. There was no way Ashley Griffin was jealous of anybody. Especially me. My mind flailed like a six iron sailing into a golf pond. "Why would Ashley Griffin be jealous of me?"

Jack's face flushed, his top lip and bottom lip pressed together. "She caught me looking at you. Well, staring really."

If the declaration that Ashley Griffin had been jealous of me was difficult to wrap my head around, the admission that Jack had been staring at me, me, was absolutely mind blowing. "Why were you staring at me?" In all those years back in high school, I was convinced that Jack Thompson didn't even know I existed. And now to hear him say he was staring at me? *WTF?*

Jack shrugged. "What, you think I never noticed how you would look at me? It seemed like every time I turned around, you were there." *Fair.* Jack's eyes twinkled like diamonds. "I mean, come on, you were a cute girl. I was a teenage boy. What can I say? I was intrigued."

I had to hold on to my chair to keep myself from falling over. *Jack Thompson thought I was cute????*

"Anyway, I want to apologize. Truly." Jack looked me right in the eye. "I would do anything, Mary, anything to take it all back."

I had to take a deep breath to give myself a moment to calm down. If I would have known back in high school what I had just found out, my entire life would have been completely different. Somehow, I gathered my wits and made my lips move. "It was twenty years ago. We're both adults now. You've changed, I've changed." I didn't need the horrors of the past tainting the present. I just wanted to forget high school and move on. "What's done is done."

Jack's eyes drifted over my fingers. My bare fingers. Fingers that were not wearing any rings.

"You're still single?" His lips pressed together, his eyes like a lion stalking prey.

"I am."

"Never settled down?"

"I don't settle," I said.

Jack smiled. Lion fangs peeking out between his lips. "You ever get close? To settling I mean."

"I was serious about someone once. A long time ago. A guy I

met after college. He was a nice guy. A fantastic guy, actually, but it ended badly."

Jack took a slow sip of his drink. "What happened?"

"We just didn't fit."

"Sorry about that."

"I'm not. You live and you learn, right?" I took another sip of my coffee. "What about you?" I asked. "Ever get married?"

Jack shook his head. "I was engaged, though." He held up two fingers. "Twice. Well, three times if you count Charla."

"Charla?"

"You know that saying, what happens in Vegas, stays in Vegas? Well, she didn't stay." Jack's face made it clear he didn't want to elaborate.

"You bought her a ring?"

Jack frowned. "I think so."

"Well, it seems to me that if you put a ring on a woman's finger, she should count. Even if her name is Charla."

Jack passed me a napkin, which I used to wipe away the pistachio flavored cold foam from my chin. "So let me guess," I said. "All these women you thought you were in love with, not a fit?"

"Something like that." Again, Jack seemed less than eager to elaborate. Instead, he peered out the window where a Bill Murray look-alike in a yellow fedora swatted his putter across the green. Jack asked, "So if golf isn't your game, what is? Actually no, wait, don't tell me, let me guess."

"Okay."

Jack contemplatively rubbed at his chin. "Full contact karate."

"Nope."

"Big game hunting."

"Not that one either."

"Ah, I got it. Cage free shark diving."

"Aw, so close."

Jack pushed aside his cup and leaned over the table. "Okay, you stumped me. What, Mary Burns, is your special skill?"

I twirled my spoon in my latte. "You really want to know?"

"Very much so."

"Pickleball."

"Pickle-what?"

"Pickleball."

"What exactly is pickleball?"

"You've never played pickleball?"

"Does it involve shots of vodka and suggestively eating a pickle?"

"Wait, what?"

"If not, then never mind."

"Pickleball is one of the fastest growing sports in the country." I pointed to the old couple next to us. "Especially for retirees." The old woman gave me a dirty look.

"Sounds ... injury ridden."

"Oh, it most certainly is. Very easy to break a hip."

"And how do you play this intriguingly dangerous sport?"

"Well, it's like a mishmash of ping-pong, badminton, and tennis."

"So all the racket sports had an orgy?"

"Pretty much."

"And this is something you play."

"I don't just play, I coach. The Casselberry Senior Center. I volunteer."

"You're a volunteer coach?"

"I give lessons every Tuesday." I got an idea. "Want to learn?"

"Tuesday? That's tomorrow."

"So it is."

Jack leaned back in his chair, fingers drumming on the table-top. "Would I need to bring any safety gear? A helmet maybe. Hip pads?"

I looked Jack dead in the eye. "I've got everything you need."

I PACED THE LINE OF PICKLERS LIKE A DRILL SERGEANT
inspecting new recruits. Dick and Mabel, the couple Janet and I
played before, lined up closest to the net.

Beside them were Lewis and Lucille, whose children had
stuck them in a retirement home, so this was their only chance to
get out. Next was Dorothy, a retired math teacher who always
kept score incorrectly.

Then came Howard, who suffered from a severe case of
forgetfulness, so even though he had been coming for months, he
always thought every lesson was his first.

Edna was next. Edna loved to bake, but refused to stand near
the no volley zone, which in pickleball terms, we call "the
kitchen", so the group had fun teasing her about it.

And finally, last but not least, our pickleball virgin, Jack.

"Okay, paddles up," I commanded. The group raised their
paddles, except for Howard, who was watching a butterfly. I made
a mental note to bring a whistle for the next class.

"Today we're going to practice dinking, and then apply our
lessons in a game." The class stood attentively. "Who can tell me
why we dink?"

Howard raised his hand. "My name is Howard."

"Nice to meet you, Howard." I turned back to the class.
"Dinking. Purpose. Any ideas? Go."

Edna stepped forward. "Dinking is like foreplay."

Some days at the Senior Center were true trials of patience. I
could tell this was going to be one of those days. Edna's husband
had died years ago. She confided in me once that she hadn't had a
single date since. She had later followed up with me to clarify that
by date, she meant cuddle time. And then later still she had
followed up again to clarify that by cuddle time, she really meant
sex. I had told her I had gathered as much.

"Okay, thank you for that, Edna." Not wanting to encourage
her, I was about to explain the true purpose of the dink shot when
Jack raised his hand.

"What do you mean, dinking is like foreplay?" he asked. I shot him a look and mouthed the word, *No!*

"It's all about getting into rhythm," Edna explained. "You know, toy with 'em a little. Tickle their ..."

"Okay, we get it, Edna, thank you," I said.

Edna gave Jack a wink. As much as I tried to fight it, disturbing visions of Edna, naked, engaged in "cuddle time," popped into my head.

To my horror, Edna continued. "You know, give 'em a little backspin. A little topspin. Give 'em a little somethin' on the front side. Give 'em a little somethin' on the back side."

She had the class's complete attention. Even Harold's.

"Then, when they least expect it, WHAM!" Edna smacked her fist in her palm. "Go in for the big shot."

I really needed to get myself a whistle.

"Okay," I said, raising my voice to regain everyone's attention. "Fine. Yes. I guess. Dinking is a little like foreplay. But it's also about patience. Biding your time. Testing. Exploring your opponent's strengths and weaknesses."

Lewis raised his hand. "What if you don't have any weaknesses?"

"Lewis, everyone has weaknesses."

"Do you have weaknesses?"

I could see Jack looking at me, a grin on his face. "This isn't about me," I told Lewis. It would be a shame later if he accidentally tripped over a pickleball and broke a hip.

I saw Jack with his hand raised. *Good God.* "Yes, Jack." This wasn't just a trial of patience. This was a reenactment of Dante's journey through hell.

Jack asked, "If you really want to score, why not just take your big shot right away? Why wait?"

"That's called banging," I explained. "Going hard and fast."

"Bangers hate dinking," said Edna.

"But do dinkers hate banging?" Jack asked. I would have given my left ovary for a whistle at that point.

Dorothy raised her hand.

"Yes, Dorothy."

"Are we still talking about pickleball?"

"Yes," I said. "I think."

Howard raised his hand. "My name is Howard."

I smacked my head with my palm. After taking a deep breath, I said, "Let's just play a game."

"I'm on his team!" Edna shuffled over to stand next to Jack.

"Fine. Howard, you're with me. The rest of you, over there." I pointed to the other courts.

Once everyone was in position, I took the first serve, Edna receiving the ball first. She dinked the ball back at me, soft and low, just over the net. The ball bounced in the front section of the court, the kitchen, and Howard dinked it back toward Jack.

Jack deftly dinked it back, as if he had been playing pickleball since the day he was born. The rally continued, with Jack perfectly finessing every shot. He had the control of a fighter pilot, the touch of a maestro, and a nose for the ball like a sommelier.

"You're quite the dinker," Edna cooed.

"You should see me bang." Jack countered. This time, he was the one who winked.

That's when Edna's teeth fell out. Literally. I'm not exaggerating. Edna's teeth physically fell out of her mouth and scattered all over the court.

"Hold up everyone!" I yelled. But the *PLINK* and *PLUNK* of the pickleballs persisted. Damn, I needed a whistle.

"We have another dentures situation!" I shouted louder, so everyone could hear.

The pickleballs fell silent. After Jack and I finished helping Edna collect her scattered teeth off the cement, I said, "Edna, you better sit this one out. Jack, we're going to have to get you a new partner."

"New partner, huh?" Jack looked over in my direction, smiling. "I think I found one."

It's hard to put my feelings at that moment into words. Joy?

Maybe. Elation? Perhaps. Eternal bliss? That's the one. It was the feeling that finally, after all these years, everything suddenly, magically was falling into place. But it was even more than that, too. It was a feeling of relief. The feeling that everything was going to be okay. The Universe wasn't really out to screw me over at every turn. It was like a twenty-year weight had lifted off my shoulders. Happiness, true happiness, was finally within reach.

"Hey Jack," a familiar voice said from behind me.

"Hey Janet," said Jack.

"My name is Howard." said Howard.

"Janet?" I blinked a couple times to make sure the vision of Janet I was seeing was really real. "What are you doing here?"

"I came to see Jack." And then, as if they knew that words alone were not enough to make me understand, Jack and Janet graciously provided me with a physical demonstration. Jack walked around the pickleball net, went over to Janet, leaned in close, and gave her a hug.

"Come on, Jan." *He calls her Jan?* "You and I are over here." Janet pulled out her pickleball paddle as Jack set up on the far side of the court.

On her way over to join him, Janet pulled me aside, leaning in close to whisper. "So remember when I told you Jack helped me get my car out of the mud, while you were in the hospital?"

I pursed my lips. "I remember."

"Well, we got to talking and, Mary, you will not believe it, but Jack Thompson is not a bad guy. His medical practice sponsors this charity 5k for sick kids. He volunteers as a cook at a homeless shelter and goes on missions to Mexico to rebuild after hurricanes. He's like some sort of master carpenter or something. He's not just nice, he's amazing."

"I see." And see, I did. I saw the twinkle in Janet's eyes and the way her cheeks turned bright pink as she talked about him. I saw the way she looked across the court at Jack's toned and tanned legs. *Aaaaahhhhhh!!!!!!!* Yup. Janet showed all the signs. My best friend was falling for the man who both haunted my nightmares and made me have to change the sheets the next morning when he showed up in my dreams. Janet was falling for Jack.

There were so many questions, I didn't know where to begin. "So when ... where ... how ..."

"After you got trampled at the reunion, and he helped me get my car out of the mud, we started talking and hanging out. Nothing serious, of course, but ..." Janet trailed off.

She still had the look in her eye. The same look she always got. The one right before she fell head over heels for some misfit guy and then had her heart ripped out, tossed on the ground, and bludgeoned with a sledgehammer.

Janet had always been a good friend, and I knew she would never do anything to hurt me. Not on purpose, at least. If I would have told her I was still angry at Jack for what he did to me, everything would have ended right then and there. If I had given Janet even a hint that I was still interested in Jack for myself, she would have backed off immediately. But at that point, I wasn't even willing to admit my true feelings to myself, let alone admit my delusional feelings to someone else. Even if that someone else was my best friend.

Janet must have seen the torment on my face though, because she reached over and grabbed my hand. "Mary? What's wrong? You look like you're going to pass out. Maybe you should go sit down."

"I'm fine."

"You're not upset I'm talking to Jack, are you? He told me he apologized and the two of you made up. But if you're still mad at him for what he did back in high school ..."

Why did everyone have to keep dredging up high school? Why couldn't everyone just let me suppress my emotional traumas so I could let it all out in one self destructive life spiral during a midlife crisis like everyone else?

"Of course I'm not still mad at him," I said. "What kind of person holds on to something like that for twenty years?" *Me.*

Janet cocked her head, studying my face as if she could see

right through my skull and into my brain. "You don't still have feelings for him, right?"

"Feelings for him?" I barked out a laugh. "Janet, you're my best friend. You've known me my whole life. Better than anyone. So you, of all people, know I don't have any feelings." I did my best to make a smile.

"So, are we going to play some pickleball here or what?" Jack waved his paddle from the other side of the court.

Janet gave me a big hug. "You're the best friend anybody could ask for." She skipped to join Jack, an extra bounce in her step, leaving me with Howard.

Turning back to my partner, I said, "Well, that's it then. I guess it's just you and me."

"My name is Howard!"

WHEN THE LESSON WAS OVER, JACK WENT TO CHECK ON Edna, who was still attempting to reassemble her teeth. Janet came over to my side of the court, while everyone else was busy packing up their gear. "So? What do you think? We make a pretty good team, huh?"

I looked at Janet like she had just asked me to solve an algebra problem in Mandarin Chinese, using sign language. True, they were a phenomenal pickleball team. In pickleball, Janet could be lethal. And Jack, well, apparently, he really was good at everything because he looked like he had been playing pickleball his entire life.

But other than pickleball, Jack and Janet couldn't have been more wrong for each other. Janet had a history of falling for the wrong guy and then going too far, too fast. And I still wasn't entirely sure if Jack had really changed. Jack and Janet talking on the phone and hanging out as friends was one thing, but anything more than that was a disaster waiting to happen. I was about to tell Janet exactly that when Dick and Mabel walked over.

"Hey Mary, guess what Dick gave me." Mabel held up her middle finger. For the life of me, I had no idea why Mabel was flicking me off. Then I realized it wasn't her middle finger she was showing me, it was her ring finger. With a ring on it, big and sparkly. "Dick proposed!"

The commotion had drawn a crowd, and the other senior pickleballers oohed and aahed appropriately.

Dick put his arm around Mabel's shoulder. "And to think, we wouldn't have even met if it wasn't for you, Mary." It was true. After introducing Dick and Mabel at one of my pickleball classes, I was the one who encouraged Dick to ask Mabel out. And then encouraged Mabel to say yes to Dick's invitation.

"There's going to be an engagement party," Mabel announced. "And everyone's invited."

Dick said, "As you can see, we are very old. So most of our friends are dead now. We could use all the support we can get, so the first round is on me!" There was an eruption of applause.

Mabel turned back to us. "You two are coming, I hope."

"Of course! Wouldn't miss it," Janet answered. "Right Mary?"

"Right. Sure. Of course."

A sly look spread across Mabel's face as she leaned in close to Janet. "And bring your new friend, Jack, too."

Chapter Ten

After pickleball, Janet suggested we all stop for drinks, and I badly needed one, so we did. On the drive over, I decided I needed reinforcements, so I called Ralph to join us. It was a new place called the Axe 2 Grinder. The reviews said the food was edible; the drinks were cheap, and they had axe throwing, which for some reason sounded like a good idea at the time.

While Ralph and I grabbed a table, Jack went to fetch a bucket of beer at the bar and Janet went to get the waivers for the throwing cage. It was like a batting cage, except instead of swinging at baseballs with a bat, you hurl axes at chunks of wood with a bullseye painted on them.

While we were still alone, Ralph leaned in close. "So let me get this straight. Janet and Jack. They're *together* together?"

"Well, not *together* together. Just together, I think. Janet told me they were only hanging out."

"You know it's your fault, right? You were the one trying to get Janet to find someone to hook up with, and now it looks like she found someone. Karma." Ralph was right. It was the Universe f-ing with me.

"I'm still not entirely sure how it happened," I said. Which was the truth. I still couldn't believe it myself. The boy who had traumatized me in high school, had resurfaced after twenty years, now an incredibly handsome, amazing, nice smelling man, and somehow, I, like a complete idiot, had aligned the stars, the sun, and the moon to create the perfect storm situation which brought Jack and Janet together.

"You have to do something," Ralph said, stating the obvious. "They would be horrible together."

"It would be a disaster," I agreed.

"Jack Thompson is a complete asshole," said Ralph.

"Once an asshole, always an asshole," I agreed, though I still needed to investigate that assumption for myself.

Over at the bar, we watched as the female bartender leaned over the bar talking to Jack, smiling and batting her eyes, the top half of her unbuttoned shirt allowing her surgically enhanced bosom to practically spill out onto Jack's nuts. The bar snack variety, just to be clear. And then there was another table of horny MILF's checking out his butt.

"I don't even see what women see in him." Ralph looked like he was trying to give Jack a brain aneurysm telepathically.

"Well ..." I began.

"Well, what?" Ralph raised an eyebrow.

"He is a doctor."

"Doctors are self absorbed pricks." Ralph had a thing against all doctors. I think it was some kind of doctors versus lawyers thing.

"Janet says he makes balloon animals for children."

"What kind of balloon animals? Like a snake? Because if it's a snake, that doesn't count."

"No, not a snake, the good ones. Monkeys and giraffes and stuff."

"Monkeys?"

I nodded.

"Giraffes?"

I nodded again.

"I wonder if he can do a tiger?"

"Probably."

"I love tigers."

I patted Ralph on the back. "I know you do." Ralph's favorite animal was a tiger. In fact, he was wearing an Aloha shirt with a tiger shooting lasers out of its eyes that very night.

"You know what else Janet said Jack is good at?"

"I don't think I want to know. He doesn't play the ukulele, does he?" Ralph had recently started taking ukulele lessons on YouTube. He was extremely proud of himself. Though for the life of me, I did not know why.

"No, not the ukulele. Janet says he plays acoustic guitar. Jimmy Buffett mostly."

"Hell. I love Jimmy Buffett. Now I want a cheeseburger."

"Jack is good at everything. I mean everything."

"What an asshole."

"He bakes soufflés. Chocolate soufflés. Who does that?"

"Jerk."

"And he builds things. With his hands."

"What things?"

"I don't know, wooden things. Probably toy trains for orphans. And pergolas."

Ralph shook his head. "Total prick."

"Do you know, he studied massage in Bangladesh? Bangladesh!"

"How do you even know that?" I tried my best to stay cool under Ralph's judgmental gaze, but he knew me too well. He saw right through the charade. "Oh my God, you're still obsessed with him."

"No," I said. Even I thought I sounded unconvincing. As a lawyer, Ralph had developed a sixth sense when it came to reading people's true intentions and figuring out the truth. So while my bluff had worked well enough for now with Janet, Ralph wasn't fooled.

"You want him for yourself." The way Ralph said it made it clear it wasn't a question.

"Better me than Janet," I blurted, before my self respect filter could kick in. "He'll chew her up and spit her out."

"Mary, think about it. You said he's a gynecologist. What kind of man makes a career choice to look at women's vulvas all day?"

"You know I dated a chiropractor once. His back rubs were fantastic." My eyes got dreamy.

Our conversation was interrupted by a waitress hoisting a large tray of food. "Your cute friend over there ordered a couple of apps for the table."

"Apps? What apps?" Ralph was visibly salivating at the mouth.

The waitress set the platters down. "Pulled pork nachos, mac & cheese balls, fried pickles."

Jack gave us a thumbs up from the bar, then resumed talking to the big breasted bartender.

Ralph saluted him. "Perhaps I judged the fine Dr. Thompson a wee bit too hastily." Ralph stuffed his mouth with an entire mac and cheese ball. "I'm just surprised Janet didn't go after Gary instead."

"Gary?"

Ralph nodded. "The dungeon master. Your painter. You told her he told you to tell her he said 'hi', right? That's total code for Mary, please set us up."

I had a major Homer Simpson Doh moment. I had been so focused on thinking about Jack, the thought of Janet and Gary still having any interest in one another never even occurred to me.

Ralph slathered one of the tortilla chips with pulled pork and nacho cheese. Thankfully, he was careful to avoid the sour cream. "I mean, she was in love with him back in high school. Almost as bad as you were in love with Jack." Ralph took a bite of a fried pickle. "Pretty sure he was really into her too."

"How could you even tell? He was so quiet. And lanky. And nerdy."

Ralph scooped another nacho chip into a puddle of barbecue sauce. "Didn't you ever find it odd that whenever we found a dragon's cave, you and I would get incinerated and Janet would end up with all the treasure?"

Before I could interrogate Ralph further, Janet came back with the waivers. "We're good to go. The axe throwing cage is all ours."

Janet nodded her head toward the bar, where Jack was coming over with the beer bucket. "So. Ralph." She was smiling ear to ear. "What do you think?"

"That drinking and sharply edged weapons are not a good mix."

"No, I mean about me and Jack. I think I might ask him out."

Ralph had his lawyer's face on. Like he was cross-examining a witness trying to catch them in a lie. "I don't think you should rush into anything," he said. "Maybe, you know, keep your options open. Play the field."

"Yes," I agreed. "What Ralph said."

"I've played the field," Janet replied. "Outfield. Infield. Pitcher. Catcher. Ball boy. I'm tired of playing the field. Maybe I need to think about settling down. My biological clock is ticking."

Ralph and I exchanged a look.

"Janet ..." I began.

"No Mary, stop. I know what you're going to say." *Run away as far from Jack as you can. So I can have him.* "You're going to tell me to take things slow. That I always rush into a relationship and things go too fast and then I end up getting hurt."

"Right," I agreed. "That's exactly what I was going to say. Verbatim. Every time you get involved with someone, you think you're in love and then before you know it, you're lying on your bathroom floor freebasing rocky road ice cream. Literally, every time."

"Not every time," said Janet. "Sometimes it's mint chocolate chip."

Ralph came in for the assist, swallowing another bite of fried mac and cheese. "For once in her life, Janet, I think Mary's right. Jack isn't ..." Ralph tapped his throat to get the rest of the mac and cheese down. "Wow, that's gooey."

"I know Mary's right," Janet said, capitalizing on the pause in the conversation. "Which is why I'm doing a thirty-day plan."

"A thirty-day plan?" I asked.

"A thirty-day plan," she confirmed. "I saw it on TikTok."

Ralph coughed. "What's a thirty-day plan?"

"Thirty days of friendship only. No intimate physical contact. No kissing. Certainly nothing below the belt."

"And this is a real thing?"

"Supposedly they do it in Gen Z." We all rolled our eyes. "That way, you get to see if you're compatible. See if you really connect. Without all the sex stuff and hormones messing with your head."

I had to admit, the idea made sense. Even if it was a Gen Z thing.

Before Ralph and I could probe further, Jack arrived with the beers.

"A toast," he said, distributing the bottles. "To old friends." We clinked bottles, then poured beer down our throats.

"To new friends." Janet hoisted her bottle, and we drank again.

"To making good choices." Ralph looked pointedly at Janet. Then at me.

"To friends who intervene when you don't make good choices." I looked pointedly at Ralph.

"Now who's ready to get their axe on?" asked Jack.

"Whoo! Me!" Janet raised her hand. Jack passed out the remaining beers from the bucket and we headed for the cage.

———

ONE OF THE MANY LIFE LESSONS I HAVE LEARNED OVER the years is that you should never make an important life decision when you are too tired, too angry, or too drunk to think clearly. Especially when you are all three. For example, signing up for a "free" four days, three nights exclusive vacation offer where they try to sell you a time-share in Branson, Missouri. Or going all-in on a new hair color you ordered online from Vietnam. Or plotting strategies to orchestrate the manipulation of your best friend's love life, as well as your own.

But, after getting home late that night from Axe 2 Grinder, and seeing Janet flirt with Jack all night, I was too drunk, too tired, and too pissed off to remember any lessons, life altering or otherwise. I started texting Gary as soon as I got home.

MARY:

r u up???

it's mary

mary yearns

sorry spel correct

of course it does not correct spell

burns

mary burns

the greige lady

I mean walls

not me

i'm not greige

just my walls

actually just looked in the bathroom mirror

fluorescent lighting

I actually am greige

in my defense have not slept

and way 2 much bears

not bears

no bears here

I looked for a bear emoji to include but couldn't find one. I found the beer glass emoji however and used it generously.

🍺 🍺 🍺 🍺 🍺 🍺

beers

2 much beers

way way

I added more beer glass emojis for good measure. Then I found the bear one after all and added a bunch of those too.

Purrfect had been waiting up for me when I got home, wearing a look of disapproval that would have made a Catholic nun proud. She looked even more disappointed in me when I didn't go straight to bed, or at least open up a can of tuna. She settled for a good ear scratching, though.

As I ran my fingers through her fur, the screen on my phone lit up, three dots pulsing beneath my last message. Gary was typing a response. Then he wasn't. The three dots disappeared. Then they came back. Then they disappeared again. This went on for about ten more minutes.

I figured he was probably debating on whether he should just block me or report me to the texting authorities as unauthorized spam. Then, finally, Gary's message came through.

NEW PAINTER:

no

No? I had totally forgotten what my original question was that he responded "no" to.

MARY:

no what?

NEW PAINTER:

no I'm not up

u asked if I was up

I am saying no I am not

MARY:

seems like u r

NEW PAINTER:

bc of u

why r u txting me

MARY:

bc i need you

There was another long pause, even longer than the first one.

NEW PAINTER:

what exactly does that mean?

😄😄😄😄😄

Eww. Yuck. I quickly clarified.

MARY:

not what u r thinking perv

not that desperate btw

NEW PAINTER:

g thx

😔😔😔😔😔

MARY:

meet at the house tomorrow?

pls?

pleasepleasepleasepleasepleaseplease?

NEW PAINTER:

ugh

MARY:

how soon can u b there?

NEW PAINTER:

I thought u fired me

MARY:

changed mind, u r unfired

NEW PAINTER:

not how it works

MARY:

u been fired b4???

NEW PAINTER:

no

MARY:

then how do u know

don't you want $$$

NEW PAINTER:

not that desperate btw

MARY:

g thx

After another long pause, Gary texted again.

NEW PAINTER:

what u want me 4

MARY:

better 2explain in person

NEW PAINTER:

sounds dangerous

MARY:

it is

tomorrow pls

1st thing

NEW PAINTER:

can't tomorrow

MARY:

new job??

NEW PAINTER:

something like that

MARY:

whatever they're paying, I'll dble it

NEW PAINTER:

not getting paid

MARY:

then I'll triple it

why are you not getting paid? Is it illegal????

it's something criminal right?

NEW PAINTER:

no

MARY:

is the Russian mob involved?

NEW PAINTER:

am doing it 2 b nice

MARY:

ah

i see

pro boner

NEW PAINTER:

r u?

a little surprised

MARY:

autocorrect, meant to say pro boner

NEW PAINTER:

got it the first time

MARY:

ugh

autocorrect again

u know what I mean

NEW PAINTER:

actually don't know

growing concerned

pretty sure don't want to know

sleeping now, good night

MARY:

I know u r not sleeping bc you have been
texting me 4 past 20 mins

NEW PAINTER:

bc phone won't stop dinging

MARY:

u still have ding for text tone???

NEW PAINTER:

let me guess u have a schwing

MARY:

pro boner joke

funny

u r a real funny guy

NEW PAINTER:

seriously, going to bed

have to be somewhere in morning

Then I got an idea. Not just a good idea, a great one. Better than my hook up Janet at our high school reunion idea, better than my schedule a gynecology appointment with my high school crush idea, even better than drinking a full bucket of beer and throwing sharp axes in a cage. I texted Gary again.

MARY:

I will help u

There was another really long pause. Then the dots appeared. Disappeared. Appeared again.

NEW PAINTER:

u want to help me?

MARY:

we can make deal

I help u with pro boner job

pro boner

pro boner

pro boner

wtf

pro b-o-n-o

then we talk after

deal?

NEW PAINTER:

if I say yes will you let me sleep

MARY:

yes

NEW PAINTER:

ok

text address in morning

MARY:

It's a boing btw

NEW PAINTER:

huh?

MARY:

my text tone is a boing

like a cartoon spring

NEW PAINTER:

ha

MARY:

goodnight Gary

NEW PAINTER:

goodnight Mary

MARY:

goodnight Jim Bob

NEW PAINTER:

you are really weird

MARY:

no

just really drunk

I sent a couple more beer emojis and bear emojis for good measure, but Gary's texts stopped. No little dots. No new messages. My battery was in the red, so I plugged my phone into the charger and got ready for bed.

Once again, Purrfect snuggled up next to me on my pillow. Apparently, it was our new routine. It wasn't long before I fell into a deep sleep.

So deep that I didn't hear my phone boing.

When I woke up the next morning, there was a new message waiting for me.

NEW PAINTER:

wear comfortable shoes

Chapter Eleven

The next morning, I put on some old clothes I didn't mind getting paint spilled on and a pair of comfortable shoes, then mapped the address Gary sent me. It was in the middle of nowhere, miles from civilization. The kind of place you would invite someone if you didn't want anyone to hear their screams. My first thought was to revisit my Gary is a serial killer theory.

"If I don't come back later, call the police," I told Purrfect. The look on her face made it clear she was perfectly content to let my dead body rot in the woods, never to be found.

I had to take a series of dirt roads to get there. Pine trees stretched for miles. For a serial killer looking for a secluded place to lure their prey, it was perfect. The GPS finally brought me to a log cabin with a green roof. A boardwalk trailed off into the woods. There was a post next to the building, with a sign attached —"Nature Center."

"God damn it," I said, to no one in particular.

I got out of my car wearing the painter overalls Gary had let me borrow, the ones I had not yet returned. Even though I was wearing old clothes, I figured the overalls would provide an additional layer of protection, considering my track record with paint.

Before I even got all the way out of my car, I was drenched with sweat. It was the kind of day when the bright sun reached down from the blue sky and punched you in the face. The air smelled like swamp. Blood plump mosquitoes buzzed my head like I was a giant monkey on top of a skyscraper. In the trees, I spotted a flock of buzzards, waiting for the next thing to die.

I found Gary dousing himself in bug spray, leaning against the handrail along the boardwalk. He was dressed in a floppy hat, cargo shorts, a long-sleeved sun shirt, and hiking boots with neon yellow laces. I think he was going for a big game hunter out on safari look, except instead of lions and tigers, it was squirrels and butterflies.

"This isn't a painting job, is it?"

Gary slowly shook his head, the smile on his face widening. "I didn't think you'd show." He looked down at my shoes. I was wearing my brand new white pickleball sneakers, the most comfortable footwear I owned. I figured when we started painting, I would take them off and go barefoot.

"You're going to want to change out of those," Gary said. "They have rubbers you can borrow inside."

Blink

"This really is a pro boner job isn't it?"

"Rubber boots," Gary clarified. "Like snow boots."

In the distance, a bird screeched. Like a hawk gutting a mouse. Entrails hanging from its claws.

"Funny, when I was listening to the radio on my way over, I didn't hear them mention anything about a blizzard." I looked up to check the sky, just in case. The sun was like a heat lamp slowing, roasting the entire state like a rotisserie chicken. Or rotisserie flamingo, since it was Florida.

"It's not snow you have to worry about, it's mud. You got anything on under those?" Gary tilted his head toward my overalls. His overalls, technically.

"I can't help but wonder what answer you're hoping for," I

teased. I surprised myself when I realized I was pleased when he blushed.

On the drive over, I had repeated the mantra "please Mary, just be nice, please Mary, just be nice" a thousand times, out loud, to coerce my brain into submission. I needed to stay on Gary's good side. And I would not let the temperature, bugs, or Gary's lack of disclosure sour my mood.

I stripped off the overalls, revealing the shorts and old t-shirt I was willing to sacrifice to the paint gods.

"I thought you didn't like Justin Bieber." Gary pointed to my shirt, which featured a tattooed Justin on the front, and at a bunch of concert cities and dates on the back. At least this time I was wearing a bra.

"I have yours back at the house," I said. "This is the only shirt I own that I don't mind getting splattered with paint."

"You really hate Justin Bieber, don't you?"

"You have no idea."

The truth was, I had no intention of ever helping Gary paint. I only wore the old clothes to make him think I was going to help. Then I was going to fake an injury or something. Really, all I wanted was a chance to talk.

"I hope you're not allergic to mosquitos." Gary tossed me the bug spray. "Or bees."

A sense of impending doom started buzzing around in my head. Like a mosquito. Or bees. "What exactly are we doing here, anyway?" I eyed the dense thickets of trees surrounding us. I was fairly certain it was the location where they filmed that movie with Leonardo DiCaprio, the one where the grizzly bear mauled him and left him for dead.

"Nature hike." Gary's voice was supernaturally chipper for someone who had just uttered the words nature and hike in the same sentence. "Come on, the other chaperones are inside with the kids."

"Kids?" I preferred the thought of hiking with grizzly bears.

THE INSIDE OF THE CABIN LOOKED LIKE SOMETHING straight out of a horror house. The first thing I saw when I stepped inside was a stuffed bear in a glass case, jaw gaping and claws poised for attack.

But the bear wasn't the only dead animal in the room. A coyote, an otter, a raccoon, and an owl all stared back at me with dead black eyes, a slight smile on their frozen faces. Like they knew what was coming and couldn't wait to watch.

"Okay everybody, start gathering your groups!" A uniformed park ranger, Sarah, according to her name badge, tried to wrangle the children that were running and jumping all over the room. I can't say which was more horrific, the dead animals or the screaming children. "Everyone settle down." Sarah waved her hands in vain. "Please."

A little freckled girl squealed as she knocked a porcupine off a display case. Quills scattered like buckshot.

"Dad!" a small voice rang out. I turned just in time to see a little boy charge toward us. I barely had time to duck as he leaped at Gary. His tiny arms wrapped around Gary's neck in a choke-hold. They wrestled. Fighting for his very life, Gary flipped the kid over and set him on the ground. Then Gary gave the little boy a noogie.

"Dad, did you see the snakes?" The boy dashed back over to his compatriots, who were banging on glass cases filled with large, hairy spiders and poisonous looking snakes.

"Dad? You have a kid?"

"His name is Kyle." For some reason, Gary seemed proud.

"You didn't tell me you had a kid."

"You didn't ask."

Kyle reached into one of the aquariums and pulled out a snake. I assumed it wasn't a poisonous one, or if it was, some responsible adult would intervene.

"He just turned eight."

I looked at the pandemonium swirling around me. When I first entered the cabin, Ranger Sarah had been a young, perky brunette. I had a feeling by the end of the day, she would be completely grey. "So this job you tricked me into, what exactly are we doing?"

"Field trip chaperone." Gary swept his arm across the surrounding mayhem. "As you can see, they could use the help."

As I would later learn, the Summer Ultimate Kids Camp was one of the best summer camps for six to twelve-year-olds in all of Central Florida. Or, more specifically, it was the only summer camp that was affordable and still had an open spot left by the time Gary realized summer camps fill up quickly and he better get off his ass and make a reservation.

The Summer Ultimate Kids Camp had a sports day, a movie day, a creative arts day, and if it wasn't raining, they rigged up the slip and slide every Friday. Best of all, there was a weekly field trip. Each new destination was more amazing than the last. For example, the trip to the zoo, where one year Happy the hippo got it on with Helga in front of the entire class. Entertaining and educational. Then there was the trip to the water park. The one with the Raging River, the Lazy River, and what the camp counselors christened the River of Pee, because that's where they let the preschoolers swim.

But of all the field trips, throughout the entire summer, the trip to the Nature Park was the one trip every single child looked forward to ... the least. Inevitably, someone got stung by a wasp, someone passed out from heatstroke, or someone lost a shoe in the mud. That's why there was plenty of room for another chaperone.

I looked around the room of dead animals and screaming children, the horrific reality of my situation fully sinking in. One eye on the exit door, I told Gary, "I have limited experience with kids."

"Really? I never would have guessed," Gary deadpanned. "It's easy. If you see a kid in one of those orange shirts..."

I realized all the children were wearing matching orange shirts.

Gary continued, "Just tell them to sit down, shut up, or keep their hands to themself. Watch." Gary pointed to a kid wearing an orange shirt, carrying an alligator skull, chasing other kids around the room. "Maxwell, keep your hands to yourself!"

Maxwell ignored him, gnashing the jaws of the skull up and down to make it bite another kid's face.

Gary frowned. "Okay, so I'm not exactly a pro myself. Speaking of pros ..."

A woman walked over. "Hey Gary, who's this?" She was holding the hand of a little girl who looked the same age as Kyle.

Gary introduced us. "Mary, this is Karen, Karen, this is Mary." Gary stepped back, as if he had just combined potassium chlorate and sulfuric acid and was waiting for the explosion.

Karen was wearing one of those mom hats, with the mom visor. She also wore mom shorts. Mom shoes. And a mom shirt. A fanny pack strapped around her waist completed the ensemble.

Karen stuck out her hand. I shook it firmly. The smile on her face never moved.

"Karen is the other chaperone in our group," Gary explained.

"This is my daughter Cary." Cary stared at me unimpressed, the same look I got from Purrfect. "Which one is your son or daughter?" Karen asked.

"None of them, thankfully. I don't have any kids. I'm just along for the ride."

It took Karen a moment to process this news. "Lovely." Karen said the word 'lovely" but the tone in her voice suggested something else entirely. Still, the smile never moved.

"Okay everyone, who's ready to start exploring!" Ranger Sarah had pulled out her megaphone, a sound strategy if she had any hope of being heard over the cacophony of noise. Even better than a whistle. A cheer erupted from the children. A groan erupted from the adults.

As we made our way toward the exit, I pulled Gary aside. "Remember, you and I need to talk."

"Plenty of time along the way," Gary reassured me.

As we stepped outside, Ranger Sarah handed us orange T-shirts that matched the ones the campers were wearing. "So we know who's in our group. You can change in the restrooms around the corner."

"Great!" said Karen.

"Great!" I said. Although I tried, I couldn't quite match Karen's zeal.

After changing into our new T-shirts, I joined Karen in front of the bathroom mirror. I squinted a bit, like when you peek at an eclipse, just in case the bright orange color seared my retinas.

"These shirts suck," I said.

"What did you just say?" Karen furrowed her eyebrows.

"These shirts." I pinched the material near my shoulders. "They suck," I said again.

Although I didn't mean to offend her, the look on Karen's face made it clear she took it as a personal affront. "No, they don't."

"But they do."

"They do not." Karen gave me a look like I had just farted on a crowded elevator and then pressed the emergency stop button.

"They literally say suck." I pointed at our reflections. Our bright orange shirts had the letters "S.U.K.C" emblazoned in neon yellow straight across the breast.

"That stands for Summer Ultimate Kids Camp," Karen explained.

"That may be what it stands for," I said, "but that's not what it says."

Karen and I stood quietly for several moments, reflecting on our reflections. I could tell Karen was trying to come up with a way to refute reality, but was coming up blank.

Finally Karen said, "We should join the others. I'm sure the kids are anxiously waiting."

"I'm sure."

We left the bathroom to join the anxiously waiting kids.

THROUGHOUT HUMAN HISTORY, THERE HAVE BEEN many grueling journeys filled with human suffering and strife. In 1521, Ponce de Leon trekked through alligator infested Florida swamps, battling the heat and humidity while searching for the Fountain of Youth. In 1804, Lewis and Clark marched 8,000 miles to the Pacific Ocean, traversing treacherous mountains and rivers, faced with deadly illness and dangerous wildlife. In 1846, members of the Donner Party's tragic expedition endured blizzards and starvation, trapped in the Sierra Nevadas, ultimately forced to resort to cannibalism to survive.

Now I'm not saying the nature walk was anything like those terrible journeys. But I'm not saying it was un-like them either.

"Okay troops!" Gary pointed to the first line on the Nature Hike Checklist. "Our first mission is to find a ladybug and count its spots."

"Yay!" Cary fast clapped.

"Cool!" Kyle pumped his fist.

"How fun!" Karen's face beamed with delight.

It took all my effort to keep from vomiting. You see, the Summer Ultimate Kids Camp nature hike was not just an ordinary death march, it was a competition. As Ranger Sarah had said, "Like a scavenger hunt, except instead of collecting objects, you're collecting observations." When she said it, I really really really wanted to punch her in the crotch.

The nature hike comprised a series of trails crisscrossing the nature preserve. A letter marked each trail. We started on trail "A". By the time we got to "Z", our checklist would be complete.

"How do we know if it's a ladybug?" Kyle asked.

"Oh, that's easy," I answered. "Just turn it over and look between its little bug legs."

Karen gave me a dirty look. "We need to take this seriously, Mary. The first team back with all the correct answers wins a prize."

"Maybe it's a hat to match our shirts," I said. "Or even better, a matching hat and matching socks. Then we would totally suck!" Gary, Karen, Kyle, and Cary all looked at me in their bright orange S.U.K.C shirts. None of them seemed amused.

Eventually we found a ladybug. I was going to turn it over, but after seeing Karen's face, Gary shook his head and made a slashing motion across his throat.

When we counted the spots, I came up with eleven. Gary counted nine. We went with Karen's number, which was seventeen. Then, when Karen saw Gary's handwriting, she volunteered to write all future answers going forward. She also generously offered to hold the checklist for us and read all the questions. And although not verbally stated, but universally assumed, Karen would also take on the responsibility of answering all the questions, either with or without the input of the group. Preferably without.

We hiked from trail "A" to trail "B" answering more questions along the way. Trails "C" and "D" meandered along a small stream.

"Next question," said Karen. "List three things that can make a stream's water turn brown." The stream beside the trail was indeed brown, the same color as iced tea.

"I know this one," I said. "Fish poop. Frog poop." I pointed to the river of tea. "Kids, what other animals poop in a river?"

"Beavers?" Kyle suggested.

"Excellent Kyle. Beavers. Beavers probably poop in the water all the time." I turned to Karen. "Fish poop, frog poop, and beaver poop."

Karen said, "I'm going to write leaves, sticks, and mud." And that was the end of that.

I leaned in close to Kyle, "Speaking of sticks in the mud."
Kyle giggled.

"How about a little break?" Gary suggested, pointing to a
couple of benches along the path. "I think some of us need a time
out." He looked at me when he said it.

Karen looked at her watch. "Maybe just a quick one. Five
minutes. Tops."

Chapter Twelve

Gary pulled a handful of granola bars out of his cargo shorts. "Who's hungry? Sorry, they may be a little melty." I was hungry, but not hungry enough to eat melted food that came out of Gary's pants. "At least take a water." Gary pulled a couple of bottles from his pack.

I had been guzzling water all morning to mitigate the pounding in my head from the previous night's hangover, but I still felt dehydrated. I downed the first bottle in a couple of big gulps. Gary handed me another.

"Thanks."

"You know those are bad for the environment, Mary," Karen noted. "You should really use reusable water bottles." I considered pointing out that, technically, it wasn't me who brought the Earth-destroying plastic water bottle, but I was pretty sure Karen would blame me, regardless.

While everyone else enjoyed a snack, I strolled over to the edge of the creek, sipping my sea turtle murdering water bottle. To Karen's credit, there were indeed a lot of sticks and leaves in the creek and I didn't see any poop floating by, beaver or otherwise. A bit of a breeze rustled the leaves and a blanket of shade shielded me from the sun. The water babbled as it splashed against the rocks. The air smelled like pine. I wondered if that was what relaxing felt like.

The reason I had stepped away from the group was to give myself time to think. I needed to get a moment alone with Gary, so I could convince him to help me with my plan. The plan? It was simple, really. Janet plus Gary equals Mary plus Jack.

You see, Janet and Gary should have been together from the beginning. Janet liked Gary back in high school, so there was already an attraction, or at least the potential to rekindle one. They were both nice. They were both kind of nerdy based on the Dungeons and Dragons thing. And best of all, Gary had a kid and Janet talked about having kids of her own one day all the time.

Really, the more I thought about it, the more I convinced myself they were perfect for each other. Almost as perfect together as me and Jack. If I could just convince Gary to go along with it, nature would take its course. I shut my eyes and concentrated, trying to decide what I would tell Gary when I cornered him.

"Having fun?"

Startled, I jumped. With my eyes closed, I didn't realize Gary was behind me. Just as my body pitched forward, toward the brown murky creek, Gary grabbed my waist and pulled me back from the edge. My back sank into his chest and his arms wrapped around me.

"Sorry." His voice was a whisper in my ear. "I didn't mean to sneak up to you."

I wiggled loose and turned to face him. My heart thumped in my ears. "What did you say?" I had been so busy trying to force myself to relax, I hadn't heard him.

"I asked if you were having fun," said Gary.

Fun was not the first word that came to mind, but I needed Gary on my side, so I played nice. "Well," I said, "It doesn't completely ..." I pointed to the letters on my chest. S.U.K.C.

In the distance, we heard something that sounded like a cross between a growl and a honk. Only louder. And more reptilian.

"What is that?" I asked.

"Alligators," Gary answered. "You might not want to stand so close to the water. It's mating season."

"Great, we're in the middle of nowhere, surrounded by horny alligators. How do you even know that?"

"I was in scouts."

"Of course you were."

"I made Eagle Scout."

"I'm sure that impressed all the girl scouts."

Gary almost smiled. "You said you wanted to talk?"

"Well," I said. "Remember the other day? You told me to say hi to Janet for you."

"I did." Gary nodded, confirming my recap of his request.

"So I did that. I told her. I told Janet you said hi." That was as far into my plan as I had gotten before Gary almost made me fall into the horny alligator inhabited creek.

"Thanks for telling her," said Gary. "And, um, did she say anything back?"

"She said to say hi to you, too."

"Thanks for relaying her greeting," Gary said.

"You're welcome," I replied.

Karen made a huffing noise and kept glancing at her watch. As if looking at it repeatedly would make time speed up.

"Was that all?" Gary asked.

"No."

"What else then?"

"Is there a bathroom around here?"

"Janet asked you to ask me about a bathroom?"

"No, Janet didn't ask about a bathroom, I'm asking." I started doing a potty dance, which involved angling your knees toward one another and bouncing up and down on the balls of your feet. After consuming two dolphin strangling plastic water bottles, I really really had to pee and the flowing water of the creek wasn't helping.

Gary pointed to the creek. "You could pretend you're a beaver."

"Hilarious. I'm being serious. I really have to go."

"You see that tree over there? Or that one. Also that bush." Gary randomly pointed at various trees, bushes, and shrubs. None of which looked like an acceptable bathroom.

"Sure, it's easy for you boys. You just unzip your fly and whip it out."

"It's not really a whipping motion," said Gary. "It's more of a gentle gathering and positioning. It's not like you're wrangling a fire hose that's flailing about."

"Maybe not in your case. You know they make little blue pills for that."

"Trust me. I don't need any pills." Our eyes snagged. Like a swath of tangled vines in the middle of a forest and a pair of untied shoe laces on a pair of hiking boots. A flash of warmth crept all the way up my spine, where it pooled in the creases around my neck.

"Good for you then." I looked into the trees, which grew thicker and more tangled as they went deeper off the trail. "I'm not going in there. There are probably spiders."

"There are definitely spiders."

"And snakes." I looked at the surrounding ground to make sure one of them wasn't slithering up on us right then and there.

Gary nodded. "Snakes and spiders, for sure. But you should really be more concerned with the bears and the wild pigs."

"Wild pigs?" It was like we were taking a nature walk through a National Geographic documentary.

Gary pointed to a patch of mud along the bank of the creek on the other side. It looked like a tribe of preschoolers armed with pails and shovels had attempted to create a replica of the grand canyon. "They dig up the dirt to find grubs."

"Okay," I said. "So let's just play this out. Let's say I go over there behind that bush. I pull down my pants. I squat down. I start to pee. You following along so far?"

"Unfortunately."

"A wild pig comes along, catches me with my pants down, literally. What would a former Eagle Scout have me do?"

"Not former. Once a scout, always a scout." I was not at all surprised. "Drawing upon my Eagle Scout expertise, I would suggest you stand up and make yourself as large as possible. Raise your arms. Try to look intimidating."

I narrowed my eyes and pursed my lips.

"Exactly. Just like that." Gary continued, "Just don't be threatening. Especially if it's a momma hog and has babies. They can be very aggressive if they feel threatened, especially when they're protecting their young."

"So intimidating, but not threatening."

"Exactly." Gary nodded. "Now if's a bear, lie down in the fetal position and slather yourself with honey. That way, the rest of us have more time to escape."

"Can I at least pull my pants up first?"

Gary shrugged. "Your funeral."

———

At Karen's insistence, we "picked up our pace." That's when I learned that the only thing more fun than walking through nature is walking through nature at a picked-up pace. Somewhere along trail "E", she stopped asking for input on the checklist, and just entered the answers herself.

Deeper into the woods, we came to a three-way intersection. The "F" trail wound to the left. The "G" trail twisted to the right. Trail "H" pointed straight ahead. The woods were quieter here. The trees were darker. It felt like the middle of nowhere.

"I think we should take 'F'," Karen said decisively.

Gary's Eagle Scout instincts were kicking in. I could see it in his eyes. "I'm not sure," he said. "I think 'G' is a more direct route."

Just to keep things interesting, I said, "We should totally do 'H'."

"Hey, I've got an idea," Karen said, pressing her hands together like she was about to lead us all into prayer. "Why don't we divide and conquer? Gary and I can go 'F'. And Mary, you can go straight to 'H'." Karen gave me another one of her prize worthy smiles.

"Hey, here's another idea," I said. "How about if Gary and I go 'H', and Karen, you can go 'F' yourself?"

Gary's eyes widened and his cheeks puffed out as he pressed his lips. He looked like he had just blown out of an airlock in space and had to hold his breath.

"I want to go with her," said Kyle.

I looked over, and to my surprise, Kyle pointed at me. "You want to come with me?" I looked at Gary for help.

But Gary only smiled and said, "Okay with me."

Karen had her hands on her hips. "Well Gary, what's it going to be, 'F' with me or 'H' with Mary?"

"I'm going 'G'," Gary said, then marched down the trail to the right by himself. Without looking back, he said, "Try to be back before dark. And watch out for alligators. And wild hogs. And bears." His voice trailed off in the distance. "Maybe panthers."

Once Gary disappeared into the trees, Karen and I squared off, feet firmly planted, hands clenched on our hips. No words were needed. The stakes were clear. First one back to the nature center would be the winner. The winner of what, exactly? I wasn't sure. But the prize didn't matter. Beating Karen was all that did.

"Come on, Cary," Karen grabbed her daughter's arm and practically yanked her off her feet. Cary yelped. They disappeared down the trail at an even greater "picked up" pace.

Kyle and I stayed where we were, watching them go. "They're totally going to kick our asses," I said.

"I know," Kyle agreed.

"Why'd you want to come with me, anyway?" I started hiking down trail "H", Kyle on my heels.

"You're funny," he said after a few moments. "And weird."

"Didn't you want to hang out with your girlfriend? What's her name? Cary?"

"She's not my girlfriend." We continued walking. He didn't say anything to me, and I didn't say anything to him. We just soaked in the peace and quiet of the forest.

"Sorry about the girlfriend comment back there," I said after we walked a bit more. "I didn't mean girlfriend like *girlfriend* girlfriend. I meant, why didn't you want to go with your friend, who happens to be a girl?"

"She's not my friend." Then, after a quiet pause, he said, "She doesn't even like me."

"What makes you think she doesn't like you?"

"She said I was gross."

"Why did she say that?"

"I don't know."

"Were you picking your nose or something?"

"No."

"Were you scratching your butt?"

"No."

"Sniffing your butt?"

"No."

"Sniffing her butt?"

"You're weird."

"You said that already."

We continued walking down the trail at a leisurely pace, much less "picked up" than before. Kyle didn't seem to be in any hurry, so I followed his lead. Turns out he was formulating questions. After a long spell of more silence, he asked, "Are you my dad's girlfriend?"

I had just taken a sip of water and sprayed it all out in front of me.

"Oh no, no way," I answered. "Absolutely not."

"So you're just his friend, that's a girl."

"I'm not entirely sure about that either."

"You're not sure if you're a girl?"

"I'm definitely a girl. A woman technically."

"So you're not his friend?" Kyle frowned.

"No. I mean yes. Sort of. We're friendly-ish. It's complicated."

"Weird."

We kept walking. Then I had an idea. Perhaps this was my opportunity to get a little more background info on Gary. Info I could use to help me with my plan to set him up with Janet.

"So your dad, does he have another girlfriend?"

"No."

"Does he ever have a girlfriend?"

"I don't think so."

"What about your mom?"

"She's not here anymore."

"So you just live with your dad?"

Kyle nodded.

"Do you ever visit your mom?"

Kyle shrugged. "Some times. My dad takes me to see her."

"I see."

"How long have they been div...," I remembered to choose my words wisely. The kid was only eight, and he seemed a bit sensitive. Especially after the whole girlfriend thing. "How long has your mom been gone?"

"Since I was a baby."

"Sorry. That sucks. My mom went away when I was twelve." It's never easy on a kid when their parents split, no matter how young or old.

We continued walking in silence for a long time after that. Eventually, I could see the green roof of the nature center just ahead, over the tops of the trees.

Before we reached the end of our journey, Kyle stopped. He clearly had something else he wanted to say.

"What is it?" I asked.

"I think my dad needs a girlfriend," he said.

I had thought he was going to ask how many points we were going to get on the scavenger hunt quiz or ask me to change the brown water answer back to beaver poop. I wasn't expecting that at all. "How come you think that?"

"He's by himself a lot. That makes him sad. And then that makes me sad."

"Yeah. I was actually just thinking I might be able to help with that."

"Really?"

I said, "I'm certainly going to try."

We continued walking toward the cabin. After a few more steps, I felt his hand grab hold of mine.

WHEN WE GOT BACK TO THE NATURE CENTER, GARY, Karen, and Cary were already there, waiting. Karen gave me her biggest smile yet, a victory smile. Honestly, I didn't even care.

"I guess I can call off the search parties," Gary said. "We were starting to worry." I could tell by the look on Karen's face that the term "we" did not include her.

Regardless, I decided to play nice. "Did you turn in the checklist yet? Did we get our prize?"

That's when Ranger Sarah walked up, checklist in hand. "Hey there team, looks like you forgot to finish one of the questions. We need all the answers before I can give you your prize."

"I thought we got them all," Karen said. "What question is it?"

Ranger Sarah pointed at the checklist. "What do mosquitoes, ticks, and leeches all have in common?"

I looked over at Gary. He looked over at me, the tears already brimming in his eyes. In order to keep from laughing, he was biting down on his lower lip. I surreptitiously caught Kyle's atten-

127

tion, and then pointed at the letters on my shirt, mouthing each one in turn. "S.U.K.C."

Kyle turned to Ranger Sarah and raised his hand.

"Yes, Kyle?" asked Ranger Sarah.

"They all suck?"

Karen's entire body clenched. If I could have wedged a piece of coal up her ass, I would have gotten myself a diamond.

"Way to go!" Ranger Sarah gave Kyle a high five. Then she passed out our prizes. An annual pass so we could repeat the nature walk again and again all year round as many times as we wanted.

* * *

As everyone was getting ready to leave, saying their goodbyes, Gary pulled me aside. "Thank you for coming," he said. "I appreciated the help. Really."

"No problem," I said.

"Kyle seems to really like you."

"He's not so bad himself. For a kid, I mean."

Across the parking lot, the kids and chaperones started loading on to the bus. "That's my ride. I guess I better go." Gary lingered a moment longer. "Did you really come out here just to tell me you told Janet I said hi?"

Forced to confront the truth of my intentions, I suddenly realized how utterly ridiculous I had been. Did I actually believe I could pull off a matchmaking plan that would cause anything other than broken hearts and mass destruction? I wasn't a matchmaker. I was a match breaker. There was no way I had any business meddling in other people's relationships. I couldn't even handle a relationship of my own.

"Mary? Is that really all you wanted?" Gary was waiting for an answer. I could see Karen eyeing us from a bus window. She was breathing so hard she was fogging up the glass.

I mean, seriously. So what if Janet had a crush on Gary back in high school? It had been twenty years. Janet had changed a lot in the past twenty years. Clearly, so had Gary.

"Well," I said.

The idea that they would just magically hit it off, so Janet would forget all about Jack, was insane. Ludicrous.

"Well?" Gary frowned.

To pull something like that off would require master planning. Precise execution.

"Mary?" Gary stood there waiting.

Gary and I would have to be joined at the hip for weeks. Plotting and planning. Day and night.

"What else were you going to talk to me about?"

And we would have to get started immediately, before things with Janet and Jack progressed. It was a long shot, sure. But look at what was at stake. People's lives were on the line. Okay, maybe not their lives, per se, but their love life for certain.

The bus honked, and Karen stepped down to the bottom step by the door. "Gary, everyone's waiting!"

Could I really just sit back and watch? We're talking long-term happiness here. Quality of life. Fulfillment. Life partner stuff. Really, if you thought about it, it was my duty, my responsibility to intervene. What kind of friend would I be if I just sat back and watched Janet throw her life away?

And then what about Kyle? An innocent child. Really, he's the one who sealed the deal. He was concerned about his father being lonely. Would I just ignore the suffering of a child? When there was the perfect woman just waiting for him, standing there right in front of his face?

Gary waved his palm in front of my face. "Maaar-yyy. Hello? Anybody home?"

That's when I made my final decision. I was going to go all-in. No turning back.

"Mary, I've got to go. Was there something else you wanted to say?"

I put my hand on Gary's arm and took a deep breath. It

looked like he was holding his. "There was one more thing I wanted to ask you," I told him.

Gary still looked like he was holding his breath. "Ask me then. Ask me anything."

So I asked him. "What are you doing tonight?"

My battle with the universe was just getting started. And it was time for me to start putting points on the board.

Chapter Thirteen

T he Fresh Foods market was always busy at that hour. Located along the main road, it was a convenient spot for people to pick up groceries on their way home from work. People like Janet. The bookstore where she worked was only a block down the street. And every Thursday, after her shift ended, she would stop at Fresh Foods to grab dinner.

"How do I look?" Gary seemed nervous. Probably because I was staring at him and frowning.

"You look great," I said.

Getting here hadn't been easy. And I'm not talking about the drive. I'm talking about convincing Gary. Naturally, he had been resistant at first. And last. And every moment in between. I started with the truth, telling Gary that Janet had a crush on him. I told him that Janet was single, and I thought the two of them would be a great fit, just leaving out the part about how Janet liking him had been twenty years ago, and the "single" was the filing status on her tax forms. No need to make things more complicated than they were already.

"I don't know about this," said Gary.

"That's okay," I told him. "Because I do."

"You don't think this is, I don't know, desperate or something?" We were standing in the cheese section. Gary picked up a wedge of gorgonzola and grimaced.

"It's not desperate," I said. *It was totally desperate.* "We just want things to happen organically."

"Maybe we should stand over in the organic section then," Gary quipped.

I took the cheese out of his hand and put it back on the shelf. "This is serious."

"Sorry. Of course."

I stepped back to give Gary a better look. Per my instruction, he was wearing a nice green shirt, Janet's favorite color, and a nice pair of khaki slacks. I felt I had to be specific because, with my luck, he would have shown up in paint stained cargo shorts and S.U.K.C. shirt.

"You sure I look okay?"

"You look great."

I studied Gary a moment, like a museum patron assessing a piece of modern art, trying to decide if the art piece was the artist's actual attempt to be brilliantly creative, or they were just messing with everyone as some kind of hoax. Gary shifted his weight back and forth on his feet.

"Hmm."

"Hmm?"

I brushed an errant hair from his eyes and straightened his collar. "You clean up nice," I said.

"I do?"

I nodded. "You look hot, actually."

Gary tugged at his collar and wiped his hand across his forehead. "Well, I am sweating. I think I might have a fever."

"The other kind of hot. The good kind of hot." I gave Gary a wink. "Like a block of ghost pepper havarti." Gary's face turned from pink to red. "Now let's go find some tortilla chips."

"Why tortilla chips?"

"They're Janet's favorite food."

Gary followed me to the snack aisle, where I found a bag of

tortilla chips and added them to our cart. He eyed the bag doubt-fully. "And what exactly is it we're doing again?"

"Meeting Janet," I explained. We had already been over it a million times.

"But she doesn't know we're meeting her?"

"Not yet. Now we need tofu."

"Tofu?" Gary wrinkled his nose.

Fresh Foods had one of the largest vegan selections in the area, which is why it was Janet's favorite place to shop. We found a shelf of tofu products next to the produce. There were tofu cubes. Tofu bricks. And tofu nuggets. It was as if we had died and gone to vegan tofu heaven, or as it was called by non-vegans, hell.

"What is it exactly? Tofu? It looks kind of squishy."

I pulled a package of tofu from the shelf and read the back of the label. "Coagulated soy milk curds pressed into blocks of varying firmness."

"Sounds amazing."

I pointed at the tofu. "Add one of those to your cart."

Gary made another face. "Does she prefer soft, firm, or extra firm?"

"I'll let you do your own research on that one big guy." I patted Gary on the back. "But since we're trying to make a good impression here, I think you should go with the extra firm."

Gary took a package of extra firm and placed it in the cart.

"Now on to the magazines." We stopped the grocery cart in front of the magazine racks and started perusing the titles. "We need something ..." I fished for the proper word. "Intellectual. Sophisticated. Refined."

"Refined?"

"Show her how ... civilized you are."

Gary gave me a funny look. "Like what?"

"I don't know, something about engineering or science. We need to make her think you're smart."

"As opposed to ..." Gary trailed off.

"You know, just a painter."

"What's wrong with being a painter?"

"Nothing. Nothing's wrong with being a painter. It's just, if you were, I don't know, like, say, a doctor, for example. You would have had to go through medical school, take on a certain degree of responsibility. Being a doctor implies intelligence. Being a doctor implies wealth."

When I looked over at Gary, he had his arms folded. He didn't look thrilled.

"Look, no offense, but being a painter, well, let's call it a blank slate. We need to fill in the blanks. For Janet I mean."

"You said Janet was single, right?"

"Yes. I did say that."

"And you said she liked me."

"I said that too."

"Why don't you just call her up and say hey, you and Gary should go on a date."

"That would seem desperate."

Gary waved at our surroundings. "And this isn't?"

"Gary. We've been over this a hundred times."

"I only counted ninety-seven."

"Think of it like an open house."

"An open house?"

"An open house. It's a real estate analogy since I'm a real estate agent. You see, most people think the open house is about the house."

"It's not about the house?"

"No."

"Even though it takes place in the house, which has been specifically opened, for the purpose of people going in to the open house."

"Exactly. You get it now." I'm not sure that he really did, but I continued anyway. "What the open house is really about is the prospective buyers. Seeing the house is just a lure. A decoy. The prospects think it's about one thing, but really, it's about something else entirely."

"So what is it about, then?"

"Finding the right match for the real estate agent hosting the open house," I said. "Assessing fit and interest of potential clients. If the buyer displays the right profile," I pointed to the items in the grocery cart.

"Lactose intolerant vegan?"

"The agent digs a little deeper. How many bedrooms are you looking for? Do you want a pool? What's your budget? That first meeting, the 'open house' if you will, that's when both parties decide if the relationship should move forward. That crucial first meeting when buyer and seller decide if they'll go all the way."

"What kind of real estate agent are you again?"

"The kind that invests the time and energy to find the right match."

"Seems like a lot of work."

"Trust me Gary, I'm a professional. This is what I do."

Gary and I continued looking over the magazines. "How about this one?" He held up a True Crime magazine with a feature story titled "Stalkers!"

I rolled my eyes. "Speaking of professional guidance, we should probably work on your write-up. You know, highlight your feature set. Tell buyers, in this case Janet, what makes you stand apart. What would you say is your best trait?"

Gary shrugged. "I don't know, my personality?"

"It's definitely not your personality."

"Ouch."

"Don't take it personally. You just never want to say you have a good personality. In the dating world, personality is another word for loser. What else do you have?"

"I'm generous?"

"Generous means clingy."

"Is attentive okay?"

"I'm afraid we're moving into stalker territory now."

"I think we're already there."

Gary pulled a copy of Architecture Today off the magazine rack and held it up for me to see. "What about this one?"

The cover featured a dream house, sleek and modern, with perfect landscaping and a mountain view. "Excellent choice," I said. "Architects are totally sexy. All those bold angles and sexy curves. Architects are even better than doctors."

Gary put the magazine in the cart.

I rearranged it so it wasn't covering up the extra firm tofu. "You know I wanted to become an architect once."

Gary pushed the cart down the aisle. "Why didn't you then?"

"Algebra. Math and I never got along. That's why I got into real estate and interior design. I love a good project. Nothing better than taking something boring and plain, and transforming it into something spectacular."

Gary nodded. I still wasn't sure he was buying any of it, but at least he was still playing along.

We were passing through the frozen food section, which sparked an idea. "Frozen dinners! We almost forgot about the frozen dinners. The frozen dinners are the most important part. It lets the woman know you're single. She sees a pot roast or a jar of Béarnaise sauce and it's all over."

"By the way, how do you even know I'm single? How do you know I'm not already dating someone?"

"What do you mean?"

"When you told me that Janet was interested. How did you know I wasn't already interested in someone else? I didn't pull out any frozen dinners on the nature hike."

"No, just granola bars. From your pants. Which was super appetizing, by the way."

I tried to stall answering him by stacking half a dozen random frozen dinners in the cart. When Gary continued looking at me, waiting for an answer, I admitted, "Kyle told me. And he told me about his mom."

"He told you about his mom?" Gary looked surprised. Shocked, actually.

"Kyle told me everything. You know, I'm just trying to help here. Help you. Help Janet. I thought you two would be great together, but, you know, I don't want you to do anything you don't want to do."

Gary took a moment to consider everything I'd been telling him. "I suppose I've got to get back out there at some point, right?" He rubbed at the finger where his ring used to be. I don't think he knew he was doing it. For a fraction of a second, a hint of doubt almost snuck its way into my brain but I squashed it immediately.

"Let's go find a nice bottle of wine," I said before Gary could change his mind. I headed for the wine shelves near the back of the store, Gary pushing the cart behind me.

ONCE WE GOT TO THE WINE SECTION, WE TOOK A FEW moments to survey the shelves. I grabbed a random bottle. The label said it was a French Syrah. I wasn't a wine expert, but it seemed like it could work.

"Now with this we accomplish three objectives," I explained. "First, it's expensive, so she'll think you have good taste. Second, it's French, which suggests romance. Third, if this blows up in our faces, you and I can go back to Aunt Catherine's house and get tanked."

I caught a flash of something in Gary's eyes when I said the part about him and me going back to Aunt Catherine's house and sharing a bottle of wine. I figured he must have thought the idea that something like that would ever possibly happen was completely ludicrous. Which it was, of course. Absolutely ridiculous.

I held up the bottle. "So, what do you think?"

"I'm more of a beer guy."

"Really? What a coincidence. I'm more of a beer gal."

The beer cooler was right next to the wine shelves. Gary

pointed to it. "Stouts or lagers?"

"Neither," I said. "I'm a sour girl all the way."

Mischief danced in Gary's eyes. He pulled a six-pack from the cooler, then placed it in the cart. "So what would you think if you saw this in here?"

I recognized the packaging immediately. It was from one of the local breweries, FoxPaw Brewing. The beer was aptly named SourPaw. "I would think you have superb taste. That's one of my favorites."

"So you've been to FoxPaw?"

"I know the head brewer, Mike," I said. "I go there all the time."

FoxPaw Brewing was on the way home from the real estate office. Me and some of the other agents would go there after closing a big deal. They had a great beer selection, terrific truffle tater tots, trivia nights, even karaoke.

Gary said, "We should go sometime."

"We?" Gary had caught me off guard. "By we you mean you and Janet. Right?"

He hesitated before answering. "Right. By 'we' I meant me and Janet. Obviously."

"Obviously," I agreed.

I took the six-pack of SourPaw out of the grocery cart and put the wine in the cart instead. "Janet will be here soon," I said. I did a quick review of the grocery cart to make sure we didn't miss anything. Tofu, check. Tortilla chips, check. Frozen dinners, wine, and architecture magazine. Check, check, and check. "We should get into position."

"If you say so." Gary's hands gripped the cart like he was holding on to one of those Coast Guard sea rescue ladders they drop from a helicopter. Hovering over a school of hungry sharks.

"You've got this," I said, trying to sound confident for both of us.

Gary positioned his cart near the front entrance so he could spot Janet when she arrived. I took my position near the cheese.

The trap had been laid. The snare had been set. When Janet arrived, she would see Gary standing there with his cart. The plan was to let her recognize him, then make the first move. They would start talking, laugh about old times, then nature would take its course.

We waited.

And waited.

And waited some more.

After thirty minutes, I abandoned my cheese post and returned to Gary, hiding behind a floor display of acid reflux pills.

"Are you sure she's coming?" Gary was still death clutching the grocery cart. His knuckles were ghost white.

I checked my watch. Janet should have gotten off work over thirty minutes ago. "I'll text her."

MARY:

hey, u still at work?

JANET:

book signing

stuck here till 10

why?

MARY:

nvmnd

Touché universe. Touché. After everything we had done to prepare, Janet wasn't coming.

"Time to move to Plan B," I announced.

"Plan B? What's Plan B?"

I did not know what Plan B was. "Plan B is, well, Plan B is even better than Plan A."

Gary asked, "If Plan B was better than Plan A, why didn't we just start with Plan B to begin with?"

Because I'm making this up as I go.

Chapter Fourteen

The Book Belle bookstore where Janet worked was a nerd's wet dream. Rare comic books hung on the walls like posters. Collectible toys, movie memorabilia, and anatomically inflated action figures were staged on the shelves and counters. Oh, and they had books too.

Gary's eyes glazed over as soon as we walked inside. "What is this place?" I suspect his tofu package went from extra to super firm.

"The Book Belle," I said. "This is where Janet works." After high school, Janet had gone to college and majored in literature, which basically qualified her for absolutely zero actual jobs. So she ended up getting a job at The Book Belle, and had worked her way up the ranks.

"Janet works here?" Gary was like a little boy that just found out his best friend's mom worked at a candy factory with unlimited free samples.

I nodded, "Yup."

Ever since people started getting their books online, cheaper than any small business could afford, independent bookstores like the Book Belle had to get creative. And Janet was a genius in creative marketing. It was her passion that had kept this place afloat, even as most of the other bookstores around town had gone the way of the dinosaurs. Speaking of which, on the shelf above us, a tyrannosaurus rex chased a flux capacitor fueled DeLorean about to run over Frankenstein.

We weaved our way through the labyrinth. Books of all sizes, shapes, and colors packed the shelves. New and used. Fiction and nonfiction. Cook books. Romance novels. Science Fiction and Do-It-Yourself.

There were dozens of spaceships hanging from strings pinned to the ceiling, an epic space battle milieu. Stormtroopers and Klingons and Transformers waged war across the shelves.

"This place is awesome." Gary stood in awe as an electric circus train transporting plastic lions, tigers, and bears twisted through a mushroom themed village of gnomes, defending their village against an onslaught of Smurfs.

"Okay, Charlie, you can go play in the chocolate factory later. Right now, we have a job to do."

It was good to see him smile. Weird that he was smiling at all the nonsense, but still good.

"And what exactly is the job? Specifically?"

"I'll tell you," I said. And I planned to as soon as I figured it out myself.

I looked around the bookstore, desperate for inspiration. Based on what I was seeing, we could either make Janet walk the plank off a spaceship into some sort of desert sinkhole creature with tentacles and teeth, or hop across yellow blocks in a plumber outfit and bounce on the head of a big green dragon until it pooped gold coins out its butt.

"Hey, look at this." Gary pulled a random book from a random shelf next to where we were standing. He held it up for me to see. *Modern Architecture*.

"Holy shit, you're brilliant." I punched him in his arm.

"Ouch."

"We're going back to Plan A."

"I thought you said Plan B was better than A."

"The situation is fluid."

"I have no idea what any of this means."

"Lucky for you, I do." I looked around at the surrounding shelves. "You have the architecture book, so that covers the sexy intellectual angle. But Janet's favorite books are supernatural romance."

Gary made a face.

"You're not secretly a werewolf, are you?"

"Not that I know of. But it has been a while since my last lycanthropy screening."

"Is that the one where you bend over and cough?"

"No, that's for vampirism."

"Here." I handed Gary a book with a cover that showed a raven haired woman, breasts bursting out of her evening gown, flanked by a half naked, muscle bound werewolf on one side and a half naked, muscle bound vampire on the other. It was called *Blood Moon Lust*.

"People read this stuff?"

"Janet does. Follow me."

I led Gary through the bookstore. I added Wealth Investing, Vegan Cooking, and the Kama Sutra to the stack in his arms as we went.

"You know, technically, I already know how to do all these things."

I stopped and spun around so quickly that Gary almost dropped the pile of books on my toes. "Wait. All of them?"

A bit of a smile curled on Gary's lips. "If this plan of yours gets Janet to go out with me, then you can ask her later to verify."

I'm not sure why, but my heart started beating like I was being chased by a pack of werewolves and vampires through the woods. I had to stop for a moment, hand braced on a shelf.

Concern clouded Gary's face. "Hey, Mary, I was just kidding?" He paused, then added, "I don't really know how to cook vegan."

I slapped Gary on the arm.

"Maybe I should get a self defense book. Karate or kung fu?"

I noticed we had stopped in the poetry section, and I got an idea. "This is perfect." I pulled a big leather bound volume from the shelf, then put it on top of the other books. Gary looked like a pack mule overladen with supplies, about to topple over from the weight.

"What's that one?"

"French poetry."

"Janet likes French poetry?"

"Nobody likes French poetry. But women like sensitivity. You know, all that touchy-feely nonsense. And French poetry is about as fluffy as you can get."

"I don't speak French."

"That's the beauty of it. Neither does Janet. You could speak Portuguese and she wouldn't know the difference."

"I don't speak Portuguese either."

I stepped back to survey my handiwork. As I looked over the collection of books, I thought Plan B, which was now Plan A, might actually be even better than the original Plan A after all.

Janet loved books. Once she saw Gary shared her passions, she couldn't help herself but fall head over heels.

Take that universe. Mary Burns was on the board.

The twinkling lights from the gnome village gave Gary's eyes a warm glow. Standing there with the heavy stack of books in his arms, I could see the muscles in his biceps flexing under the weight. My eyes drifted to the title on the spine of the book just under the French poetry. *Kama Sutra*. My heart started beating faster again. *I already know how to do all those things.*

"Oh my God, Gary, Gary Wright? Is that you?" We both turned as Janet appeared, her eyes wide and hands poised for clapping. "I can't believe you're standing here in my book store after all these years!"

I quickly scanned their faces. Janet was genuinely thrilled. She looked like she was about to explode. And was that smile on

Gary's face as real as it seemed? *Holy hell. This might actually work.*

Janet said, "I need a hug Gary, give me a hug!"

Quickly, I motioned for Gary to pass me the stack of books. He did. But as soon as he pulled away, my knees buckled, and it took all of my strength to stay upright.

Throwing out my back was worth it, though, because before Gary could even brace himself, Janet leaped into his arms and wrapped her hands around his neck. In a good way, not a strangling way to be clear.

"It is so good to see you again!" she squealed. "I can't believe it." After sufficiently smothering the poor man, Janet stepped back to get a better look. "You look a-maze-ing," Janet gushed. "I mean, wow." Janet looked like a teenage girl who just got pulled up on stage at her very first Kpop concert.

She started fanning herself with her open hand and breathing in gasps. "My God, Gary Wright, I can't believe it, after twenty years. What are you doing here?"

Something seemed to click in Janet's brain.

She looked at me.

Then looked at Gary.

Me again.

Then Gary.

A big smile stretched across Janet's blood flushed face. "You're here with Mary?"

"No," I said before any more assumptions formed in her head. "We just came here together, as friends, because Gary, Gary wanted to ..." My brain must have decided it had enough excitement for one day and was going on strike effective immediately. I demanded it get back to work, but it only held up a picket sign that read F-YOU.

"I'm here for the book signing," Gary pointed to the book signing flyer taped to the wall. It was like he had ridden in on a white horse, his shiny metal armor gleaming in the sun. Not unlike the King Arthur figurine in the mythology section beside us.

"Yes, the book signing," I agreed. Meanwhile, the books in my hands were slipping. The hard cover edge of the architecture book was cutting into my hand like a razor.

"So you're here to see Lance Boyer, then?" Gary and I stared at Janet as if she were speaking French. Or Portuguese. "The author here signing books," she explained.

"Yes," I said. "Lance Boyer. Of course."

"Mary was kind enough to give me a ride," Gary added.

"As friends. Since we're friends. Just friends," I reiterated.

Janet turned to Gary. "I didn't realize you were into that kind of thing," she said.

"Oh yes," I interjected. "Gary's a big fan. He's read all of Lance's books."

"I see." Janet nodded. "He's so inspirational. So brave."

"Very brave," I agreed. "Very inspirational. He really inspired Gary. Isn't that right Gary?"

Gary nodded. "For sure. He inspires me every day."

I tried to shift the weight of the books in my arms from my left side to my right side, as my left shoulder went numb.

"Here, let me help you with that." Janet grabbed some books out of my hands, holding them up for inspection. "Don't you have enough sex books already, Mary?" Janet shook her head at me like a nun who had just caught a catholic school boy with a dirty magazine hidden under his bible. "And *Blood Moon Lust*, you have to finish *Night Lust* and *Star Lust* first. It's a trilogy, so you have to read them in order."

I caught Gary's smirk out of the corner of my eye.

"I have no idea what you're talking about," I said.

"You asked to borrow them from me just last week."

Eager to change the subject, I said, "What's the name of Lance's new book again? The one that he's signing?"

Janet put her hand on Gary's shoulder and gave it a squeeze. "It's called *Coming Out*."

"Wait, what?" Gary looked like he just got the results back from a lycanthropy screening. All positive.

"*Coming Out*," Janet repeated, then turned to Gary. "If you liked his other books, you're really going to love this one." Janet took Gary's hand and gave that a squeeze, too. "I'm so glad you came. But we should hurry if you want to get a seat. Lance is going to start speaking any minute now. Follow me."

WE FOLLOWED JANET THROUGH AN ARCHED ENTRANCE with the words Somewhere Over the Rainbow tacked to the wall in fanciful colored letters. The arched portal led to another section of the store. Here, a rainbow mural swept across the ceiling, where it continued down the far wall. Leprechaun figurines were protecting a pot of gold from Jason and Freddy action figures, complete with a hockey mask, chainsaw, and claws. I assumed this was where the books focused on Irish folklore, LGBTQ, and unfortunate summer camp incidents. Perhaps there would be something here about our nature walk adventure one day.

The small stage was tucked into a cozy corner just past the rainbow room, facing several rows of folding chairs set in a semicircle. Lance Boyer sat down on the stool in the middle of the stage. Beside him was a small table with a glass of water, a pen, and a stack of his books. Lance was a beef slab of a man, like a tree trunk dressed in flannel. He had the beard of a lumberjack, the neck of a wrestler, and the biceps of an "after" model from some wildly successful new testosterone treatment.

Gary squirmed in his seat. He leaned over to whisper in my ear. "This is bad. Really bad. We should just sneak out and go."

"It's not that bad," I said.

"It's not?"

"No," I said. "Things could be way worse." I had meant it to be reassuring, not foretelling. *Whoops.* My bad.

Janet stepped on stage beside Lance, holding a microphone. She leaned down and whispered something in his ear. When she stood back up, she looked directly over at Gary, smiled, and gave him a big thumbs up.

"Definitely bad," Gary hissed. He tried to rise out of his seat, but I grabbed him by the thigh and squeezed, holding him in place.

"Ouch, that's going to leave a bruise."

Janet turned on the microphone and addressed the dozen people in the room. "Thank you all for coming. Tonight we welcome to the Book Belle stage, author Lance Boyer, whose previous works include *Under the Rainbow* and *Living with Pride*. He's here with us this evening to read a small excerpt from his latest book, *Coming Out*, and then he'll be happy to pose for photographs and sign any copies of *Coming Out* that you purchase here in store tonight."

The audience erupted in applause as Lance took the microphone and stood up from his seat. He towered over everyone, especially with the added height of the stage.

The applause finally ebbed, and the room fell silent.

Lance took a deep breath, bowed his head. When he looked up again, there were tears in his eyes.

"My latest book, *Coming Out*, is really the culmination of a lifelong journey. Like all my books, it's about making brave choices. It's about not being afraid to take chances. It's about living your best life." Lance pointed to Janet. "Our lovely host here has asked me to dedicate tonight's event to someone here in the audience this evening. Someone who, I'm sure, has had to make brave choices."

"On no." Gary tried to stand up again, but I squeezed his leg harder.

"Someone who, if he's read all my books like Janet says he has, is probably not afraid to take chances. Someone who, since he's here tonight, must be living his best life. Gary? Gary, can you stand up please?"

The audience started clapping. Gary and I stayed frozen in our seats. The audience looked around, waiting for the guest of honor to stand. Janet gestured enthusiastically for Gary to stand from the side of the stage. I'm sure Gary wanted to give me a different gesture.

"I told you this was bad." Gary looked at me accusingly.

"And I told you they could be way worse. Which now they are."

I let go of Gary's leg. Slowly, he stood. The audience applauded. Gary made the brave choice to soak it all in, unafraid, making the best of his life situation. He even gave a little wave.

On stage, Lance said, "Gary, may this book give you the courage to follow in my footsteps." When the applause faded away, Gary returned to his seat.

Lance sat back down on the stool, opened *Coming Out*, and began reading. "The Alaskan air was frosty that morning. Although it was now spring, the ground was still a blanket of white. Fresh flakes of snow clumped on the green trees of the pine forest."

"What is he talking about?" whispered Gary.

I replied, "I have no idea."

Lance continued, "I waited at a safe distance. Camera ready. My heart beating out of my chest. Because soon, after a winter long slumber, the magnificent brown bears of the vast wilderness would be ..." Lance paused for effect, then continued. "... Coming out."

Lance held open the book, revealing photographs of brown bear cubs playing in the snow. The audience oohed and aahed as Lance flipped through his photography book, each picture more magnificent than the last.

AFTER THE BOOK SIGNING, WHEN AUTHOR LANCE Boyer and the other customers were long gone, I placed a signed copy of all three of Lance's photography books down on the checkout counter. I was buying them for Gary. I figured it was the least I could do.

While Janet was totaling the sale, I flipped open *Under the Rainbow*. It was a series of photographs of the active volcanos of Hawaii, red lava and black rock juxtaposed with colorful rainbows in the sky. Lance really had an eye for natural compositions.

Living in Pride was a photo-journal of Lance's time following a pride of lions through the Serengeti, in the Arusha region of Tanzania. Lance was truly living his best life. To be honest, I was jealous. Being eaten by lions or mauled by bears or falling into a volcano sounded like pretty good options compared to what I was dealing with.

Gary and I had stayed to help Janet clean up. Gary swept the floors, and I busied myself putting the books we gathered earlier back on their proper shelves.

I wanted to give Gary and Janet a little time to themselves. And the time alone together seemed to pay off. I heard Gary's voice in the distance, laughing with Janet about some lost memory from days back in school. Looking down at the remaining stack of books in my arms, the cover of the *Kama Sutra* stared back up at me. The Universe was mocking me again.

On the other side of the store, I heard Gary still laughing with Janet. I watched from afar as he hoisted a stack of folding chairs over his shoulder. Clearly, Gary was no longer the lanky, acned, scrawny nerd geek he was twenty years ago. And yes, some women might even think he was attractive. And yes, perhaps, maybe, possibly, I was one of those women. But it didn't matter what I thought. It only mattered what Janet was thinking.

"Where do you want me to put these?" I heard Gary ask. Somehow, Gary now balanced two armfuls of chairs on his shoulders.

"Oh, you can put those in the game room," said Janet. "It's right through that door over there. Follow me." Janet looked over in my direction, and I pretended I was reading the book in my hands.

"How does she even bend over that far?" I asked a Dr. Ruth bobblehead, surrounded by the collectible cast of the Rocky Horror Picture Show.

"Hey Mary," called Janet. "I was going to show Gary the game room. Why don't you come too?"

I followed Janet and Gary to the game room in the back of the bookstore, over a faux drawbridge beneath a mural of wart covered trolls. Tables and chairs lined up in rows down the middle. There was a poster of a Minotaur on the wall, replica weapons in plastic cases, and a life-sized suit of armor propped in the corner.

"This is where we hold our Dungeons and Dragons nights," Janet explained.

"Dungeons and Dragons?" Gary had a glint in his eyes. And possibly a package of super firm tofu in his pants. Out of the corner of my eye, I caught Dr. Ruth nodding.

"We have all the handbooks and modules. Dice, props, miniatures. Everything you would need." Janet said, "Hey, maybe someday we can all get together and play."

Chapter Fifteen

I bent over.

I stuck my butt in the air.

I spread my legs.

Behind me, Johan barked orders. "In! Out! In! Out!"

I tried to look back at him, between my spread legs, but my boobs were in the way. They tumbled down, or up, I suppose, in my inverted position.

It was the morning after the book signing. After I got home, it took me three quarters of a bottle of Pinot Grigio to fall asleep. It was not a restful sleep. It was a sleep haunted by dreams. Disturbing dreams.

In the last dream, I was sitting in a chair on the beach. The rocks, the sky, the sand were all black and white. I sat at a table as the ocean crashed behind me. On the table was a checkered board filled with chess pieces.

Sitting across from me was the Universe, draped in a black hooded robe. Every move I made, she countered. Every piece I played was taken from me. I woke up to the sound of Her laughing.

"Get on your hands and knees," Johan demanded. His thick

accent and sharp tone left no room for debate. Suitably positioned, my bottom quivered like a jello mold.

Johan moved in front of me. Looking up, it was hard not to stare directly into his bulging crotch.

After waking up from my Universe chess dream, I decided I needed to blow off some steam. Engage in some physical activity. Get a little spiritual stimulation, so to speak.

So I went to see Johan. Whenever I needed a little physical release, Johan always delivered. *And then some.*

By that point, he had been working me over for nearly thirty minutes. Sweat clung to my sagging breasts. Wetness dripped down my aching thighs. I was going to need a long, hot shower after Johan was done with me.

"I thought yoga was supposed to be relaxing," Janet hissed, moving from Cat pose to Cow pose beside me.

"Downward Dog!" Johan yipped. "Butts higher. Glutes tighter. Legs straight!"

Johan marched us through another series of positions only suitable for a twenty-one-year-old, jointless acrobat. Then, mercifully, the yoga class ended.

Janet and I hit the showers, then went to our lockers to change. As I pulled on my panties underneath my towel, I noticed Janet looking over at me, grinning. Not only grinning, her eyes were sparkling.

"What?"

Janet kept grinning as I pulled on a pair of shorts.

"*What?*" I asked again.

"So."

"So?"

"How's it going with you and Gary?"

"What do you mean, me and Gary?"

"You two are cute together."

I made a face. And it wasn't just because of Janet's completely erroneous and grossly misguided assumption. It was also because there was an older woman changing at the bank of lockers across from us. The woman was naked, naturally. And by naturally, I mean nature was on full frontal display.

I averted my eyes, refocusing on Janet. "Gary and I aren't cute together. Gary and I aren't anything together. Gary and I aren't together at all."

Janet still had the stupid grin on her face. "Okay. Sure."

Unfortunately, I caught another sideways glimpse of the naked woman. And I take back that comment I made earlier about *my* boobs sagging. Compared to the naked woman, mine were as pert as a plastic surgeon's twenty-two-year-old mistress.

Stuffing my own boobs into my bra, I said, "I'm serious, Janet," a little louder than I intended. "I just gave him a ride to the book signing."

"If you say so."

"I do say so."

"I heard you say so."

"Good. Because I said it."

Even though I was being extremely careful not to look behind me, I caught a glimpse in the mirror. The naked older woman's cooch looked like Gandalf's beard.

WE STOPPED AT THE SMOOTHIE BAR ON OUR WAY OUT of the gym. Janet ordered us two vegan Green Monsters, a special kale and spinach mixture blended in house. Mine tasted like vomit flavored paste.

Eager to shift the focus away from Janet's utterly insane, warped perceptions about me and Gary, I asked, "What about you and Jack? Have you seen him again?"

Janet shook her head, the grin finally fading. "Not since pickleball. I called him yesterday at work but that nurse of his, Kelsey, put me on hold until I hung up. I don't think she likes me."

As I attempted to suck my smoothie, my level of hope, unlike the green chunks in my straw, started to rise. It seemed, perhaps, I still had a window of opportunity to course correct fate's failings. Despite the mishaps at the grocery store and the book signing. Maybe there was still a chance for me to make things right.

Then Janet said, "At least I get to see him again on Saturday."

"Saturday?" My voice cracked just a bit. I pretended I was choking on the smoothie. Which wasn't hard to fake. "What's going on Saturday?"

"Jack's medical practice is sponsoring a charity 5k. He asked me if I wanted to volunteer."

I looked at Janet as if she had signed up for a colonoscopy but declined the anesthesia. "Volunteer for what? Do psych evals on anyone who would willingly run a 5k?"

"I'm handing out ribbons at the finish line. And then, for the winners, I get to put a medal around their neck." Janet got a dreamy look in her eyes. "I told Jack if he won, he might even earn himself a kiss."

Janet kept talking as we made our way to the parking lot, but whatever words came out of her mouth never made it into my ears. The vision of Janet putting a medal around Jack's neck and then kissing him was almost as horrifying as when the naked woman bent over to pick up her sock. It was a sight you could never unsee.

When we got to Janet's car she said, "You should come too. Maybe bring Gary along." Janet's grin returned. "Even if you two aren't *together*, together." Janet made quote fingers.

Even though I was annoyed by Janet's persistent delusion that there was something going on between Gary and me, I recognized the moment for the opportunity that it was.

So I matched Janet's grin. "Good idea!"

THE NEXT DAY, I WENT TO WORK SETTING MY NEW
Gary Plus Janet Equals Mary Plus Jack plan into motion. It was a
good plan, but a risky one. There could be blood. Definitely
sweat. Probably tears. In fact, Ralph already had tears. Or his face
was just melting in the heat. We were outside. During Summer. In
Florida. The temperature was roughly the same as the surface of
the sun.

We were dressed in our brand new running shirts, running
shorts, running socks, and running shoes. Even though the sports
store guy said the material was breathable, damp polyester stuck
to our skins like fly paper. And we hadn't even started running
yet.

Ralph propped his foot up on the back of a bench, presum-
ably to stretch. "Now I know why I never took up running. Or
jogging. Or walking. How could anyone do this on purpose?"

Admiring the way my new sports bra held my boobs in place,
I said, "Beats me."

Convincing Ralph to take part in my plan had not been easy.
When I first approached Ralph with the idea, his exact words had
been, "that would be a hard no." Then there had been talk of the
four horsemen of the apocalypse, and catastrophic climate change
in hell. Something involving Satan, Hitler, and Justin Bieber
making snow angels together.

I had to pull out my Sadie Rosenberg card.

Sadie Rosenberg was a girl Ralph met in law school. One year,
Janet and I went to visit his dorm room during fall break. He'd
been fawning after this girl all semester, but she was way out of his
league, and he knew it. So he asked for my help. And I gave it to
him, saying, "Someday, and that day may never come, I will call
upon you to do a service for me. But until that day, accept this
assistance as a gift." I had done the *Godfather* accent and
everything.

We took a trip down to the barbershop where I ordered a
complete makeover. We scoured the sales racks at Macy's for a
new wardrobe. I even made Ralph memorize a script. By the time

I finished with him, the ugly warted frog had become a handsome prince. When Ralph asked her out, Sadie said yes. It ended up being a one-night stand and there was an alleged pregnancy scare, but a deal's a deal. I sat on that favor for years, saving it for a rainy day. And now, it was raining.

While Ralph finished stretching, I surveyed the battlefield, Red Bug Lake park. The jogging path circled the entire complex, winding through the ball fields and tennis courts, tracing the near side of the lake. Above me, the osprey nested in the light towers. Near the lake, a pair of sandhill cranes searched for an early dinner. And of course, all over the park, there were bugs. Lots of bugs. Red bugs, green bugs, and an assortment of other colors. The kind of bugs that flew up your nose, the kind that flew into your mouth, and the kind that waited for you to drop your guard so they could crawl into your pants.

I saw Gary on the baseball field closest to the sand volleyball courts. Earlier that morning, Ralph had called to ask Gary if he wanted to meet for a beer under the guise of a potential painting job. When Gary told him he couldn't because he was coaching Kyle's little league practice, I did a quick pivot, and the rest of the plan organically fell into place.

"Over there," I told Ralph. He lifted his hand above his eyes to block out the sun.

Gary's little league team spread across the baseball diamond. Kyle was staring up at the clouds in left field. His not-girlfriend-not-even-friend-friend Cary from the nature hike was playing shortstop. I saw her mother, Karen, watching from the bleachers.

"Great," I said.

"What now?" asked Ralph.

I tossed my head in Karen's direction. "Karen, one of the moms. I think she has a thing for Gary."

"Must be going around," Ralph said, just loud enough for me to hear.

"What's that supposed to mean?" I demanded.

"Nothing. Nothing at all."

Ralph had a tell when he was lying. He would either cover his mouth or rub his forehead. Over the years, I had amassed enough poker winnings from his failed bluff attempts that I could sign Purrfect up for one of those fancy pet day cares. Which I did. Once. But after only forty-seven minutes, one of the pet sitters called me and said that Purrfect wouldn't stop hissing at Lulu the chihuahua and then scratched Moose, the Doberman Pincher, so I had to come back and pick her up immediately.

"You said the word *nothing* like you mean *something*."

"Is that what you heard?" Ralph yawned and rubbed his forehead.

"Well, if you meant *something* when you said *nothing*, then you're making *something* out of *nothing*."

"Or you're making nothing out of something," Ralph shot back.

Tired of Ralph's imaginatively inaccurate innuendos, I said, "Let's just get this over with."

As we made our way toward the baseball field, I saw Gary madly motioning in a right to left motion with both arms, in a hopeless attempt to indicate the proper counter clockwise path one should take when running the bases on a baseball field. The oblivious little boy who had just hit the ball sprinted past third base in a huff and was rounding toward second with a full head of steam.

"So let me make sure I fully understand this plan of yours," said Ralph, as we drew closer to the field. "When practice is over, you and I jog past the baseball field. Gary sees us. Warm salutations and greetings ensue."

"Something like that."

"Then Gary says, hey there, Mary, Ralph, so awesome to see you two again. Love those matching running outfits you're sporting. Say, what are you two doing here in this unbearable Florida heat? Why aren't you at home playing Call of Duty and drinking gin and tonics like a sane person would do at six thirty on a Thursday evening?"

I crossed my arms.

Ralph continued. "Then I say, we're here torturing ourselves because Mary is bat shit crazy, and then we all go out and you buy us beer, and we talk him into going to some race thing with Janet."

I was not amused. "Ralph, this is important," I said. "It's important to me, and it's important to Janet."

"Why would Janet want Gary to go to this running thing anyway?"

"Because she's in love with him."

"I thought Janet was doing the thirty-day thing with Jack."

"Janet's only doing the thirty-day thing with Jack because she isn't doing the thirty-day thing with Gary. Yet. Weren't you paying attention?"

Now Ralph crossed his arms.

I took a deep breath and continued. "Look, we jog on by, he sees us, he asks us what we're doing, you say, 'oh, we're training for this charity thing for sick children.' Then Gary says, 'oh wow, what a wonderful cause, can I help sick children too?' And then you say, 'why of course Gary, yes you can, the more the merrier, why don't we all help sick children together?'"

Ralph nodded. "Yes, yes, that's exactly how I see this playing out. I love the voices, by the way. Your Ralph voice really captures my essence. Might want to work on your Gary though. I don't remember him having an Australian accent." Ralph was always very critical of everything. "Can I ask another question?" Ralph asked. Which in itself was a question, though I didn't point that out.

"If you must."

"What kind of sickness are we talking about here?"

"Huh?"

"The children. What kind of sick children are we helping, just in case he asks?"

"I don't know. Bubonic plague or something. Probably. It's got to be one of the bad sicknesses if people will go out in this heat."

"Okay, fine. Let's say, by some miracle, your ridiculous plan works and Gary plays along. Then, not only do I have to make sure Jack doesn't win, you want me to make sure Gary finishes fast enough to earn some kind of trophy?"

"Medal," I corrected.

"Fine, medal."

"Gary doesn't have to win a medal. All I want is for him to finish the race ahead of Jack."

"Have you seen Jack and Gary? Jack can probably run circles around Gary, while simultaneously bench pressing him and giving him a wedgie."

"You're thinking of high school Jack and high school Gary." Then I added, "In case you haven't noticed, Gary has kind of... bulked up."

"So how am I supposed to stop Jack from winning, exactly?" Ralph asked.

It was a good question. So good that I didn't exactly have an answer for it. So I said, "You're a smart man. I'm sure you'll think of something."

"Like toss a banana peel on the ground so he'll slip and crack his head open?"

"No cracked heads, please."

"Remove a manhole cover so he falls into the alligator infested sewers?"

"I'd prefer no plans that involve alligators."

"How about I Tonya Harding his kneecap?"

"Ralph, you're overcomplicating things."

"I'm overcomplicating things?"

"It's very simple, really. Remember what happened after cownado?"

"It's a moment I'll never forget." Ralph held his hand over his heart.

I ignored him. "Remember what Jack did? He swooped in like the hero. Because he's a doctor. It's what he does. All you have to do is pretend to pass out or something."

"If we go through with this, I will not have to pretend."

"Jack will stop to help, and Gary will just cruise on by to victory. See?"

"Not really."

Out on the baseball field, Kyle was chasing a butterfly, the second baseman was adjusting himself, and the catcher was making a sand castle in the clay next to home plate.

Gary shouted, "Okay everybody, I think we'll call it a day. We'll see you all again next week. Don't forget your water bottles. Billy, is that your cleat?"

As the parents collected their players, I turned to Ralph. "It's go time."

Ralph slumped his shoulders and sighed.

WE SET OFF FROM THE BACK CORNER, PAST THE outfield, and adjusted our pace to time our arrival to coincide with the moment Gary stepped off the clay. The jogging path was about two and a half miles total, but Ralph and I only had to run the short stretch that rounded the back side of the baseball diamond, then cross the sidewalk between the restrooms and the dugouts.

Ahead, on the baseball field, Gary collected an errant ball and a discarded glove near first base. Then he angled toward the opening in the fence to exit the field.

Instinctively, Ralph and I quickened our step, powering through the stiffness in our joints. At this point my body was on autopilot, my stride automatic, my brain in a zone. I was a huntress, springing across the grasslands to devour my prey. Every muscle in my body was taunt and flexed.

Gary passed through the dugout out onto to the sidewalk. Ralph and I had timed our arrival perfectly, like a Rube Goldberg Machine, where every domino and playing card fell into place.

We were only seconds from interception.

Gary turned.

That's when Karen appeared, right in front of us, forcing Ralph and I to skid to a halt.

"Mary?" The look of disgust in her eyes only flashed for a second. "It's sooooo good to see you again." Karen's voice sing-songed up and down the scale. "What are you doing here?" Karen flashed her trademark smile. Piranha-like.

"Yes, what are you doing here?" Gary's face was a mix of many things. Surprise. Suspicion. Intrigue?

Ralph recovered the ability to speak before I did. He said, "Training." His face was the color of a Carolina Reaper. "Mary's helping me get ready for a 5k this weekend."

"It's ... *huff* ... a charity ... *puff* ... race ...*huff* ... for sick children." I made a mental note to stop at the nearest emergency room on my way home and ask them for an IV and oxygen.

"Oh, you guys are doing the Family Fun Run?" Gary pointed to the flyer taped to a post beside the dugout. It showed stick figures of a mom, a dad, and two kids with round heads and big smiles, in some sort of running pose. I thought using the words family and fun and run all in the same description was a blatant conflict of interest.

"Yes," Ralph answered. "The Family Fun Run."

"What a coincidence," Karen cooed. "We're going too."

Between gasps of oven baked air, I wheezed, "We?"

Karen's smile stretched wider. "Gary and I."

"Karen signed me up last week." Gary looked about as excited as Ralph did when I had registered him.

"I told him it was for charity," Karen explained. "You know, for the children."

"Right, the children," Gary nodded.

"Can't say no to the children," Ralph agreed.

Karen said, "So, Mary, I never imagined you as much of a runner." She looked me up and down like an MMA fighter sizing up the competition during ring introductions.

"Oh, but I am," I said. "I run all the time. I love running."

Karen's head nodded, but her eyes bore into my soul. "I did track and field back in college. All-conference in the two hundred meters." Karen wore her smug smile like a linebacker's mouth guard.

Gary asked, "So Mary, does that mean you're running for charity too?"

"Me? Oh no, no. No way. Not me. I would have loved to, but the registration deadline passed this morning." It was true. I had submitted Ralph's registration fee just under the wire.

"Gee, that's too bad," Karen pouted, her lips out like a baboon. "Would have been fun to see what you still got."

"Oh, I got plenty," I assured her. Gary and Ralph exchanged a look, as if questioning the rules of time and space.

Karen elevator eyed my running outfit. "So I see." Clearly I was going to have to take this woman out. I wondered how serious Ralph had been about his ability to pull off a Tonya Harding.

"Wait a second," said Gary. "Karen, didn't you say you had extra tickets?"

"I did?" For the first time, Karen looked like she got caught off-guard.

"Yeah," continued Gary. "You told me you had extra tickets, and you didn't want them to go to waste, which is why you invited me to go."

Slowly, the piranha smile crept back on to Karen's face. "You know, I would love to give one to Mary, but we need the other tickets for the kids."

"That's not a problem," Ralph chimed in, pointing to the

flyer on the post. In big bold letters, the flyer proclaimed, "Thompson Family Fun Run: Kids Run Free!"

After reading it, Karen had the same expression on her face as the one she had when I pointed out that our camp shirts sucked.

"Then it's settled," Gary proclaimed. "We can all run together."

"I think that's a great idea," Ralph agreed.

"Remember, it's for the children," said Gary.

"For the children," Karen mumbled.

"For the children," Ralph agreed.

Chapter Sixteen

The morning of the Fun Run, I rolled out of bed at the crack of dawn. Technically, it wasn't really a roll. More of a stumble and a trip. Purrfect had decided the floor right beside the bed was a good place to stop and lick herself.

As I shuffled through my morning routine, every muscle and bone in my body protested the rude awakening, but I powered through. I had been up half the night thinking, mind racing. Now it was time for my body to race, too. I had a job to do, and I would not let sheer exhaustion stop me.

I fed Purrfect a can of cat food and made a banana kale protein shake for myself. When I grabbed my keys to go, Purrfect seemed annoyed that I was leaving so early. But then every other day, she would seem annoyed that I was leaving so late. Our relationship was still in the love/hate phase, skewed toward hate.

When I got to the park, it looked like the circus was in town. Tents lined up and down the sidewalks. Food trucks parked along the road. A clown made balloon animals ... for the children.

As I made my way across the parking lot, I saw vendors hawking protein bars, gym memberships, and chiropractic adjustments. I picked up a coupon from an amiable lady who was advertising her pet therapy services. I figured Purrfect had some issues to work through and could use the help.

As I navigated my way through the chaos, the humidity made it feel like I was wading through a bowl of warm soup. The sun was barely up over the trees, but the pavement was already hot enough to grill pancakes. It wasn't long before sweat puddled in my cleavage and my spandex sports bra started chaffing my nipples.

When I arrived at the registration area, I scoped out the scene. Like a grand master surveying the chess board, making sure each piece was strategically placed.

Jack, the king piece, held court in the sponsors tent, chatting with Nurse Kelsey. I'm not sure what kind of piece she was supposed to be. Whichever one is closest to a shameless, slutty whore. *Bishop maybe?*

I watched them from afar, assessing the situation. Nurse Kelsey threw herself at Jack like she was stranded on a deserted island without her vibrator. She wore a formfitting crop top that showed off her perky boobs and washboard abs. Her spandex running shorts left nothing to the imagination. Even from where I was standing, I could tell her bikini lines were freshly waxed.

Pulling my eyes away from Nurse Kelsey, I found the Queen of the chessboard at the snack table, cutting up bananas and oranges. Janet wore a neon yellow T-shirt that said VOLUN-TEER, completely oblivious to what was happening in the sponsor tent behind her.

That's why Janet plus Jack would never work. Jack was like some kind of rock star, surrounded by bra flinging groupies, throwing themselves at him wherever he went. And as Janet's best friend, I couldn't stand idly by and let her get hurt. Just like she had rescued me from Jack twenty years ago at prom, it was now my turn to rescue her.

My attention shifted to the pawns in the game, Gary and Ralph. Ralph's assignment was to run interference, keep Karen far away from Gary, so I could get Gary close to Janet. Then I could get close to Jack. Ralph had been readily agreeable to the idea, which was strange, because Ralph was never agreeable about anything.

I spotted Ralph and Karen chatting by the playground. Kyle and Cary were playing on the swings, taking turns pushing each other back and forth. For not friend-friends, they seemed to get along just fine. I didn't see Gary, but at least he was nowhere near Karen, which meant Ralph was doing a good job distracting her. So far, so good.

Keeping an eye out for Gary, I entered my name on the sign-in sheet at the registration table. Susan, the receptionist from Jack's office, collected my ticket. She wore a yellow VOLUNTEER T-shirt, just like Janet. Luckily, she didn't seem to recognize me.

"Are you green or are you purple?" Susan asked, holding up two numbered race bibs. One race bib was green. The other one was purple.

"What's the difference?" I asked.

"Purple is for the Family Fun Run," Susan answered.

Out of curiosity, I asked. "What exactly is supposed to be fun about it?"

"There's a massage station at the halfway point. For foot massages. One of the other sponsors is a podiatrist." *Figures.* Susan continued, "There are misting stations all along the route, and a water balloon toss at the mile markers, you know, in case you want to cool off." Susan's smile was too big for this early in the morning. "Best of all, at the end, they're giving out ice cream sundaes." Susan paused for dramatic effect. "With sprinkles!"

"What about the green one?" I asked, pointing at the other running bib.

Susan's smile faded. "The green one is for the competition runners. That's the race where they're giving out medals." I looked over at the sponsor tent. Jack wore a green bib. *Because of course he did.*

"Is there a foot massage station in that one?" I asked.

Susan shook her head.

"Misting stations?"

Susan shook her head again. "But that course goes right past the lake. You just have to watch out for the alligators along the bank. And the snakes. Oh, and somebody said they saw a wild boar over there earlier this morning."

I opened my mouth to ask my next question, but Susan must have read my mind because she said, "The green race doesn't have any ice cream either."

Susan held out both bibs. One purple. One green. "So what'll it be?" It was the equivalent of being asked if I wanted to go to the spa for the full body hot stone massage or get a swift kick in the vagina.

I glanced back over at Jack, still wearing green. If I was going to get close to him, obviously I had to enter the same race that he did. The purple race bibs all seemed to be worn by children in strollers, overweight housewives, or elderly seniors with walkers and colostomy bags.

I chose the vagina kick.

As I was pinning the green bib to my chest, taking care not to puncture a boob, a familiar smell wafted my way. Vanilla scented massage oil. Cherry-flavored lube. The sickly sweet scent ripped open old memories before I even heard her voice.

"Mary? Mary Burns? Is that you?" The voice weaseled into my ears and wormed into my brain. Burrowing past the logic and reason parts, boring directly into the fight-or-flight survival zone. The part that cave women used to fight off hungry dinosaurs. Or horny cave men.

Somehow, even though I was already soaked, my body sweat doubled, every pore like a fire hose. My heart felt like it was trying to claw its way out of my chest. "Oh my gosh, Mary Burns, I can't believe you're here!"

I slowly turned to find myself face to face with Ashley Griffin, Jack's old girlfriend from high school. The girl responsible for the most humiliating moment of my entire life.

"It is sooooo good to see you again," Ashley squealed. Before I knew what hit me, her arms wrapped around me in a giant, *I'm pretending it's so good to see you again,* hug. It was like being in a group hug with a dead corpse, a penguin, and a vampiric Eskimo. An icy chill shuddered through my body as her hands brushed my bare skin.

Ashley said, "I can't believe it. Mary Burns, after all these years. What are you doing here?"

Momentarily dumbstruck, I pointed at my green runner's bib. "Running?" I didn't mean it as a question, but it squeaked out that way. "What are you doing here?" I asked. It was a minor miracle that the rats and mice in the area didn't mistake my voice for a rodent mating call, and come swarming out of the trees.

Ashley thumbed toward her yellow T-shirt, stretched tight over her double D surgically enhanced, probably bionic, bosom. "Volunteering?" Ashley mimicked my cracked inflection and mouse like tone.

Just when I thought things couldn't get any worse, Ashley said, "You remember Bridget and Heather, right?" I hadn't noticed at first, but two of her mini-skirted goons from back in her cheerleading days flanked Ashley.

Bridget, wearing a matching yellow VOLUNTEER shirt, smirked. "Good to see you again, Mary."

Heather, also in yellow, asked, "How's your leg?" She was referring to the leg that she, Ashley, and Heather had caused to break when they dropped me from the top of the cheerleading pyramid.

"All better. Good as new," I squeaked, glancing toward the trees to see if any rats were stampeding.

"Glad to hear it," said Heather.

"For sure," said Bridget.

All I wanted to do at that moment was scamper away like a beaten dog, tail tucked between my legs. But both my body and my brain were paralyzed. I couldn't talk. I couldn't move. It had been over twenty years since that night at prom, but I was still traumatized. I wished for a sinkhole to form under my feet and swallow me whole. Put me out of my misery for good.

The dictionary defines a miracle as an extraordinary event that defies the laws of nature, attributed to divine intervention. For example, bringing the dead back to life. Oceans parting to create safe passage. Justin Bieber releasing a new single that doesn't make you want to vomit. I never believed in miracles before. But I did after what happened next that morning. And it wasn't some supernatural presence that created the miracle. It was Gary.

"Mary, there you are! I've been looking all over." I felt his hand on my shoulder, gentle, but firm. "The race is going to start soon. We should go stretch." I felt his hand slip down from my shoulder to take my hand. He pulled me away, just like Janet did all those years ago. I couldn't believe it. Gary saved me.

We kept walking through the gathering crowd of runners and spectators, Gary leading me by the hand. He only let go once Ashley and her friends were well behind us.

"You have quite the grip." He rubbed his palm, flexed his fingers.

"Sorry." I didn't realize I was holding on to him so tight.

We found a spot with a bit of shade under a sprawling oak tree. Gary grabbed one foot and pulled it back behind him, stretching his quads. Stretching seemed like a good idea, so I followed his lead. Across the lawn, I spotted Ashley and her henchman slinking back over to the sponsor tent.

"You okay?" Gary asked.

I nodded. Even though I wasn't okay. Not okay at all. "You remember Ashley Griffin? Jack Thompson's girlfriend?"

"How could I forget?" The look on Gary's face suggested he remembered her just about as fondly as I did. He bent over to touch his toes.

"Thanks for rescuing me." When I bent over, I could barely reach my shins.

Gary nodded. "I was over at the registration table and saw them talking to you. You looked like you could use a friend."

I needed more than just a friend at that point. When I woke up that morning, I was determined and focused. I knew the odds were against me, but I had faith that somehow, some way, I would distract Janet from Jack. But after one thirty-second encounter with Ashley, all my confidence had melted away like a sand castle hit by a tidal wave. I looked down at my hands. They were shaking.

"Want to talk about it?"

"Not really." Mercifully, Gary didn't push.

I dug deep for my last tattered scrap of resolve, forced a smile. "I'm fine, really. Just looking forward to the race."

"I guess you really do love running." Gary pointed at my green bib. "At first, I thought you said you enjoyed running just to get under Karen's skin."

I had been so thrown off by my encounter with Ashley that I had forgotten all about the harsh reality that there was still a race to be run. "Where's yours?"

Gary unzipped his warm-up jacket, revealing a purple bib underneath. "Kyle and I are doing the Fun Run together."

"With Karen?"

"Yeah. She thinks you're the competition, you know."

"The what?"

"Competition."

"Competition for what." Realization came in like an upper-cut. "You mean she thinks I'm competing with her for YOU?" Gary's sheepish grin confirmed the truth. The laugh shot out of me like a cannon. "She thinks ..." I waggled my finger between us.

"I'm afraid so."

I searched Gary's face for any sign that he was joking. He was not. *Karen thought I was after Gary???* The idea was ridiculous. Ludicrous. Completely out of the realm of any conceivable possibility. I said, "Never in a million years."

"Not in two million," Gary agreed, shaking his head.

"Three million," I added, driving home the point. A wooden stake through a vampire.

We could see the playground from where we were standing. While Ralph took turns pushing Cary and Kyle on the swings, Karen was going through her pre-race routine. Jogging in place. Deep breathing exercises. Jumping jacks.

"I think that's why Karen is taking this race so seriously," said Gary. "Like whoever wins this race will win my affections."

"That's insane," I said.

"Insane, right? If I was going to hand out any affections, it wouldn't be based on a race."

"Oh, no?"

Gary shook his head.

I was genuinely curious, so I had to ask. "What would it be based on?"

"I'm thinking cage match."

"Bare knuckle?"

"Is there any other way?"

I allowed myself a moment to indulge in the fantasy. The roar of the crowd. The glare of the lights. Blood. Sweat. Tears. I imagined punching. Throwing one fist and then another. Left, right, left, right. But it wasn't Karen's face I was imagining. It was Ashley's.

"You're smiling," Gary said.

"I am?" I hadn't realized I was smiling. "Can't I smile?"

"Not like that, no." Gary must have seen the bloodlust twinkling in my eyes. "You know," Gary started. "When I saw you show up at little league practice, I thought." His voice trailed off.

"You thought what?"

"I thought you were going to try to convince me to go on some sort of crazy scheme."

"Crazy scheme?"

"Yes," Gary said again, his face serious. "Crazy scheme."

"My schemes are never crazy," I replied. "Well, maybe a little crazy. What kind of crazy scheme?"

"Oh, I don't know. Like, hey Gary, let's go spelunking in this abandoned mine shaft. Janet's really into caves."

"That's ridiculous. I don't like enclosed spaces."

"Or, hey Gary, Janet loves circus performers. Why don't we dress you up as a clown and shoot you out of a cannon?"

"Actually, that's kind of brilliant. You should have brought that one up sooner."

Gary crossed one foot behind the other and leaned sideways to stretch his hip flexors. "So you're not really here just because you have some sort of plan to set me up with Janet?"

It took every ounce of my being to keep a straight face. "I'm not trying to trick you, Gary. Janet really does like you."

"I know she liked me. As in past tense. Twenty years ago in high school."

"So you knew Janet had a crush on you in high school?"

"I am capable of recognizing when someone is flirting with me." Gary's eyes lingered on me a bit. "Unless, of course, it was your idea to join the Dungeons and Dragons club."

"No, that was definitely all Janet."

"I figured."

And that's when it happened. The eureka moment. Realization came crashing in like a collapsed mine shaft on top of a spelunker's head. "It wasn't just Janet who liked you. You liked her too."

At first, he didn't answer. Then, "She was the first girl I ever loved."

I couldn't believe what I was hearing. I always knew that Janet was in love with Gary back in high school, but I didn't realize that he had been in love with her, too. It was all just too perfect. Long-lost loves, reunited at last. Soul mates, adrift in the endless universe, finally pulled together by fate. Or, technically, me. But it was no longer about me anymore. It was no longer about Jack. Cosmic destiny was at play.

"But that was a long time ago." Gary resumed his stretching, bending forward in a lunge.

"It's never too late for love," I said. Trying to convince Gary. Trying to convince myself. "How come you never made a move?"

"I made a move. The night of senior prom. I asked her to dance."

Every second of that night was still etched in my brain like it had happened five minutes ago. But I never remembered seeing Gary that night. And since I spent most of that night with Janet, surely I would have noticed. "Janet never told me."

"She probably forgot all about it."

"You never forget your first dance."

"We didn't dance."

"Janet said no?"

"No. She said yes."

"Wait. So Janet said yes when you asked her to dance, but then you didn't do any dancing?"

Then Gary explained. "We were on our way to the dance floor when she saw you."

"Saw me?"

Gary nodded. "Saw you with Jack." It all made sense then. I had been alone when Jack approached me that night. Just standing off to the side, minding my own business. Janet and Ralph had gone off to get some punch. That must have been when Gary asked her to dance.

"I saw what happened," said Gary. "I saw the whole thing."

I didn't know what to say.

But Gary did. "I'm sorry that happened."

"Yeah," I agreed. "Me too."

A voice amplified by a megaphone shattered the lingering silence. "All Fun Run runners, please report to the purple banner. The Family Fun Run is about to begin."

A few seconds later, a second megaphoned voice rang out. "All competitive runners, please report to the green banner. The Competition Race is about to begin."

Gary's eyes drifted back down to my green bib. "You know, I bet they would let you switch over to purple. That is, if you wanted to switch."

Over Gary's shoulder, I could see the volunteers setting up the ice cream sundae station. In the distance, misting stations released a cooling mist of water vapor into the breeze.

"You can run with Kyle and me," said Gary.

It was a tempting offer, I had to admit. And not just because of the ice cream. It made absolutely no sense, but a tiny little voice in the deepest, darkest recesses of my subconscious brain told me Gary was the better choice. The safer choice. The right choice. Even though Gary had almost gotten me killed multiple times.

But just as I was about to take Gary up on his offer, I glimpsed Jack leaving the sponsors tent, heading toward the green banner flapping on the horizon. He wore his green racing bib like a sponsor's badge on a race car.

Another megaphoned voice rang out, "All runners report to your designated starting areas. The races are about to begin."

"Mary?" Gary waited for my decision.

I told the tiny voice to keep its mouth shut. "I think I'll stick with green," I said. Gary may have been the safe choice, the easy choice, but too much was at stake. I couldn't afford to take the safe and easy route. I had a job to do, no matter how hard or how difficult. It was too late to turn back now. Besides, no risk, no reward, right?

Gary smiled, but it was a smile that didn't quite reach his eyes. He said, "Okay. Good luck then."

"Yeah. You too."

He turned to leave.

"Gary. Wait."

He stopped. Turned.

"Maybe I'll see you after?"

"Maybe." The smile still didn't reach his eyes. And now it wasn't on his mouth either.

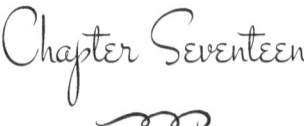

Chapter Seventeen

I made my way through the crowd of runners, submersing myself in the current of green bibs flowing toward the green banner. I spotted Jack near the starting line and snaked my way toward him.

"Mary!" Jack's eyes did a double take when he saw me wearing the green bib. "I didn't realize you were so hard core."

"My core is always hard," I replied. I wasn't sure what exactly that was supposed to mean, and based on his confused expression, I don't think Jack did either. Before he could put too much thought into it, I said, "Although it has been awhile since I ran a 5k." *Awhile, as in never.*

Jack frowned. "The Family Fun Run is the 5k. Us green bibs are doing the fifteen."

"Fifteen?"

"Fifteen," Jack nodded.

"Fifteen, what exactly?" I asked, once again expecting an answer I would not like.

"Fifteen K," Jack explained. For a moment, I held onto a sliver of hope that the "K" in this nightmare scenario stood for "Kahula" shots. Or Krispy Kreme donuts. Alas, it did not stand for either.

I took a deep breath, trying to maintain my slipping grasp on my sanity. "And remind me again how many miles that is?"

"Nine point three two," Jack said, a bit too enthusiastically for my taste.

"Nine miles?"

"Nine point three two." Jack must have seen the look of terror on my face because he waved his hand in the air as if running nine point three two miles was the equivalent of a leisurely stroll through the park.

Without even attempting to be subtle, Jack looked me up, down, and all over. I could have sworn his eyes even paused on my spandex wrapped hips. "Somebody in as good a shape as you are, it'll be a piece of cake." I would have given my left ovary for a chance to sit down and eat a piece of cake at that moment, instead of running nine miles. *Whoops, sorry, nine point three two.*

When I was a kid, my dad would take me to one of those fancy art house movie theaters, the Enzian, off Highway 17-92. It was the kind of place that hosted Avant Garde festivals and showed documentaries about foreign directors, and you could have a glass of Chardonnay while watching movies with subtitles.

My dad loved serious movies. Films, as he called them. I think he thought if he made me watch enough of them, his appreciation would rub off. It didn't. One day we went to see *Chariots of Fire*. It's a movie about two guys who ran on the beach a lot. And then, against all odds, they win a gold medal at the Olympics or something. I think it won a bunch of Academy awards.

Anyway, my dad loved it. Maybe because it was so freaking long, he had enough time to drink three glasses of Chardonnay. I, on the other hand, was bored out of my mind. I couldn't have told you any of the details about the movie five minutes after we got out of the theatre. The whole thing went in one side of my brain and right out the other.

Except for the music. The music I remembered. The music I never forgot. There was a scene where the two dudes were running along the beach. In slow motion. Not that they were actually running slowly. I mean, the special effects made it seem that way.

As they were running and jumping along the edge of the water, the music was playing in the background. Legs pumping through the sand. Feet splashing in the water. The music was timed perfectly with every step. Cymbals crashed at the end when they raised their hands in triumph.

That same music started playing in my head as I lined up with the other runners.

Buuum Baaah. Buuum Baaahhhhhh

The synthesizer started thrumming a slow steady beat.

Tap tappa tap tap. Tap tappa tap tap

The snare drum tap danced in rhythm, pushing the pace.

Doo doo doo doo, doo doo doo doo

Then came the piano. Plucking the melody like it was tiptoeing through a field of tulips, hop scotching up and down the scale.

The memories of the music fueled me. Inspired me. Like those runners in that film, I too could rise up and overcome the hurdles life threw at me. Stick my middle finger in the face of fate. Poke the Universe in the eye and emerge victorious. I was invincible, as long as I had a dramatic soundtrack playing behind me.

A race official wielding a megaphone and fondling an air horn positioned himself about twenty yards from the line.

Jack crouched beside me, back arched like a jungle cat. His leg muscles were as taut as steel beams. The man was a god among men. No wonder Kelsey was shaking her ass and wagging her tits in the sponsor tent. No wonder Ashley Griffin and her thugs crawled out of their holes to volunteer. No wonder Janet had been smitten with Jack. And I was determined to smite her smit.

Uninvited, an image of Gary popped into my head. Staring after me. Standing there in his purple bib. Like a lost little puppy left out in the rain. I felt guilty for not turning around and going back to explain it to him. Tell him it was nothing personal, just part of the bigger plan.

I looked back up to find Jack smiling at me. He gave me a thumbs up. "Good luck Mary."

"Yeah," I said. "You too."

"One minute runners! One minute!" The guy with the megaphone raised his air horn, thumb poised on the trigger.

The race was about to begin.

I stuffed all that guilt and doubt back down into the pit of my stomach. I had made the right choice. Gary was a big boy. He could take care of himself. And if he couldn't? Well, it sounded like Karen was more than willing to help him out.

"Thirty seconds!" the race official slurred through the bullhorn, his voice mangled by the third rate amplification. He probably found the bullhorn on a clearance rack at Big Lots.

I knew I would never win that race. The other runners were younger, stronger, and probably didn't have brand new running shoes that were already giving them blisters.

But I didn't have to win. All I had to do was finish. Even if I had to crawl across that finish line on bruised, bloodied stumps. If I could finish, Jack would notice. If I finished, no, *when* I finished, Jack would be impressed.

"On your mark," squealed the bullhorn.

As the runners jostled for position at the starting line, the rest of the world fell silent. Like the scene in the movie, everyone moved in slow motion. Toes sliding up to the white chalk line. Bodies leaning forward. Every nerve in my body was tingling, ready to leap into action. Every one of my senses was on high alert.

"Get set!"

The image of Jack's face when he saw me wearing the green bib came to mind. It was a look of wonder. It was a look of respect. Jack must have seen something in me he had never seen before. For the first time, Jack had seen a glimpse of who I really was. A woman who was determined. A woman who was brave. A woman who was strong. Perhaps the 'Queen of the Geeks' from high school was not so geeky after all.

All I had to do was finish.

All I had to do was finish.

All I had to do was finish.

BBBBWWWWWWAAAAAAAA!!!!!

Big, bold, and brassy, the blast of the air horn shattered the morning still. The snakes all jumped. Wild boars fled in terror. Somewhere, an alligator pooped its pants.

The runners surged forward like a horde of Southern Baptists at a Cracker Barrel after Sunday morning church. I tracked Jack weaving through the masses, surging toward the vanguard. I kept pace with him for a good three minutes. Okay, three seconds.

As runners passed me on all sides, I saw Jack pulling away from the masses, joining the fastest runners out in front. Sweat poured down my forehead, stinging my eyes. I couldn't help but blink, and when I opened my eyes again, Jack was gone. He slipped over the horizon and vanished in a cloud of dust.

It didn't take long for the breath in my lungs to feel like it was on fire. My heart pounded like a jackhammer. My knees felt like they got hit with a jackhammer and my leg muscles felt like they were disintegrating under my skin. I channeled all my focus on putting one foot in front of the other, the soundtrack of *Chariots of Fire* still playing in my head.

Kilometer one was anguish.

Kilometer two was agony.

Kilometer three was "what the hell are you doing are you insane?"

Despite the pain, I soldiered on. Determined, I decided my mind would simply overpower my weak, useless body through sheer force of will.

By kilometer four, I had found a rhythm, my body in the zone. The rhythm I had found was Step, oh my God, ouch. Step, oh my God, ouch. Step, oh my God, ouch. The zone was the WTHAYDYGTKUA zone. The 'what the hell are you doing, you're going to kill us all zone'. Like that red area on the pressure meter in the main control room of a nuclear power plant, the quivering needle slipping over the line from the orange section to the red, seconds away from apocalyptic Armageddon.

By kilometer five, my heart was beating so fast it felt like it was going to dislodge from my chest. Then take off, turn around, and go get some ice cream. My lungs were a puddle of kerosene jelly that had been lit on fire with a blowtorch, then thrown into an erupting volcano.

I made it further than I should have. For someone whose primary sources of exercise were an occasional yoga class, playing pickleball with senior citizens, and a dedicated regimen of fork lifts. Forks laden with ranch drenched fried pickles. Up and down from plate to mouth.

I never saw the gopher tortoise hole. Probably because my eyes were blinded by the sweat and the tears. I didn't feel it when my ankle rolled. Probably because the bottom half of my body was numbed by pain. What I felt was the ground, rushing up to meet me when I tipped forward and face planted on the trail. Jagged-edge gravel tore into my knees and elbows. A random twig stabbed me in the thigh.

It took everything I had left just to roll over. Staring up into the cloudless sky, I had a moment of clarity. This was my penance. A punishment for my sins. What kind of person covets their best friend's boyfriend? What kind of person tricks a somewhat clumsy but otherwise innocent man into helping her with her sinister schemes? I deserved the pain and the suffering that had befallen me. For all the evil I had wrought, in thought, word, and deed.

Somehow, I made it to my feet, taking a moment to let the waves of pain subside. Everything hurt. My left knee was bleeding. My elbows were the color of strawberries. I tried to walk, but as soon as I stepped down, my right ankle throbbed. I tried hopping, but only made it two hops before I fell back down on the ground. I considered crawling, but as soon as I put any weight on my hands, the gravel tore into my palms. Unable to walk, alone and defeated, I did the only thing I could do.

I sat in the dirt and cried.

The Universe was right to put me back in my place. There in the dirt. Beaten. Bruised. Bloodied. I had gotten exactly what was coming for me. Justice had been served. I sat there for I don't know how long. Waiting for the snakes or the boars or the alligators to come along and put me out of my misery.

"Mary?" The voice sounded faint, like it came from a dream. Turning my head, I saw Jack jogging down the trail toward me. "Mary!" He rushed to my side. As soon as he saw my bloodied knees and swollen ankle, he sprang into "doctor mode." Delicate fingers traced over my injuries. Tender hands attended to my wounds.

I reached out to touch his arm just to make sure he was real. "Jack? What are you doing here?"

"Janet didn't see you at the finish line, so she asked me to come find you."

"You ran all the way back to find me?"

"I took a shortcut across the field." Jack's eyes got wide as he examined my foot. "Your ankle's the size of a grapefruit." *More like a small watermelon.*

Jack cupped my damaged foot in his hands, fingers gently probing. "We need to get your leg elevated and get you some ice. Here." Jack guided my body backward, so I was laying down, his hand supporting the back of my sweaty head.

Once I was prone, nimble fingers untied my shoelaces. Strong hands tugged off my shoe. Sliding his hands down my calf, Jack carefully pulled my sock loose and my red throbbing foot burst free. It felt like a root canal with a migraine.

"Yikes," Jack said, poised over my foot like he was disarming a bomb that was about to go off. "Does this hurt?" Jack prodded the eggplant colored lump that was once my foot.

"I don't think so."

"How about this?" Jack gave me another good poking.

"Nope."

"This?"

He could have smashed my foot with a hammer, and I wouldn't have noticed. "I can't feel a thing."

Jack studied my Frankenstein foot a moment longer. "I don't think it's broken. But you shouldn't put any weight on it."

Then Jack took a deep breath. His face got serious. "I'm afraid I have some bad news." Jack put on the expression I imagined he would use when he had to deliver a traumatic diagnosis, like 'I'm sorry, you're having triplets' or 'the tests came back positive for herpes.'

"What is it?" I asked.

"I'm afraid I can't let you finish the race."

"What? Oh, no!" On the outside, I was a woman who was having triplets and had herpes. On the inside, I was a woman who had just won a lifetime subscription to the ice cream of the month club.

Jack stood up and extended his hands. "Here." I grabbed onto him and he pulled me to my feet.

Once I was stable, balancing on my one good foot, Jack asked, "How much do you weigh?"

"What?" I had to hop a bit to get my balance. "Why do you need to know my weight?"

"I'm trying to decide if I should carry you over my shoulder or have you climb up on my back."

"You want to carry me?" Normally, I would have been happy to climb on Jack's back and his front, for that matter. But then the logistics of what he proposed sank in.

"One thirty? One thirty-five?" *I wish.*

I stuck my fists on my hips. "Don't you think that's a little personal?"

"It's okay Mary, I'm a doctor."

"Does that line usually work for you?" I asked.

"Actually, it does. But a woman's weight isn't usually what I'm asking for when I say it."

My face flushed the same color as my ankle. "It doesn't matter what my weight is," I said, eager to shift the conversation.

"You don't have to carry me, because I'm going to finish this race."

I took a few steps down the path to prove my point. The first step was torture. The second step was torment. The third step was listening to a Justin Bieber concert without a Q-Tip to stab out your eardrums.

"Mary, don't be ridiculous. Here." Before I knew what was happening, Jack scooped me up in his arms, pulling me in close to his chest. It was like snuggling up to a brick wall. His pectorals were even harder than they looked. It was hot outside, but the heat of the sun was nothing compared to the inferno that was slowing burning up inside me. Parts of me I didn't even know still existed started getting all warm and fuzzy.

But as Jack held me close, I realized with sudden clarity that my entire body was covered in dirt and dripping with sweat. Surely I smelled like a middle school boys' locker room. Jack, on the other hand, didn't smell like sweat at all, despite having just run nine point three two miles. In fact, he smelled like vanilla and cherries. *Almost like ... no, he must have gone over to the Family Fun Run festivities for a sundae.*

Jack shifted my body in his arms, and I could feel the bulge of his biceps against my hip. He angled me toward him, so my face was close to his.

"You okay?"

"Yeah, I'm okay." I was better than okay. Curled up in Jack's arms, my head was naturally positioned to stare right into his luscious pink lips. *Wait? What?*

"Are you wearing lipstick?" Jack's lips were smeared with a pink pastel substance.

"Huh?" Jack looked confused.

"It looks like ..." Realization set in. "Did Janet kiss you?" I remembered that one of Janet's volunteer duties was to hand out medals to the winners. She had told me she was going to give Jack a kiss if he won.

Jack touched his lips, coming away with a smear of pink on

his fingertips. "Yeah, that was Janet," Jack answered. "What can I say? Your friend can't keep her hands off me, I guess." Jack wiped the rest of the lipstick away with the back of his hand. *So much for Janet's GenZ inspired thirty day friendship only plan.*

The heat building inside of me instantly went cold. Like a bucket of ice cold water tossed in my face.

The moment was further ruined when we saw the cloud of dust on the horizon. Moving fast. Moving toward us. A golf cart materialized out of the cloud, charging down the trail. It slid to a halt, kicking up gravel.

Ashley Griffin jumped out. "Jack!"

"Ashley, what are you doing here?" Jack dropped me like a sack of potatoes. I barely had time to get my feet under me, hopping on my one good foot.

"I saw you run off before the medal ceremony and I got worried." Ashley's eyes sliced toward me. "Everything okay?"

"I'm fine," Jack said. "But Mary hurt her ankle pretty bad."

"Oh no. That's terrible, I'm so sorry." Her voice dripped with something that was definitely not sympathy. She turned to Jack. "Do you need a ride back?" Then to me Ashley added, "Sorry Mary, there are only enough seats for two."

Jack took a moment to validate the golf cart's seating capacity, then said to Ashley, "You're going to have to take her back to the sponsor tent. Help her get some ice on it and find something to wrap it with in the first aid kit."

For once in our lives, both Ashley and I could agree on something, loathing the idea of sharing a ride together in a golf cart. Not to mention, the thought of Ashley getting anywhere near my ankle made my stomach turn. I had to think quick.

Then it came to me. Whenever Purrfect wanted something, a back rub, more tuna casserole, a seat on my lap so she could shove her butt in my face, she would make her eyes all big and watery, then stick out her bottom lip. Like an orphan begging for scraps on Christmas morning, in the middle of a blizzard. *Please sir, may I have another cat treat?* I made that same face at Jack.

"What's wrong?" Jack frowned, his voice deepening with concern. I may have overdone it just a tad.

"Oh, it's nothing," I replied. I made my eyes bigger and jutted out my bottom lip a bit more.

"Are you having a seizure?"

"No, it's just, well, I'd really feel better if you took me back in the golf cart," I told Jack. "You know, since you're a doctor."

Ashley opened her mouth to protest, but before she could say anything, Jack said, "Yeah, I suppose that makes sense." Jack turned toward Ashley. "You're okay if I drive her back, right?" Ashley's face did not look like she was okay with that plan. Not at all.

"But like I said, there's only room for two," Ashley stammered.

Jack pointed across the park. "It's not that far to the finish line if you cut across the field. Just watch out for the fire ants."

Ashley looked like she was about to vomit.

"Come on, Mary, I'll get you fixed up good as new." Jack offered me his arm, escorting me to the golf cart, his hand supporting the small of my back. My hand in his hand, he helped me into the seat. When I looked over at Ashley, her eyes were daggers made of ice.

Jack climbed into the driver's seat and turned the key in the ignition. He must have pressed down on the accelerator a little too hard, because the tires spun in the gravel, bathing Ashley in a cloud of dust.

As we took off, Jack driving me toward the finish line, I turned around in my chair and waved. Even through the thick cloud of dust, I could clearly make out Ashley flicking me off.

WHEN WE GOT TO THE VOLUNTEER TENT, JACK wrapped my ankle super tight with tape from the first aid kit, then drove me to my car in his golf cart. Along the way, we passed the finish line for the Family Fun Run. I spotted Gary and Kyle eating ice cream, and Janet was there, too. They were all talking and laughing. Gary must have dribbled ice cream down his face because I saw Janet dab his chin with her napkin.

Once we got to my car, Jack helped me slide behind the steering wheel, letting me wrap my arms around his shoulders.

"I'll call you later," said Jack. "Check in and see how you're doing. If you need anything, and I mean *anything*, you just let me know." I briefly considered asking him to drive me home and tuck me into bed, and make me a margarita, and then a chocolate sundae, but thought that might be pushing it.

Chapter Eighteen

The next morning, that extra jolt of adrenaline was still coursing through my system because I was wide awake before the alarm even went off. I hopped out of bed, literally, and made Purrfect a scrambled egg topper for her breakfast. She chowed it down, then pulled out the sad cat face, so I made her a second egg.

My ankle was feeling much better. After plenty of ice, and a couple extra strength Tylenol, I felt good as new.

As I finished blending my kale protein smoothie, I took a moment to reflect on my unexpected run of good luck. Even though I ran into Ashley Griffin, hurt my ankle, and didn't finish the race, all in all, the prior day was a success. Things didn't go exactly as expected, but in the end, my plan worked.

Now all I had to do was keep the momentum going. Things were falling into place. I just needed to give them a bit more of a nudge. Order would soon be restored, and everyone would live happily ever after.

Feeling refreshed, rejuvenated, and recharged, I headed over to Aunt Catherine's house, where I was pleasantly surprised to find the renovations progressed, despite my absence and neglect. In the front yard, Leo, my landscape guy, had replaced the sod that Gary ruined with his van. He also finished planting the flower beds and added a fresh layer of pine bark mulch. The air smelled like a mountain forest as I walked up to the porch. Curb appeal, check.

Once inside the house, I took a moment to appreciate my genius. The all greige walls created the perfect blank canvas. It was plain now, sure, some might even say boring, but that was only temporary. Adding furniture, window treatments, and some tasteful art pieces would completely transform the house.

I made my way to the kitchen. The new slate grey cabinets looked fantastic. So did the stainless steel appliances. The only thing left to do was rip out the God forsaken wallpaper. As I knew they would, the tiny pink roses and green vines clashed horribly with the rest of the kitchen. I needed to get rid of it as soon as possible.

When I called Gus to confirm the final invoice, I had asked him if he would get rid of it for me, but he said he wouldn't touch any kind of wallpaper with a ten-foot pole. I reminded him he didn't have to use a pole of any size to take it down, but that didn't sway him to my cause.

Standing there, trying to figure out my next move, I had another eureka moment. Purrfect and I would move in to Aunt Catherine's house. With the walls painted, the flooring down, and the kitchen cabinets and appliances in place, I could start working on all the other things that were vital to selling a house. The furnishings, decorations, and staging.

I would tear out the damn wallpaper myself, in between everything else. If I was staying there, I could focus all my extra attention and effort on the cause. The sooner I had everything finished, the sooner I could list the house, sell it, and never look back. The more I thought about it, the more it all made sense. With things finally going my way, I would capitalize on the momentum and plow full steam ahead. Seize the moment. Rule the day!

I went straight back to my apartment and packed. The good

thing about living the lifestyle of a minimalist celibate nun is I had little to box up. A couple of outfits, my pickleball gear, some pots and pans for the kitchen. And of course, Purrfect's cat supplies. I had already planned on renting furniture for staging, so I called the rental place and paid for rush delivery.

———

THE NEXT DAY, I SPENT MOST OF THE AFTERNOON experimenting with different configurations and arrangements until I found the perfect placement for every piece of furniture. I placed hooks for the artwork, measured for curtains, and installed blinds. I staged knick knacks on dressers and books on shelves. I shopped for throw rugs, decorative pillows, and faux flowers for the dining room. In the bathroom, I installed a gold flaked mirror I found at a yard sale. Turning cheap things into something spectacular was my specialty.

When I ran out of ideas to delay dealing with the wallpaper, I pulled up an A.I. chatbot and asked it if Home Depot rented flamethrowers. Turns out they do not. Taking a break to put my foot up, I sat on a rented chair in my inherited house with my inherited cat, glowering at the rose and vine monstrosity. Unable to stomach it any longer, I took a stab at the wallpaper myself. A literal stab, that is, with a knife.

After slicing off a corner, I plucked the edge with my fingers and pulled. It was like pulling off one of those extra sticky price tags they put on with superglue. I would pull free a tiny scrap of a piece and then it would tear and I would have to scrape up a corner or an edge all over again.

After about twenty minutes of effort, only a small circle of wallpaper had come loose, peeling away in a thousand tiny bits. By that point, it wasn't just my ankle throbbing, my back ached from bending over and my knees felt like they were made of rust after all the squatting. I limped across the kitchen and plopped down in the chair again to consider my options. At the rate I was going, it would take years to scrape off all the wallpaper, the equivalent of a moderate prison sentence. I considered having Gus just knock down the walls with a bulldozer. *Does a house really need a kitchen, anyway?*

Purrfect watched me from the counter, seeming to enjoy my misery. The wallpaper shouldn't have even been there. Gary was supposed to get rid of it when I hired him to paint the house. Yet there I was, an unsatisfied customer, staring at a job he never finished. The more I thought about it, the more my frustration grew. It was a matter of principle. When someone hires you to do something, you do it. You finish the job no matter what.

I grabbed my phone and texted Gary's number.

MARY:

hey

NEW PAINTER:

what's up?

everything ok?

MARY:

need to talk about the wallpaper

NEW PAINTER:

I'm at little league practice

talk later?

I didn't respond to his last text. I didn't want to leave anything to chance, so I snatched up my keys and started marching toward the door. It had nothing to do with wanting to see Gary again, just to be clear. I swear.

WHEN I GOT TO THE PARK, I WAITED IN THE PARKING lot to surveil the scene. The sun was so bright it pierced Charlotte's tinted windows like they were plastic wrap. I cranked the climate control all the way to blizzard. Charlotte hissed as frigid air billowed out of the vents like a tornado.

I waited until little league practice ended, and the parents collected their dirt stained, sweat soaked children. I saw Karen go out onto the field to wrangle Cary. They walked back toward the dugout with Gary and Kyle. *Ugh.* The last thing I needed was Karen distracting Gary from Janet, when Gary was supposed to be distracting Janet from Jack. That's when I saw the yellow Corvette roll into the parking lot, its engine rumbling like a tiger. I would have recognized it anywhere. *Ralph???*

I sunk down in my seat to avoid being seen. The Corvette pulled into a parking spot, then Ralph got out and waved. *What the heck???* Before I knew what was happening, Karen sprang from the dugout and pranced over to Ralph. I stared, dumbfounded, as they hugged. For a split second, I considered the possibility that I had somehow slipped into another dimension.

After the generously warm greeting, Karen fetched Cary, and they all squeezed into Ralph's car. The doors closed. The tiger growled. Ralph, Karen, and Cary all rode off into the sunset together. I was definitely in another dimension, for sure.

It took me a moment to process what I had just witnessed. Ralph and Karen? Together? As in *together* together? To be fair, I had told Ralph to keep Karen away from Gary, without specifying the techniques. Whatever I might have thought of his methods, I had to admire Ralph for not half-assing it. Ralph full-assed it all the way. Making a mental note to interrogate Ralph later, I made my way over to the baseball field.

When Gary saw me, he didn't seem surprised. "Great," he said, slipping a baseball glove on one hand. He punched his ungloved fist into the leather with a *SMACK*. "You're just in time to help."

"What exactly am I helping with?" I eyed the baseball he was holding suspiciously.

"Swing practice." Gary smiled.

"Mary!" Kyle dropped his bat and ran over to greet me. I was shocked when he grabbed onto my legs for a hug. Gary's smile only widened. Much like Purrfect, I think he enjoyed my discomfort.

"So how many home runs did you hit today?" I asked, looking down at the small human wrapped around my lower torso.

Kyle took a moment to think, squinting in the sun. "Zero," he announced.

"You'll get a bunch next time, I'm sure," I said..

"You haven't watched me play, have you?" Kyle picked his bat up and skipped to home plate.

"So you want to play outfield or catcher?" Gary asked from the pitcher's mound.

"Neither?" From Gary's face, I could tell that wasn't one of my options.

"Catcher it is," Gary said. He got me a glove from his coach's bag and helped me slide it on to my hand. "All you have to do is stand behind home plate." Gary pointed. "Then try to catch the ball if it comes to you."

"I know how to play catcher," I replied.

"You play baseball?" Gary looked amused.

"My dad made me play when I was little," I explained.

"Interesting," said Gary.

"Not really." Before we started playing golf together, my dad made me play little league in an attempt at daddy-daughter bonding. I spent a lot of time on the bench.

As I moved behind home plate, I could tell Gary had his doubts. "What, you don't think I can do this?" I asked.

Gary shrugged. "I never said that."

"But you're thinking it."

"How do you know what I'm thinking?"

"I think you're thinking it right now."

"I think you think too much," Gary said.

"I think I think just enough."

"I guess we'll see," said Gary. "Okay Kyle, let's show Mary what you've got."

We took our positions. Out on the pitcher's mound, Gary held the ball up in the air, waiting for Kyle to set his stance. Kyle hefted the bat with both hands, resting it on his shoulder as he set his feet.

"Okay now, keep your eye on the ball." Gary twisted the ball in his hand, waiting for Kyle to stay still. "Just before it crosses over the plate, that's when you swing."

Kyle nodded, the batting helmet flopping back and forth on his head.

Gary pitched. Kyle missed. I picked the ball up off the ground and tossed it back. This went on for the next five minutes.

Finally, I couldn't take it anymore. "His grip is too low," I told Gary, pointing down at Kyle's bat. I squatted down, so that Kyle and I were face to face. "Hold the bat like this." Gently, I adjusted the position of his hands. "Move up a little. There. Now step back from the plate a bit. Give the ball a little more space."

I put my hands on Kyle's shoulders and tugged him back another step. "Now, as soon as the ball comes down, right about here." I drew an imaginary line in front of him. "That's when you swing." A flock of vultures perched on the fence for a front-row seat, their beady black eyes fixed on the proceedings.

"Pitch it," I ordered Gary, backing up a step.

Gary didn't look very confident. Neither did the flock of vultures. "Okay. Here goes nothing."

Gary tossed the ball. It sailed through the air, an easy backspin making it float in slow motion. In unison, the vultures turned their heads to watch the ball rise, then fall, gravity pulling it toward home plate.

As soon as the ball reached the spot I had shown him, Kyle jerked the bat backward as hard as he could pull, building momentum in the windup.

Crack!

I felt the wood smash into my knee and I dropped faster than a lead balloon carrying a grand piano filled with bowling balls.

Then, even faster than it had launched in reverse, Kyle's bat surged forward.

Thwack!

It was a perfect strike. Wood impacted leather. The ball rocketed forward.

Gary never had a chance. Before he could even process the fact that his son had finally hit a pitch, the baseball plowed into his groin with testicle crushing brute force. Gary screamed like a banshee, then dropped to his knees. Fueled by adrenaline, dazed by his first taste of success, Kyle forgot to drop the bat as his body swung around.

Still doubled over from the searing pain in my knee, my head was now at the same height as the spot where I had told Kyle to smash the ball.

I looked up.

I saw a blur of lacquered wood.

I heard the crunch of wood on flesh.

I felt the splash of liquid, warm and sticky.

My head began spinning. A ballerina out of control, twirling and twirling, faster and faster.

Then it wasn't just my head spinning. I was spinning. The ground was spinning. Everything was spinning.

The last thing I saw were the vultures, also spinning in the air right above me, slowly circling in their descent.

WE SAT ON THE SPLINTER LADEN WOODEN BENCH inside the dugout. The air smelled like clay and sweat, but the tin roof shielded us from the sun. Luckily, there was plenty of ice left in the cooler. And a few juice boxes, too. I sipped on a grape juice while wearing a bag of ice on my head. Gary nursed an apple juice with a bag of ice on his crotch. Kyle sucked on a fruit punch, his straw sucking air like a cat fur clogged vacuum.

"Nice hit, by the way." I toasted Kyle with my juice box.

Gary shot me a look, his face red and blotchy. Probably a side effect from the intense groin pain.

"What?" I shrugged. "It was." I gave Gary an apologetic smile. I wasn't sure how much he blamed me for the impromptu circumcision. "Thanks for chasing away the vultures, by the way. I thought I saw them calling dibs on my body parts."

"I couldn't let that happen," said Gary. "Your corpse would have impeded the base runners." Gary repositioned the bag of ice on his privates. "You going to be okay?"

"I think so." Nothing was broken, that I knew of, and the ice had brought most of the swelling down. I still had a lump on the side of my head the size of a turnip and my knee was now the same shade of Periwinkle as my ankle.

We sat a bit longer, nursing our wounds and sipping on juice boxes.

"Are we still going swimming?" Kyle asked. "You promised we could go swimming if I hit the ball."

"He definitely hit the ball," I noted.

"Maybe I can turn on the sprinkler in the backyard after dinner," Gary offered.

"What are we having for dinner?" Kyle asked, swinging his legs back and forth on the bench.

"We'll have to stop at the store and get something."

"Can we have pasta?"

The fight drained out of him. Gary said, "We'll see."

I still hadn't asked Gary to finish the wallpaper and somehow, after the baseball to the groin incident, it didn't seem like the right time to ask. I had to get Gary in a more relaxed setting. Or at least wait until the crotch swelling eased.

"Aunt Catherine's house has a pool," I said cheerfully. Gary's expression was less cheerful, more suspicious.

"Who's Aunt Catherine?" Kyle asked.

"My aunt," I answered.

"She'll let us swim in her pool?"

"She's dead," I explained.

Gary was already shaking his head. "Mary, it's already been a long day. A long week, actually. I just want to go home and rest. Plus, I still have to make dinner."

"I'll make dinner," I said. "Whatever you want to eat."

"You know how to cook?" Gary looked doubtful.

Somehow, I kept my reassuring smile in place. "I'm an amazing cook. I love to cook. I cook all the time." Turning to Kyle, I asked. "What's your most favorite meal ever?"

I figured asking an eight-year-old what he wanted to eat for dinner was a low-risk question. Spaghetti maybe? Elbow macaroni? Cheese raviolis perhaps? All I would have to do is throw some noodles in a pot, boil them, and throw it on a paper plate. Bon appétit!

"Anything I want?" Kyle asked.

"Anything you want," I confirmed. I noticed the vultures still sat on top of the fence watching me and smiling. One of them licked its beak.

Kyle took a moment to think, drumming his fingers on his chin. "Osso Buco," he said at last.

"Os-so what now?" I thought maybe the bat to the head affected my hearing. I looked at Gary for confirmation.

"We went over to Karen's house for dinner last week and that's what she made us." Looking over at Kyle, Gary said, "I guess it made an impression."

"So *Karen* made this osso busso thingy?"

"Yes, but you don't have to do that." Gary pulled another apple juice from the cooler and tossed me another grape. "Kyle, Mary's not making Ossu Buco. We'll just order pizza."

"No." At first I wasn't sure if I had said it or one of the vultures did. I had never made Osso Buco. I had never tried Osso Buco. Five minutes earlier, I didn't even know that Osso Buco was a thing that exists.

"If Kyle wants Osso Buco, then that's what I want to make," I announced.

Kyle's eyes lit up with excitement. So did Gary's, but in a different way.

"Are you sure about this?" Gary asked.

"Of course I'm sure." I figured if Karen could make Osso Buco ... *how hard could it be?*

Chapter Nineteen

I raced straight to Aunt Catherine's house while Gary and Kyle swung by their place to grab bathing suits and a change of clothes. When I walked in the house, Purrfect must have used some sort of telepathic cat voodoo power to foretell the impending disaster I had set in motion because she made a noise that sounded like the meowed version of *what the hell were you thinking* and then bolted out the back door.

The truth was, I didn't cook, I couldn't cook, and the last time I tried to cook anything more complicated than a box of ramen noodles, I nearly burned down my apartment. After a diet of microwave pizza, frozen pot pies, and Chinese takeout, I wasn't sure if I could cook Osso Buco if my life depended on it. And my life did depend on it, a life of happiness and joy spent with Jack, or a life spent miserable and alone staring at ugly kitchen wallpaper.

After pacing back and forth across the kitchen for a solid ten minutes trying to tamp down a panic attack, the first thing I did was search for a recipe. Scouring social media, I learned that Ossu Buco is a traditional Milanese dish comprising veal shanks braised in white wine, onions, and various herbs no normal person has ever heard of. And according to rocketkitty90210, Osso Buco is a flavorful but extremely complex dish, and a great way to showcase one's culinary mastery.

The second thing I did was call every food delivery service in the greater central Florida area. Unfortunately, it turns out, Osso Buco is not a very popular takeout or delivery menu item. It is also not available in the frozen food section of Publix. Or Whole Foods. Or Aldi.

That's as far as I got because the doorbell rang. I opened the door to a face full of flowers. At least I think they were flowers. Some of them may have been weeds. Gary held the fist full of flower-like plants at arm's length. "These are for you."

"You brought me flowers?" *Why did Gary bring flowers?* I invited Gary over to talk business. Wallpaper business. Distracting Janet business. That's it. There should not have been any flowers involved.

"I picked them," Kyle beamed, peeking out from behind Gary's leg.

"They're a housewarming present," Gary explained.

Phew. Gary didn't bring me flowers. He brought the house flowers. I wasn't sure if I felt relieved or jealous.

"It was Kyle's idea," Gary said, patting the top of Kyle's head. "He said boys are supposed to bring girls flowers. He kind of insisted. And then I figured maybe they would be a nice compliment to all that greige."

"They're beautiful," I said, taking the bundle of weed looking flowers from Gary's hand. One of my fingers got stabbed by a thorn. I could feel the sneeze attack already building. I found an empty vase, filled it with water, and let the weed flowers soak.

Meanwhile, Gary and Kyle embarked on a self-guided tour. I watched as they wandered. Gary was wearing khaki shorts, flip-flops, and an ocean blue Aloha shirt speckled with surfboards and palm trees. The shorts showed off the bottom half of his tanned legs. The color of the palm trees made his grey-green eyes really pop. I had the sudden urge to pour a bottle of tequila in a blender and make us a pitcher of margaritas. But margaritas didn't pair well with Osso Buco, I assumed, so I restrained myself.

After he had a few moments to look around, Gary said, "It looks amazing in here. I can't believe the difference." *Did Gary Wright just give me a compliment?*

"Well, I am a professional," I said.

"That's quite the setup." Gary pointed to the dining room table, a walnut stained behemoth with big chunky legs. The chairs were foam grey, with high backs and pewter buttons up and down the sides. The place settings were Wedgewood china, the stemware Reidel. In the center was a towering spray of white orchids, flanked by vanilla candles encased in frosted crystal. "I guess I should have worn my tuxedo."

"That's not where we're sitting," I explained. "That room's just for show."

Gary pointed to the artwork on the wall. "Oh look, a Gustave Caillebott."

"If you say so." It was a print I ordered online, then put in a frame I found at a garage sale. In the painting, smears of muted blue waves lapped at a sandy shore, a rock strewn cliff jutting up behind them. I had no idea who painted it, I just liked how the colors matched the chairs. "You know that artist?"

"Well, not personally, obviously, since he died in the eighteen hundreds. But I know his work."

"Impressive."

"Well, I am a professional," said Gary.

An involuntary laugh barked out of me. "A professional painter."

"Exactly." Gary seemed to delight in my confusion. "Not all painters just paint houses, you know."

I pointed at the piece of professional artwork, elegantly framed *by me*, on the wall. According to Gary, a Gustave Caillebott. "Are you trying to tell me you paint like that?"

"Not impressionism, no. And certainly not as good as Gustave. But I do paint landscapes. Mountains. Beaches. Trees."

I tried to picture in my mind what some of Gary's so-called paintings could look like. Again, a child's finger paint creation came to mind. Smeared browns and blues and greens. Yellow and orange, most likely. Actually, probably a lot of reds.

"I can show you sometime if you want."

"Sure," I said, just to be polite.

"Oh, I almost forgot. I left something in the van." Gary ran back to his van and returned with a brown paper bag cradled under one arm. He reached into the bag and exhumed a bottle of wine. "I also brought this." As he pulled out the bottle, I couldn't help but notice the curve of his biceps under his shirt. "Look familiar?" Gary asked.

The biceps or the bottle? The biceps I clearly remembered from the time I found him not wearing a shirt in Aunt Catherine's backyard, when he was hosing off his paint brushes. But the label on the wine bottle looked familiar too.

"The one we picked out at the grocery store," I guessed.

"The Syrah from France. When we were stalking Janet," Gary added. "Well, when you were stalking Janet, and tricked me into helping you."

"Trick seems like a strong word," I said as I took the bottle of wine from his hand.

"Strong but accurate," said Gary.

"And last, but not least." Gary reached back into the grocery bag. "I brought this in case you were in the mood for something other than wine." He pulled out a six-pack of SourPaw, the beer from FoxPaw, the local brewery. "I believe you said this one was your favorite."

"Awww, you remembered." *He remembered???* Before I knew what I was doing, I reached out and patted his upper arm like he was a dog that had performed a trick. *There's that biceps again.* Gary's jaw ticked as his eyes darted down to where my hand touched his arm. And then when our eyes met again, his cheeks turned at least six shades of pink. *Was his jaw always that jutting? Were his lips always that full?*

"Look!" Kyle's voice broke the spell. Purrfect lingered in the hallway, scoping out the intruders as if plotting the best way to evict them.

"Oh, that's just Purrfect," Gary said, his voice drawing long on the purr.

"Can I pet her?" Kyle's eyes lit up.

Purrfect looked up from her paw licking, tongue still protruding, suddenly concerned. She gave me her *don't you fucking dare* look. I gave her my *payback's a bitch* look.

"Can I, Mary?" Kyle looked like a kid on Christmas morning waiting for permission to tear into a stack of presents.

"Sure," I told Kyle. "She really loves her belly rubbed." Purrfect hated her belly rubbed. "But you have to catch her first." I wasn't sure how old Purrfect was when I involuntarily inherited her, but she still had her cat like reflexes and could outrun an Olympic track team if she wanted to, especially if the Olympic track team was trying to rub her belly.

Kyle accepted the challenge with a leap and a shriek. Purrfect bolted upright with a leap and a shriek. All four paws pedaled at the slick laminate flooring like a drag racer burning rubber. Lots of spinning. Not a lot of forward progress. Her paws barely found purchase just as Kyle lunged. Purrfect squealed in terror. Kyle squealed with glee.

"Well, that should keep them busy for a while."

When I turned back around, Gary pulled two bottles from the six-pack. "Should we open a couple of these before dinner?"

"Absolutely," I said. "That will give me an excuse to show you the kitchen."

After making our way across the house, I paused dramatically at the entrance to the kitchen so Gary could take it all in. The last time he had been here, everything was still original to the house. Linoleum flooring. Formica countertops. Kitschy kitchen relics from the long distant past. It was like walking into one of those period exhibits in a history museum. A history museum dedicated to bad kitchen taste.

Since then, everything got upgraded. The pink cabinets ripped out by the root and replaced with a modern slate grey. Gus had pulled apart the formica countertops with a crowbar, then replaced them with a metallic pearl granite. The new faux oak flooring I selected was pristine. Not a single nick, scrape, or stain. The entire room was transformed. Except the wallpaper. Wallpaper that refused to peel off. Wallpaper that refused to die. Like a cockroach scurrying around in the wake of an atom bomb.

"Well?" I asked. "What do you think?"

Gary took his time as he circled the kitchen, looking everything over with a critical eye. "I like it," he said at last. "You did an amazing job. Really." *Another Gary compliment!*

I handed Gary a beer. He took a long sip. "But I see what you mean about the wallpaper. Doesn't really match your new vibe.."

"Gee, you think?" I took a sip of my beer, too.

"I still think you should keep it, though." Gary traced his finger along one of the vines.

"You're serious?" It was like he had some sort of wallpaper fetish or something. *Is that even a thing?*

"It's authentic." Gary tilted his bottle for emphasis.

"Dated." I tilted mine for rebuttal.

"Classic," said Gary.

"Old," I countered.

"You know what they say?" Gary pointed at the wallpaper. "Retro is the future."

I rolled my eyes. "They don't say that. No one says that. It's two completely different styles. You put them together and they clash."

The dimple on Gary's left cheek made an appearance. His sea foam green eyes twinkled.

I could tell he was up to something. "What?" I asked, taking a sip of SourPaw to brace for whatever he said next.

Gary pointed to my beer bottle. "What was the first sour you ever had?"

"This one," I said. "I tried it at the brewery. And the only reason I even tried it is because Mike, the owner, was giving out free samples."

"What did you think when you first saw it on the tap list?"

"What do you mean?" I wasn't sure where Gary was going with this. If he was trying to convince me of something, he would fail. Once I made up my mind, it didn't change. Ever.

But Gary persisted. "What did you think when you first saw that FoxPaw Brewing made a sour beer?"

"I thought it was the stupidest thing I ever heard of."

"But then you tried it."

"Of course I tried it. It was free."

"And you liked it."

"Not at first. At first I thought it was terrible. But then Mike, the owner, made me savor it a little. Hold a sip in my mouth so the flavors could swirl around on my tongue. I don't know, I guess it kinda grew on me."

"And now you like it."

I shrugged, refusing to answer him. It was a stupid point, and I had no intention of helping him think he made it.

"If I remember correctly," Gary said, "In the grocery store, when you were stalking Janet ..."

"When we were stalking Janet," I interjected.

"When you tricked me into helping *you* stalk Janet," Gary continued. "You said, and I quote, this happens to be one of my favorites."

"Beer and wallpaper are two completely different things."

"Fair enough. The point is, just because two things don't seem to go together, that doesn't mean they can't work."

I thought Gary was done with the lecture, but apparently he wasn't quite done galloping around on his high horse. "A Spring flower poking up out of a snowdrift. Sunbeams filtering through the shadows. A majestic mountain, looking high over a storm-tossed ocean. Juxtapositions. That's the thing I like about painting," said Gary.

"Okay, Bob Ross, my kitchen will not be your happy little

accident." If Gary was trying to convince me to keep the wallpaper, he had failed miserably. Failed spectacularly. "It would never work."

"Well then," Gary said. "I guess I'll just have to show you."

Reluctantly, I joined Gary on the other side of the kitchen. We stood next to the wall with no counters or cabinets. Just wallpaper, as far as the eye could see. There were so many flowers and vines it felt like we were in the middle of a meadow, on a mountain in spring. Maybe if we drank enough SourPaw, we could reenact the Sound of Music.

"Look," Gary's voice brought me back to the present. "We keep it here."

"We?"

"On this accent wall."

I shook my head vigorously. "The green vines clash with the greige."

"I'll repaint the walls. Get rid of the greige."

It was a good thing the vines were only in wallpaper form. Otherwise, I might have used one of them to strangle him. "I already told you. I like the greige."

Gary kneeled down and pointed to one of the tiny pink roses. "Here, look."

Against my better judgement, I knelt down beside Gary, our bodies now close. The scent of mint and jasper lingered on his body like a protective shield. Actually, no, not a shield. Shields keep things off. The smell coming from him was the opposite of a shield. A magnet. Meant to pull things close. I had the sudden urge to gorge myself on chocolate mint ice cream between shots of jasper flavored gin.

Gary pointed right at the heart of the flower, which was colored a deep shade of red. "This one. This color here. We blend classic and contemporary." *We again?*

Gary stood up and offered me his hand. I took it. He pulled me to my feet. Sparks of electricity seemed to pass from his skin to my skin, then ricochet through my entire body. I must have stood up too quickly, because a rush of warmth raced up through my chest and into my head, then back down my body again, pooling between my legs.

"Come here." Gary put his hands on my shoulders, taking a position behind me. Gently, he pulled me back until I had a good vantage point to take in the entire room. He leaned close, lips nearly brushing against my ear. "Just picture it." That smell again. Mint and jasper. "We repaint the walls." *We.* "Draw off the colors of the wallpaper to counter balance the grays."

I tried to envision what Gary was describing, but I found it hard to concentrate. I felt faint. If it wasn't for Gary's firm grip on my shoulders, I would have toppled over for sure.

Gary whispered in my ear again, and the warmth that had been gathering in the lower half of my body start bubbling up like a long dormant volcano. "I think it could work."

I've always had an eye for design, since I was a little girl. My teacher featured my dinosaur themed decoupage during Parents' Night in kindergarten. When I was in middle school, my Animal Farm diorama won first prize in the county art show. Colors. Patterns. Textures. If something in a room was missing, I knew exactly what it would take to complete it. If someone needed help to pick out a new color, I could find the perfect match to suit their tastes. No one ever taught me. It just came to me. Instinctively. I could see it all in my mind.

When I looked again at the center of the rose, it all clicked. Gary was right. The darker red would complement the slate grey perfectly. Maybe a few accent pieces could play off the green of the vines.

When I pulled away to face him, Gary's hands slipped from my shoulders. I was surprised how quickly I'd gotten used to the feel of them on me and as soon as they weren't, it felt like a part of my body was missing.

"What do you think?"

I took a deep breath to settle my pounding heart. "I think ... you might be right."

"Maybe we can talk more over dinner?"

"Dinner?"

"The Ossu Buco," Gary reminded me. "You were going to wow us with your cooking skills. How's it going, by the way?" We both glanced at the oven, which was clearly lifeless, dead, and empty. *Like my soul.*

"Well, I got as far as looking up a recipe," I said. "And I found two of the seventy-five spices it requires in my pantry. Speaking of which, do you know what marjoram is? I mean, does anyone *really* know what marjoram is? Does it actually exist or do the people who write these recipes just like to mess with our heads? And what about bay leaves? Is that like a leaf that somebody pulled out of an actual bay? And don't get me started on rosemary."

"Um, I didn't?"

"Who likes rosemary? Nobody likes rosemary. Rosemary is disgusting. That guy who wrote *Rosemary's Baby* probably named the mother Rosemary because the herb rosemary is the spawn of Satan."

I was spiraling. I needed to stop spiraling. I wanted to stop spiraling. But I was so far gone I didn't think I could. When I looked back up at him, Gary had that deer in the headlights look. I had that driving a jacked up four-wheel-drive pickup truck with a shotgun rack in the back, foot heavy on the gas pedal look.

"Mary, it's okay. Just take a breath." Gary put his hands up, like a police negotiator talking to someone on the ledge of a tall building. "Did you cook anything yet?"

I dropped my head in shame. "No."

Gary surprised me when he said, "Good. Honestly, the thought of eating baby cows grosses me out. And Kyle's favorite foods are chicken nuggets and macaroni and cheese. It's a low bar to impress him."

"Who said I was trying to impress *him*?" I said.

"If not Kyle, then who were you trying to impress?" Gary asked, a twinkle in his eye.

"Well, certainly not *you*," I answered. "I've already done that with my hiking and baseball skills."

"Don't forget your cat rearing skills," Gary added.

"Oh yeah, that's at the top of the list for sure."

To punctuate the point, Purrfect scrambled across the kitchen floor, Kyle in hot pursuit. Purrfect paused just long enough to flick me off with one paw, then raced into the dining room. From the dining room, we heard a crash. Then a high-pitched meow. Then the sound of breaking glass.

Taking pity on me, Gary said, "Why don't you go deal with whatever just happened out there, while I look in the fridge to see what I can muster up for us to eat."

"No way," I said. "I invited you here. I should be the one cooking."

"Mary." The way he said my name felt like he wrapped me in a blanket, all soft, warm and cozy. "It's fine, really. I like cooking. Do you have any chicken?"

I nodded.

"How about tomatoes?"

"Yeah. I think so." Luckily for me, I had put in a grocery order the prior day. I had a bunch of food delivered so I wouldn't have to go out shopping and stay focused on the remodel. For the first time in my entire life, I actually had a well-stocked refrigerator.

"Maybe if you play your cards right, I'll show you how to make grandma's homemade sauce. Just never tell her because then she'd have to kill you." Gary thought about it some more. "And then kill me."

Chapter Twenty

When I returned to the kitchen, I discovered Gary had been hard at work. He found chicken and cheese and tomatoes and bread crumbs. *Chicken Parmesan!* He had the ingredients laid out on the counter, like a celebrity chef in front of a studio audience. I set up Kyle in the other room watching television. Purrfect sat on top of the refrigerator, silently criticizing everything Gary did.

"Here you go." Gary pulled out another beer for me. I stepped toward him to grab it. At the same time, Gary stepped forward to hand it to me. We ended up face to face, closer, I think, than either of us had intended. We both just stood there, staring. His jaw ticked. That warm and fuzzy feeling bubbled up again in my nether regions.

I took the bottle. "Thanks."

He didn't move.

I didn't move either.

We were so close I smelled lemons and oranges on his breath, remnants from the SourPaws we were drinking. In the air all around us, I smelled garlic. A pan of chopped garlic simmered in olive oil on the stove. "Are you expecting a vampire attack?" I asked.

"You never know," said Gary. "I like to be prepared, just in case. One of those Eagle Scout things, I suppose."

We were still standing face to face. Somehow, our bodies drifted closer. I took another sip of my SourPaw to occupy my lips, just in case they got any impromptu urges. Looking over at the display of ingredients, I said, "That's quite the layout."

"I thought we could do it together," said Gary. His eyes twinkled in the glow of the kitchen lighting, hinting at something more than cooking. *Or was I just imagining things?* I took another sip of SourPaw in a feeble attempt to quench the fire building in my tummy.

"Come. I'll show you what to do."

GARY LAID THE CHICKEN BREASTS ON A CUTTING board, then I whacked them with a mallet.

"I'm pretty sure it's already dead," he said, leaning over my shoulder.

Once flattened and tenderized, Gary dipped the pulverized chicken in an egg wash, and I coated it in flour. Gary sprinkled on the bread crumbs. I sprinkled on the Parmesan cheese. Gary added salt. I added pepper.

"Is now a good time to add the marjoram?" I asked.

With the chicken breaded and seasoned, Gary fried each piece in oil. Then I placed each piece in a baking dish. Gary spooned homemade tomato sauce on each piece of chicken. I added a slice of mozzarella cheese. Gary added fresh basil and the sautéed garlic. I sprinkled on more Parmesan cheese.

"Now can I add the marjoram?" The exhaust fan from the oven must have blown a wisp of hair across my forehead because, before I knew what was happening, Gary reached up and brushed it away from my eyes. The gentle touch of his fingertips on my skin made the entire length of my arms break out in goosebumps.

Gary stepped away from the pan and smiled. "Knock yourself

out." I'm not sure Gary's recipe actually called for marjoram, but he was kind enough to humor me.

When we finished assembling the ingredients, I had to admit, the final product looked pretty darn good. We still had to bake it, of course, but I could tell it was going to be the best chicken Parmesan ever.

"Not bad," said Gary. "Not bad at all."

"We actually make a pretty good team," I said. "If only we were this good at setting you up with Janet."

Gary froze. "Right," he said, finally. Avoiding eye contact, he used a wooden spoon to reposition the chicken in the baking dish, then placed it in the oven. "If only."

He took another sip of SourPaw.

Then another after that.

As Gary put the oven mitt back on the counter, I tried to get a bead on what he was thinking, but his face was impossible to read. If I hadn't known better, I might have thought that Gary was *glad* our plans had fallen short. *Glad* he wasn't with Janet.

Stupid Karen. It had to be her. Maybe there was something between Gary and Karen, after all. But then, as I thought about it some more, that wouldn't explain why Gary was going along with my set-him-up-with-Janet plan. Spending all of his free time with me just to get with someone he wasn't interested in didn't make sense. *Unless ...*

No.

No way.

Absolutely not.

Surely Gary wasn't just playing along because ... I couldn't even finish the thought. Ever since the day I hired him to paint Aunt Catherine's house, it had been one disaster after another. Surely he could see that he and I didn't fit. Surely, he knew that anything beyond our current business arrangement would be an impossibility.

"We should make some pasta to go with the chicken," I said,

changing the subject. "Do you prefer penne or linguine?" I filled up a pot of water and set it on the stove.

"Penne," Gary said. "Penne is better at soaking up the sauce."

"Exactly," I agreed. "Whenever I try to eat linguine, it just slides off the fork."

While we waited for the chicken to brown and the cheese to bubble, I mixed up a salad and Gary sprinkled garlic on a loaf of bread. He was still acting funny. All quiet and serious. I decided I would just confront him right then and there. Ask him point-blank if he was even interested in Janet at all. And if he wasn't interested in Janet, who *was* he interested in? "Gary ..." I began.

"Hey, come check this out." Gary crouched down, studying the wallpaper. "You should see this."

What now? I joined Gary on the other side of the kitchen. There were pencil marks on the wall. Drawn numbers. Sketched letters. Faded lines scribbled between roses and etched among the vines.

"What are those?" I had to squint to make anything out.

Gary traced a sequence of markings up the wall. "Looks like measurements or something." He held his finger over some scrawled pencil marks I could barely make out. "Three feet, ten inches." Rising up the wall, Gary found more pencil markings. "There are dates, too. And initials." Then he turned to me. "Who's HB?"

At first, the letters didn't register. I was too busy wondering why Aunt Catherine let some hooligan vandalize her ugly kitchen wallpaper. Then it hit me. H.B. When I looked again at the markings, it felt like I was staring at a ghost. "Henry Burns." It took everything I had to keep it together.

"Who's Henry Burns?"

I had to gather myself before answering, blink back the tears that were building. "My father."

I followed the measurements as they climbed up the wall, each year's mark higher than the last. I could picture my father as a young boy standing there, Aunt Catherine lining up the pencil on the top of his head. "He told me he used to spend summers at his aunt's house when he was a kid. This house. Right here." I wiped away the tear dripping down my cheek with the back of my hand. "Sorry. It's stupid. That was a long time ago, I know."

"It's not stupid." Gary grabbed the tissue box from the counter. The resulting nose blowing was reminiscent of a flock of Canadian geese playing trombones in a Labor Day parade.

"You and your dad, you were close?"

I nodded. In those days, I tried not to think about my dad too much. The hurt was still new. He had died only a few years before. I missed him terribly. I didn't even talk about him with Janet. But for some reason, I started talking about him with Gary. "He was the one that raised me after my mom left."

"Is she still around?"

"Somewhere," I said. "After the divorce, she and the guy she was with moved to California. Got married. Then divorced. Rinse and repeat. Rinse and repeat."

"You ever talk to her?"

"She sends me birthday cards."

"Love hurts," Gary said. The way he said it made it seem like he knew from experience.

"Love sucks," I agreed. With Kyle's mom no longer in the picture, I figured Gary must be dealing with demons of his own. I could see it in the way he looked back at me. Not just a mirror, but a magnifying glass. Taking my pain and sending it right back at me tenfold.

"Was it ever good? Between your parents, I mean."

"They fought like cats and dogs," I answered. "My dad was a good guy, but he could never make her happy. No matter what. It was never enough."

Pulling myself away from the wallpaper, I decided it was a good time for another drink. I found a corkscrew in one of the kitchen drawers and a pair of plastic cups we could use as wine glasses.

Gary opened the Syrah and poured me a cup. "You know

you're not doomed to become her, right? You're not your mother."

I shrugged. "When I was little, people would tell me I was just like her. And every time they said it, I thought to myself, God, I hope not."

It was like my mouth was on autopilot, spilling secrets previously locked away and buried, never meant to see the light of day. But that night, somehow, some way, Gary made me feel comfortable enough to keep talking. He made me feel like I could tell him anything.

Gary poured a cup of wine for himself too. He looked over at me with a serious look on his face. "And that's why you're still waiting for Mr. Right."

"I'm not waiting for Mr. Right, Dr. Freud," I said. "I'm waiting for Mr. Perfect." *A doctor who drives a red BMW, and gives massages and bakes chocolate soufflé.*

"Sounds like Mr. Impossible," Gary said.

Not impossible, I thought. Just complicated. *Because I have to steal him away from my best friend first.*

Gary raised his plastic cup. "Cheers."

I tapped my cup to his, then took a sip, the wine loosening my tongue. "Really, they never should have been married in the first place."

"Why do you say that?"

"He was a carpenter. She was a VP at a marketing firm. He was into baseball. She was into reading the *Wall Street Journal*. He was into being a good dad and faithful husband. She was into screwing other dads and husbands." There I was again, over sharing about the checkered past of my traumatic upbringing.

"Love is complicated," said Gary.

"You're telling me."

It seemed like Gary had more to say, but whatever it was, he let it go. We both settled into the silence, leaning against the kitchen counter, once again, close.

As we both just sat there staring at the oven, it felt like my senses shifted into overdrive. The scent of Gary's mint and oak cologne mingled with the smells of baked marjoram and simmering garlic. I took another sip of Syrah, notes of blackberry and pepper tingling on my tongue. I could both feel and hear the steady thump of my heart beating.

You know that feeling when something is happening to you, but it's like you're outside of yourself? Like it's happening to somebody else. Like I was watching old home movies of someone else's life on VHS cassette. Leaning forward on the edge of my seat. *What's going to happen next?*

Mint. Oak.

Garlic. Smoke.

Smoke?

Gary and I both looked over to where the oven was doing its best impression of a smoke machine at a heavy metal concert.

"Gary!"

He sprang into action, donning a pair of oven mitts, then dumping the flaming pan into the sink. Dousing the flaming wreckage with the kitchen faucet, charred chicken fumes billowed across the entire room.

DINNER WAS A DISASTER, SO WE IMPROVISED. GARY borrowed a couple of fans from the neighbors, which we set up near the windows to blow out the smoke. Kyle and I went online to order delivery from the Thai place. We ate pineapple fried rice on the patio, out by the pool, while we waited for the smoke to clear.

We were all famished, so it wasn't long before empty containers littered the table. I watched Gary take his last bite, then waited for him to finish chewing. "So. What did you think?"

Gary furrowed his brow, like I had just asked him to solve an algebra problem. "It's good," said Gary, poking a stray piece of pineapple with his fork. "I never realized how well pad Thai goes with garlic bread and margaritas."

"I agree." With the chicken Parmesan off the table, literally, and the wine long gone, I had decided a pitcher of margaritas wasn't such a bad idea after all. I also made Kyle a virgin Pina colada.

"When can we go into the pool?" Kyle asked.

"As soon as you help with the dishes," Gary answered.

Everyone pitched in to help. I washed. Gary dried. Kyle dumped the empty containers in the trash and then wiped down the table.

As I handed Gary another plate, I couldn't help but notice he was humming. "Is that a Justin Bieber song?"

Gary's face flushed, caught red-handed. "Sorry. I forgot you have some sort of weird Justin Bieber thing."

It suddenly occurred to me I still hadn't returned the T-shirt he let me borrow back when we first met. "I still have your T-shirt up in my closet. I'll give it back to you before you leave."

Gary waved me off. "Keep it. It fits you way better than it would ever fit me."

"Thanks, I guess." It was a gracious gesture, though it was a bit of a double-edged sword. I mean, it was a comfortable T-shirt and all, but it had Justin Bieber on it. I handed Gary another wet plate. "So you actually like Justin Bieber?"

"I mean, he's okay, I guess." Gary's eyes shifted back to the plate he was drying. He stayed quiet for a few moments, like he was going over something in his head. When he looked back up at me, he said, "I got it when I was with Ann."

"Kyle's mom." Gary had only ever mentioned her the one other time. On the nature hike of doom. I remembered thinking that he must have loved her very much. Not that I had any direct knowledge or experience on the subject. It just seemed that way. A gut feeling based on a vibe.

Gary's nod was the only response that I got. Then he went right back to drying the plate. I told you how Gary made me open

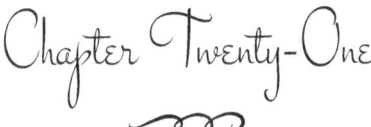

Chapter Twenty-One

The warmth that had been sitting in my chest and my knees and every body part in between now went ice cold. "Me go swimming?" That wasn't part of the deal. When I invited Gary over, I was expecting just Kyle to go swimming. While Gary and I sat down at a table, fully clothed, and planned our next move to woo Janet.

"I don't have a bathing suit," I said, thinking fast. It was the truth, too. I had left my bathing suit back at my apartment. And even if I had a bathing suit, I certainly wouldn't be prancing around half naked in front of Gary. "You brought your swim suit too?" I asked, just to clarify his intentions.

"Well yeah. Of course," Gary said, as if him prancing around half naked in front of me was never in question. "You don't have a swimsuit?"

"I never brought it with me," I explained. "It's still at my apartment." My breath quickened and that warmth in various parts of my body suddenly returned.

"But you have a pool." Gary pointed to the pool out the window, as if I didn't realize it was there.

"Correction. Aunt Catherine had a pool. This was her house. Not mine."

"But didn't you move in?"

"Temporarily. Just until I'm done renovating so I can sell it."

Gary looked at me like I was a crazy woman. "Why would you go back to an apartment when you now have this home?"

"Houses aren't homes," I said. It was a common mistake. One of the many myths propagated by the financial services industry. "Houses are assets," I explained. "A piece of property to be bought and sold."

"So you're definitely not staying?"

"Certainly not." I had no intention of staying in Aunt Catherine's old house. Permanent relationships with a piece of real estate required commitment. Hard work. Maintenance. Things break. Every weekend turns into fulfilling obligations. No, thank you. Much better to keep things simple. "I never stay in one place. Buy, fix, flip, sell. Then leverage the profits for the next one."

"That explains a lot," said Gary. He had on his Freud face again.

"Will you please go swimming with us?" Kyle asked.

"I don't like to swim," I said. Which was true. I didn't like being wet or even damp in general.

"This is Florida. You have to swim," said Gary. "I think it's a state law or something."

"Then call the swimming police." There was no way I was going swimming. No way in hell. "Besides, even if I wanted to swim, I couldn't because I don't have a bathing suit. As I already explained."

Gary's face brightened. "I have an idea."

"What idea?" I had a feeling I would not like the idea.

GARY FETCHED A LADDER FROM HIS VAN, THEN positioned it under the attic.

"If you find another vagrant cat up there," I said, "I'm having the entire house exorcised by a priest."

"Can you hold this steady?"

"What exactly are you planning to do up there?" I asked Gary's butt as he climbed.

"The last time we were up here, I saw a bunch of boxes. One of them was labeled Clothes," Gary called down.

I spotted Kyle at the far end of the hallway, waiting patiently. He was already in his bathing suit and swim floats. The inflatable orange rings hugging his arms were almost as big as his head.

Thump

The sound came from above me. "You okay up there?" I hollered.

"Yeah," Gary called back.

Crunch

"Everything's great!"

Thud

When I looked back down, Kyle was much closer, now in the middle of the hallway. I hadn't even seen him move. He was still staring at me.

Crash

"You sure you're okay?" I glanced back up through the opening into the attic. I couldn't see anything. It was like a black hole. Or a portal to another dimension.

"Everything's under control," said Gary. "It's all good."

"It doesn't sound like everything's good," I shouted. This time, when I looked back down, Kyle was standing right next to me.

"Holy hell," I yelped. Remember the eighties horror movie *Children of the Corn*? With the creepy kids with the white hair, standing in the middle of the cornfield? Yeah, it was like that.

Kyle just stood there for a while, staring at me. Thank God he wasn't an albino, or I would have really freaked out. I could tell there was something on his mind. "Everything okay Kyle?" I asked.

"Purrfect ran away from me." Purrfect ran away from me too, in most situations, so it didn't surprise me. But Kyle seemed to take it personally.

"Yeah," I said. "She's antisocial. Kind of an asshole, really." It occurred to me I probably shouldn't use the word asshole in front of a kid, but that cat was already out of the bag, so to speak. "Sorry. I didn't mean asshole. I meant, ass." The word 'ass' probably wasn't any better.

Kyle continued studying me for a moment, then asked, "You don't have a kid I can play with?"

"No, God no. I don't have any kids. Not that there's anything wrong with you. I mean, not you, you, as in you personally, I mean kids in general. Or you personally. I think." I was blathering again. Talking to children was not a life skill that I had much opportunity to develop. As you can probably tell, I kind of sucked at it.

"How come you don't have a kid?" Kyle asked.

How about a thousand reasons? "Because I'm not married," I explained.

"My dad's not married."

"I know."

"He has a kid."

"He does."

"He has me." Kyle pointed at his chest. I may have been pretty dense occasionally, but I'm pretty sure Kyle took me as a fool.

"Well," I said. "That's different. He was married."

"My mom's gone now."

"I know. Sorry."

Kyle nodded again. I looked back up into the black abyss that was the attic door, wondering where Gary disappeared to. He needed to get back down quick. Kyle was asking a lot of questions and at that rate, it was only a matter of time before he was going to ask me to make him a flow chart and Venn diagrams to explain the birds and the bees.

"Were you ever married?"

"No. Absolutely not."

"Why?"

How about a million reasons? "I just haven't found a nice man yet."

"My dad's nice."

"Well, yes. Yes, he is." My brain scrambled for a new topic to change the conversation. But I did not know how to converse with an eight-year-old, as evidenced by the past five minutes we had been standing together in the hall.

Then it occurred to me. This was my chance. My chance to get some inside information. I still didn't know Gary all that well. Did he go on a lot of dates? Was he even interested in getting serious with someone again after what must have been a very difficult divorce? It had taken my dad years to get back out there after what my mother did to him.

It made me wonder once again what happened between Gary and Kyle's mother. How bad were the scars? How likely was it really that Gary would follow through on our plan to woo Janet? I thought it was a safe assumption that Ann was the one who had done the leaving. Gary didn't seem like the leaving type. Gary seemed more like the getting left type. Regardless, this was my chance to get the inside scoop.

"I bet you and your dad were excited to come over," I said. "So you could swim."

Kyle nodded.

"Have you and your dad ever gone over to anybody else's house to go swimming?"

Kyle shook his head. "We just swim at our house."

"Wait. You have a pool at your house?"

Kyle nodded. At the park, after baseball practice, when Kyle had asked Gary to go swimming, I assumed he meant the public pool at the park. So that was why I offered for them to come over. If Gary already had a pool at his house, why did he accept my invitation to come here?

"Is your pool broken or something?" I asked.

Kyle shook his head.

"And it has water in it?"

Kyle nodded.

"Is it like filled with sharks? Or alligators? Or piranhas or something?"

Kyle shook his head again. Then he looked me dead in the eye and said, "Are you and my dad going to kiss?"

Luckily, I had made another batch of margaritas while Gary was fetching the ladder from his van. I picked my cup up off the floor where I had staged it while holding the ladder, then took a nice big gulp. I needed to buy myself enough time to plan a response. "No," I said, as the tequila warmed the back of my throat. "No, of course not. Why would you ask that?"

"Is my dad going to kiss you?"

"No. No one's going to kiss anyone." I took another gulp of margarita and instantly regretted it, because now my glass was empty. Luckily, the sound of Gary's voice saved me.

"Hey Mary," Gary called down from the attic. "You might want to come up here and take a look."

"Be right up!" Grateful for the distraction, I scampered up the ladder.

———

As soon as Gary grabbed my hand and hoisted me up through the opening, I asked, "What's wrong?" I was afraid he had found a magic portal to hell, letting in an army of cats. And inquisitive children.

"Nothing's wrong," Gary said. "Just a lot of boxes to sort through. I figured it would go faster if we worked together." Gary swept the beam of his flashlight so it illuminated the far side of the attic, where the boxes were stacked on top of each other from floor to ceiling. Gary took a step toward them, and the floor creaked.

"Make sure you stay on the crossbeams," I warned. "Otherwise you could fall through."

"Thanks for the tip." Gary tiptoed across the attic, springing from beam to beam.

"You realize you're wasting your time, right?"

"How do you figure?" Gary asked, pulling a box off the stack.

"It's probably all junk."

A box tucked under each arm, Gary balanced across a wooden board like a tight-rope walker in Cirque du Soleil. We each opened a box and started digging.

I pulled out a pair of polyester orange pants. "Even if we found a bathing suit in here, it would never fit." Gary pulled out a faded denim jacket. "And even if it fit, I wouldn't wear it." I pulled out some green corduroy slacks. "And even if I wore it, I would never let you see me wearing it."

Gary pulled out a mint green tablecloth. "So you're proposing we go skinny dipping?"

"If you want me to go skinny dipping, we're going to need another pitcher of margaritas." Not giving him time to form a mental picture, I said, "Plus, there's a small child present. I wouldn't want to traumatize him. You'd have to take out a massive loan to pay for all the therapy."

Gary's flashlight pointed at the boxes, so I couldn't see his face. Was he smiling? Frowning? Was his face stuck in a silent scream of terror? It felt like Gary stayed quiet for an eternity. I hoped he wasn't dwelling on that stupid skinny dipping thing. It was only a joke. I mean, really, there was a child down there. Plus, I hadn't waxed my bikini lines in weeks. There were a thousand reasons Gary Wright, and I would not be skinny dipping any time soon. Or ever. A million reasons. *Damn it, now I was dwelling on the skinny dipping thing.*

While I had been trying to wrestle my thoughts back under control, Gary grabbed another armful of boxes. For the next twenty minutes, we searched box after box. It was like Christmas morning, except instead of wonderful gifts and presents, it was old smelly boxes full of junk. We found pillowcases, towels, and a coffeemaker with a cracked glass carafe. The one thing we didn't find was a bathing suit.

"Why do you care if I go swimming, anyway?" I asked as Gary handed me another box. By this time, there were only a few left to search.

"Kyle's not a strong swimmer yet, so if he goes in the pool, I have to go in with him."

"And what does that have to do with me?"

"Well," said Gary. "If you come into the pool with me, I figured it would give you time to explain." Gary frowned as he pulled an ancient-looking brassiere out of his box.

"Explain? Explain what?" I asked.

"The real reason you're trying to set me up with Janet?" His face bathed in illumination from the flashlight, Gary met me eye-to-eye.

I had to do damage control, but something inside of me knew it was already too late. Like Kate Winslet, pulling out a roll of duct tape as the Titanic slipped under the waves. "I told you why I was trying to set you up with Janet," I said, heart thumping faster in my chest. "She was obsessed with you."

"Twenty years ago."

"Yes, but ..." My brain scrambled like an NFL quarterback with no offensive line.. "You and Janet are still a good match."

"Well," Gary said, his voice little more than a whisper. "It will be hard to match us when she's already dating Jack Thompson."

And there it was. The gig was up. All my plans came crashing down like a house of cards. "Gary ..." I scrambled for the right words, but everything I tried to say ended up caught in my throat.

"Hey, look at this," Gary announced cheerfully. "A bathing suit." He pulled out a piece of clothing from the box, letting it dangle from his fingers. "I guess it's your lucky day."

It didn't feel like my lucky day.

Not lucky at all.

When Gary said he found a bathing suit in Aunt Catherine's boxes, I was expecting some sort of old lady bathing suit. Full body coverage. Polka dots. Ruffles. But this bathing suit must have been from Aunt Catherine's glory days. When she was young, wild, and carefree. And enjoyed the feel of spandex between her butt cheeks. I suspected that maybe Aunt Catherine had once had a side hustle working as an exotic dancer.

I stared at myself in the mirror. The bathing suit was a two-piece. In a leopard print. The bottom didn't even come close to covering my ass. Kind of like when my dad asked Janet about the funny smelling "cigarette" he found in my backpack. Janet had covered my ass then, about as well as Aunt Catherine's bathing suit did now..

The top had a plunging neckline, that might as well have gone all the way down to my belly button. It looked like something Farrah Faucet or Bo Derek would have worn in a pinup poster, taped to the wall in a horny teenage boy's bedroom.

I could see a lot more of my body than I wanted to see. Which meant that Gary would see a lot more of my body than I wanted him to see. Although now that he knew about Jack and Janet, he probably wouldn't want to see me at all. Under other circumstances, I would have just cut my losses. Let Gary and Kyle go swimming while I put on a pair of cozy pajamas and locked myself in my bedroom with another pitcher of margaritas.

But now that I knew that Gary knew about Jack and Janet, I had to know how much he knew about Jack and Janet. And the only way to do that was to play nice in the sandbox. Or, in this case, play nice in Aunt Catherine's pool. Resigned to my fate, I wrapped a towel around the entire length of my body and went outside to succumb to the humiliation.

Chapter Twenty-Two

The first thing I saw when I stepped onto the deck was Gary, propped in the corner at the far end of the pool. His arms stretched out along the edge. His bottom half was submerged under the water, but his top half was on full display. Rounded shoulders. Curved biceps. His skin glistened with moisture. *Wow!*

"Mary, watch!" Out of nowhere, a blur of motion charged toward me. Kyle bolted past, leaped in the air, and cannon balled into the pool. The resulting splash sent a spray of water in every direction. Including Purrfect's direction. Now drenched and dripping, she scrambled inside the house, probably to go rub wet fur all over my pillow.

When Kyle resurfaced, his smile stretched ear to ear. "Did you see that, Mary?" His orange inflatables bobbed in the waves.

"Yeah. Wow. Nice splash."

"You made it." Gary stretched his arms out in front of him and used his legs to push off the wall. He slid through the water like a shark. A shark with extremely well developed latissimus dorsi muscles, not to mention the calf muscles and glutes.

As Gary dipped under the water, his body now skimming the pool floor, I wrapped the towel even tighter around my body.

Even though it was stifling hot and suffocatingly humid, my body had a chill.

Popping up near the steps, Gary emerged from the pool, water flowing over his body like a raging river pounding against the rocks. Whole body dripping, he took one hand to slick the hair back out of his face. The world moved in slow motion, like the opening of *Baywatch*. Some poor person is drowning, but sure, take your time. You got to give people a good look at the abs, right?

"You okay?"

"Huh?"

Gary stood right in front of me. "I was beginning to worry you ran away."

"I considered it. Believe me."

"Can you hand me a towel?" Gary pointed to the pair of towels on the table. As I handed one to him, I hoped he couldn't hear how loud my heart was pounding. "Just need to grab the margaritas."

Gary wrapped the towel around his waist, then disappeared into the house. When he returned, he was holding two freshly poured margaritas, salt lining the paper cup rims. "I figured you could probably use another drink." Gary's chest was still dripping. Beads of moisture nestled in the crease of his pecs.

"You figured right," I said, taking a cup from Gary's hand.

Gary took his margarita back over to the pool and marched down the steps into the water. Holding his cup above his head, he waded into the deep end, cozied into the corner, and waited for me to join him.

"Just jump right in," Gary urged. "It feels fantastic."

"I'm not really the just jump right in type," I called across the water. "I need to get used to it first, before I can commit."

"Sounds about right." Gary held his cup in the air. "Cheers!" He took a long sip. Taunting me. I watched as his tongue flicked over his lips, scraping at the salt remnants.

I took a sip of my own. The tartness of the lime juice and the sting of the tequila washed down the back of my throat. The puddle of warmth that I was becoming all too familiar with started oozing through my body again.

What am I doing? Now that Gary knew that Janet and Jack were together, what was he still doing here? There was no way my plan could possibly work after that. I should have turned around and gone back inside. *Unless ...* Maybe Gary was sticking around for some ulterior motive. Maybe he was still in love with Janet and didn't really care if she was seeing Jack or not. I had to find out what he was up to. Perhaps, just maybe, the plan wasn't completely dead after all. Besides, I had gotten this far. *Can't turn around now.*

The hour of judgement was at hand. Time to sink or swim.

Still clutching the towel around my body, I poked my toe in the water, then claimed an exploratory foothold on the pool step. I took my time acclimating to the water, swishing my foot back and forth. It wasn't because the water was cold. In fact, the pool felt like a warm bath. Baking in the Florida sun all day, the swimming pool had become a giant hot tub.

It wasn't the water I needed time getting used to. What I needed was time to think. I needed time to figure out what I was going to say to Gary. I needed time to figure out what Gary was up to. I also needed time to figure out how to make an invisibility machine so Gary wouldn't see me in Aunt Catherine's rated R bathing suit.

"Hey Mary, watch this one." Kyle lined up for another run. Once he saw he had my attention, he dashed toward the pool and jumped in for another big splash.

That's when I knew what I had to do. Like Kyle, I just needed to go for it. Throw caution to the wind and dive right in. I would find out what Gary knew, or at least, what Gary thought he knew, and deny anything and everything unless he had some kind of proof. And then if that didn't work, I would simply join a convent and live out my remaining days as a leopard print bikini wearing nun.

Downing the rest of my margarita in one gulp, I ripped off the towel and dove into the water. Except it was more of a belly flop, with the grace of a breaching narwhal that was drunk and had vertigo. For one horrible moment, I feared I had given myself a concussion when my cheek hit the water, and Gary would have to scoop me up off the bottom of the pool and resuscitate me with mouth to mouth. I could picture Purrfect sitting on the deck, pointing and laughing.

But somehow, miraculously, my flailing arms propelled me to the far side of the pool next to Gary. I took a moment to gather my breath and my thoughts. And my sanity.

"I can see now why you don't go in the pool," Gary teased.

"I told you I wasn't much of a swimmer."

"Swimming? Is that what you call that?"

I swooshed my arm and sent a spray of water toward Gary's face. Ducking under the surface of the water, the splash sailed over Gary's head right into Purrfect, who had only recently returned from the house. Howling in disgust, Purrfect raced back inside.

When Gary emerged again, he was on the other side of the deep end, well out of harm's way. "Nice suit, by the way."

"Gee thanks," I replied, with all the fake sincerity I could muster.

"You look good in cheetah print," Gary said. "Yellow and brown spots seem to suit you."

I frowned as I looked down at my bikini top. "I thought this was leopard print?" It was at that moment that I realized not only was the bathing suit hideous looking, it was also generously see-through when wet. Hopefully Gary would mistake my nipples for leopard spots. Or cheetah spots. Or Justin Bieber horns.

"No, I'm pretty sure that's cheetah," Gary said. "I think leopard spots are bigger and less rounded." *Okay, he definitely saw my nipples.*

Leopard. Cheetah. I didn't care if they were the spots of a purple polka dotted alien species from outer space. The less time

Gary spent looking at my bathing suit, the better. So I continued my new strategy and just went for it.

"So," I said.

"So," Gary echoed. He swam to my side of the pool, arms sweeping through the water in long graceful arcs. The muscles in his arms looked like steel cables, taut and quivering.

"So, what do you know about Jack and Janet?" I asked. "Or what do you think you know?"

Gary waded in place, the current from the pool jets nudging him toward me. "I saw them together."

"Of course you did. They're friends."

"It looked like they were more than friends." A lock of Gary's wet hair stuck to his forehead. I felt an urge to reach out and brush it off to the side, but I restrained myself.

"What do you mean, more than friends?"

Gary drifted closer, then propped his elbow on the deck next to me. "I saw him at the closing ceremony. Janet put a medal around his neck."

"Yes," I said, doing my best to keep my voice from cracking. "Of course she did. She was a volunteer. That was her job." I looked down into the depths of the pool. Perhaps if I slipped underneath the water and held my breath long enough, Gary would get bored and go away.

"I saw the way she looked at him."

"Putting a medal around someone's neck requires advanced hand eye coordination. If she wasn't looking at him, she could have poked his eye out or something."

"She hugged him."

"Janet is a friendly person."

Gary wasn't just looking at me, he looked through me. Watching every breath. Analyzing every blink. Across the pool, a green and blue dragonfly lazily hovered over the water. Across the yard, a bright red cardinal hopped along a tree branch. In the sky, a large white cloud shifted into the shape of a hippopotamus wearing a tutu. Or maybe it was a giant mushroom wearing a top hat. Or maybe it was just a shapeless blob of white, fluffy nothingness. Like my soul.

"Mary." Gary's voice brought me back to reality. "How long have you known?"

As much as I wished I could transform myself into a dragonfly or a cardinal or a fluffy white cloud and just fly far away, I knew I had to own up to what I did. I had to tell Gary the truth.

"Since the beginning," I confessed. "They connected at the high school reunion, and it was my fault."

If Gary was surprised, he didn't show it. He only nodded, as if what I was saying made any kind of sense. Really, he looked numb. Mentally numb. Emotionally numb. At the time, I thought that was our lowest point. The level of trust between two people sinking to somewhere between zero and negative infinity. Little did I know there was still a long drop ahead.

"I made her go to the reunion because I was trying to give her a distraction, take her mind off her ex. Things sort of fell into place. Or out of place, I guess."

It was like I had pulled loose the first stone in the dam. Once the first lie had seen the light of day, they all came rushing out at once. "They're not right for each other," I blurted. "Janet should be with someone kind. Someone caring. Someone like ..." I looked back up into Gary's eyes. "Someone like you."

For a moment, his eyes softened. His jaw was no longer clenched. The color in his cheeks, his lips, his nose all came back. Maybe there was still a scrap of our tentative friendship left.

"So you were using me to get her away from Jack." It wasn't a question. He stated it as fact.

"Yes." A wave of shame washed over me. The guilt of everything all hitting at once. The staging at the grocery store and book signing farce. Using a children's charity event for my own selfish needs. If my conscience had been a little green bug sitting on my shoulder, it would have bitten me on the earlobe, and then kicked me in the nose. "I'm sorry."

"Mary."

I kept staring into the water. I couldn't even look him in the eye. Maybe if I was lucky, a giant octopus would reach up and pull me down into the depths.

"Mary, look at me."

I did.

"Why are you sorry?"

Why was I sorry? I wasn't sure I heard him right. I had tried to use Gary to wedge my best friend apart from the guy she was seeing. A guy I wanted for myself. Of course I was sorry. What kind of person wouldn't be sorry? What kind of person did Gary think I was?

"Why should you be sorry?" Gary said, his voice rising. "Jack Thompson was an asshole. No. Jack Thompson *is* an asshole. Guys like that never change."

The intensity in Gary's voice gave me pause. Jack Thompson was an asshole, sure. No one would argue that. But Jack had changed. When I talked to Jack at the driving range, he apologized for what he had done to me back in high school. He bared his heart and his soul. He'd been sincere; I was sure of it. People change. Jack had changed. *Hadn't he?*

"You were just trying to protect your friend," Gary said. "Honestly, I don't blame you. I would have done the same thing." Elbows still propped on the pool deck, Gary's hands curled into fists. The anger was plain on his face.

"Gary?" There was a darkness in his eyes.

Gary took a deep breath, clenched and unclenched his hands. When he turned back to me, the darkness was gone, replaced by pain.

"Gary, are you okay?"

"You weren't the only one he humiliated, you know," Gary said. "Back in high school, Jack and his football buddies liked to have their fun. None of us were as big as he was. None of us were as strong. I guess the kids like me were easy targets. The chess kid who played dungeons and dragons. The kid who made the mistake of wearing his Eagle scout uniform to school."

"You wore your uniform?"

Gary nodded.

"To school?"

Gary nodded again. "Right after I earned my final badge. It was something I was proud of. Until Jack saw me wearing it." Gary trailed off. Now it was his turn to stare into the pool.

"What did he do?" I asked.

It took a while for Gary to answer. When I looked into his eyes, they were like portals into another world, bursting with feelings and thoughts and emotions bottled up so long they were now ready to explode.

"It was after gym class," Gary began. "They broke into my locker while I was in the shower. When I came out in a towel, Jack was wearing my Eagle scout uniform. Making fun of me. When I told him to give it back, he asked me what I was going to do about it. His friends grabbed me before I even got close. They pulled off my towel. Threw me outside. Locked the door so I couldn't get back in."

"My God." I didn't know what else to say.

"After a while, one of the coaches heard me crying."

"What did they do to him?"

"Nothing."

"Nothing? What do you mean, nothing? He should have been suspended. He should have been expelled."

Gary shrugged. "When coach asked me who did it, I told him I didn't know."

Gary's shared memories brought back memories of my own. I knew what it was like to be humiliated. I knew what it was like to just want to pretend it never happened and move on.

"It was a long time ago." Gary's voice was little more than a whisper. "Whatever doesn't kill us only makes us stronger, right?"

"Right," I lied. After hearing Gary's story, I can't say I was surprised. Jack Thompson was a bully. That was never in doubt. The question now was whether Jack had changed. I had changed. Gary had changed. Why couldn't Jack?

After that, we got out of the pool and toweled off. As I was changing into dry clothes, I felt a little dizzy. That last batch of margaritas was wreaking havoc on my wits. When I came back downstairs from changing in Aunt Catherine's bedroom, I could tell right away that Gary was feeling it too.

He said, "I'm going to book an Uber. There's no way I should drive right now. I thought maybe I could just leave my van here and then pick it up tomorrow morning. If you don't mind."

"Yeah, no problem, good idea." But then I had another idea. A better idea. "Or," I said. "You and Kyle can just stay here tonight. I mean, I have two extra rooms. Might as well get some practical use out of them." I was pleasantly surprised when Gary didn't immediately say no. To sweeten the pot, I added, "The furniture rental place I used even decorated one in a space theme, with a rocket bed and everything. Kyle would love it."

"Forget Kyle. I'm taking the rocket bed for myself."

GARY DIDN'T END UP IN THE ROCKET BED. AND NO, HE didn't end up in my bed either, in case you were wondering. Instead, Gary and I both ended up on the couch, flipping through dozens of stations of nothing worth watching on T.V.

I paused at station 1001-2. "A western?"

Gary made a face. He looked at the station guide app on his phone. "What about a murder documentary?"

I made a face, stopping the remote on 342-3. "Ooh, here's a winner. Mexican soap opera." We both made a face.

After flipping through another two dozen stations, with absolutely nothing catching our mutual interest, I said, "I have an idea."

Gary looked doubtful. "What?"

"Game shows."

"Game shows?"

"Game shows. Specifically, Family Feud. Everyone loves Family Feud. Or at least, no one hates it."

"The Steve Harvey version?"

"Of course, the Steve Harvey version. Although the Richard Dawson cringe factor is pretty good, too."

Gary smiled. "True."

I don't know how late we stayed up watching old Family Feud reruns. We took turns answering the final round questions, with one of us getting the top answer almost every single time. Finally, there was something that we were both good at. And even better together. By two in the morning, we had agreed to drive out to Los Angeles or wherever they filmed the show and sign up as contestants the very next day.

"I have to pee," I announced.

"I'll save your seat." Gary yawned as he patted the couch cushion beside him.

I wasn't gone long, but when I came back, Gary was asleep. I decided to let him be, tucking one of the couch pillows under his head and draping my favorite fuzzy blanket over the top of him. It was also Purrfect's favorite blanket, so it wasn't long before the two of them were both curled up underneath it.

Just as I turned out the light and was about to go get in my bed, I heard Gary's voice. "Mary?"

"Yeah."

"Are they serious? I mean, really serious, Janet and Jack?"

"No," I answered, with enough conviction to convince us both. "Not yet, at least. Janet keeps telling me she wants to make sure they're friends first."

Gary nodded. "I just don't understand what she sees in a guy like Jack."

Um ... he's gorgeous, he's rich, he's athletic, he's a doctor, he drives a BMW, he's an expert chef and masseuse.

But I didn't say any of those things. Instead, I just shrugged.

"He's not good enough for her," said Gary.

"He's not," I agreed.

"He'll end up hurting her."

"I know."

We both stayed quiet for a long time, lost in our own private torments. Even though we couldn't see each other with the lights out, it felt like we were finally, truly, seeing each other for the very first time.

Gary's voice came from the darkness. "We have to stop them."

Chapter Twenty-Three

The Lake Eola farmer's market occurred every Sunday morning in the heart of downtown Orlando. Tents and tables lined the sidewalks, which circled the lake, in front of the big colored fountain. I stopped to sample some buffalo ranch dip with a pretzel stick, smiling as I reflected on my sudden turn of fortune. Finally, Gary was on my side. He was going to help me get Janet away from Jack. *Willingly!*

As I walked through the crowds, the buttered kettle corn and smoked brisket tacos smelled like victory. Through the din of mango smoothie slurping and a guitar player strumming Fleetwood Mac's "Dreams", I could almost hear the sound of the Universe in a slow clap, a begrudging acknowledgement of a match well played.

I found Gary in the artist section, next to the guy selling succulents attached to pieces of driftwood. It was the group of tents in the very back, past the homemade candle vendors and the self-published authors. Across from the one vegan food truck. It was the part of the farmer's market where only the most devout friends and family dared to go.

Gary was still setting up when I got there. He smiled when he saw me, and I smiled when I saw him wearing the Yale T-shirt again. The one that showed off his biceps.

"You came."

"Of course I came."

"I got you a coffee." Gary handed me a cup. "Just in case."

"Just in case?"

"I didn't think you'd show up." Gary looked at me like he was still trying to figure out if I was just an illusion.

In truth, it had been a close call. Really close. What I wanted to do that morning was stay snuggled up in bed. But when Gary called and suggested we meet up at the farmer's market so we could come up with a plan to distract Janet from Jack, I couldn't let the opportunity slip through my fingers.

"I pegged you for a Caramel Macchiato girl." Gary watched as I took a sip.

"Good guess." I was, in fact, a Caramel Macchiato girl. Caramel Macchiato's were my all-time favorite. At least until fall when they rolled out the pumpkin spice. A few more sips and my insides felt like Purrfect's belly after a day of hunting lizards. Warm and fuzzy.

Somehow, even though we barely knew each other, Gary could read me like a book. I was never exactly a prolific dater, but no man in the history of my love life had ever come close to being able to read my mind. Even when I wanted them to. Like when I was hungry for Thai food, but my date would take me to the sports bar for a burger.

"Would you mind helping me unload these bins?" Gary pointed to a stack of large plastic containers.

"Sure." When Gary suggested we meet up at the farmer's market, he had been a bit sketchy about the details. All I knew for sure was that I was there to "help out."

Gary opened the top bin and pulled out a piece of painted canvas. "Here," Gary said, handing me one of his paintings. "Put this one in the front. There should already be hooks for hanging."

I took the painting from him and made my way to the front of the tent. "To the left or to the right?" I asked. The two support posts that held up the front of the tent were filled with tiny holes to adjust the height of the legs. There were hooks in the top and middle holes, just big enough to fit into the clasps on the back of the frames.

"Left," said Gary. "Wait, which one is that again?"

I turned the painting around so it was facing me, and for the first time, got a good look at Gary's handiwork. "It's a tree," I said.

"What kind of tree?"

"I don't know. A green and brown one. With branches. And leaves." When Gary cocked his eyebrow, I said, "Sorry, I'm not a professional arborist." I turned the painting around so Gary could decide what kind of tree it was for himself.

"Twisted Oak," Gary said. "Put that one on the right." Then he turned around and rummaged through the bin for another painting.

As I hung Twisted Oak on the middle hook of the right post, I had to admit that Gary's painting wasn't half bad. It was actually kind of good. The tree, an oak tree, I presumed, rose from a windswept hill, branches twisting and turning in every direction. A blackening sky loomed overhead. In the shadows of a swatch of dappled sun, yellow daisies poked up through the weeds. There was a certain darkness to the painting. But also beauty. And hope.

We spent the next thirty minutes arranging Gary's artwork all over the tent. The pieces that weren't framed sat in bins so passersby could sort through them at their leisure. But in the whole time we were setting up, there were no passersby.

As Gary hung a painting of a cypress tree dripping with Spanish moss, I took a moment to admire another piece he had set up by the cash box on the table. It also showed what I assumed was an oak tree, limbs reaching out and curling in on themselves like an animal's talons. Like the Twisted Oak painting, a coming storm clouded the sky in this one. Nestled in one branch, a patchwork of twigs and thatch cradled a tiny blue bird, its feathers ruffled in the breeze.

I was so lost in the colors and the textures I didn't realize that Gary was looking over my shoulder, standing close.

"That one's called Last Flight," he said.

"Sounds ominous."

Gary shrugged. "It's just a name."

"But nothing happens to the bird, right?"

Gary's eyebrow quivered. And a small smirk curled his lips.

"Something happens to the bird, doesn't it?"

"Mary, it's only a painting."

"Yes, well, maybe you need to work on your picture naming."

"I'll keep that in mind."

Gary followed me as I strolled through the tent, looking at his other artwork. It was mostly landscapes. A quiet river snaking through a leafless forest. A snowcapped mountain melting in the morning sun. More trees. Lots of trees. Splintered branches. Hollowed trunks. Yellowed leaves.

"You know, some of these are pretty good. A little dark. But good."

"Some of them?"

"Well, they're all good. But a couple of them, I don't know." I struggled to find the right words. "It's like they're saying something."

I guess I had found the right words because Gary smiled. "Thanks."

"How long have you been painting?" I pointed to Last Flight. "Painting artwork, I mean. Not houses."

"A few years," Gary answered.

I did the math and made an educated guess. "After Anne was gone."

For a moment, Gary's face was as dark as the sky in Twisted Oak. "Yeah."

I was tempted to ask him about her, curious to know what happened between them. But if Gary wanted to talk about it, I decided it would be better to let him bring it up. I had heard enough divorce horror stories from Ralph to understand it was a topic that was usually better left locked away in the dark.

Sensing it would be best to change the subject, I said, "Well, they really are good. I'm surprised you haven't been doing it longer. Especially since you were already a house painter."

"Actually, I started painting houses at the same time I started doing these." Gary rearranged the painting on the front post. "Wright Stuff Painting was my uncle's business. He let me come on part time when I needed to, well, do something productive. Then last month he retired. So now, well, I guess I'm running his business all on my own."

Gary, being relatively new to the house painting business, certainly explained a lot. No wonder he felt compelled to express his personal opinions about my choice of color palette. And as an artist, I guess I could see why he might have been captivated by the classic kitsch of Aunt Catherine's wallpaper. Mr. Wright was getting more and more interesting by the day. "What did you do before you started painting?" I asked.

"I was an architect."

"You were an architect?" I felt my jaw drop.

"Mary, please. I got a perfect score in AP Calculus. Me being an architect should not be a big surprise."

Gary was right. It shouldn't have been a surprise. Gary was super smart. Probably a genius. Back in school, he was probably the smartest kid in our class. He could have done anything. I asked the question that had to be asked. "How did you go from being an architect to painting houses?"

"Long story," Gary deflected.

I looked around the tent. There were no customers. In fact, there hadn't been a single customer since we finished setting up. The only person even close to the tent was a woman in a Metallica t-shirt walking a chihuahua, and she didn't seem like the art buying type. "I think we've got time."

Gary could tell I wasn't going to just let it go without an

explanation. He took a deep breath and seemed to brace himself. "When Ann and I first got married, before Kyle was born, I worked for this big architecture firm. They had clients all over the world." Something about the look on Gary's face reminded me of the little blue bird from his painting. "I traveled a lot. Australia. Dubai. Bangladesh. Do you know where Bangladesh is?"

"Actually, I do." I had looked it up. *Where Jack learned massage.*

"Yeah, well, it's an eighteen hour flight." *Something definitely happened to that little blue bird.* "Once Anne was gone." *Something bad.* "I had to be there for Kyle." *Something tragic.*

My head felt like a helium balloon that had drifted off into space. I had to blink a few times to make my eyes refocus.

Deftly changing the subject, Gary pointed to the paintings on the display rack. "So you really like my work? You're not just saying that?"

I pointed to Last Flight. "That one's my favorite. I really like the colors. Especially how the dark tones blend with the light." I walked over to get a closer look. "Like these red lines weaving through the bark of the tree. And this splotch of purple between the blacks and the grays." I pointed to the corner of the canvas. "This bit of yellow here. The sun fighting through the darkness."

I took a step back so I could take it all in. "You know what I think?"

"I'm afraid to ask."

"I think the little blue bird turns out just fine. I think she buckles down, rides out the storm."

Gary only smiled, not confirming yes or no.

"I think she's holding on to that hint of sunshine. Holding on to that last glimmer of hope. Last Flight means it's the last time she feels like she has to run away. Because she learns to overcome the darkness. She doesn't have to be afraid." When Gary didn't answer, I asked, "What do you think?"

"I think you should take it."

"What, the painting?"

Gary nodded. "I want you to have it. Put it up in your aunt's house. After all, those gray clouds would go perfectly with the greige."

"Oh no, I couldn't. You should sell it. Somebody is going to come along any minute now and snap that one up for sure."

I followed Gary's eyes as he looked around the vicinity of his tent. There was no one even looking in our general direction. Except the woman in the Metallica t-shirt, waiting for her chihuahua to poop.

"I wouldn't hold your breath," Gary said.

I pointed to the tent at the end of the row. "Well, it is hard to compete with the neon unicorn portraits," I admitted. "Especially the ones where they're sliding down rainbows."

Gary cast a sidelong glare at the tent at the far end of the artist's section, where the neon unicorn artist, a twenty-something year-old with dragon tattoos and nose piercings, wrapped up another sale.

"I have an idea."

"Oh, oh." Gary looked nervous.

"No, this is a good idea this time. Really."

Gary still didn't look so sure.

"When I was walking over here, I saw one of the food trucks was selling funnel cake. With whipped cream. And chocolate sauce."

Gary looked at his watch. "Its nine am."

"Funnel cake is basically a big, flattened donut without the hole."

"So?"

"So let's get some breakfast."

THE FARMER'S MARKET GOT BUSIER AS THE DAY WORE on. The playground filled with laughing children. Happy couples strolled through the gardens holding hands. Joggers and dog walkers packed the sidewalks..

Gary asked Michelle and Joan, the couple in the tent next to ours, to watch his stuff while we got a funnel cake. Michelle made jewelry out of bottle caps, and Joan made bracelets out of hemp. In return for their tent minding, we offered to bring them back some funnel cakes too.

As we walked past a table piled high with crates of zucchinis, Gary asked, "Have you been here before?"

"Not in a long time," I answered. "When I was little, my dad and I would come every December to see the lights. They would set up Christmas trees all around the water, and the fountain would light up red and green." Memories of holding my dad's hand as we peered up at all the colors and sipped hot chocolate came rushing back. *Boy, did I miss him.*

As we waited in line for the funnel cakes, the mist from the fountain drifted over the breeze. Out on the lake, a flock of swan shaped paddle boats drifted back and forth. More swans, real ones, floated on the water or curled up under the cypress trees.

"You know you're actually not that bad," I told Gary, after he paid for the funnel cakes and we waited for our order.

"Gee, thanks?" he replied.

"What I mean is, Janet would be lucky to have someone like you. We just need her to see that you're better than Jack. Even if she doesn't see it for herself yet."

"So we go back to the original plan, then?" Gary asked. "Get Janet to fall for me. So she forgets about Jack?"

"It's the only way," I said. "We just need to emphasize your good qualities. Let Janet see you for who you really are."

"My good qualities?"

"Yes," I said, trying to think of reasons Janet might be interested in Gary. "You're good at painting. Artsy stuff. Not so much the houses. Or naming paintings. That could use some work. But you were also an architect. So that's something I suppose."

"How does any of that help?"

"You're a great dad," I added. "Like super dad level, for sure."

"Super dad?"

"Super dad," I confirmed. "But for Janet to see you as a better option than Jack, you're going to have to meet him head to head. Show dominance in his domain. Strength against strength."

"So what, like gladiatorial combat? Or a Medieval joust?"

"Do you know how to gladiator combat?"

"Not exactly."

"Have you ever jousted?"

"Only in D&D."

"Oh yes, dungeons and dragons. The key to every girl's heart." Gary wasn't giving me a lot to work with. "What sports are you good at?"

"Hmm, let me think." Gary stroked his chin contemplatively. "None."

"Do you play golf?"

"I just said I didn't play sports."

"Golf isn't a sport. It's a recreational activity."

"Tell that to Tiger Woods."

"I will the next time I see him. Can you run a 15k?"

"Can you?"

I threw him a look. "There has to be something you're good at. I mean, other than dungeons and dragons."

"Order forty seven!" The funnel cake food truck guy didn't look very patient, so I grabbed our order and we headed back toward the tent.

"There is one thing," Gary said, as we stopped at the dip tent. I balanced the three plates of funnel cake in one hand while I used my free hand to sample the Habanero Lime.

"What one thing?" I asked, dipping a second pretzel into the Barbecue Cheddar.

"Pickleball."

"Pickleball?" I nearly spit out my sample of the Cucumber Dill.

"Yes," Gary said. "It's like a mish mash of ping-pong, badminton, and tennis."

With my brain temporarily paralyzed, my mouth switched to autopilot. "Like all the racket sports had an orgy."

Gary frowned. "Gross."

"You really play pickleball?"

"Kyle got into it from school. Now we play together whenever we get a chance."

"Are you a banger or a dinker?"

"Dinker for sure."

"Somehow I'm not surprised."

"You play pickleball?"

After grabbing a pretzel-full of Avocado Chipotle, I said, "Of course I play pickleball. I play all the time."

"You bang or you dink?"

"I bang and I dink." I gave Gary a wink. But then he looked at me funny. So I winked again. And then I must have got an eyelash in my eye because my eye started itching really badly. Like someone was rubbing my cornea with sandpaper. So I started blinking really fast to get it out.

"Mary, are you having a stroke? Blink once if you're okay. Blink twice if I should call 9-1-1. Okay, ah, what does four blinks mean? Is your brain malfunctioning?"

"Gary, my brain has never been more functional in my entire life."

"Well, that's concerning."

"No, that's perfect. We'll challenge them to a match." The dip tent lady was looking at me suspiciously, so I waited until she turned her head. Then I sampled the Teriyaki Sriracha.

"A pickleball match?"

"A pickleball slaughter. Here, try the Bloomin' Onion." I handed Gary a dip laden pretzel.

"Wow, that is good. You and I on a team?"

"Me and you on a team. We'll destroy them. Annihilate them. Make them rue the day they were born."

"Or maybe we just settle for some nice, friendly competition. This Parmesan Spinach isn't bad."

My mouth full of Horseradish Crab, I caught a glimpse of the dip tent lady heading our way.

"Sir? Miss? Would you like to purchase any of the dips you sampled?"

I pretended not to hear her, scooping up a pretzel full of Bacon Chive as we fled.

Chapter Twenty-Four

On our way back to Gary's tent, we had to pass through a gauntlet of vendors and solicitors, handing out pamphlets and flyers for various charities and events.

"Would you like a free credit score review?" Someone tried to hand me a flyer.

"No thank you, we're good."

"Let me tell you how solar panels can cut your electric bill by eighty-six percent."

"I think we'll pass."

"Can you take a moment to save the whales?"

I pushed the clipboard out of my face. "No, I don't want to save the whales," I snapped.

"What do you have against whales?" Gary asked.

"I have nothing against whales. My funnel cake is getting cold." I started marching back toward the tent, but Gary hadn't moved. He had a look on his face that reminded me of that little blue bird again. Bracing for a coming storm. "What's wrong?"

"That day in the grocery store, you asked me what my best trait was. Remember?"

"I guess." I had done my best to erase that total disaster from my memory.

"What do you think it is?"

"What do I think what is?"

"My best trait."

Out on the lake, the sounds of laughter provided a welcome distraction. I watched for a moment as a man and woman climbed into a swan boat; the man taking the woman gently by the hand. "I don't know," I said, trying my best not to look Gary in the eye.

"I mean, there has to be something about me that Janet is supposed to like, right?"

"Can we talk about this later? I told you, the funnel cakes are getting cold." Looking down at the three plates, the ice cream was already melting, and the sprinkles were sliding off the top.

Gary didn't budge.

"Fine," I said. "You want to know your best trait? I'll tell you your best trait." But the thoughts swirling in my head were about as coherent as the melting ice cream. "You said it was your personality, right? Back in the grocery store?"

Gary nodded.

"I suppose you have a pretty good personality."

"You said personality wasn't important."

"Well, no, what I meant was, personality is important, in an established relationship, just not in the initial, you know, attraction phase."

"Attraction phase? Is that the phase we're in now?" There was a bit of a twinkle in Gary's eye.

I tried to steady my accelerating heartbeat, but my cheeks flamed in bright scarlet despite my best efforts. "I think we blew right past the attraction phase. Now we're in the ... retraction phase, when you try to figure out how to undo everything that went wrong."

It took more willpower than it should have to pull my eyes away from him. I tried to focus on a pair of swans swimming side by side out on the lake. When I turned back toward him, Gary still hadn't looked away. And the twinkle was still twinkling.

"Why are you looking at me like that?"

"Like what?"

"Like you have something to tell me."

"I do." Gary paused for a moment, but kept staring at me. "You still have some Teriyaki Sriracha dip on the corner of your lip." Gary batted his grey green whirlpool. My heart started doing round off back handsprings inside my chest and every molecule in my skin fizzed like a shaken up can of ginger ale.

"So that's it then?" asked Gary. "I have to rely on my personality?" The look on his face pinned me to the sidewalk. *Curiosity. Amusement. Danger.* He reminded me of the way Purrfect looked when I caught her toying with a lizard she caught on the pool deck. Enjoying a little pre-meal entertainment.

"Well, no, the situation isn't that bad," I said, distracting myself with a pair of swans gliding across the lake. "I mean, you're nice too. You're not bad looking."

"You think I'm not bad looking?" Gary's Cupid's bow twitched and his front teeth grazed over his bottom lip.

I had to clear my throat to keep from coughing. "It doesn't matter what I think," I said, avoiding a direct answer to his question. "It matters what Janet thinks. She's the only one that matters."

"Janet." Gary's eyes widened.

"Yes, Janet," I repeated.

"No, Janet." Now he was pointing.

"Huh?"

Gary pointed behind me. "Janet's here."

I spun around to peer at Janet, passing out pink pamphlets in the line of pamphlet pushers to each passerby. From what I could tell, she hadn't seen us yet.

"What do we do?" Gary's voice dropped to a whisper, even though Janet was at least twenty yards away.

"I don't know?" I whispered back. Run? Hide? Go back and

sign up for a whale saving expedition to Antarctica? I couldn't let Janet see Gary and me together. The last thing I wanted was for Janet to get any more crazy ideas that Gary and I were anything more than friends. If Janet saw Gary and me together, the plan would be ruined. I might as well just book my passage to Antarctica and hurl myself into the path of the first harpoon I could find.

"Mary?" A man's voice called my name, but it wasn't Gary's voice.

Slowly, I turned.

Jack stood in front of me with a stack of pink papers under his arm. Apparently the same flyers Janet was distributing. His eyes drifted down my body, settling on my feet. "How's the ankle?"

"Better," I said. "Thanks."

Jack turned to Gary. "You look familiar."

"We went to the same high school," Gary explained.

"Larry?"

"Gary."

"The dungeon dude." Jack's eyes drifted between us. Back and forth. Back and forth. "Are you two ..."

"Friends," I said. "Just friends."

"Good for you." Jack clapped Gary on his back, almost launching him into the lake.

"That's a lot of funnel cake."

I remembered I was still carrying an armful of funnel cake, the ice cream now completely melted.

"She didn't eat breakfast," Gary explained.

"Hey Janet," Jack called. "Look who's here!" Jack waved Janet over.

When Janet saw me standing there with Gary, she handed the rest of her pink papers to the whale woman and bolted our way.

"Mary! Gary!" Janet scooped me up in one of her signature hugs. Then it was Gary's turn. She wrapped her arms around him and plowed her breasts into his chest. "What are you two doing here?" Janet purred, her eyes darting back-and-forth between Gary and me.

"Gary's an artist," I said. Somehow, my hand ended up on Gary's arm, but I wasn't sure how it got there. "He has his own tent and everything."

"Ooh, an artist, that's amazing," said Janet.

Jack seemed less impressed. "Let me guess, dragon and wizard stuff?"

Gary pursed his lips. "I paint landscapes."

"Oh, so like flowers. And trees," Janet guessed.

"Sometimes mountains." I saw Gary cast a sideways glance at Jack and brace himself, like he was expecting Jack to come over and give him a wedgie.

"Well, good for you," said Janet. "Artistic expression is a great way to get in touch with your inner feelings."

"Way to touch those feelings, dude." Jack clapped Gary on the back again. I thought I heard his spine crack.

"You should see some of his stuff." I pointed toward Gary's tent. "He's fantastic."

"I'd love to," said Janet, as she patted his arm in the same spot where my hand had just been.

"What's with all the flyers?" Gary pointed to the stack of pink papers still in Jack's hands.

"Jack's helping me hand out flyers for the bookstore," said Janet.

"Here." Jack handed Gary a pink flyer, as if to show their technique. "This sounds like your kind of thing, Larry." Even though surviving puberty may have transformed Gary from a small boy into a capable man, standing next to Jack, he seemed to shrink back inside himself.

"Yes Gary, you should come," said Janet. "And bring Mary with you." Janet gave me a wink. I gave Janet a bird.

Jack handed me a flyer, too. "You two should definitely come. Janet and I are going to be there."

When I looked down at the pink paper, the first thing I saw

was an illustration of a scaled dragon, wings aloft and breathing fire. Below it, an armored knight deflected the flames with his shield.

Dungeons & Dragons Night
The Book Belle
Thursday 8pm

Gary and I stared at the flyer. Then at each other. Back to the flyer. Then each other again. I could tell we were both trying to stifle a smile.

"Maybe there will be a chance for gladiatorial combat," Gary said.

"Or jousting," I added.

"Anything's possible," Janet said. "That's what's so fun about role playing. You can do whatever you want. So you think you can make it?"

Gary beat me to it. "It's a date."

Jack and Janet followed us back to Gary's tent. Along the way, we passed a man selling homemade salsas and hot sauces and a woman in an aloha shirt making tropical fruit smoothies served out of hollowed out coconuts. As we turned down the path that branched toward the artist's section, I spotted a man selling pet supplies, so we stopped. I browsed through the hand knitted dog sweaters, bedazzled collars, and chew toys made of caribou antlers.

"Hey Mary, look." Gary held up a cat sized pink bandana spotted with stars and embroidered with the letters PURR-FECT. "It's perfect."

"No," I corrected him. "Puuuuuurrrrfect." After completing the purchase, I told Gary, "She's going to hate it."

"When you put it on her, you should get portraits done. Use them for your Christmas cards or something."

"That would be perfect," I agreed.

"No," Gary corrected. "Puuuuuurrrrfect."

———

When we got back to the tent, Gary asked Michelle and Joan if any customers came by while we were gone. Michelle looked at Gary as if he had sprouted a second head. I passed them their funnel cakes, which were now piles of soggy fried dough soaked through with melted ice cream.

Janet floated amongst the racks that displayed Gary's work, her mouth agape in amazement. "Wow, look at all the paintings! You did all this?"

Gary nodded.

"These are fantastic!"

Jack remained outside Gary's tent, his attention focused on the paintings of rainbow sliding unicorns instead. The tent that also contained the rainbow sliding unicorn artist, who was currently bent over in a short leather skirt, packaging up another sale. The mermaid tattoo on her inner thigh was on full display.

When Jack noticed me noticing him, he quickly shifted his attention back to Gary's work. "Yeah Lare, super cool." He made an effort to browse through a few of the paintings. "Lots of trees. And flowers."

Janet said. "Jack, you should buy one."

Jack wrinkled his nose. "You want me to buy a painting?"

"You don't have to do that," Gary said.

Janet shook her head. "No, he wants to, right Jack?"

Jack made his best attempt at a smile. "Right. Sure. I think they're great."

"Which one do you want?" Janet's face was aglow.

"I don't know, you pick," said Jack.

"Which one speaks to you?" Janet asked.

The look on Jack's face clarified that none of the paintings spoke to him. Except maybe the rainbow sliding unicorn paintings, because I noticed his eyes kept drifting that way.

"Jack, you really don't have to buy anything." Turning to Janet, Gary said, "Take whichever one you want, Janet. It's on me."

Janet waved him off. "Don't be ridiculous. Jack can afford it." Taking Jack's hand and pulling him deeper into the tent, Janet asked, "Which one do you think?"

Jack looked like Janet was making him choose which of his limbs to sever with a rusted hacksaw. "Fine." Jack pointed to the first painting he saw, the one directly in front of him. "How about that one?"

It was Last Flight.

"Yes! I love it!" Janet clapped her hands with glee. "Especially the little blue bird. He's soooo cute!"

Gary tried to intervene. "Actually, that one's already taken. I was going to give it to Mary."

"Ah," Janet smiled at me and winked. "Gary's giving you one of his paintings, huh?"

"No," I blurted. "Gary's not giving me anything." I liked the painting, sure, but what I did not like was the look on Janet's face. She was clearly beginning to think there was something going on between Gary and me, which would only make matters worse. I had to do whatever it took to keep the plan on track. "You should take it, Janet. It would look perfect in your place. Maybe Gary could come over and help you hang it on the wall."

"Actually," said Janet, "I was thinking Jack could put it in his office."

"You were?" Jack wrinkled his nose.

"You can put it in one of the exam rooms. That way your patients will have something nice to look at while you're, you know ..." Janet pointed at my crotch. "While you're examining their hoo-haw." I don't know why she chose my crotch for a visual reference point. And who the hell calls it a 'hoo-haw?'

"Great," Gary put on a smile, but his tone reminded me of

the dark clouds in the painting. Under his breath, he mumbled, "Just what every artist dreams of."

When Jack and Janet weren't looking, I slid in beside Gary and wrapped my hand around his arm. "It's okay," I whispered. "You can paint me a new one." I could feel the muscle in his forearm tense.

When he turned to look at me, his mood seemed to have brightened. Like the glimmer of yellow in the swirling dark skies. "Deal."

As Gary was wrapping Last Flight in bubble wrap, and Jack was reluctantly pulling out his wallet, Jack said, "So Lare, did you get roped into going to this engagement party thing too?"

"Engagement party?" Gary looked confused. Which was understandable. Because he didn't know about the engagement party. I hadn't told him. The last thing I wanted to deal with was Jack and Gary at the same event, in the same room. My plan was to divide and conquer, not combine, and have a nervous breakdown.

Jack continued, "Yeah. Some old couple, Mary and Janet, play pickleball with."

Gary looked at me sideways, eyes boring into me. "I never got an invitation."

"I figured you wouldn't be interested." I picked at my funnel cake, which was so drenched with melted ice cream it disintegrated when I poked it with my plastic fork.

"Yeah, well, I don't blame you." Jack handed Gary a hundred-dollar bill. "Karaoke night. It's going to be a nightmare."

"Yeah, see? Karaoke night." Looking up at Gary, I said, "You'd be miserable."

"What are you talking about, Mary?" Janet helped Gary tape the last piece of bubble wrap around the frame. "Gary was the captain of the Glee Club back in high school." *Damn it, I had forgotten about that.* "Hey Gary, remember our duet?"

A sly smile crept over Gary's face. "How could I forget?"

A weird feeling settled in my stomach. At first I thought it might have been too much dip sampling. But then I realized the uneasy queasiness in my stomach wasn't the Habanero Lime. Or the Chipotle Avocado. Even Horseradish Crab. It was dread. Things were spinning out of control, and I wasn't sure I was going to be able to wrangle the chaos. I felt like a circus clown juggling meat cleavers while riding a unicycle on a tightrope over a cage of tigers.

"Well," I said. "Even if he wanted to come, he can't. I'm sure Gary has to get home to Kyle. You know how hard it is to find a good babysitter these days."

"Actually, Kyle has a sleepover at his friend's house tonight, so I'm good," said Gary.

"Then it's settled," Janet declared.

"Sorry dude." Jack hit Gary with another back clap.

Chapter Twenty-Five

B y the time I got to the brewery that night, the engagement party was well under way. Dick, Mabel, and their guests dominated the far corner of the room. Janet, Jack, and Gary had already secured a table, a little too close to the karaoke machine for my liking.

I had planned to get there earlier, but after I helped Gary pack up his paintings when the farmer's market ended, I went home and jumped in the shower, standing there until the hot water ran cold, hoping for some sort of inspiration. Some brilliant idea to survive the night, without all of my plans completely falling apart.

Somehow, I had to get Janet to notice Gary, and make sure it was crystal clear that Gary and I were not even remotely, or possibly or potentially, together. Then, as if that weren't difficult enough, I had to get Jack to notice me, without noticing what I was really up to.

When no lightbulbs magically popped up over my head, I got out of the shower, got dressed, and flopped down on my rented couch. Purrfect jumped on the coffee table and stared at me, but didn't come up with any bright ideas either. Miraculously, she hadn't ripped off the pink bandana yet. She was probably still trying to figure out a way to slip it off and then use it to strangle me.

I lingered in the front entryway of the brewery for a couple of moments, gathering my courage and my strength. Edna, from pickleball class, was up on stage singing a Rod Stewart classic.

If you want my body ...

As she sang, it looked like she was doing some sort of Channing Tatum *Magic Mike* routine.

It wasn't only Edna's singing and dancing I had to prepare myself to endure. Even from across the room, I could see Jack, Gary, and Janet talking and laughing. I could only imagine what they had been discussing before I arrived.

"Hey Mary!" The owner of FoxPaw Brewing, Mike, called me over. Mike always let me sample the newest beers before they were officially put into rotation. He and I had become friends over the past couple of years, and not just because I tipped well. I helped Mike sell his old house after his divorce, and then find a reasonably priced condominium. I got him a sweet deal on both, so he had enough money left over to start his new brewery. Now, he was living the dream.

"You gotta try the latest," Mike said as I moseyed over to the bar. He set a shot glass sized beer sample in front of me.

"What is it?"

"PuckerPaw."

"PuckerPaw?"

"I'm still working out the name. It's SourPaw conditioned with espresso beans and vanilla." Mike smiled devilishly when he saw the concerned look on my face. "Then aged in bourbon barrels."

I know exactly what you're thinking. Because I was thinking about it too. The idea of a sour beer, combined with the taste of coffee and vanilla mixed with bourbon, sounded like somebody had let Dr. Frankenstein into the brewhouse. It's like those houses at Christmas that put out a light-up Santa Claus, a nativity scene with the baby Jesus, and a giant blow-up of the Grinch all together on their front lawn. Blasphemy. I mean, pick a lane, right?

"Try it," said Mike. "Trust me." Just as I was about to push the glass away from me in disgust, something Gary said when we were arguing over the wallpaper in Aunt Catherine's house came to mind. He said that sometimes, just because things don't seem to go together, they actually end up making something better than if they were just kept to themselves.

I put the glass to my lips. As soon as the beer hit my tongue, my mouth exploded with complimentary flavors. It was sweet, and it was sour. It was light, but also rich. Somehow, all the flavors came together perfectly. It was like a seventy-piece orchestra playing Pearl Jam while Michael Jackson moonwalked across my tongue.

"See? Told you."

I downed the rest of the sample, holding the glass up over my mouth to suck down every drop.

"Want a full pour?"

"Absolutely."

Mike poured me a pint. "Just be careful. It's twice as potent at Sourpaw. Too many of these things and your friends will have to carry you home."

"Speaking of my friends, I guess I better get this over with."

"You going to do Justin again tonight?" Mike asked.

"Not a chance," I replied.

Taking another sip of liquid courage, I made my way across the room toward the engagement party. Edna was just finishing her song, which drew an enormous round of applause from the crowd. Judging by the smile on Edna's face, I could only assume that she interpreted the outpouring of applause as the crowd thinking that she was indeed sexy, and they were letting her know.

"Mary, you made it!" Mabel was taking the microphone from Edna just as I arrived. "Mary Burns everyone!" The crowd once again applauded, although the applause was neither as loud nor as long as the applause letting Edna know how sexy she was.

"Everyone? Can I have your attention?" Mabel made her way to the center of the stage. "Can I have your attention, please?" The murmurs faded, and a hush fell over the crowd. "I'd like to take a moment to thank the person responsible for bringing us all together here tonight. If it wasn't for her, none of us would be here. Mary?"

I was so busy watching Janet split her attention between Jack and Gary that I didn't realize everyone else was looking at me.

Mabel held up her beer. "Cheers, Mary." Everyone raised their glasses and took a sip. I swallowed down a mouthful of the PuckerPaw as Mabel continued, "I just wanted to say thank you, Mary. Thank you for giving me Dick."

"Huh?" I almost spit out my drink.

Everyone in the entire brewery was staring as Mabel continued. "Now, Dick is waiting for me every Friday night after bingo. I wake up with Dick every morning. And Dick is the last thing I see every night before I go to bed. I fell in love with Dick thanks to Mary. And I've had a smile on my face ever since. To Mary!" Again Mabel raised her beer glass. But this time, everyone was too busy staring at me to follow suit. I downed the rest of my beer in one long chug.

By the time I made it back to the bar, Mike already had a second PuckerPaw waiting for me. "That was some toast."

"Is that what that was?" I took a gulp of the freshly poured beer.

"Hey Mary," Janet followed me to the bar. "Gary asked if you could get him a SourPaw while you're over here and Jack wants a Blue Hawaiian."

"It's a brewery, Janet," I said. "They don't have rum or blue Curaçao. They have beer."

"Oh. Jack's not much of a beer drinker. He only likes fancy drinks."

I gave Mike our order and as he was pouring the drinks, I noticed Ralph and Karen had arrived, holding hands. I still couldn't believe they were together. Ralph was the epitome of the stereotypical bachelor. I never thought he would settle down. And Karen, well, Karen was ... Karen.

"So who's your friend?" asked Mike, eyes focused on Janet.

"Oh, this is my best friend, Janet. Janet, this is Mike, the owner."

"Pleasure to meet you, Janet." Mike extended his hand and Janet took it.

"Pleasure to meet you, too."

Janet brushed the hair out of her eyes and smiled. "So you own this place? It's amazing. You must be so proud."

Mike shrugged. "It's been great to see all the hard work pay off. Can I get you something?" Mike pointed to the beer menu behind him.

Janet shook her head. "I'm more of a cider girl."

"Well then, you're in luck. Just a second." Mike disappeared into the walk-in cooler behind the bar. When he returned, he carried a pint glass full of a pink translucent liquid. "You like strawberry?"

"I love strawberry." Strawberry was Janet's favorite. Janet took a sip and from the way her eyes rolled back in her head, I was pretty sure she liked it.

"That's fantastic. What is it?"

"It's my new strawberry cider recipe, StrawPaw." After seeing our faces, Mike said, "Yeah, still workshopping the name."

"Well, whatever you want to call it, it's delicious. You should make more."

"I've been experimenting with a watermelon recipe. And a dragon fruit."

"I love dragon fruit," said Janet.

"Then maybe you could come back and taste test for me."

"Absolutely. I'll be back for sure."

As we left the bar with a fresh round of drinks, I couldn't help but notice that Janet had an extra bit of a spring in her step. Once we were out of earshot, Janet stopped me and leaned in close. "That Mike guy is cute."

I glanced back at the bar. Mike was looking our way. He smiled. "Yeah, I guess so," I agreed.

"Is he single?"

"Divorced. But he was a client of mine, so don't even think about trying to set me up." Mike was super cute. Super nice too. But I had a strict rule about mixing business with pleasure. So I would never even consider dating a client.

"Who said I was trying to set *you* up?" Janet winked.

Before I could fully process what Janet said, Ralph and Karen spotted us from the entryway and made their way over. Karen actually hugged me. I assumed she had sustained a head injury and didn't recognize my face.

"You doing Bieber tonight?" Ralph asked.

"Absolutely not."

We made our way back to the engagement party, where I was horrified to find Gary flipping through the song sheets. "What are you doing?" I hissed.

Gary flashed a pair of doe eyes at me. "Just seeing what they got."

Mercifully, a distraction arrived in the form of Dick and Mabel. "So are you kids having a good time?" Mabel and Dick each had a beer in hand. They seemed to be having a good time. A really good time. We all nodded enthusiastically and gushed about how wonderful of a time we were having.

But the reality was that things were not all that wonderful. I had this sense of impending doom hanging over me, like I was starring in a horror movie and I just started walking down the stairs into the pitch black basement.

"So when's the wedding?" Ralph asked.

"As soon as possible," Dick answered. "We're old. Time's a wasting. We could drop dead any minute." Dick chugged the rest of his beer and signaled a waitress for another.

"The problem," explained Mabel, "is that all the venues are booked. It's impossible to find anything last minute."

Jack said, "I know a place."

We all shifted our gaze simultaneously.

"The ranch."

Blink

"The reunion place."

Blink

"Where Mary got run over by the cows." The trauma of being physically assaulted by a herd of cattle remained fresh in my psyche. I still had nightmares, waking up drenched in sweat, the smell of cow lingering on my skin.

"That place would be perfect," Ralph agreed. Apparently, he had no concern whatsoever about returning to the scene of my humiliation.

"I have a friend who's friends with the person on the reunion committee who booked it. If you want, I could call her?" Jack offered.

"Would you? That would be amazing." Mabel grabbed Jack and gave him a big hug. A big long hug. I mean a really big, really long hug.

Gently prying himself loose, Jack asked, "When would you want to do it?"

"We're flexible," gushed Mabel.

"And old," Dick added.

"As soon as possible," Mabel said.

"Old." Dick tapped his watch, then feigned death by tilting his head, closing his eyes, and sticking his tongue out. Then he downed at least half of the new beer the waitress handed him in one long slurp.

Jack pulled his phone from his pocket. "Then I guess I better call Ashley right away."

"Ashley?" asked Janet.

"Yeah," said Jack.

"Ashley Griffin?"

Jack nodded.

"You have Ashley Griffin's number saved on your phone?" Janet frowned.

Jack shrugged. "She's an old friend."

Before Janet could press further, Jack headed off to make the call. When Mabel and Dick moved on to socialize with the next table, Ralph put his arm around Janet's shoulders and pulled her in close. "Everything okay?"

It took Janet a moment to pull her eyes away from the door. "With me and Jack? Things are going great. I mean, they're good. Everything's fine."

"You went from great to good to fine in the span of two seconds."

We all waited until Janet felt compelled to elaborate. "I mean, we have our differences, of course. Just like any two people do."

"What differences?" I asked, doing my best to sound supportive.

"Nothing important." Janet laughed, but stopped when she saw that no one else was laughing with her.

"Television shows," said Gary.

"Television shows?" asked Janet.

"Someone told me once," Gary glanced my way, "That you can judge the status of a relationship by the couple's T.V. watching habits."

"Like how?" Janet frowned.

"Do you watch the same things?" Gary asked.

"Well. Not exactly," said Janet.

Taking the baton from Gary, I asked, "You don't watch T.V. together?"

"No. It's just, I guess we never seem to find something we both want to watch." Janet's face looked like she was trapped in an elevator with someone who had just eaten a family sized crock pot full of baked beans. "But that's not a big deal. I'm sure most couples like different shows."

Janet fixed her eyes on Karen and Ralph. "I mean, I'm sure Karen doesn't like those old lawyer shows you're always watching, right?" Ralph loved lawyer shows. Especially the classics like Matlock and anything with Angela Lansbury.

"Well, no, they're not my favorite," Karen admitted. "So we take turns. I watch one of his shows, then he watches one of mine."

Ralph nodded, then said, "We binge watched six episodes of Doogie Howser reruns just the other night."

"A doctor show?" Most times, Ralph refused to acknowledge that doctors even exist. Like Bigfoot.

"Actually, I kinda liked it." Ralph gave Karen's hand an extra squeeze.

Gary and I traded glances. We both remembered that night we made dinner. Well, we both remembered that night we burned dinner. Then, after we got out of the pool, we watched old episodes of Family Feud while Kyle slept. For some strange reason, I found myself wishing that Gary and I could just go back to Aunt Catherine's house right then and there, curl up on the couch, and watch some more.

It seemed like Janet's head was floating somewhere in outer space. "The other night when Jack came over, all he wanted to do was watch football. So I just sat at the kitchen table and played sudoku."

"Well, I'm sure you two have plenty of other things in common," said Karen. "What else do you enjoy doing together?"

I braced myself to hear something I didn't want to hear, but Janet only shrugged. "To be honest, Jack is so busy at work we hardly do anything at all. We went to the movies last weekend, but it was one of those super hero ones where everyone just runs around in tights and blows things up."

Karen and I both wrinkled our noses. "Yuck."

"We've been out to eat a couple of times, but Jack always wants to get sushi."

"You're vegan," I pointed out.

"Exactly." Janet pressed her fingers into her temples.

Karen leaned in from across the table, dropping her voice low. "I hate to be blunt here, Janet, but what exactly do you see in that guy? Ralph told me about what a jerk he was in high school."

The entire table fell silent, beer mugs frozen mid-sip. We watched as Janet's gaze drifted across the crowded brewery. There, leaning against the exposed brick wall like a GQ model who'd wandered off set, was Jack, still deep in conversation on his phone. Ashley Griffin must have said something amusing because Jack smiled, his perfect white teeth lighting up the entire room. His rolled-up sleeves were fighting a losing battle against those unfairly generous biceps, and the way he ran his fingers through his perfectly tousled hair should have been illegal. A waitress carrying a tray of beer flights nearly walked into a potted palm, her head swiveling owl-like to steal another glance when Jack wasn't looking.

Janet, Karen, and I all sighed in synchronized harmony.

"Okay, fine. He's not horrible to look at, I suppose." Ralph made a face, but Karen was still too busy staring at Jack to notice.

Eyes stilled glued to Jack, Janet said, "I guess I just never thought someone like that would be interested in someone like me." *I could certainly relate.*

We all sat silently for a few moments, sipping our beers. While Janet seemed lost in thought, Gary caught my eye. I could tell he was plotting something.

"I'll be right back," Gary said, excusing himself.

What are you doing? I mouthed silently.

You'll see. Gary mouthed back. And before I could press further, he was gone.

I looked across the table as Janet sipped her strawberry cider. Even though I wanted Janet to realize that Jack was not the right man for her, it pained me to see her struggling. I may have been a terrible, no good, horrible, rotten person, but I was still her best friend. The last thing I wanted was for Janet to get hurt. Which is why I had been trying to get Janet to see reason ever since I found out that she and Jack were together. I knew if she kept at this, it would only get worse.

Seeing Janet's face in that moment only steeled my resolve.

I had to follow through with my plan, no matter what.

Chapter Twenty-Six

W hen Mike brought Janet a fresh cider, I looked around the brewery to see if I could spot Gary, but Gary was still nowhere to be seen. Jack was in the far corner, still on his phone. Ralph and Karen were still holding hands and making google eyes at each other. Something felt off. Like something was out of place. There was a bad feeling stirring around in my gut, and it was only getting worse.

"How's the thirty-day thing coming along?" Ralph asked Janet when Mike returned to the bar.

"So far, so good." Janet took an extra long sip.

I felt my heart skip several beats. The thirty-day thing. Day thirty would come around soon. The end of the friendship period. Then the gloves came off. Along with, potentially, everything else. And if that happened, Janet would be even more attached when he inevitably dumped her and broke her heart. If I was going to stop this train wreck from happening, I had to get my act together fast.

"What thirty-day thing?" Karen asked.

"Well," Janet began. "It's kind of hard to explain."

"No, it isn't," I interrupted. "It's actually quite simple. All of

Janet's previous relationships have crashed and burned. We're talking Hindenburg blimp level catastrophes. She goes too far too fast. She becomes emotionally attached. Suffocation ensues. And then the object of her obsession runs for the hills screaming in terror."

"It's not that bad," Janet mumbled, although her tone was so weak she didn't look convinced herself.

I continued. "So this time, Janet took a different approach. Before things go anywhere, they have to become friends. Thirty days of nothing."

"She saw it on TikTok," said Ralph.

Gary said, "It's a GenZ thing."

Karen nodded like it all made perfect sense. "So then, what happens on day thirty-one?"

A devilish grin crept across Janet's face. "I guess we'll see."

"But before then," I declared, "No hugging. No kissing. Definitely no funny business." But then I remembered what I had seen after I got hurt at the charity race. When Jack picked me up and held me in his arms. I had seen pink lip gloss on Jack's lips. Lips that clearly must have come into close contact with Janet's lips. "Although kissing is allowed now, apparently."

Janet's face contorted with indignation. "What? No, it isn't. Jack and I haven't kissed. Other than the kiss on the cheek I gave him when he won the medal. Why would you think that?"

Before I could tell Janet that I knew they were kissing because I saw the evidence on Jack's very lips, Karen asked, "And Jack is okay with this arrangement?"

"Well, he said he was." Again, even Janet herself didn't seem convinced.

"Speak of the devil." Ralph pointed as Jack returned.

"We're all set!" Jack waved Dick and Mabel over to share the good news. "Ashley made some calls and found out they had a cancellation next month. The place is all yours if you want it."

Mabel leaped into Jack's arms. "Thank you, thank you, thank

you," she gushed. Mabel was so grateful it took a combined effort from both Dick and Jack to pry her off.

Janet's mouth was smiling, but her eyes were doing something else entirely. "That was so nice of your dear friend Ashley to help."

If Jack noticed the tone in Janet's voice, he wisely ignored it. "Even better, the couple who cancelled had prepaid the deposit. Nonrefundable!"

I saw the numbers adding up in Dick's head. "So you're saying we can use the place on the cheap? Tell your friend thank you for us."

"She owed me a favor," Jack said. *A favor for what?* Janet's face made it clear she didn't look favorably upon Ashley's favor.

"So what happened? The bride or the groom got cold feet?" Mabel asked.

"Oh, it wasn't cold feet. The bride caught the groom cheating on her with the maid of honor," Jack explained. I couldn't help but notice Jack glanced my way when he said maid of honor. *Was that a wink?* I had to be imagining things.

"That's horrible," Janet said.

"Not for us, it isn't," Dick said. Dick and Mabel high-fived, then ordered another round on their tab. While they were waiting for Mike to bring them their drinks, the group talked through the logistics. Karen had a friend who was a florist, and she was pretty sure she could get them a deal. One of Ralph's divorce clients had just opened her own catering firm and a few texts later, the food was taken care of. I had a credit with the furniture rental place I used for house staging, so I offered to take care of the tables and chairs.

When Mike returned with Dick and Mabel's drinks, he also brought something for Janet.

"What's this?"

"It's a microphone," Mike explained.

"Why are you giving it to me?" Janet looked concerned. But not as concerned as I was.

Mike said, "You'll see."

Suddenly, a familiar-sounding keyboard chord played over the sound system. And a familiar-sounding voice began singing, "Now I've, haaaad, the time of my li-ife."

Ralph's face lit up and his head snapped toward Janet. "Oh my God, are you doing it? Please tell me you're doing it." All across the brewery, conversations stopped and heads swiveled as people searched for the source of the voice. Like a colony of prairie dogs scanning the plains for predators.

No, I never felt like this before ...

That's when I spotted him. Gary. On stage. With a microphone. *Please, dear God no!*

Ralph saw him too, then spun back in his seat to grab Janet by the shoulders. "You're doing it. You're really doing it." Ralph's face looked like he had suddenly found himself in the middle of Willy Wonka's chocolate factory. Without the clear and evident safety hazards and child murder. He spun back toward Karen. "They're totally doing it."

Karen was clearly confused. "Doing what?"

Jack was too. "What exactly is happening?"

I, unfortunately, knew exactly what was happening. It was the song Gary and Janet had performed during the talent show senior year. A day that will forever live in infamy. If YouTube had existed at the time, the video would have had two billion views overnight.

And I owe it all to you-hoo-ah-hoooo ...

"Go Janet go!" Ralph yanked Janet from her chair and practically shoved her toward the stage.

"They're doing the glee club thing," Ralph explained to everyone at the table. "They're actually doing the glee club thing." Ralph had more glee that the rest of the brewery combined.

The stage lights were on, so Gary was standing in the middle of a swath of white light. His hand was outstretched, beckoning Janet to join him.

The keyboard chord shifted, and the synthesizer twinkled,

signaling Janet's part. Without missing a beat, she lifted the microphone Mike had given her to her lips and sang.

The drum machine kicked in, driving the beat.

Ba bupbup bup ba baa, ba ba, bupbup, bup babaa

Janet bounded up the steps and she and Gary took their positions on opposite ends of the stage, hands outstretched toward one another and fingers wiggling.

I remembered the day like it was yesterday. It was one of those things where it's seared into your memory for eternity. Like when a president gets shot. Or a terrible catastrophe levels a piece of civilization. Or Starbucks releases a new variation of the pumpkin latte.

Janet and Gary had practiced their routine for months. Every note had been harmonized. Every step had been choreographed with surgical precision. They had watched the movie *Dirty Dancing* so many times that Janet's voice began sounding exactly like Jennifer Grey's voice and Gary's hair started feathering out on the sides like Patrick Swayze's.

Back on the brewery stage, Gary began singing about waiting for so long, and finally finding someone to stand beside him. Then Janet sang about feeling a magical fantasy.

"It's like they've been practicing the past twenty years." Ralph danced in his seat, mesmerized. We all watched as Gary and Janet came together on the stage, arm in arm, face to face. It was a perfect replica of the dance in the movie.

On the night of the talent show, everything had gone great at first too. Both Gary and Janet were on key, perfectly in tune and synthesized with the beats. Their steps were flawless. Like two gazelles floating across the stage. Until the big climax. The part in the movie where Baby leaps into Patrick Swayze's arms and he lifts her into the air.

You can guess what happened next. I could still hear the screaming. I could still hear the laughing. I could still hear the sirens. Luckily, no one got hurt too badly. Well, except for Mrs. Taylor, who was seated in the first row.

Holding my breath, I watched and waited for the inevitable.

Gary sang, "You're the one thing," shaking his hips and twirling.

Janet sang, "I can't get enough of." Janet flung her torso backward, arms flailing, then pointed directly at Gary, lips pouting.

Ralph stared in awe. "You don't think they're going to try the jump, do you?"

I shook my head. "No way. Not again."

Gary sang his part.

Together they sang the duet part.

From the left side of the stage, Janet dashed toward Gary.

Together, Ralph and I said, "Oh my God."

Gary went down on one knee and braced himself.

Janet leaped into the air, her body rising, then falling.

Gary lunged forward and caught her in his arms, then hoisted her high above his head.

Again, Ralph and I said, "Oh my God."

They started spinning. Janet had her arms and legs outstretched, her back arched. With the grace of an 80s film legend, Gary carried Janet around the stage, together singing.

This time Jack and Karen joined Ralph and me as we said, "Oh my God."

———

AFTER IT WAS OVER, GARY AND JANET WERE THE center of attention. Even complete strangers came over to tell them how amazing they were. Mike gave them a round of drinks on the house. The truth was, they were amazing together. The way they moved was so natural and free, it looked like they had been dancing together their entire lives.

Long after the dust had settled, and the crowds of adoring fans had dispersed, Gary and Janet were still smiling. I couldn't help but notice the way she was looking at him. I also couldn't help but notice the way he was looking at her. Finally, after all this time, I had gotten exactly what I wanted. Finally, after all this time, my plan was starting to work.

"You okay Mary?"

"Huh?"

Janet was looking over at me and frowning. "You don't look so good."

"Oh, no, I'm great. Good. I'm fine."

"Another great to fine in the span of two seconds." Ralph shook his head.

"I'm just tired, that's all." But that wasn't all. I was tired, sure. A little drunk, maybe. But I couldn't get the picture of Janet and Gary gliding across the stage out of my head. The way he held her against his chest when he dipped her backwards. The lines of the muscles in his arms as he effortlessly lifted her over his head. The fire in his eyes as he thrust his hips when she bent over in front of him. The way his eyes sparkled when he looked at her. *Whirlpools in the middle of the ocean.*

It was obvious to anyone paying attention that there was some kind of spark between Gary and Janet while they performed on stage. But if Jack noticed, he didn't seem concerned. "Speaking of tired, I have a delivery first thing in the morning. I better head home for the night." Jack clapped Gary on the back. "Nice moves up there, champ."

Gary smiled through his teeth. "Thanks Jack."

As Jack said his goodbyes out, I knew I had to take advantage of the fortuitous turn of events of the night. Finally, there was some positive momentum. Finally, the Universe had cut me some slack. It was clear to me that there was a budding chemistry between Janet and Gary, even if Jack and Janet and even Gary didn't have a clue. I had to strike while the iron was hot. Bend fate while it was still malleable to my will.

If I could arrange for Janet and Gary to get a little more time together, the spark that had ignited on stage would grow into a conflagration. One more idea to force Janet and Gary together, while simultaneously pulling Jack and Janet apart.

My mind raced. There was a new indoor rock climbing place near the real estate office. But then I had a vision of Gary dangling upside down from the top of a plastic rock formation, ankle ensnared by a safety rope. Or what about paintball? We could divide up into teams. Gary and Janet on one side, me and Jack on another. But then I realized paintball welts all over my body might not help my cause.

As Jack turned to leave, I became even more desperate. Things were finally falling into place and I couldn't let it all fall apart now. I decided I would find a church carnival. Bribe the pimple faced teenager manning the ride controls to get Gary and Janet stuck at the top of the Ferris wheel. But then I remembered they put those things up and take them back down in five minutes. With my luck, the wheel would break off with Gary and me still in it. Our screams fading as we rolled off into the sunset.

"Hey, wait a second," Gary said. "Before you go." Jack stopped and turned. I think Gary must have seen the panic on my face. Somehow, he knew exactly what I was thinking without me having to say a thing. Maybe all the time we had spent together had paid off. Maybe getting to know each other, really know each other, had created some sort of bond.

Gary's eyes flashed the question. Do you really want me to do this? I nodded my head. An involuntary blush painted his cheeks reddish pink. Like a paintball welt. Or blood splatter from a tragic Ferris wheel catastrophe.

"We should get together again tomorrow night," said Gary. If Jack and Janet weren't watching, I would have kissed Gary right then and there. "I have the perfect idea. We can ..."

"Tomorrow night? I'd love to," said Jack. "But I can't."

"You can't?" Somewhere in the back of my consciousness, a sad trombone player honked a lonely tune.

"I have to fly to Cancun tomorrow after my shift at the hospital."

"Cancun?"

"That sounds fun," said Karen. "Blue water beaches. Fancy

drinks with little umbrellas. Sounds like a blast." Karen turned to Janet. "Are you going to?"

Jack answered before Janet could even open her mouth. "Normally, yes, Cancun is totally amazing," Jack explained. "But I'm going for a medical seminar. So no fun for me. I'll be locked in conference rooms all day, every day, through the entire weekend. I might not even see the sun at all."

"Bummer," said Karen. Bummed seemed to be a good word to describe Janet's mood, too.

Jack quickly changed the subject. "But I'll see you all next week at the dragon and dungeon thing, right?"

"Absolutely," Ralph answered.

"Definitely." We all nodded our heads.

"Wouldn't miss it for the world," added Gary.

Jack and Janet said their goodbyes, but that was it. No hug. No kiss. Maybe I had been mistaken about the whole kissing thing after all. Jack barely even glanced back at us as he walked out the door.

Mike started wiping down counters and stacking chairs, so the rest of us said our goodbyes, too. But just as we were leaving, Gary stopped to talk to Janet. "Hey Janet, did you need a volunteer to dungeon master? It's been a while, but I'd be happy to help."

It was the dungeon master's job to create the story and set the scene for the players. Back in high school, Gary was always the dungeon master. He knew the rules better than anybody and had all the best ideas for monsters and traps.

"You still remember all the rules and stuff?" Janet's mood and tone seemed to brighten.

"Just like riding a bike," Gary reassured her.

I was pretty sure being a dungeon master was absolutely nothing like riding a bike. One requires at least some degree of physical dexterity and balance. And the other requires one to be a complete and total nerd.

"Sure," Janet said without hesitation. "If you want, I mean. That would be great."

When he looked over at me, I saw a twinkle in Gary's eye. He was up to something. As everyone else made their way to their Ubers, I held Gary back. "What are you up to?"

He only smiled. "Trust me."

Chapter Twenty-Seven

T he dragon stretched across the width of the road, munching on a bone poking up from the dirt. It lifted its head and blinked, its yellow eyes blazing. It never stopped chewing.

"Look." Gwain, the bard, pointed, his voice a frantic whisper.

Periwinkle, the halfling, and Gronk, the half-orc barbarian, had stopped about twenty yards back. That was on purpose. If the dragon attacked, Gwain would be incinerated first.

Gwain held up his hands in a gesture of peace, then called back to his fellow adventurers. "It looks wild."

"Of course it's wild," Gronk hissed, tightening her grip on her magic purple shield. "It's a dragon."

"What do we do?" Gwain averted his gaze, as if making eye contact would set the beast off.

"Turn around and run," said Periwinkle, her half sized frame dwarfed by the towering presence of the dragon.

"We're not going home." Gronk pointed past the dragon. "We're almost there."

Just down the road, the thatched roofs of Serenity Vale could be seen on the horizon. According to the rumors, it was once a peaceful place, where elves, dwarves, and humans lived together in harmony. But now, raiding bands of goblins and ogres terrorized the countryside after the notorious Witch Queen overtook the local castle. It would take a band of brave and hardy adventurers to explore the dungeons, defeat the monsters, and liberate the castle from the Witch Queen's grasp.

Gwain pulled the lute from his back, prepared to strum an enchanted tune to calm the beast's nerves. Periwinkle removed the magic ring from her pouch, ready to slip it on and turn invisible. Gronk backed further away from the dragon, figuring that the time it would take to eat both Gwain and then Periwinkle would give her more time to escape.

"Never fear, I, Sir Jack, the Badass, shall smite the dragon," Sir Jack stepped forward, his gleaming silver armor sparkling in the sun. Sir Jack was a new companion they had met, along with the forest elf, Caryn, renown for her knowledge of the wilderness and her ability to take really long, boring hikes without complaining.

"Your name is Sir Jack the Badass?" Gwain the bard rolled his eyes.

"Yes!" Sir Jack proclaimed proudly, as he raised his sword and advanced toward the dragon.

Periwinkle, the halfling, stepped in front of Sir Jack and raised her fur covered palms. "Whoa, wait a second Sir Jack."

"The Badass."

"Fine, wait a second Sir Jack the Badass. What do you think you're doing?"

Sir Jack lowered his sword. "Smiting the dragon?"

"You're going to kill the poor dragon? It's just sitting there minding its own business. What did the dragon ever do to you?" Periwinkle was one of those annoying, self righteous vegan halflings. The kind that only ate turnips and refused to let her fellow compatriots attack the monsters to collect treasure, even if the monsters wouldn't think twice about eating them.

"But it's a dragon." Sir Jack looked confused.

Blink

"And I'm a knight."

Blink

"Knights slay dragons."

Blink

"Don't they?"

"Maybe we should just shoo it," Gwain made a shooing motion with his lute to demonstrate the technique.

"You want to shoo a dragon?" Caryn's pointy Elven ears twitched.

"Then I'll sing it to sleep," Gwain offered.

"No!" the rest of the party all answered together as one.

WE HAD BEEN SITTING AT ONE OF THE GAMING TABLES in Belle's Books for almost an hour, but our Dungeons and Dragons game was barely getting started. We got a late start because, before we could do anything, Gary had to explain the rules to Jack and Karen, making sure they understood how to play. Then, Janet helped Jack create his knight character, and Ralph helped Karen create her Elven druid. My job was to place the figurines on the map Gary had custom drawn by hand.

"I thought the whole point of this thing was to kill the monsters and take all their gold and stuff," said Jack.

"There's more than one way to win," Gary explained.

"Like we could make friends with the dragon and then he might give us all dragon rides," Janet offered.

"Or I can sing my magic song." Ralph suggested for about the thousandth time already. Bards, the type of character Ralph used, were known for singing songs of enchantment, so Ralph had brought his ukulele with him, just in case. He'd been dying to show off the new Hootie and the Blowfish song he learned.

"No!" we all said again.

As dungeon master, Gary had the seat at the head of the table. From the smug look on his face, he seemed to enjoy his position of authority. And if I'm being honest, I was kind of enjoying it too. Something about a man in power, I guess. Even if that power is only dungeon mastering.

Gary looked down the table toward Jack, who was sitting right beside me. When we were first getting situated, Jack had pulled the chair out for Janet. A true gentleman. Seizing the opportunity, I slipped in and sat down instead. Somewhat less gentle, I admit. Janet ended up taking the last open seat. The one right next to Gary.

"You see, Jack, the cool thing about Dungeons and Dragons is that it's a roleplaying game, so you get to choose whatever actions you want to take. You're in control."

"Sure thing Gare. That is *super* cool." Jack's face got very serious, and he nodded solemnly. I think if I would have opened a dictionary in that moment and flipped to the word "patronizing", Jack's picture would have been right there under the verb tenses.

"Well, if we get to choose our own adventure," Karen announced, "the action I choose is to grab another beer. Do I have to roll the dice for that?"

"Only if you're trying the growler of jalapeño lager, Mike asked us to taste test," I said. Judging by the look on her face, Karen liked that idea about as much as when Janet suggested she look through the prop bin for a pair of Elven ears.

Ralph got up to help Karen. "Anybody else want a beer?" We all raised our hands.

"Jalapeño lager?" We all lowered them.

While Ralph and Karen went to fetch another round from the cooler, I moved my half orc figurine back another space, away from the dragon. By my calculation, I was now out of the range of its fire breath. Just to be sure, I nudged the bard figurine a tad bit closer.

Wanting to support Gary's efforts, I said to Jack, "That's what makes D&D so interesting. It's all fantasy, of course, but the choices you make as your character often reveal the real you."

Gary and I exchanged a knowing look. Because that was our master plan. To get Jack to reveal his true self to Janet, through the actions of his character in the game. Gary had meticulously planned the entire thing. Would he ravish the woodland nymph when she lured him into the forest? Would he abandon his fellow adventurers to save himself during the Minotaur ambush? And in the ultimate battle, would he sacrifice himself to save Periwinkle, the halfling? Or take the bait and go after the magic sword. Even though it had been Gary's plan, I had to admit it was quite brilliant.

Jack humored me with an amused smile, then took another sip of his colorful Blue Hawaiian drink. Somehow, I got the impression that my Dungeons and Dragons philosophy was not the thing that was amusing him, however. I couldn't help but notice the way his teeth scraped over his bottom lip when his eyes flashed to my lips. If I didn't know better, I would have thought he was ogling me like I was the woodland nymph.

Pulling his eyes away from me, Jack surveyed the hand-drawn map stretched across the gaming table, then turned his attention to the assortment of miniature figurines representing the positions of each of our characters. "Tally ho, ye fellow adventurers. Let us hasten to vanquish yonder dragon forthwith."

"Why are you talking like that?" Ralph wrinkled his nose.

Jack shrugged. "I thought we were supposed to use voices?"

"No." Ralph and Gary both answered immediately. I forgot to mention that the entire time we had been playing, Jack had been using a British accent. Like a knight. It was kind of cute. And I thought sexy. But also very annoying to some people, based on Gary and Ralph's response.

"Can I though? Use my knight voice?" Jack asked, using the British accent once again.

"Yes," said Janet, Karen, and I all together.

Jack was like a sexy James Bond. Except instead of a shaken, not stirred martini, he was throwing back his third Blue Hawaiian, the blue hue from the Curacao stained on his jutting upper lip.

"What's this over here?" Jack pointed to the section of the map to the left of the road.

"That's the swamp," I explained. While Gary was drawing the mountain range and coloring in the river on the other side of the map, he had let me draw the swamp lands with green and brown-colored pencils. To be honest, I was kind of proud of it. I had put in a bunch of creepy looking gnarled trees and colored in little bubbles in the swamp water to suggest something lurking beneath the surface. Gary said it was good. No, wait, I think his exact words had been, "really good." And he would know because Gary was a legitimate artist.

As Karen and Ralph returned with our beers, I asked, "Hey, does anybody here know why the swamp water is colored brown?"

Karen raised an eyebrow. "Dragon poop?"

I pointed at her with my plastic dagger and winked. "Bingo."

Jack picked up his knight figure and put it next to the swamp. "Fine, if we can't kill the dragon," He gave Janet a sideward glance. "We'll sneak around through the swamp. Can we do that?"

"You can try to do whatever you want," Gary explained. "But whether you succeed is up to the dice." Gary handed Jack one of the fancy dice, the one with twenty different sides.

Jack looked around the table. "What do you all think?"

I shrugged. "I don't know Jack. You're the leader. It's up to you. Everything that happens tonight is all on you."

The day before the Dungeon and Dragon's event at Janet's book store, Gary had come over to Aunt Catherine's house bright and early. While Kyle went swimming and tried to groom Purr-fect with my hairbrush, Gary and I hunkered down at my rented kitchen table and planned it all out. At the beginning of the game, I would suggest that Jack lead the party, a role which he would readily accept. With the responsibility of making the ultimate choices, the ultimate outcome of our adventure would fall on him. And for every wrong move Jack made, Janet would have a front-row seat to bear witness.

"I think we should go through the swamp," agreed Janet. "Just as long as you don't hurt the dragon."

After playing with Janet all those years in high school, Gary and I knew her tendencies and preferences. She couldn't stand the idea of hurting an animal. Even an imaginary one that was trying to kill us imaginarily. So while most D&D adventures involved swords and sorcery, monster maiming and creature killing, Gary's dungeon mastering games were always more evolved. In order to win the quests in Gary's games, the characters would have to solve riddles, or navigate mazes, or outwit complex traps. There was always a peaceful solution to every problem, if you were creative enough to look for it.

"I'm not so sure about the swamp idea," said Karen, pointing to my swamp drawing. "Look at those bubbles. They look ominous." I high-fived myself in my head. "If Serenity Vale is anything like Florida, there's going to be all kinds of alligators and snakes in there. Maybe worse." Karen seemed to enjoy playing in character, drawing on Caryn, the forest elf's wilderness expertise. Not to mention the fact that Karen herself was a veteran of S.U.K.C.'d.

"Definitely worse." I pointed again to the green bubbles.

Ralph traced his finger along the penciled road, to the right of where the dragon figurine was looming on the map. "What if we go around it, along this wall?"

"Or we turn around and go back. Leave the poor dragon in peace. What if it has little baby dragons back in its lair or something?" Janet patted the tiny dragon figurine on its pewter head.

"What do you think, Mary?" Jack asked. Sitting right beside him, I could smell the rum on his breath. His cheeks were flushed red and his eyes flashed fire. Like a dragon. I hadn't realized we sat that close. Had I subconsciously scooted my chair closer toward him? Or was his chair somehow closer to me? The expression on Jack's face made me think of a steel trap. Once you stepped inside, you could never get back out. At least not without gnawing off your own ankle first.

"Keep going," I said, picking up my Gronk figure and setting it down at the far edge of the map. "Too late to turn back now. No risk, no reward, right?"

"If you say so," said Gary. His face was as unreadable as a dragon scroll written in algebra equations.

"Onward then, brave adventurers, tally forth to the right!" Sir Jack the Badass stepped away from the gurgling swamp and headed for the cobblestone wall to the right of the dragon's position. A sign posted a warning, "Thou Shalt Not Trespass, Lest Yee Be Shot!", with a scrawled etching of a bow and arrow.

In the distance, a herd of horned beasts grazed in the pasture. The strange creatures emitted a long, low, guttural sound, as if in mocking, but otherwise left the adventurers alone. The dragon also left them alone, thanks to some magical lute playing by Gwain, the bard, who sang to the dragon that *"I only want to be with you."*

Once Sir Jack, Gwain, Periwinkle, Caryn, and Gronk were safely past the dragon, there were a series of other trials and tribulations to overcome.

There was the lost goblin whelp, who could have been used to force the goblin tribe to help defeat the Witch Queen, but, per Sir Jack's suggestion, was returned to his family after Periwinkle's plea for mercy.

There was the magic potion that could have been used to make Sir Jack invincible, but was used to heal the wounded village elder who had given Periwinkle his last turnip.

And of course the climactic scene where Periwinkle was bewitched by the Witch Queen, made to believe that friends were enemies and enemies were friends, and the witch queen's henchmen trapped Gronk in the dungeon. It was up to Sir Jack to choose which one he would save. But instead of choosing one of his companions over the other, Sir Jack sacrificed himself to save them both, surprising the Witch Queen so completely that she just gave up and left the castle on her own and the adventure was over rather suddenly.

Gary had created the Serenity Vale adventure as one big test. Each step in the adventure was supposed to be more difficult than the last, testing Jack's morals and character. The entire night had been carefully orchestrated to reveal all of Jack's flaws. Expose his true nature for everyone to see. But if the Dungeons and Dragons game was a test, Jack passed it with flying colors. An A+.

When the game was over, the town of Serenity Vale had been saved, the Witch Queen had been vanquished, and Sir Jack the Badass was hailed as a hero. And then when the town leaders tried to give Sir Jack his reward, the real Jack asked Gary if his character could just donate the treasure to the goblin orphanage. Things could not have gone any worse.

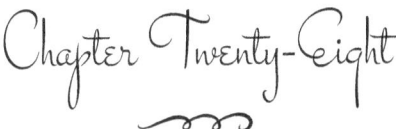

Chapter Twenty-Eight

R alph had to get Karen home to relieve the babysitter, who was pulling double duty with both Cary and Kyle, so Gary and I volunteered to stay behind and help Janet and Jack clean up.

As I was helping Gary fold the map, I glimpsed Janet and Jack out of the corner of my eye. They were across the bookstore near the information desk, laughing and talking. The sight of the two of them so happy and content made me sick to my stomach.

As I swept Cheetos crumbs into a dustpan, Gary pulled me aside. "Maybe he isn't so bad after all? Maybe we were wrong?"

I took another chug of jalapeño lager, then opened my mouth as wide as possible to let the air cool my tongue. "Maybe."

Jack's game had been flawless, always two steps ahead. He was like Bill Belichek with a camcorder. Like he knew what play we were running before breaking huddle. As much as I hated to admit it, Gary was right. Jack had made all the right moves. He was kind, thoughtful, generous. Sir Jack the Badass. Perhaps the name suited him after all. "He was kind of ... perfect."

"They seem happy together," said Gary. The sound of laughter carried across the shelves like nails on a chalkboard.

"You okay?" Gary asked.

I wasn't okay. Nothing was okay anymore. It took every ounce of my being not to scream.

Gently, Gary pried the jalapeño lager cup from my grip. "Janet promised Mike we would let him know what we thought," I explained. "It's my scientific duty to use proper size sampling."

"I think maybe you've sampled enough."

Gary set aside the cup and took my hands in his. The touch of his fingertips sent a sizzle down my center. "Maybe you should sit down for a minute." A soothing warmth radiated from Gary's hands into my hands. Up my arms. Into my head. I caught myself studying the curves of his shoulders like there was going to be a pop quiz later. "Mary?"

I had to close my eyes to keep the world from spinning. Too much jalapeño lager. Way too much. How scientific of me.

"Mary, look at me." I didn't want to look at Gary, but my eyes opened anyway. I could feel my hands still wrapped inside his hands. And for some reason, I still hadn't pulled away. "If Janet sees us like this, she might get the wrong idea. You'll blow your chances."

"I don't want to be with Janet," said Gary. "I want to be with you." His eyes sparked, little fireworks blasting off inside the whirlpools.

It was like watching one of those romance movies on the big screen, munching on popcorn and sipping a Coke. Look up there. This is the big declaration. Where the hero declares his feelings for the heroine. And oh, hey look, the heroine is me.

Or maybe it wasn't a romance movie, it was a horror movie. Or a comedy movie. Maybe a mutant combination of all three.

For several seconds, or minutes, or decades, neither one of us blinked. "Mary?" Gary was still standing in front of me. And this wasn't a movie. It was very much real life. "Say something."

"I have to go to the bathroom." Spinning away from him, I hurried away as fast as my feet could carry me. I was moving so fast I didn't see the cart with the books that still needed to be put away. I crashed into it and the cart toppled over, spilling paperbacks all over the floor. I didn't stop though, I just kept moving.

When I reached the back of the bookstore, I stumbled into the bathroom and slammed the door, grabbing onto the sides of the sink with both hands to steady myself. I hadn't lied to Gary. I really had to get to the bathroom. But it wasn't because I needed to pee. I had to get to the bathroom so Gary wouldn't see me come apart. I had to get to the bathroom so Gary wouldn't see me shatter into a million pieces like a stupid, blubbering fool right in front of him. Staring into the mirror, my cheeks were red and my eyes glazed over like wet asphalt after a monsoon.

"What the hell is wrong with you?" I shouted into the mirror. It took all of my willpower to keep my hands at my sides so I didn't punch my reflection in the face.

You probably think I was upset because the plan to expose Jack had crumbled. You're most likely thinking that I was on the verge of tears because I finally realized I would never have Jack for myself. But that wasn't why I was upset. I wasn't upset about Janet and Jack. I was upset about Gary.

Staring into the mirror, I wondered how I could have let it happen. I was too busy obsessing about Jack and Janet to see what was happening right in front of my face. He had fallen for me, and I had ignored all the signs and let it happen. True, Gary and I had more in common than I first thought, but there was still no way that Gary and I could ever work. Honestly, he deserved better than anything I could ever give him, anyway.

I wiped away the tears on my cheek, then stared myself in the eye. Gary and me. Me and Gary. It could never work. *Could it?* I blew my nose with a big wad of toilet paper. I couldn't even believe that I was contemplating the possibility.

Gary and I had fun together for now, sure, but life isn't all fun and games. Life is hard. Life is complicated. It's hard enough to survive on your own. Surviving together, with someone else, your partnership, your union, better be air tight. No room for doubts. No foothold for division. Because once that first crack forms, no matter how small, it grows, and it grows. And it keeps growing and growing until everything falls apart.

Better not to risk it at all.

When I came out of the bathroom, Gary was nowhere to be seen. I didn't see Jack or Janet either. I assumed Gary was embarrassed by his momentary lack of sanity, and was now hiding alone by himself in a closet. Jack and Janet were probably in another closet. Making out. All of which was fine by me. The last thing in the world I wanted at that moment was to see, hear, or talk to anyone else.

I returned to the cart I knocked over and picked up the books. It was a pleasant distraction. But a completely useless one. I couldn't stop thinking about what Gary said. The entire plan, the entire time, was to get Janet to realize she belonged with Gary. How could that possibly happen if Gary was really interested in me? No wonder all our efforts had crashed and burned. No wonder the past few weeks had been one disaster after the next.

One of the books I picked up off the floor was a contemporary romance. The front cover was a pastel colored drawing of a handsome man and a beautiful woman looking dreamily into each other's eyes. They were happy. They were smiling. The look of true and everlasting love sparkled on their stupid faces.

What a joke. Like that actually ever happened. If any of those books were actually anything close to the truth, they would have to be shelved in the horror section.

As I finished stacking the books back on the cart, I told myself it was all for the best. Now that we had officially failed to break Jack and Janet apart, Gary and I could each go our separate ways. It was better for everyone. Safer for certain. Besides, I didn't even care about Janet being with Jack anymore. Turned out, Jack wasn't such a bad guy after all. He really had changed. Janet was lucky to have someone like him. I was wrong to interfere.

I finished picking up the books and began weaving the cart through the shelves. When I heard Gary and Janet talking, I turned around and went back the other way. I couldn't face either of them. I picked up one of the books to put away in the Self-Help section. *Making Better Choices*. I couldn't help but laugh out loud.

Janet was a big girl capable of making her own choices. Right or wrong, they were her choices to make. Just like it was *my* choice to decide what I wanted in *my* life. And if the choice I made was to live my life as a hermit in Antarctica, then that was my choice to make.

It was better, before, I decided, when I put all my time and my energy into work. Buying houses. Fixing houses. Selling houses. At least then you can see the actual fruits of your labor. At least with real estate, all your investments of time and emotion and hard work actually paid off.

When I looked back up at the shelf, the Dr. Ruth bobblehead was staring at me again, shaking her head in pity. *Fuck you Dr. Ruth*. So what if Gary had feelings for me? So what if I had feelings for him?

Feelings are temporary. Feelings fade. The kind of relationship that I wanted, the kind that doesn't end up in misery and suffering and tears, needed more than just feelings to survive. A solid relationship needed iron clad unity. A solid relationship needed both people to always be on the same page. A solid relationship required two people who were perfect for each other, so nothing could ever rip them apart.

I could still hear Gary's voice coming from somewhere across the rows of shelves. He was still talking to Janet. I couldn't make out what they were saying, but I could hear his voice. I decided I had to stop running. I had to go back and confront him and tell him the truth. Gary and I would never work. No matter how he felt about me. No matter how I felt about him.

I had to tell Gary that what he thought he was feeling for me wasn't real. The last thing either of us would want to see happen is for us to get together and then break apart. Like his ex-wife, Anne. Like me and Greg. Or my parents. The world was already cruel enough as it was.

I paused at the end of the Dr. Ruth aisle, resting my hand on the shelf so I could gather my strength. Taking a deep breath, I rehearsed what I was going to say. I would tell Gary that now that we knew Jack and Janet were truly happy together, it might be best if we just went our separate ways. Now that we knew Jack had changed, and that he was a decent human being, there was no reason for us to continue playing games. We had to separate before things could get any more awkward. Turn around now, well before the point of no return. That way, no one would get hurt.

"Good choice." His voice came from behind me, a whisper in my ear.

When I turned around, Jack and I were standing face to face. "Good choice?" *Could Jack read my mind?*

"That one there." Jack pointed to the book where my hand was resting. The Kama Sutra. *Because of course it was.*

"Are you okay?" Jack asked.

"What makes you think I'm not okay?" I said.

"It's looks like you've been crying." Jack was looking at me, just as curious as I was looking at him. Had I been crying? It was only then that I realized I had been.

I considered Jack's question. Turning it over and over in my mind. "I'm fine," I said, after realizing, really, that I was. "I'm good. Actually, I'm great."

"Good." His eyes never wavered. "That's great that you're great."

"I am."

Jack nodded. "I'm doing pretty great too." When he spoke, the now familiar scents of vanilla and oak rolled off his tongue. I had lost count of how many Blue Hawaiians he had. Just like I had lost count of how many jalapeño lagers I had myself.

Jack's eyes shifted back to the spine of the Kama Sutra, the devil dancing on his lips. "You know…" Jack started saying.

I held up my hand to stop him. "Let me guess. You traveled to India. Learned to master every technique."

Jack's smile was like a shark's smile. All gleaming white flesh rending teeth. "Actually, it was the city of Patna in Bihar. Me and some buddies from med school went backpacking across Asia." He shrugged it off like hiking an entire continent was nothing more than a walk in the park. "It's not all about the positions, you know. It's also about love and family."

I looked up at him. Although he was much taller, I met him eye to eye. For the first time, I noticed he must have broken his nose at some point, because it listed a bit to the side. And his eyes weren't entirely blue. There were flecks of brown and grey. Was he wearing contact lenses? There were faint pock marks on his skin, almost hidden beneath the stubble on his cheeks. Old scars from what must have been a lingering case of acne. Jack Thompson. Football stud. Homecoming King. Zit face. *Probably all the steroids.*

"So that's what you learned from the Kama Sutra, Jack? How to love? Raise a family?"

There was that shark smile again. Shark eyes too. All black and treacherous. "Among other things." Jack leaned in as my back pressed against the edge of the shelf, his hand coming to rest right next to mine. "Mostly, I learned about the art of living a fulfilled and harmonious life."

"Fulfillment and harmony?" I snorted out loud. What a crock of B.S. "Please Jack, enlighten me. What's the secret to a harmonious and fulfilled life?"

Jack shifted his stance, his hips now pointed toward mine. "Well, first, live every day to the fullest. Don't be afraid to take risks." It was like his crotch was shooting off an electromagnetic pulse. Activating all of my nerve endings. Lighting up my whole body from inside.

I tried to back away further, but I was trapped against the shelf. Like a swimmer in the ocean, the shark coming under the water, jaws open wide.

Jack reached up and brushed away the clump of hair that had fallen down into my eyes. The gentle touch of his fingertips made every square inch of my skin break out in goosebumps. "To live in harmony, you can't be frightened of the consequences. To be truly fulfilled, you have to seize opportunity when it comes." I didn't realize I was staring at my feet until Jack's hand gently lifted my chin. "You were always one of those shy girls, Mary. Timid. Afraid. I'm not being critical. Just stating facts."

I wish I could have summoned the outrage to refute him. I wish I could have looked him dead in the eye and told him he was wrong. But he wasn't wrong. Jack was right. When it came to love. When it came to being honest with myself. When it came to allowing myself to feel genuine feelings, I was a coward. I had been one my entire life.

Somehow, Jack was even closer now. The shark coming in for the kill. "But here's the thing, Mary. You're not that same little girl anymore. Are you? No, I can tell that you're not. You're a big girl now. Ready. Willing. Able. To go after what you truly want."

It was like I had gone to get my teeth checked and the dentist had shot up my entire body with Novocain. I thought my knees were going to buckle. It felt like my head was swimming in an ocean of jalapeño flavored beer. My mouth was surely dripping drool. One more second and Jack was going to have to scoop me up off the floor and give me mouth to mouth. "You learned all that from a book?"

"I didn't learn that from a book."

"No?"

"Nope."

"How did you learn it, then?" My heart was beating so loud and so fast I could barely hear the words coming out of my mouth.

"Practice."

I wasn't sure which one of us moved forward first. Did Jack step toward me? Or did I step toward him? Before I knew what was happening, his face was right in front of mine. Our lips touched. Then pressed together tight. Like we both had a mouth full of magnets, pulling us together against our wills.

I was vaguely aware of my hands on his shoulders, his muscles tense and stiff underneath. I was vaguely aware of his hands moving down my lower back, pulling my body against his.

I didn't know which one of us started it.

What I did know was that neither one of us pulled away.

At first.

Somehow, a sliver of logic and reason wormed its way into my brain. *What the hell are you doing?* I was kissing Jack. Jack was with Janet. I was kissing the man who was with my best friend. I lifted my hands to his chest and nudged him away for separation. It seemed like he had to battle his own demons to break away, too.

"Jack, oh my God, I'm so sorry." I couldn't believe what I had done.

If Jack was even one millionth as sorry about what happened as I was, it was hard to tell. In fact, he almost seemed … amused.

"Whoops," said Jack. "Sorry about that. I forgot. You're with Gary."

Shark eyes. Shark mouth. Shark soul.

The laugh erupted out of my body like an air horn at a foot race. "Gary?" I laughed again, this time even louder. "You thought I was with Gary? Gary and me? Please. Gary and I are complete opposites. He loves floral print wallpaper for God's sake. Burns dinners. Terrible at sports. He even likes Patrick Swayze movies. Gary and I would never work."

On the outside, I was talking to Jack. But on the inside, I was talking to myself. I wasn't trying to convince Jack I didn't have feelings for Gary. I was trying to convince myself.

Even as the words were coming out of my mouth, I knew I was the single worst human being in the entire history of humanity. If there had been an award they gave out for the most despicable person on the entire planet, they would have engraved my face on the trophy.

But as if that wasn't bad enough, I kept going. "If Gary and I were together, it would be a disaster. Clearly I'm not serious relationship material. The first and last time I made the mistake of letting myself get close to someone, it blew up in my face. And obviously Gary doesn't belong in a serious relationship because his wife, Ann, divorced him."

Yeah.

That.

I actually said *that*.

If I could go back in time, I would have materialized out of the space-time continuum, run over to myself, grabbed the Kama Sutra off the shelf, and crammed it down my throat just to keep myself quiet. But despite the Michael J. Fox figurine standing on the shelf next to the Delorean above me, there was no going back.

I knew what I had done was bad. But I didn't realize how bad until I saw Jack's eyes widen in surprise. The moment I realized he wasn't looking at me. He was looking past me.

Behind me.

Slowly, I turned.

Janet and Gary were standing at the end of the aisle, staring at us in shock. For a long time, no one said anything. We all just stood there in silence. Plenty of time for the entirety of the betrayal to fully sink in.

Gary was the one who eventually broke the silence. "Ann didn't divorce me, Mary. She was diagnosed with metastatic breast cancer after Kyle was born. She didn't leave me. She died." Gary's voice was little more than a whisper. He looked as if all the life had been sucked right out of him. All the happiness. All the joy. Sucked right out of him. By me.

I think I remember opening my mouth, intending to say something, but I couldn't even form a single word.

It's not like it would have mattered, anyway.

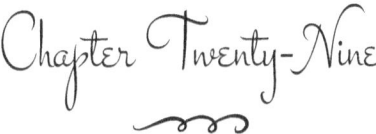

Chapter Twenty-Nine

"I'm a horrible, horrible person." I cradled my chai latte in my hands because it was still too hot to drink.

"Yes," said Ralph, without looking up. He was reading the copy of *The New Yorker* he found on the table while sipping the caramel Frappuccino I bought him. With extra whipped cream and three shots of espresso.

"Ralph."

"Mmm."

"Can you put that down, please?"

Ralph refused to look up from his magazine. "I'm trying to read about the changing work standards for millennial knowledge workers in the hybrid economy."

"Ralph, talk to me. Please." I was desperate.

"Fine." Ralph lowered the magazine and finally looked at me. "Are you familiar with the term quiet quitting?"

"What?"

"Quiet quitting."

I bunched my eyebrows together. "I've heard of loud quitting."

"Quiet quitting is when you just check out, mentally and

emotionally, but you don't tell anybody." Ralph resumed reading his magazine.

"Ralph."

"I'm actually doing it right now." He never looked up from his magazine.

"Fine. What do you want me to say?"

Ralph wiped a dab of whipped cream off his upper lip. "What else is there to say?" He had a point.

I looked down at the steam rising out of my cup, wishing I could assume some sort of vapor form and drift away into noth-ingness. I took a slurp despite the heat, scalding my tongue. Perhaps a little taste of hell. A preview for the eternal torment I would most likely and deservedly be banished to.

The micro dose of caffeine did nothing to clear the fog. I had spent the entire night pacing and crying and impotently trying to make phone calls. Janet and Gary must have blocked me. Every call and text I made disappeared into the abyss. Maybe Jack high-tailed it back to Cancun for another medical seminar. Even I had to admit that sitting in a conference room listening to lectures about vaginal diseases sounded like a pretty good alternative to facing the reality of what I had done.

The only person who would talk to me was Ralph. He agreed to let me buy him a coffee in exchange for hearing me out. Although apparently hearing me out did not include any return conversation, or pretending that I still existed. While he knew about the plan to break up Janet and Jack, which he agreed with, by the way, he didn't know my ulterior motive was to steal Jack for myself. So while he was a willing accomplice for half of the plan, he was mad at me for using him for the other half, just like I used everyone else.

"I messed up, okay. Bad. Real bad. I'm sorry. If I could take it all back or change it, I would, but I can't." I didn't bother wiping away the tears from my cheeks.

Ralph took a sip of his latte, then kept reading.

"Please Ralph. I need you to help me figure out how to fix it.

Did you talk to Janet?" In the rare circumstances in the past, when Janet and I would get into a fight, a bad one, she always went running to him first.

Finally, Ralph's eyes flashed over the top of his magazine. He had on his lawyer's face. Like I was a witness on the stand under interrogation, and he was just waiting for me to confess my guilt. "We were on the phone last night for over three hours. I lost a lot of sleep. You know how I need my rest." Ralph was the kind of person who needed a solid eight hours or he would turn into the Grinch.

Ralph pointed a finger at me. "Here we were thinking Jack was the bad guy in all this. That he was going to be the one to hurt her. But it was you. Janet said that Jack said that *you* were the one who kissed *him*. He told her it was all *your* fault."

That night at the book store, everything that happened was still a bit of a blur. Between the jalapeño lagers and the emotional roller coaster ride, I still wasn't sure exactly what happened or how it happened. *Did I lean in to kiss Jack first? Or did he kiss me?* I figured it didn't matter who started it. I was the one who put all the pieces in place for it to happen.

Ralph shook his head. "I can't believe you would do that, Mary. Was it really all your fault?"

The lump in my stomach worked its way up into my throat. I took a deep breath and nodded. "It was my fault. Everything was my fault. You're right, Ralph, he's not the bad guy. I am."

If Ralph got any satisfaction from my admission, it didn't show. If anything, he looked even angrier. I suppose it would have been easier for him if it were Jack's fault. But it wasn't Jack's fault. It was mine.

"Well, Janet must have believed Jack because they're still together, I guess." Ralph buried his face back in the magazine, letting me suffer in silence some more. "Despite your best efforts."

When I was a teenager, for a while my dad thought it was a good idea for me to go to church. So we went, religiously, for almost six months. One time, I even went to confession. Baring my soul in the little wooden booth. I remember sitting there, wearing my saddest, most pathetic, most repentant face. Just in case Father Tom could see me through the little cross shaped holes in the partition.

When he peered over the top edge of his magazine again, I put on that same face for Ralph. It must have worked, because his frown relaxed ever so slightly. "Look Mary, you and Janet have been best friends for too long to let something like this ruin everything. Even if you were a completely terrible friend."

I kept my eyes glued to my coffee, still making my "choir girl face." He was right, of course. I was horrible. I was awful. Terrible. Deplorable. And more. But Janet and I had been through tough times in the past too. Some day, when she let me, I would get down on my knees and beg for forgiveness. I would do anything and everything I had to do to win back her trust. Our friendship had endured over thirty years, and one minor, okay, major, mistake wouldn't ruin everything. *Right?*

I peeked up from my coffee, bottom lip drooping. "You really think?"

Ralph plopped the magazine down in his lap. "Look, just give Janet time. She'll come around when she's ready." Ralph's lips twisted into something that was almost a partial version of a smile. "Maybe, when I talk to her next time, I'll even vouch for how pathetic you looked when you admitted what a terrible friend you were."

"You will?"

Ralph nodded. But although his words made me feel a little better, my stomach was still doing back flips. The undeniable feeling in my gut that something was still horribly wrong hadn't gone away. Like the world was about to spin off of its axis and spiral off into a black hole.

That's when it hit me. Janet wasn't the one I was really worried about. Before I knew what I was doing, my mouth said, "And what about Gary? Will you also talk to him?"

Ralph's frown returned. "What about Gary? And what in the world could I, or anyone else, possibly say to him?"

I knew I was pushing my luck, but I went for it, anyway. "Maybe you could ask Karen to ask him to call me?"

Ralph's eyes narrowed, and his frown returned. "Are you serious right now? Don't you think you've tortured the poor guy enough?"

"I just want to make sure he's okay."

"Of course he's not okay. Janet told me what you said about him, too. Something about you and Gary being a disaster? Something about him being unfit because his wife died, and you accused him of getting a divorce?"

I bowed my head in shame. "She heard all that?"

"Yeah. She heard that. She heard everything. She and Gary both." Ralph shook his head and checked his watch. "I'm late for a deposition." He stood up and turned to go, unable to even look me in the eye.

But after a few steps, he must have had second thoughts. Took pity on me. He turned back just before he walked out the door. "Look Mary, I think Janet will come around. Eventually. But as far as Gary's concerned, I think you need to just let him go. I don't see how you can fix what you did to him."

I watched as the door closed and Ralph disappeared into the parking lot.

An overwhelming feeling of loneliness washed over me. More powerful than anything I had ever known. My heart physically hurt, like it was crumbling inside my chest. It felt like my lungs were shrinking. I couldn't breathe. I don't know if it was a panic attack or anxiety or a complete mental breakdown. All I do know is I wanted to run away as fast as my legs could carry me, or fall down on the floor and sob, or jump up on the table and scream all at the same time.

I had to focus on taking slow, deep breaths until my heart stopped racing. I had been by myself for a long time, of course. Ever since my dad had died. Loneliness wasn't anything new. But I had never felt anything like that before. Not in my entire life. I was sad, hopeless, and lost.

Sitting there, thinking about Gary, I tried to wrap my head around the fact that I would never see him again. I tried to picture my life without him. Without Kyle.

I couldn't.

The thought of never seeing Gary again was too painful to comprehend. How was I going to get through it? How could I survive? And that's the moment I realized it. Sitting there on that couch in the coffee shop alone.

Gary had told me he wanted me, not Janet.

That's when I realized it.

I realized I wanted him, too.

Was Gary perfect? No. No one is. But he was funny. And kind. And caring. I liked talking to him. I liked listening to him. He was a great dad. He was a great partner. He was a great friend.

I don't know how long I just sat there, not knowing what to do. If I could just talk to him one more time, maybe I could explain what had happened. Maybe I could come up with some sort of excuse?

But I knew, deep down, there was no excuse for what I had done. Even if I loved him, it was too late to undo what I had done. Ralph was right. I put Gary through enough pain and torment. If I truly loved him, I needed to just let him go.

I know you were expecting a happily ever after.

I hate to be the one to break it to you, but not every story ends happily.

Sometimes, the ending just sucks.

Chapter Thirty

It took me a few days to pull myself back together. After using up what little remained of my PTO days, I sulked back into the office. There were papers to sign, ads to post, and an inbox full of email. My eyes went straight to the receipt from Wright Painting Services, waiting near the top. I clicked open. It was an itemized list for the work Gary did at Aunt Catherine's house. All business. Nothing more. Nothing less.

It had been a while since they had seen me, so Bonnie and Joyce were eager to catch up. Bonnie was planning a trip to Pigeon Forge and asked me if I had ever been to Dollywood. Joyce was planning a train trip through the mountains of Switzerland and asked me if I had ever worn snow shoes. I wasn't in the mood for chit chatting, so I politely excused myself and hunkered down in my cube with a pair of noise cancelling headphones. The gray partitions walled me off from the world. For the first time in the history of modern office furniture, sitting there in my cubicle felt cozy and safe.

For the rest of the afternoon, I threw myself into my work. Left alone with no one to bother me, I could finally get things done. I scoped out half a dozen properties, got a new listing from a web referral, and returned the backlog of calls to clients and brokers.

I would have loved to have tried the quiet quitting thing, but the remodeling costs for Aunt Catherine's house were piling up and I had a feeling the credit card companies wouldn't be so quiet if I quit paying their bills. Gary's invoice alone wiped out a sizable chunk of my bank account.

Putting all my time and energy into my job turned out to be the best thing I could have done with myself. The more I thought about real estate, the less I thought about Janet and Jack. The less I thought about Gary. I kept crossing things off from my marathon length To-Do list until well after Bonnie and Joyce had gone home. To spend time with their families. Something I didn't have to worry about. I didn't even realize how late it was until the janitor turned off the lights.

That night, I plopped down on the couch and turned on the television. You'll never guess what came on. Family Feud. Because of course it would. Steve Harvey was on fire. Every other answer was probably going to end up on YouTube.

At least Gary wasn't there to call out the answers before I did. To be honest, it was kind of nice to get some quality time for myself. I could lounge around in my pajamas without worrying about my hair or my make-up. I could eat an entire half gallon of pistachio ice cream, with no one judging me. There was no one there to smell me, so I didn't even have to shower.

I knew my luck was finally shifting when Purrfect jumped up on the couch with me and didn't even hiss. Granted, she stuck her butt in my face and whacked me in the head with her tail, but I considered that progress. Once I felt better, I also got my appetite back, even after all the ice cream.

I had put in a long day, and I had accomplished a lot, so I treated myself. I ordered an extra large, extra cheese pizza from Antonio's, which had their dough shipped in straight from New York, so it was way better than any of the chain places around town. At the last minute, I asked the pizza girl to add spinach, you know, so it would be healthy. The best part was I didn't have to share it with anybody, so I could have the whole thing to myself.

Later, as I was sitting in the bathroom picking spinach out of my teeth, I had a moment of clarity. Like a lightning bolt straight from the sky. I knew exactly where I had gone wrong. I had been distracted by all the distractions. Distracted by feelings. Distracted by relationships. Distracted by love. I had been so busy crafting plans and hatching schemes I had gone completely off track. Book signings? Nature walks? Dungeons and Dragons? Distractions all. A complete waste of time.

What I *wanted* didn't matter. What I *needed* was all that did matter. And what I needed was to focus on work. As I continued sitting there waiting for the pizza and my stomach to reach some sort of compromise, I decided right then and there that I would put all of my focus on work from now on. My number one priority was finishing Aunt Catherine's house and getting it sold. Before the bank repossessed my car.

Sitting there waiting for the pizza to figure out which way it was going next, I realized that when you let yourself fall victim to spending too much time with someone, you lose sight of what really matters in life. Like making money. Paying bills. And checking out the balance of your 401k every couple of hours to see how much longer you have to earn a paycheck before you can quit civilization, run away to a remote tropical island, and drink strawberry daiquiris all day. Where you never have to see or talk to anyone ever again.

Jack had become a distraction.

Gary had become a distraction.

Even Janet, my best friend, had become a distraction.

What did I know about relationships? Nothing. Which is why I never should have gotten involved at all. I must have been out of my mind for wasting so much time with Gary. We never had a chance. Like burning a candle from both ends. No, not a candle, a stick of dynamite. Eventually, inevitably, it was going to explode. Like eating an entire pizza with extra cheese and spinach.

A WEEK WENT BY. JANET NEVER CALLED ME BACK. JACK never called me back. And no, Gary didn't call me back either.

The good news was that because everyone I knew and cared about had abandoned me, it made it a lot easier to uphold my new oath. It's easy to avoid distractions when they never come your way.

Over those next few weeks, I focused all of my time and energy on getting Aunt Catherine's house ready for the market. I rearranged the furniture a couple hundred times. I switched out the flowers in the clay pots on the porch. I scrubbed down the wallpaper with a non-bleach cleaner and a soft sponge so the little pink blossoms really popped, careful not to touch the penciled measurements. The new owners would surely erase them, but I couldn't do it myself.

When things were as close to perfect as I could get them, I planned an open house, advertising all over Central Florida. I started printing a stack of flyers on the office copy machine, but then it jammed on me, backed up like a gastrointestinal track trying to digest an entire cheese and spinach pizza.

Bonnie helped me fish a mangled piece of copy paper out of the inner bowels of the machine. "So you're really going to sell it?"

Joyce must have seen the puzzled look on my face because she added, "You put so much work into it. Seems a shame to let it go."

I had put a lot of work into that house. And I had to admit, the place had really come together. Purrfect was happy there, obviously. After all, he had stayed even after Aunt Catherine was gone. Not to mention the pool was perfect for entertaining. Especially if someone came over that had kids. But I didn't have to worry about that anymore. I doubted I would ever entertain anyone ever again.

"Of course I'm going to sell it," I said, using two hands to extract a crinkled sheet from the feeder tray. "I don't need a lot of space for one person. And a big house like that means there's more to take care of and keep clean. Why wouldn't I sell it?"

"Sentimental value?" Joyce offered.

"I have no sentiments." I wadded up the crinkled piece of paper and threw it in the trash. "That's the problem with society today. Houses are things that shouldn't evoke any kind of emotion. They're assets. Investments to be bought and sold. And if I don't sell my Aunt Catherine's place, my asset is going to turn into a liability real fast."

Bonnie and Joyce must have read my expression because they said nothing more.

Once the copy machine was ungummed, I finished printing out the flyers and passed a few around to the other agents in the office. I wrote the access code for the front door on each of them so they could show Aunt Catherine's house to their clients, even if I wasn't there.

"You'll come first thing in the morning when I have the open house, right?" I asked Bonnie and Joyce to bring their clients over early, so I could use them for a dry-run.

"Sure, I have a retired pastor who wants to move to this area with his wife and mother-in-law," said Joyce.

"And I've got a family from Miami with four kids," said Bonnie. "They've been looking for a house with a pool."

"Great," I said, as I packed up my things to go. My plan was to stuff all the flyers under doormats and tape them to light poles. But then I thought of an even better place to distribute the flyers, with high foot traffic and a captive audience. A new plan formed.

I WAITED UNTIL SUNDAY, THE DAY OF THE FARMER'S market at Lake Eola. I got there first thing in the morning, to stake out a suitable spot in the flyer line. Those free colon screening people were vicious, so I had to establish my territory early.

That's what I told myself. But I think we all know why I was really there.

I handed out a few flyers, then caught myself drifting further and further down the line. Past the acupuncture lady. Past the save the whales dude. Past the 'You're All Going to Hell Unless You Find Jesus' guy at the very end of the line.

I handed out a few more flyers, but it was hard to concentrate. I tried to look past all the swans nesting under the trees, but I couldn't see Gary's tent from where I was standing. *Was he even there?*

No distractions. No distractions. No distractions.

I repeated the words in my head over and over, commanding my brain to focus. No distractions. But I was too weak. I handed my entire stack of flyers to a confused woman pushing a stroller, then marched toward the back of the park. I didn't even stop to sample the pretzel dips.

As I made my way around the vegan food truck, I saw Michelle and Joan set up in the same spot as before. But the space next to them was empty. I looked everywhere, spinning like a top. I saw the woman with the unicorn and rainbow paintings. The driftwood and chicken wire guy was there. So was the woman with the sea shell wind chimes. But there was no sign of Gary.

"Mary!" Joan waved me over, her arms covered with bands of woven hemp.

Michelle's mouth was stuffed with funnel cake as I stepped under their tent. Swallowing, she said, "What are you doing here?"

"I was looking for Gary."

"Bout time you came around." Joan turned to Michelle. "You owe me twenty bucks." Turning back to me, Joan said, "I knew you'd come to your senses eventually."

My voice squeaked out of my throat. "He told you what happened?" A wave of shame washed over me.

"He did," Joan confirmed. "That was pretty dumb."

"Really dumb," said Michelle, nodding.

"I know." Kissing Jack wasn't just pretty dumb, or really dumb, it was stupendously idiotic. And then, adding insult to injury, what I said about Gary was even worse.

Michelle must have recognized the torment I was feeling because she put down her funnel cake, walked over, and gave me a big hug. "It's okay hun. We all do dumb things sometimes. Especially to the people we love." Michelle turned toward Joan with a meaningful look.

"What?" Joan held up her hands. "How was I supposed to know you were allergic to marshmallows?"

"Because we've been together for twenty-three years."

"You never once talked about marshmallows."

"Because I'm allergic to them."

Joan set her fists on her hips. "What about that time we went camping at that nudist colony? The guy in the Winnebago made s'mores."

While Michelle and Joan continued to debate the topic of Michelle's gelatin allergy, I was rewinding my brain to the point in the conversation right after Michelle hugged me, when she said, "We all do dumb things sometimes. Especially to the people we love."

"Wait a second," I said, interrupting a contentious story about an unfortunate Thanksgiving jello mold incident. "Why did you say that part about doing dumb things to the people we love?"

"Haven't you been listening?" Michelle raised an eyebrow. "She tried to poison me with a marshmallow. How dumb is that?" Then she whirled on Joan. "Unless you did it on purpose. You know that life insurance policy we had expired twelve years ago?"

"No, not the dumb part," I interrupted once again, before the debate continued to spiral. "I'm talking about the love part. Who said anything about love?"

At that point, both Michelle and Joan rolled their eyes. If synchronized eye rolling had been an Olympic sport, they would have won gold. Joan said, "Oh Mary, please. It was obvious the day you were here."

"Plus, he talks about you constantly," said Michelle. "It's always Mary did this to me, and Mary did that to me."

"Gary talks about me?"

Joan snorted. "All the time."

Michelle added, "He still does. Even after everything."

Gary still talks about me? I couldn't believe what I was hearing.

"Did you really out him at a book signing?" Joan asked.

"That was an accident," I answered. "He won't return my calls."

"That's because Gary's stubborn," Michelle said.

"See? They're perfect together." Joan elbowed Michelle in the ribs.

"Although after all he's been through, you can't really blame the guy." Michelle smiled as she took Joan's hand. "I mean, if something ever happened to you, I would never open my heart ever again. Too painful to risk getting hurt." Michelle's forehead crinkled. "Unless you poisoned me with another marshmallow. Then I would use the life insurance money to go on a cross-country tour of nudist colonies."

Interrupting once again, I said, "Do you know where Gary is? I really need to talk to him."

Joan and Michelle exchanged a serious look, then got quiet. Not even another marshmallow reference.

"What?" I asked. The look on their faces made me queasy.

Michelle said, "He went to see Ann today."

"Ann?" *Gary's wife.*

Joan nodded. "It would have been their anniversary today."

The lump in my throat was the size of a watermelon. Somehow I asked, "Do you know where she is?"

THE GRAVES DIDN'T LINE UP IN STRAIGHT, TIDY ROWS like I expected. Some had headstones sticking up out of the grass.

Others only had a plaque sunk into the ground, weeds poking up along the edges. Every once in a while, there was a bigger tomb, some with intricate carvings and others with angels on top carved in stone. There were lots of flowers. Roses. Lilies. Carnations. Most of them were dead and rotting, left behind by loved ones as a last farewell.

I would have expected grey skies and thunderclouds to match my mood. But the sky that day was bright blue, the sun a vibrant shade of canary yellow. As I picked my way through the grave sites, I saw an older woman standing next to a grave, just staring off into space. She wasn't crying. Her shoulders didn't sag or slump. She just looked numb. I imagined she was there to see her husband. The man she had probably spent her entire life with, and now he was gone. At least she had had someone to grow old with, I thought. At least she had had someone to love.

I found Gary on a bench in the shade. Towering oaks with sprawling branches blanketed the area in shadows. For a minute I considered making some sort of grand gesture. You know, like in the movies. But I didn't have a boom box to lift over my head. I didn't own a guitar and I couldn't sing a song. So I decided to just be ... normal ... for once. I just walked over. Silently begging the Universe to not let me screw it up. Tears already forming in my eyes.

I just stood there in front of him, waiting for him to say something or even move. I suppose I was lucky he didn't immediately run away screaming. At least that was something, I thought. After a few moments, I sat down on the bench beside him. He still didn't run, but he didn't say anything either. He just sat there quietly, looking off into the distance.

I sat there too. I kept hoping he would say something first because even though I had been racking my brain the entire drive over, I still didn't have a clue what I could say to make everything right.

Again, I started simple. "I'm sorry."

Somewhere in the distance, a bird chattered. Across the cemetery, a groundsman raked leaves. Across the infinite cosmos, a billion new galaxies were born and a billion old galaxies died.

Gary stared at the line of ants foraging through the dirt at his feet.

"Say something," I begged.

"Say something? You want me to say something?" Gary's eyes were empty. "What do you want me to say?"

What did I want him to say?

Like I had any clue. I couldn't figure out I wanted to say to him, let alone figure out what I wanted him to say to me. Did I want him to say that he had accepted my apology? *Sure, that would be nice.* Did I want him to say that he had forgotten all about the horrible things that I had done and everything could go back to how it was? *If only.* Did I want him to yell at me and scream at me and tell me he never wanted to see me again? *No, please no, anything but that.* Even if it was exactly what I deserved.

Raking the back of my hand over my face, wiping away the tears, I said, "I want you to say to me what you said before."

I could see the gears shifting in his head, not quite locking into place. "And what exactly did I say before that you want me to say again?"

"That you want to be with me." I tried to steady my racing heartbeat, but every blood vessel in my body felt like it was about to burst.

When I first got there, Gary wouldn't even look at me. Now, he wouldn't look away. "Why would you want me to say that?"

"Because then I can say ..." I dug deep. "... that I want to be with you, too."

Gary's eyes flared. The whirlpools became water spouts, erupting high into the air. If he was still breathing, I couldn't tell. "I thought you didn't want to be with anyone."

"I didn't," I said, taking another one of those deep breaths. "Until I met you."

We were only a foot or two away from each other, sitting there on that bench, but we were miles apart. It was like one of those science fiction movies. Where the bad guys are about to blow up the good guys with their giant laser. Until the force field appears. A greenish glow that walls off the Earth and protects humanity. I watched as the greenish glow formed around Gary. Whatever he was thinking, whatever he was feeling, it was now locked up tight.

"I'm sorry I didn't realize how I really felt a lot sooner. I'm sorry that I hurt you. If I could take it all back, I would."

"But you can't Mary. You can't just take it all back. What's done is done."

"It's not too late," I started. "We'll just start over. You know, take it from the top." I fired my laser beam and Gary's force field bounced it right back in my face.

"It doesn't work that way, Mary." Gary looked at me long and hard. "At least not for me, it doesn't." His next words seeped out through clenched teeth. "Besides, like you said, you and I would be a disaster."

Gary got up from the bench.

He began walking back toward the parking lot.

I waited for him to stop.

I waited for him to turn back around.

He didn't.

Just like that ... he was gone.

I sat there staring after him, kept sitting there, long after he left.

After the cemetery, that's when I knew it was really over. Gary and I were through. The final nail hammered into the coffin, and any chance we ever had tossed in a hole and buried deep underground.

As I trudged back across the cemetery, weaving in and out of the tombstones, I realized Ralph had been right. I should have just left Gary alone. The poor guy had been through enough thanks to me. So I swore to myself I wouldn't repeat my mistakes. I made a promise to myself that I would never see or talk to Gary ever again.

Chapter Thirty-One

A couple days later, I was laying in bed, tossing and turning, my brain racing like it had been every night for weeks. No matter what I did to distract myself, I couldn't stop thinking about everything I'd done to train wreck my life. Laying there, staring up at the ceiling, the realization came to me like a vision from the divine. It was like I finally figured out the answer to the unsolvable algebra equation I had been wrestling with for eternity.

You see, I had spent all my waking hours for weeks fixing and re-fixing Aunt Catherine's house. Rearranging the furniture, testing out fresh scents on the candles, switching out tchotchkes and knickknacks. But there was always this gnawing feeling that something wasn't quite right. Something out of place. Something that didn't quite belong. Finally, I knew exactly what it was I did wrong.

I had remodeled Aunt Catherine's house in all the latest styles and trends. Black furniture. Pendant lighting. Painting all the walls greige. But that wasn't Aunt Catherine's house. I was trying to force it to be something it wasn't.

Maybe if I stopped trying to bend the Universe to my will ...

Maybe if I stopped trying to force things to be what they're not ...

Maybe if I just chilled the hell out ...

Not even waiting for the sun to come up, I grabbed the left-over paint supplies from the shed and went straight to work. I kept at it all day until my hands ached and my knees throbbed. And my stomach threatened to eat itself if I didn't take a break for dinner, especially since I had worked through breakfast and lunch.

Strolling through Fresh Foods, heading toward the single serve frozen dinner aisle, I noticed a BOGO deal on arthritis cream. I went with the extra strength for my sore muscles and joints, then remembered I needed toilet paper and tampons, too. Maneuvering past a pyramid of boxed noodles, I had to yank my cart to a halt. Out of nowhere, some idiot swerved his cart right in front of me. I almost plowed right into him. When I looked up, about to give the reckless cart owner an earful, I realized the reckless cart owner was Gary.

"Hey Mary," said Kyle, arms cradling an extra large box of Goldfish.

"Hey Kyle." My eyes flicked to his father, standing, staring right in front of me. "Hey Gary."

"Mary." Gary's head never moved.

Once I picked my jaw off the floor, I looked over at the contents of Gary's cart. Noodles. Frozen chicken breasts. A loaf of bread and sauce. "Chicken Parm?" I asked.

Gary nodded. Then his eyes passed over the extra strength arthritis medicine, extra strength toilet paper, and extra strength carton of tampons in my cart. To his credit, he didn't run away from me screaming.

For what seemed like forever, we stood there in the middle of the aisle staring at each other like two awkward teenagers at a school dance. Looking for a distraction, I noticed something else in Gary's cart. A six-pack of SourPaw glistened like an oasis in the desert. Drips of condensation dribbled down the bottles.

Speaking of six packs, Gary wore his Yale T-shirt again, the one that showcased the lines of his body as if it were made of invisible cloth. The now familiar scent of his mint and jasper cologne brought back a flood of memories and feelings. Once again, my brain went rogue. Those kinds of thoughts and feelings were only going to make things worse.

"Sorry, I'll get out of your way." I moved my cart to the left, just as Gary moved his cart to the right, so we ended up blocking each other again.

"Sorry," said Gary. This time, he moved left, and I moved right, ending with the same result.

We both pulled our carts back and continued the staring showdown.

"Why do you wear that shirt, anyway?" I asked. "You didn't go to Yale." Gary looked down at his shirt, then back up at me. "Did you?"

"Just for undergraduate," said Gary. "I got my masters in architecture at Harvard." It was one more truck load of salt rubbed into the gaping wound that was my life. All that time I thought Jack was Mr. Perfect, but the truth was, Mr. Perfect had been staring me in the face all along.

Not that where Gary went to school really made any difference. It was the fact that he went to an Ivy League school and never even mentioned it. Whereas someone like Jack bragged about everything, all the time, every chance he got.

It was also another example of how smart Gary was, and how hard he worked to get where he was in life. It was also another example of how I was so focused on what I thought was important, the things that were on the outside, that I completely neglected what really mattered.

Speaking of what was on the outside, Gary's polished presence made me acutely aware of my own sorry state. My hair looked like my head got electrocuted. My pale blotchy face was devoid of any makeup, and I wore the same baggy sweat pants I'd had on for days. If my bad behavior and poor decisions didn't drive Gary away, my B.O. would for sure.

The uncomfortable silence was mounting. I don't think either of us had any clue what to do or say next.

Luckily, Kyle did. "Can Mary eat dinner with us?"

At first, I thought the voice came from the heavens. A good samaritan angel, taking pity on the damned and the wretched. Then I realized the voice was Kyle's. Then I realized Gary hadn't immediately said no and sentenced Kyle to twelve years of time-out for even suggesting it.

Sparing Gary from having to tell Kyle no, I said, "I'd love to Kyle, but I can't. I have to get back home to finish painting."

"My dad can help you paint."

"You've been painting?" Gary's face transformed from a look of horror to concern. "What were you painting? And why?"

My poker face must have been broken because I could tell that he could tell something was wrong immediately. The look of concern on his face grew more concerning. "What exactly did you do?"

"Funny thing," I said. "And you probably know this already, since you're a professional painter and all, but did you know that when you attempt to paint a wall red, after putting on a coat of not quite dry white primer, your wall ends up pink?"

"You didn't." Gary looked at me like I had just defaced the ceiling of the Sistine chapel.

I shrugged. "I sort of did. But don't worry, I'm fixing it."

"Fixing it how? And what wall were you painting red?"

"Long story," I said.

Gary looked around the grocery store. Down the aisle, an old lady individually inspected the nutrition label on every brand of canned prunes. In the other direction, a bored stock boy affixed price tags to jars of apple sauce while jamming out to whatever he was listening to through his headphones. Gary said, "We've got time."

"You can help Mary fix her paint, right, Dad?" Kyle looked up at his father. Gary looked over at me. I looked over at the woman with the prunes, who had since moved on to analyzing raisin boxes. I figured maybe if I just ignored the situation, eventually everyone else would just go away.

But that's not what happened.

"We can make dinner at your house, Mary," said Kyle. "And then while dad fixes your paint, I can play with Purrfect."

Gary and I looked at each other again, each of us waiting for the other one to shut Kyle down. Clearly, it was a bad idea. Spending any more time together would only end up hurting us both.

It had taken me weeks to convince myself that Gary and I were permanently over. Weeks for me to process that any meaningful chance for us to be together was long gone. But now that he was there, standing right in front of me, all the old thoughts and feelings returned. And not just the old thoughts and feelings. New thoughts, new feelings too. Thoughts and feelings I had been able to conveniently deny and push back deep into my subconscious, burying them, never to see the light of day. Until that moment. In that grocery store. Pushing a cart full of extra strength toilet paper and extra strength tampons. *God damn it Universe. Damn you to hell!*

"Why were you repainting the wall red?" Gary asked again.

I dropped my eyes back on my cart in order to avoid eye contact. "Actually, I sort of realized that you may have, possibly, theoretically, been right about all the greige. It was a little ... much. In fact, Aunt Catherine's house kind of looked like a mausoleum. I figured the red would play nicely off the reflection of the sunset in the Gustave Caillebott painting.

Gary nodded, but not in an 'I told you so' kind of way. It was more of a 'I knew you'd get there eventually' kind of nod.

"My open house is Saturday, and I wanted everything to be perfect."

"You should have called me," said Gary.

"I did call you. A lot."

"Fair."

"You didn't see any of my texts?" I asked.

Gary shook his head. "Probably because I blocked you."

"Fair."

"How bad is it?" he asked.

"Hmm." I rubbed my chin as a picture of Aunt Catherine's dining room formed in my head. "I'd have to say ... bad."

"How bad?"

"On a scale of one to ten? Four hundred and seventy-two. But at least now the wall matches the little pink roses on the wallpaper in the kitchen."

A semblance of a smile appeared on Gary's face. But it disappeared quickly.

"Mary, I need you to tell me something. Honestly. No more lies."

I braced myself for whatever Gary was about to ask. "No more lies. I promise."

"What exactly did you want with Jack?"

I stared down into my cart, trying to figure out the best way to respond. I decided on the truth. "You want an honest answer? I'm not even sure."

Gary cocked an eyebrow, like he didn't quite believe me.

"It was never about him. At least not him, specifically. I think it was more the *idea* of him. Jack Thompson always had that effect on me. Me and a lot of other girls. Remember what Janet said that night at the brewery?" Gary nodded. "I think it was the idea that someone like that might be interested in someone like me."

Gary nodded, seeming to understand, or at least pretending to. "And now?"

"Now? I'm done with Jack Thompson for good. If he makes Janet happy, then I wish them the best. It's time for me to move on." I continued to look Gary right in the eye, and he never flinched. "That is, move on and repaint my dining room wall before the open house."

"You said the open house is Saturday?"

I nodded.

"This Saturday?"

I nodded again.

"Today's Friday," Gary pointed out.

"I know."

"Come on Dad, we should help." Kyle looked up at both of us, waiting for the two adults to arrive at the same conclusion he had about ten minutes ago.

Gary stared into my eyes, as if he was trying to read my thoughts. Luckily he couldn't because what I was thinking in that moment was that I really, really wanted to grab the SourPaw out of Gary's cart and guzzle all six bottles.

"I guess we better get moving then," said Gary.

At first, I wasn't sure I had heard him correctly. *Did Gary just say he would help me?* "You really don't mind helping me? After everything I've done?"

Gary seemed to consider the question long and hard. A little longer and a littler harder than I was hoping for, if I'm being honest. Then his face got serious. I could tell he was sorting through whatever he was about to say. "Mary."

"Yes?" I braced myself. When the silence lingered, I thought for sure that whatever was mending between us was about to spontaneously combust.

Gary took a deep breath, his eyes meeting mine. "If we're going to do this, let's just take it slow. No gimmicks. No games. Okay?"

"Okay." I took a deep breath of my own. "Is this what starting over looks like?" I asked.

"I suppose we're about to find out."

Earlier in the day, I had been absolutely certain that any hope for Gary and me to repair our friendship was long gone. But now? There was a glimmer of a possibility that Gary and I could still make things work. A teeny tiny itty bitty thread of hope. I had been given a second chance. This time, I would not screw it up. Take that Universe. Take that.

As soon as I got back to Aunt Catherine's house, I showered, I shaved, and I misted myself with enough perfume to mask any lingering effects of my negligent hygiene. Then I had to figure out what to wear. Something that looked nice, but not too nice in case I spilled paint all over it, which was a realistic if not probable possibility.

I decided on the red tank top I wore to the Family Fun Run. One, it was red, so if I splattered paint all over myself, there was less of a chance Gary would notice. And two, I was still pretty sure I had caught him checking out my cleavage the last time I wore it and I needed every advantage I could get.

As soon as I opened the front door, Gary's jaw dropped. "Wow."

"Wow?"

"You cleaned up." I could tell he was trying very hard to keep his eyes in a neutral position.

"Purrfect!" Kyle spotted Purrfect from the front doorway, and Purrfect spotted Kyle spotting her from where she had been licking herself in the dining room. It was like an episode of a Roadrunner and Wile E. Coyote cartoon as Purrfect jumped straight up in the air, all four paws flailing, and then took off down the hall. Kyle gleefully gave chase.

Once the chaos subsided, Gary and I resumed eye contact. "You look ..." Words seemed to fail him. But all the other parts of his body seemed to work just fine.

I smiled. "Thanks." I watched closely to see if he glanced down toward my red tank top, but the man had the discipline of a fuzzy-hatted Buckingham Palace guard.

Desperate for a distraction, Gary held up two large takeout bags of Thai food. His biceps looked like pork dumplings bulging out of his Yale shirt. "I figured I would skip the burning dinner part and just jump straight to take out. You like crab Rangoon?"

"I love crab Rangoon."

"I also got spring rolls, fried wontons, and shrimp tempura. I wasn't sure what you were in the mood for, so I got one of everything."

I made a mental note not to drool. "If we eat all of that, I'll probably be in the mood for a trip to the E.R. to have my stomach pumped."

Gary smiled as I stepped aside. "Don't worry, we can pace ourselves. We've got all night."

"All night? I thought you wanted to take things slow," I teased.

Gary tripped over the front door jamb and his cheeks turned the same color as the dining room wall we were about to paint. Bright pink. Using the bags of food as a distraction, he asked, "Where did you want me to put these? I still have to go out to the van to bring in the paint."

I pointed to the dining room table. "We're eating there tonight."

Gary frowned. "But the open house is tomorrow. You did all that work to get everything perfect."

"I figured it would be a shame to let it all go to waste." Gary was right. I did a lot of work to get everything perfect. The napkins were folded, the silverware polished, I even ironed the tablecloth. "We have to use it at least once."

While Gary went to fetch the paint, I pulled a couple of Sour-Paws from the fridge. When Gary returned, he set the paint in the foyer and then joined me at the table.

"To new beginnings." I held up my beer bottle.

"To fresh starts." Gary clinked his beer bottle against mine.

DINNER WAS AMAZING, AND IT WASN'T JUST THE FOOD. We ate, we drank, we laughed. Kyle told me all about hitting a double during his last little league game. It was almost perfect.

Almost.

As Gary and I cleaned up and Kyle and Purrfect settled on the couch to watch television, Gary asked, "So, have you talked to Janet lately?"

I took my time scrubbing a plate. "No," I answered, rinsing the plate under a steady stream of water. "She still won't return my calls." To be honest, Janet was a topic I preferred to avoid. "We should get busy painting. Otherwise, you're going to be stuck here all night."

"Doesn't sound horrible." Gary smiled. My heart practically beat right out of my chest.

Once we got going, Gary took over and did all the work. Since he was the expert, I was happy to let him take charge. I helped where I could, handing him a fresh paint brush when he needed to cut in along the edges or holding the ladder for him when he had to reach the top of the wall.

It was well after midnight when Gary finally climbed down the ladder and stepped back to assess the result. I waited while his eyes swept over the wall. Floor to ceiling. Back and forth. "Not bad," he said, nodding his head. "Not bad at all."

"I think it looks great." The greige was gone. The pink was gone. And yes, the red really popped.

"Is it hot in here or is it just me?" Gary wiped the sweat off the back of his neck with a clean paint cloth. Reaching back, his exposed triceps rippled, triggering a similar response just below my abdomen.

"It's not just you." I fanned myself with an open palm. And it wasn't just hot in Aunt Catherine's house, it was suffocating. "Gus told me the ductwork needs to be replaced. The circulation in here is the equivalent of a stagnant pool of mud." Aunt Catherine's air conditioner unit was ancient, so whenever the temperature got up there, it just couldn't keep up.

"I can look at it later." I thought to myself that Gary could look at whatever he wanted to.

Gary peeled off his painting overalls, leaving only the shorts and Yale T-shirt he had been wearing underneath. I tried not to stare, failing miserably.

"It's going to be a little wet for a while," Gary said. "But it should be completely dry in time for the open house." I watched as a funny look settled on Gary's face. "That reminds me." His teeth pressed into his upper lip. "I got you something for your open house. Be right back."

Gary went out to his van. When he came back, he had something large and rectangular wrapped in brown paper. There was even a red bow on it, the same color as the wall. "Open it."

As soon as I ripped open the brown paper wrapping, all the air whooshed out of my lungs and my heart hit the pause button. It was Last Flight, the painting of the little blue bird. I didn't even realize I was crying until Gary handed me his paint rag. I didn't even care that it was sweat soaked.

"But Jack took this one," I sputtered. "How did you ..."

"I bought it back," said Gary. "One of the nurses found it sitting in the back of a closet at his office. Still wrapped."

Without thinking about it, I jumped into Gary's arms for a hug. "Thank you Gary. Thank you so much." It was the best present I ever received. Even better than the Barbie Dream House, my dad got me one year for Christmas.

Gary's arms wrapped around me, pulling me close. I could feel the beat of his heart quicken as my body pressed against his. That time when I looked up into his eyes, he didn't look away.

I'm not sure which one of us leaned in first, but as soon as his lips pressed against my lips, a wave of heat coursed through my entire body like hot lava flowing from a volcano. From my lips, down to my chest, then oozing down lower and lower until it consumed me entirely.

I could still feel his heartbeat, the pace getting faster and faster as I splayed my hands across his chest. His shoulders tensed, the muscles like granite boulders, baking all day in the sun.

If Aunt Catherine's house was hot before, now it was on fire. I couldn't breathe. My head was spinning. The entire middle part of my body between my upper thighs and my chest was on a rocket ship ride straight into the middle of the sun.

Before I lost what little was left of my spiraling self control, I pushed away from him. "We said we were going to take things slow," I gasped. My heart sure wasn't beating slow. Neither was all the blood pumping through my body, most of it still rushing down to all the parts below my waist. The only thing slow that was happening was the flow of oxygen into my lungs because I had stopped breathing.

"Slow?" He said it like he was repeating a word from a foreign language, a word he had never heard before and didn't know the meaning. "Right. We should definitely take it slow." His mouth was saying one thing, but his eyes were on a completely different page. Actually, a different book entirely.

"It's late," he said. "Now that the painting's finished, I should finish cleaning up and go."

"Yes," I agreed. My voice was barely a whisper.

He didn't move.

I didn't move either. Once again, staring into his eyes was like getting sucked down into a whirlpool in the middle of the Bermuda Triangle, lost, gone, and forgotten.

"You're staring," said Gary.

"So are you."

"That's because you have paint in your hair." Gary smiled.

"Well, I'm staring because you have paint on your shirt."

"I do?" Gary peered down at his torso. Which, coincidentally, I was peering at too.

"Right there on your shoulder." I pointed at his hard, chiseled shoulder. Right next to his soft, kissable neck.

Was that my heart beating so loudly or did a platoon of road workers with jack hammers start reconstructing the entire Central Florida road system right outside the house?

Gary looked down at the paint on his shirt. "Oh oh, that's going to stain. This is my favorite shirt." It was my new favorite shirt, too. Ever. On anyone. "Is it okay if I soak this?"

You can soak anything you want. I didn't say that part out loud. But I was definitely thinking about it at the top of my lungs. I needed to go soak my overheated head in the pool.

In one fluid motion, Gary reached back and pulled the Yale shirt up his back and over his head. "Sink okay?"

Yes, as a matter of fact. I was sinking. My mind, straight down to the gutter.

"Mary, you okay?"

"Me? I'm great." I did my best not to look at the way his chest muscles rippled like a suit of bullet proof body armor, and the way his abdomen muscles paved a rock hard path down to his hips. I also tried not to notice the curls of hair on his chest, hair that looked so soft and fuzzy and rub-able that if I ran my hand through it, I would never want to use my hand for anything else ever again.

Well, almost anything.

Chapter Thirty-Two

T he next morning, Gary and I redefined the term "open house". We didn't finish painting until well after midnight, and it was even later by the time Gary's shirt had soaked. While I was moving it to the dryer, I asked him if he wanted to stay the night again.

"Better safe than sorry. No ulterior motives. I promise." I offered to let him take my room, but he insisted the couch was fine. Kyle, of course, got the rocket ship bed.

While I was digging out some extra sheets and a pillow, Gary turned on the television. Family Feud was playing, so I joined him. His shirt was still in the dryer, so I strategically sat on the opposite end of the couch. Not too close. Taking it slow.

Eventually, as you might expect in that kind of situation, one thing led to another. No. Not that thing. Before we knew what we were doing, we found ourselves neck and neck. In points, that is. Another friendly competition, guessing answers during the speed round. Gary won the first round, I won the second. We battled back and forth, neither one of us willing to quit. During one of the commercial breaks, I decided I would rest my eyes just a little, a few seconds at most.

I must have dozed off because the next morning, when I woke

up, I was still on the couch with Gary. He was zonked out on the other side, tangled up in the blanket. Our legs wrapped together like a pretzel.

He still wasn't wearing a shirt, and for some reason, I wasn't either. Just a sports bra and my sleep shorts. I must have gotten hot in the middle of the night and torn it off. And, let's just say, the snippets of my dreams that I could remember hadn't exactly cooled things down. They made the dream I had about Jack in his waiting room look like a rated G nursery school rhyme for toddlers.

Unconcerned about my partial clothing coverage, I sank back into the couch cushion and watched Gary sleep for a few moments. His bare chest rising and falling, the way his eyes fluttered in his dreams, the whispered sound of his breath as it passed back and forth through his lips.

"Ah-hmm." The noise came from the other side of the living room.

I whipped around to see Bonnie and Joyce standing there, eyes wide, mouths hanging open. Behind Bonnie was her client, a bald man in wire-rimmed glasses, black slacks, black shirt, and a white collar. The pastor. His hand clutched the silver cross that hung around his neck.

Next to Joyce were her clients, the young couple and their four children, each one's eyes wider than the next. The husband and the wife held each other like they were standing on the deck of the Titanic.

I scrambled up from the couch. "Bonnie! Joyce! You're here!"

The little girl pointed. "Mommy, she's not wearing her jammies."

I ripped the sheet off of Gary to cover myself, fully exposing his naked torso, his private bits barely covered by his boxer shorts. Startled awake, Gary grunted, then tumbled off the couch with a thud.

The little girl pointed at Gary. "He's not wearing jammies either."

Despite the look of horror on the faces of their clients, Bonnie and Joyce were smiling ear to ear.

Bonnie winked.

Joyce gave me a thumbs up.

The pastor made the sign of the cross.

THANKFULLY, THE REST OF THE OPEN HOUSE WENT OFF without a hitch. And after calling Karen to grab Kyle to hang out with Cary for the day, Gary stayed the entire time, helping out. During a lull in visitors, he even went back to the grocery store and bought all the ingredients to make us a gourmet brunch. Huevos Rancheros, with homemade salsa, sliced avocado, the works. Turns out, when I just got out of his way and let him do his thing, he could really cook.

Over the course of the day, a lot of people came through. No on-the-spot offers, but the changes I made to spruce up the place had them oohing and aahing. I even overheard one woman tell her husband she really liked the wallpaper in the kitchen. Gary must have heard her too, because he winked at me. I could tell by the look on his face it was one of those things he would never let me forget for the rest of eternity. *The rest of eternity?* My imagination was obviously still high on paint fumes from the previous night.

When Gary wasn't making me amazing Mexican brunches or giving me I told you so looks about the wallpaper, he busied himself touching up a few scuff marks on the walls, lubricating the windows, or vacuuming the exhaust lines for the air conditioner. He even baked a batch of cookies for the guests. Without burning them. I'm pretty sure he ate most of them himself, but nothing says welcome to your new house like the aroma of fresh-baked cookies.

Overall, it was a good day. No, a great day. In fact, it was almost perfect. The only thing missing was some billionaire investor falling in love with the house, then making a full price, all-cash offer. But by that point in my life, I had learned not to expect any of my hopes or dreams or wishes to come true. But maybe this time ...

The open house officially ended at five thirty. I was just about to turn out the lights and lock the door when I heard a knock. When I opened the door, Bonnie was standing on the front porch.

"Bonnie?"

"You'll never guess," she said, a huge smile spreading across her face.

"What?" *Was the pastor pressing charges for indecent exposure?*

"He wants to make an offer. Full price. Thirty day close."

"Thirty days?" There was a time in my life when thirty days seemed like forever. But suddenly, at that moment, it seemed like no time at all. Once again, my mouth spoke before my brain could interrupt. "I don't know."

"What do you mean you don't know? He's offering full price. You'd be crazy not to take it." Crazy, right? Maybe that's what I was. "He didn't even ask for closing costs." Bonnie started digging through her briefcase. "Now he'll probably want to douse the entire place in holy water, you know, after your little show and tell, but ..."

"There was no show," I protested.

"There was from where I was standing. And you're definitely telling me everything." Bonnie winked. "I expect details. Vivid details. The more graphic, the better."

"There's nothing to tell."

Gary came down the stairs from the second floor, from where he had been busy caulking the bedroom window frames. *Caulking?* My dirty slut brain was going haywire again. "What's going on?"

"Oh, you're still here." A devious grin swept over Bonnie's lips. "My client wants to make an offer. He said he would sign the paperwork first thing in the morning. Isn't that great?"

"Is it?" Gary looked at me.

"Yeah," I said, though I could barely muster the energy to pretend to be excited. "Great."

My phone rang. I silently thanked whatever higher power was listening for the distraction and begged them to absolve me of my impure thoughts while I had their attention.

"Hello?" It was Joyce. Her clients wanted to put in an offer too. Even better, the young couple was willing to go as high as ten thousand dollars over the asking price, as long as I could vacate the house in the next two weeks.

"Two weeks?"

"Two weeks. And that's firm. They're in a rush." *Two weeks??*

I told both Bonnie and Joyce that I needed a night to sleep on it and I would let them know first thing in the morning.

Once Gary and I were alone, he must have seen the panic building. "I thought you would be happy." He handed me the last remaining cookie. "It's what you wanted, isn't it?"

"I thought so." I took a bite of cookie, the crumbs cascading to Aunt Catherine's freshly swept floor. Except it wasn't Aunt Catherine's floor. It wasn't Aunt Catherine's house. Not any more.

I looked through the hallway at the kitchen, the kitchen where Gary had convinced me to keep the wallpaper. The wallpaper my father had stood against growing up through the years. His markings on the wall. A tangible, physical reminder of him.

I looked over at Purrfect, licking herself obscenely. In the cat bed by the stairs. Her cat bed.

I looked in the dining room at the red wall. The wall I had painted. The wall I had worked on until my wrists hurt and my back was sore. The wall that had made Gary want to come and rescue me. The wall that had given us a second chance.

Then I looked at the painting Gary had given me as a housewarming present. The little blue bird. The gathering storm. The painting Jack had taken and Gary got back. For me. Because he knew how much it meant to me.

Last flight. It was like the little blue bird was staring right at me. Through me. Right into my very soul.

I was tired of flying.

I was tired of running.

This wasn't Aunt Catherine's house anymore.

This was my house.

This was my home.

"Mary?" Gary took my hand in his.

"I'm not selling it," I said at last. "I think it's time I put down some roots."

Gary looked at me long and hard. "Good."

I should have been scared. I should have been terrified. It would not be easy keeping up with a permanent mortgage and a car payment and electric bills. Sewer. Water. Cable. Pool service. I was going to need a pool service. And I'd have to find someone to take care of the lawn.

"Mary." Gary's voice momentarily quelled the rising tide of panic. "Just breathe."

I did as I was told. I breathed. Long. Slow. Deep. Long. Slow. Deep. It must have worked because my dirty slut brain kicked back into high gear again.

"You're not mad at me, are you?"

Gary looked at me like I needed fitted for a straight jacket. "Why would I be mad at you?"

"You think I'm crazy, don't you?"

"I do think you're crazy, sometimes, oftentimes, but not for this. I knew you'd come around, eventually."

"But I almost sold it ..." I realized how close I had actually come. If Bonnie or Joyce had handed me a pen and a contract a few minutes earlier ...

Gary gave my hand a squeeze. "If you would have said that you were going to take one of those other offers, I was prepared to make you an offer myself. Then I would have insisted on a really long closing. However long it took for you to come to your senses. The sense to realize you should just keep the place for yourself."

Gary was the one not making any sense. I smiled. "That's kind, but I would never let you take on that kind of burden."

Gary shrugged. "No burden at all. Remember Rodney Banks from D&D club?"

I remembered him. One of Gary's nerd friends. "Gnome Illusionist, right? The kid who used all his spell points to create illusions of naked Elven nymphs."

"That's him. Anyway, he went to Yale at the same time I did. Now he's an investment banker. Helped me set some things up during the architect years."

I scanned Gary's face again for any sign that he was joking, but I could tell that he wasn't.

"Good old Rodney may have had an Elven nymph fetish, but he sure as heck knew what he was doing when it came to picking stocks."

For the next thirty seconds, I tried in vain to wrap my head around the reality that I was going to be a house owner. A real one this time. Not a temporary asset holder waiting for a transaction to close. No, wait, not a house owner. That wasn't the right word. Now, I actually owned a *home.*

But my sudden and unexpected sense of peace and well-being was short-lived. As soon as I heard the knock on the door, I knew things were too good to be true. There was no way the Universe was going to let me off the hook that easily.

I opened the door, Gary standing tall beside me. I half expected to see the grim reaper standing there. Or an IRS agent. Or Justin Bieber with an army of lawyers suing me for past karaoke sins.

It wasn't any of those things. The person standing at my door was Janet. Her face was red. I could tell right away that she had been crying.

"Janet?"

"Mary."

Another face poked out from behind Janet's head. It was Ralph. Janet reached one arm back over her shoulder and Ralph dutifully maneuvered a loose tissue from a tissue box into her outstretched hand. When Janet blew her nose, the resulting honk attracted every eligible goose within a twenty-mile radius.

Before I knew what was happening, Janet rushed forward and wrapped me in her arms.

As Janet settled onto the couch in the living room, Gary and I pulled Ralph to the side.

"How bad is it?" I asked.

"So far we're on our third box of tissues and fourth pint of ice cream. Though being fair, I'm responsible for at least half of the ice cream."

"You're eating ice cream too?" I noticed Ralph had bags under his eyes and his wrinkled clothes looked like he had slept in them. Ralph never wore wrinkled clothes. He dry cleaned everything.

"Where's Karen?" asked Gary.

"Long story." And from the look on Ralph's face, I could tell that it was. "A story we better save for another day. One crisis at a time."

After making Ralph swear to tell us what was going on with him and Karen later, Ralph and Gary went to put on a kettle for tea, correctly realizing that Janet and I needed some time by ourselves to talk.

"What happened?" I asked as soon as Gary and Ralph left the room.

"You were right," said Janet.

"About what, exactly?"

"He never changed, Mary. Jack Thompson is an asshole. You were right all along." Janet pulled out her phone and handed it to me. There was a video queued up on the screen.

"What is this?" I asked.

"The security camera footage from the Dungeons and

Dragons night," said Janet. "You know, the night you and Jack ... kissed."

"I remember." I really didn't feel like reliving that night, but Janet waited for me to watch whatever she had recorded on her phone.

I took a deep breath and hit play. On screen, I watched every awful moment, cursing myself for how stupid and horrible I had been. I really didn't want to finish watching it, especially when I saw Jack walking down the book aisle toward the place I was standing on the screen. Especially as Jack and I stood close to one another. Especially the part where he leaned in and ...

"Wait a second." I hit pause on Janet's phone. When I looked up, her eyes locked onto mine.

That entire night was still a blur. My mind had been going in a million different directions. I couldn't tell up from down or left from right. The truth was, my memory of everything that happened that night was still in a bit of a fog.

I hit rewind so I could play the video back on Janet's phone. Then I zoomed in and paused, advancing the image frame by frame. I watched as Jack moved toward me in slow motion, then, clearly, unmistakably, he leaned in to kiss me. In the video, I never moved.

"You see it now, don't you?"

Slowly, I nodded.

"You didn't start the kiss," said Janet. "He was the one who kissed you."

Watching it with my own eyes, I could see that Janet was right. It didn't make it any better, though. Shaking my head, I said, "I should have pushed him away. I should have stopped him."

"Yeah. You should have, Mary." Janet's eyes narrowed. "Which is why I'm still mad at you."

As my eyes settled on my feet, Janet slowly unclenched her fists. "But I think I understand why you didn't."

When I looked back up, her expression had softened. She

brushed a tear away from the corner of her eye. "I just wish you would have told me you still had feelings for him. If you would have been honest with me from the beginning ..."

I laughed out loud, though nothing about it was funny. "I wasn't even honest with myself." I took an extra deep breath, still trying to wrap my head around everything that had happened. "Not that it makes any difference now, but they were never the good kind of feelings. The only feelings I ever really had when it came to Jack Thompson were insecurity and doubt."

Janet reached over and squeezed my hand.

I squeezed her back. "Janet, you're my best friend. You've been there for me through everything, and I betrayed you. I lied to you ... I was so wrapped up in my stupid obsession ..."

"Jack manipulated both of us," said Janet. "Like we were some kind of prize in his sick, demented game. He knew exactly what to say to make me think he was truly interested in me. And then, meanwhile, he did just enough to string you along." Janet shook her head. "I feel like such an idiot."

"You're not the idiot here," I said. "Janet, I am so, so sorry. I know words aren't enough, but I promise you, I will do whatever it takes to make this right between us."

Janet moved in for another hug. When she finally released me, a slow smile crept over her face. "Whatever it takes?"

A slow frown crept over mine. "Well, I mean ..."

"Well, you can start by buying me a cider at FoxPaw." Janet's devious smile only widened.

"You liked Mike's cider that much?"

"Among other things." Janet's smile grew wider still.

Before I could question Janet further, Ralph and Gary returned from the kitchen, carrying our cups of tea. "Did you show her the pictures too?" asked Ralph.

"Pictures?"

The four of us gathered around Janet's phone. "Remember Jack's trip to Mexico?"

On Janet's screen was a picture of a Pina Colada with a pink

340

lip print on the edge, a shade of pink that looked very familiar. The same shade I saw on Jack's lips at the race. That wasn't all, though. Beside the Pina Colada was a second drink, with a very distinctive blue hue.

"Is that a ..." My voice trailed off, the reality of what I was seeing sinking in.

"A Blue Hawaiian," Janet finished. "Jack's favorite drink. There are more pictures too. Tagged to a resort in Cancun. Posted on the same days Jack said he was going to that medical conference in Mexico."

"Jack posted pictures of himself having fun in Cancun after he told you he would be working the whole time?" I scrolled through more pictures. "Not very bright, is he?"

"Jack didn't post them."

"He didn't?" I looked up at Janet, confused.

"You want to guess who posted them?"

I had a feeling I already knew. "Ashley Griffin."

I stared at Janet's phone as she scrolled through picture after picture of white sand and clear blue ocean, fancy drinks and selfies of Ashley lounging by the pool in a barely there bikini.

It took me a moment to absorb everything that Janet was telling me, and what I saw on Janet's phone.

I braced myself for Janet's inevitable meltdown. But she didn't melt down. Surprisingly, she looked like she was entirely sane and stable. Miraculously, she looked calm.

"Janet, what did you do?"

Another sly smile formed on Janet's lips. "You know that Carrie Underwood song, *Before He Cheats*?"

I couldn't help but smile myself. "You didn't."

Janet shrugged her shoulders. "I sorta did. Except instead of a truck, it was a BMW. That reminds me, Ralph, do you know any good property damage lawyers?"

Chapter Thirty-Three

T he ass stood in the middle of the road, munching on a tuft of grass poking up out of the dirt. It lifted its head and stared at us. It never stopped chewing.

"Look." Gary stopped and pointed.

"Can I pet it?" Kyle asked.

Janet and I had already stopped. That was on purpose. We were both wearing long dresses and high heels. Not exactly the kind of outfit you would want to be wearing if you found yourself in a situation where you had to run for your life. If the ass charged, we were going to need a head start.

"Careful," I warned. "It might have rabies. Or get drool on your suits." I wondered if the color red made all farm animals want to charge at you, or if that only applied to bulls. Gary's tie was the same shade of red as my dress.

Undeterred, Gary walked right up and patted the animal's head while Kyle stroked its fur along the side.

Janet looked at her watch. "We should get moving. I told Mike we would taste test his latest creations before the ceremony."

"Oh, you did, did you?" I noticed a familiar twinkle in Janet's eye.

Mike had generously offered to supply the beer kegs, at cost, for Dick and Mabel's wedding. He had been experimenting with new beer and cider recipes for a festival he was hosting to celebrate FoxPaw Brewing's three-year anniversary, FoxFest. Business was booming. So good, in fact, that he hired me to scope out commercial real estate so he could build a second location.

"It's not like that," Janet insisted. "Just doing a favor for a friend."

"Friends, huh?"

"I'm still scarred from the whole Jack-Ass debacle. I told you, I'm never dating another man again."

"Okay, if you say so."

"I do say so."

"So you said."

Speaking of asses, Gary scratched his. The animal I mean. Then he thumbed over his shoulder toward the big red barn at the end of the road. "You want to keep going?"

I looked him dead in the eye. "I do."

THE RANCH LOOKED AMAZING. AFTER THE unfortunate reunion incident, the ranch owner banished all the farm animals to the other side of the property for events. Thankfully, down wind.

Mabel looked stunning in her dress. Ethereal. Breathtaking.

Dick cried like a baby during the vows.

It was awesome. Everything. All of it.

The wedding cake had ten different layers. There were more flowers than a Swiss hillside during a yodeling festival. And best of all, enough FoxPaw beer that everyone signed up for a turn on the karaoke machine.

By popular request, Gary and Janet did an encore of their *Dirty Dancing* routine.

Edna pulled out her now infamous Rod Stewart.

I went with "Baby" by Justin Bieber. It seemed like a good idea at the time.

As the night began winding down, toward the end of the reception, it was finally time for the main event. The moment of truth. The thing that everyone had been waiting to see. It was time for the bride to toss the bouquet.

Janet, Karen, and I jostled for position. My strategy was going to be that when Janet jumped for it, I would take out her legs.

Mabel turned away from us, poised for her big throw. It seemed like the bouquet sailed through the air in slow motion.

The flower girl, Mabel's granddaughter, initially seemed to be in the right place at the right time. I may have taken her out with a hip to the solar plexus. Accidentally, of course.

To this very day, I would argue that Janet had the better position. She could have caught it if she really wanted to. But somehow, magically, it slipped right out of her hands.

And right into mine.

I stared down at the flowers in disbelief. When I looked back up, I caught sight of Gary standing across the yard, smiling.

Above us, a shooting star streaked across the night sky.

A FEW MONTHS LATER, GARY CAME OVER TO THE house. My house. He was taking me out on a surprise date. When I asked him where we were going, he wouldn't tell me. "Wear comfortable walking shoes." That was my only hint.

Well, that and the fact he asked me to drive - "Since your car has all wheel drive."

After taking my house off the market, things were pretty tight. But once I repurposed my renovation time into finding new clients and making more sales, my real estate career was revived.

I could have kept Charlotte if I wanted to, but I traded her in for a Subaru instead. Better gas mileage, more affordable, and it didn't break down on I4 in the middle of an afternoon thunderstorm.

Charlotte was a fun ride while she lasted, but after she was gone, I didn't miss her one bit.

The surprise date was a surprise all right, but not the good kind of surprise. He took me to the nature center, using the annual passes we had won.

Yay.

He told me he had planned a special hike.

Double yay.

"Oh look," Gary said. There was an information kiosk just outside the nature center. A sign read, "Today's Trivia - All About Trees!" "We should play!" Clearly, it was my lucky day.

Different trees were planted all along the boardwalk. Pines. Oaks. Cedars. Signs listed the tree names and various facts and figures. Gary filled out the trivia sheet as we walked. It was my job to stop at each sign, look for clues, and then answer the questions.

The answer to the first question was Willow. As in the willow tree.

The answer to the second question was Yew. As in the yew tree.

Gary and I had been happily dating for almost six months by then. Six months longer than I had happily dated anyone else in my entire life.

As agreed at the beginning, we had taken it slow. But it didn't take me very long to realize that he was the man I wanted to spend the rest of my life with. And every day we were together, I fell in love with him a little bit more.

It was a shame I was going to have to dump him now because he was forcing me to learn about trees.

"Here's the next question." I wondered if Gary had a secret double life as a closet arborist. "And this one is super easy. Write your name."

"My name?"

"That's what it says." Gary shrugged his shoulders.

"My name or your name?"

Gary considered carefully, even rubbing his chin. "I'll just put yours down."

"Fine. Whatever." I didn't really care what Gary wrote, as long as he hurried up and got the stupid trivia game over with. "How many questions are left on this thing, anyway?"

"This next one is the final one."

"There's only four questions?"

Gary shrugged again. "I guess."

I assumed the trivia game was designed for three-year-olds. Or extremely bored, lonely adults who had the patience of a saint, and had nothing better to do than learn about trees.

When I looked back over at Gary, he was biting his lower lip and fiddling with something in his pocket. His face was flushed, and I could see little beads of sweat on his forehead, even though it wasn't even that hot since all the boring trees created a lot of shade.

"Everything okay?"

"Hmm? What?"

"I asked you if everything was okay. You're acting funny."

Actually, Gary was acting like he had just bonged a gallon sized jug of espresso. Maybe all the oxygen the God damn trees were pumping out into the troposphere had made him lightheaded.

"Let's do the last question," Gary said, deftly changing the subject. He read the question from the trivia sheet. "The Eastern white pine is a majestic conifer known for its towering height and historical significance."

Ugh, more tree stuff.

I closed my eyes and pressed my fingers to my temples, rubbing them gently to ward off the coming migraine. Just when I thought the morning couldn't get any worse, Gary had found a way to combine history facts and tree facts together.

"Its soft, workable wood and minimal resin content fueled a

booming lumber industry and, in 1895, became this state's state tree."

In their latest annual report, the Occupational Safety and Health Administration, OSHA, reported over one hundred tree related fatalities in the United States last year. Most were from wind blown falls or accidents people had while climbing. Mine was going to be the first tree related death linked to tree trivia boredom.

I looked at the tree in front of me. It was a fine-looking tree, as far as trees go. Majestic seemed like a bit of a stretch.

"Maybe it says it on the sign," Gary offered. By this point, he looked like he was shooting up espresso through an I.V., plugged directly into his veins. And whatever it was in his pocket, he was fiddling with it constantly.

I read the sign. "Maine," I said. "It's Maine's state tree."

"What are Maine's initials?"

"I have no idea. Just write Maine."

"I'm pretty sure we can only put down the abbreviation," Gary said.

"Well, we wouldn't want the tree trivia police to come and arrest us now, would we? Fine. I'll Google it." I googled it. "The letters M and E."

"And we're finished!" For some reason, Gary's voice had gone a couple of octaves higher. I really thought maybe he was coming down with something.

"Here, maybe you should double-check my answers," Gary said. He handed me the sheet.

"I'm sure they're fine." I began heading back down the path.

"I really think you should check them," Gary said again. "In case I made a mistake."

"I trust you." I kept walking. As soon as we got back to the nature center, my plan was to throw the stupid trivia sheet in the trash anyway.

"Mary."

I stopped and turned.

"Read back the answers on the sheet. Please."

"Fine," I grumbled. I looked down at the answers Gary had written. Apparently, it was a good thing that I was double-checking after all. "You forgot the O and the W at the end of the word willow," I said. "You wrote *will* instead of *willow*, and then yew, Mary, and an M and an E. Hand me the pencil and I'll fix it."

When I looked back up, Gary was down on one knee. At first I thought his shoe was untied. Then I saw he was holding something. When I looked closer, I saw he was holding a ring.

"Read it back one more time," said Gary.

My hands were shaking so badly I could barely see the words on the page.

1. *Will*
2. *Yew*
3. *Mary*
4. *M.E.*

Epilogue

"And that, boys, is how your Grandpa Gary and I fell in love." Mary leaned back against the pillows, her two grandsons snuggled deep in her arms.

The clock on the wall said it was well past the boy's bedtime. Hers too. She could hear Gary snoring like a hog in their bedroom across the hall.

"You could have left out the kissing part." Patrick looked up at her, a frown on his face.

"The kissing part?"

"Yeah, the kissing part," Patrick said again. "The part where you and Grandpa first kissed." Jacob had looked drowsy but now he perked up, wide awake.

"Oh." Mary hadn't thought that an eight-year-old and a six-year-old would pay much attention to that. It was a good thing she had creatively edited some of the R rated parts out of the story. And now that she thought about it, perhaps the retelling of the dream she had in Jack Thompson's lobby was not exactly age appropriate.

"Come on now. Up and at 'em. Your mother and father are going to be home soon. Remember, if they ask, we were all in bed by eight thirty." Mary tried to sit up, but her tired bones wouldn't let her. That and the fact that both boys still hadn't budged. Perhaps the second bowl of pistachio ice cream had been a strategic miscalculation.

Jacob's eyes were still full of questions. "Do you and Grandpa still play pickleball?"

"We still dink from time to time," Mary said. Then under her breath she added, "And bang on special occasions."

"What about Purrfect?" Patrick looked concerned. "What happened to her?"

Mary smiled as she thought about Purrfect. In many ways, that cat was responsible for bringing Gary and her together. She took a deep breath, choosing her words carefully. "Purrfect lived a long and happy life," she said at last. "Right here in this house. With her family. Me. Your grandpa. And your father Kyle." Mary had to take another deep breath to continue. "When her time was done, she went to sleep in my arms while Grandpa rubbed her favorite petting spot. Right behind her ears."

Patrick gave an enormous yawn, which set off a chain reaction with Jacob.

Then Mary yawned too. "Okay, it's definitely past bedtime, for sure."

"Next time, can you tell us a story about Aunt Janet?" asked Jacob.

"I want to hear one about Uncle Ralph," said Patrick.

"I'm afraid both of those stories are going to have to wait until you're older," said Mary. "Much older. The Aunt Janet story is going to require a couple shots of tequila, since it involves Cancun. And another drooling ass, come to think of it. And for the Uncle Ralph story, I'm going to need you to sign a waiver."

Patrick gave another yawn, and Jacob's eyes fluttered.

"I'll tell you what," said Mary. "If you both go to sleep right away, I will tell you the story about how your mom and your dad met next time." Although, Mary thought, that one was going to need a lot of creative editing, too. And tequila wouldn't hurt either.

I Need Your Help

I hope you enjoyed reading this book. Please consider leaving a review at your favorite bookstores and your favorite book review sites. Reviews help independent authors like me find new readers, which helps us write more books.

Thank you!

M.J.

Want to hear Purrfect's side of the story? Make sure to check out **Purrfect Match**, coming soon!

When opposites attract, even nine lives aren't enough.

Purrfect of House Catherine has standards. High ones. Royal lineage. Impeccable grooming. A silk pillow for every nap. But when her human Catherine is gone, Purrfect's world crumbles. Now she's facing eviction by Catherine's greedy niece, Mary, who plans to flip the house and erase every trace of the life Purrfect once knew.

Enter Maverick. Battle-scarred. Street-smart. Rough around every possible edge. This alley cat with the mysterious past is everything Purrfect should avoid. He's also the only one who can help her, despite her constant criticism about his grooming.

With her heart and territory under siege, Purrfect must decide what matters most, preserving the perfect life she once had, or embracing an imperfect future with a tom who sees the warrior princess she's become.

A heartwarming tale of unlikely love and second chances that proves sometimes the greatest adventures begin when carefully laid plans fall spectacularly apart.

"I'm not kitten around, absolutely claw-some! A fur-bulous tale of love that crosses the garden fence. Purrfect Match is the cat's meow of romantic comedies." —Whiskers Weekly

"A paws-itively enchanting story that will have you feline good all weekend. Cat-egorically the best romance I've read this year! Two paws way up!" —The Pampered Pet Reader

Also by M.J. Fox

Purrfect Match

I Burned My Tongue in Colorado

About the Author

M.J. Fox crafts romantic comedies that capture the awkward, messy, and ultimately beautiful journey of finding love. With a keen eye for humor and heart, M.J. writes stories that remind us that sometimes the perfect love story is perfectly imperfect.

Before shifting his devotion to novels, M.J. Fox honed his storytelling skills as a writer in both the film and software industries, bringing a unique blend of creativity and technical precision to his work.

These days, when not weaving tales of love and laughter, you might find him exploring new destinations, sampling craft beers, or working off those same beers through an active lifestyle that includes hiking and spirited games of pickleball.

M.J. has found his own happily-ever-after story in Central Florida with his always fantastic wife, five usually fantastic kids, four sometimes fantastic dogs, and twelve mediocre fish. This lively crew serves as both his creative inspiration and keeps him perpetually on his toes – much like the characters in his books.

Love can be messy... but finding your next great read doesn't have to be!

Join the FoxJam Books newsletter for exclusive updates, behind-the-scenes peeks at upcoming novels, and special subscriber-only content.

Visit foxjambooks.com to sign up and stay connected.

FoxJam Books